WOMEN
AND
CHILDREN
FIRST

WOMEN AND CHILDREN FIRST

A NOVEL

ALINA GRABOWSKI

SJP LIT

A zando IMPRINT

NEW YORK

Copyright © 2024 by Alina Grabowski

SJP Lit is an imprint of Zando.
zandoprojects.com

First Edition: May 2024

Text design by Aubrey Khan, Neuwirth & Associates, Inc.
Cover design by Sara Wood
Cover photos: Photo by Margaret Durow. © 2010 by Margaret Durow
Small boat © FrankvandenBergh | iStock
Nobska Lighthouse © Judd Brotman | iStock

Library of Congress Control Number: 2023948983

978-1-63893-078-5 (Hardcover)
978-1-63893-079-2 (ebook)

10 9 8 7 6 5 4 3 2 1
Manufactured in the United States of America

The only reason that they say "Women and children first" is to test the strength of the lifeboats.

–UNKNOWN

PRE

JANE

ON THE LAST SATURDAY IN MAY, I drown in my sleep. It happens quickly. I'm standing at the edge of the ocean and when I look down into the water, the wobbly hand of my reflection reaches up to pull me under. Only it's less of a pull and more of an angry yank, like my arm's a dangling ponytail, and suddenly I'm pressed to the sand with my own hand holding me down from above. I want to scream, but my words dissolve into a stream of bubbles. I'm not ready, is what I'm trying to say. But then everything goes black.

I thought you weren't allowed to die in dreams.

When I open my eyes, I see that I've left the window beside my bed open, because sometimes I'm an idiot. The rain's coming in so heavily that when I sit up, my wet sheets stick to my chest like strands of seaweed. If I weren't a scientifically minded person, the dream plus the bedroom shower might seem like a bad omen. But I'm an unsuperstitious atheist, so it doesn't bother me.

The window won't close unless I bang my fist loudly against the glass, so I tiptoe to Mom's room at the end of the hall to see if she's still asleep. In the sliver of space between the wall and the door, I see her: not actually sleeping, but lying on top of her comforter in her underwear, tracing her chin with an unlit joint from the medical dispensary. Lately she's been wandering around the house half naked, something I don't appreciate. She says she's hot, burning up, on fire, but nothing helps—not frozen peas on her forehead or baths full of ice or a sticky balm I bought at Walgreens that smells like chemical mint. What if it's all in my head? she asked one day, after a doctor suggested meditating twice a day to prevent the flashes. It's not, I said. But even if it was, it'd still be just as real.

I close the door quietly as possible, but when it clicks I can hear the mattress bounce. "Jane?" she asks, "is something wrong?" But I'm already halfway to my own room, where the rain's blowing in so fast and thick that my duvet squishes under my sweatpants when I kneel forward to pound the windowpane shut.

OUTSIDE, IT SMELLS LIKE SEAWEED and crab shells, which means the street is flooding. The blizzard cracked part of the seawall back in January, but no one cares because it's on our side of the beach where people actually live, as opposed to the side where people "summer." Sometimes I'll walk barefoot against the rushing water with our colander, trying to catch sand dollars or horseshoe crabs (if I dry them on my windowsill, I can sell them to the souvenir shops in the harbor), and a neighbor will see me from their porch. They'll nod aggressively and say something like, "They think this is acceptable?" except they never say who *they* are or what *this* is.

It's early, seven o'clock, and no one's up yet. I straddle my bike under the remote-controlled awning that Mom uses to protect her car from the elements, since we don't have a real garage, just a driveway that doubles as our patio during the summer. I tie plastic grocery bags over my bike seat and my head, even though my hair looks stupid no matter what I do because my ancestors were frizzy-haired Irish peasants who ate too many carbs. I'm about to kick off into the street when I hear our neighbor's side door open. She moved in six months ago, a little before the blizzard. We never introduced ourselves, or brought a pie, or left a note in her mailbox, which I guess means we're unfriendly. She's pregnant—she's always been pregnant—but I've never seen a man over there. Today she's wearing an oversized shirt for sleeping and, as far as I can tell, no pants. Her legs are stringy in a way that means her hips are probably small and tight and won't easily allow a baby to pass through them. I'm never going to have a kid because I don't like being in unnecessary pain.

She rubs her big belly under her big shirt and looks out at the street. "Must be someone special," she says, and I actually look around to see who else is out on their porch this early because there's no way she'd be talking to me.

"What?"

"Must be a special boy to get you to ride your bike through this storm." The rain's making her shirt stick to her stomach, and I can see the pointy nub of her flipped-out belly button. We watch a piece of driftwood float down the street, and I wish I could grab on to it and float away from this conversation. "What's your mom think about him?"

"I'm going to work," I explain, pulling at the collar of my Village Market polo.

"Good for you." She grasps her hands beneath her belly like it might fall to the ground without the safety net of her fingers. "I hear we women can have it all these days."

I can't think of anything to say to that, which is fine because she peels open the door with her big toe and slips back inside.

NO ONE'S ON THE ROAD except for anorexic moms headed to the Y, sunburned old dudes en route to the marina, and me. Our neighbor's right, in that I'm going to see someone special, but she's wrong, in that said person is a boy.

One of the old guys rolls down his window to talk while we're at a stoplight beside the salt marsh. Overgrown cattails stoop into our lane with the rain's weight and I have to squint my eyes to keep the water from dribbling into them. "Now, what kind of boy lets his gal fend for herself in this weather?" he asks. His mouth keeps moving after he's done talking, little specks of chewing tobacco wobbling on his lip.

I try to remember the tone I used to use with my dad's fishing buddies. "The kind of boy who can't keep up."

He laughs a lot at that, slaps his steering wheel with his chubby fingers. Men love it when you make fun of other men. They think it "keeps them honest," which is apparently something they can't do themselves.

"You stay sharp, young lady," he tells me before pulling away as the light changes. He watches me in his side mirror with little pink-rimmed eyes, and I pedal extra fast to pass him, just because I can. The wind sharpens the rain against my cheeks and my water-logged socks slap against my ankles like dead fish and I remember how much I used to love this, being fast. When I want something, I block out any possibility of not getting it. That's how I used to win so many races. The other girls ran toward something stupid, like hope. I ran toward the inevitable.

The road turns into a bridge that bumps over the bay, and the bridge drops onto the smooth pavement of Main Street, which slips between the docks and candy-colored shop awnings. I sprint through the harbor on my lowest gear, the seagulls screaming above me, the stores blurring beside me, the puddles splattering under me. I'm not wearing a rain jacket, so water slides down my shirt and soaks into the band of my bra, which feels like having a melted ice pack tied to my rib cage. *Why am I doing this?* I think, like I don't already know.

The rain comes down even harder, and I keep my head down until I reach Route 5A, the only highway that runs through town. For reasons my mother calls "objectively insane," there's a stop sign instead of a stoplight where it meets Main Street. Everyone at school calls it the Murder Merge, which parents like to mention whenever someone new dies and they write yet another op-ed for the *Mariner*. Their essays are all the same: They spend a long time contemplating What's Wrong with Kids These Days, because if you die on 5A you were probably drunk or hit by someone who was, which leads the author to the same conclusion, either Bad Parenting or Not Enough Church. I don't know why they never ask one of us. The answer's simple: The world feels big and boundless when you're drunk in a fast car, and it feels small and choked anywhere they can see you.

There are so many white flags along the shoulder that it looks like a field of wildflowers from a distance. I used to feel sick whenever I saw them, and I actually did throw up once—I didn't even get off my bike, I just pedaled faster and held my head out to the side, mouth open. But last year there was some kind of anniversary related to the first flag, and then all of a sudden people started taking pictures with them. Mostly kids from school, but some strangers, too. They spilled into the road, ignoring the cars that veered into the left lane to pass them, ignoring me on my bike until I came so close that they shouted, *Watch it!* They were busy. They were writing long captions about childhood and angels and the fragility of life, they were tagging all of their friends, they were retagging their friends because they'd missed someone, they were looking sad, they were looking constipated because they didn't know how to look sad, they were holding each other close because this was Real Life, because this was Growing Up, because they wondered what it would be like if they died, if they would be called funny or nice or smart or pretty or handsome or hot. They weren't thinking that no one would call them anything, at least not for long. Once you take a picture at a kid's death site you don't come back for a second one.

When I bike past the flags, like I am now, I don't look anywhere except the straight-ahead distance.

My turn comes up fast. Water sprays up my calves as I tilt to the right, and then I'm coasting down the hill to Sandpiper Coffee Roasters. There aren't any cars in their lot except for a white Jeep with a torn-up bumper sticker on its fender that says *MILF: Man, I Love Frogs.* The shredded bumper sticker is how I know it belongs to Olivia Cushing, because I saw her mom, who also happens to be our principal, trying to scrape it off with a razor blade in the school parking lot last fall. I ride past the big window on the side of the shop and see Olivia slumped in a corner booth, her face fully planted on the table, long hair pooling over her head like a dark puddle. She's a tornado—one of those girls who makes problems not only for herself but for everyone around her. I don't believe in pulling other people into your own mess.

There's no bike rack, so I lock my bike to a nearby telephone pole, the back tire dipping into a drowned pothole. There are three floors of apartments above the Sandpiper, with rusted fire escape stairs zigzagging to the ground like stacked Zs. Rob lives here, my school's newest math teacher. He just graduated Amherst last year, but *not* UMass Amherst, Principal Cushing made sure to clarify. No one's ever out on the fire escape because of the apparently permanent sign dangling from the first landing that says REPAIRS IN PROGRESS.

I run up the stairs so fast that they wobble underneath me like a dock, the steps slippery with rain. I used to be a sprinter, but then one day I woke up and couldn't understand why I set my alarm for five o'clock every morning just to try and run faster circles than all the other skinny white girls who wanted to feel good at something. Life is too short for meaningless experiences, I told our team captain, which was maybe a bit too blunt in retrospect. Jesus Christ, she said. They're going to eat you alive out there, Jane.

I still don't really know what she meant by that.

Rob's apartment is on the sixth floor, the top floor of the building. It's scary, being up that high with only a thin metal railing behind you, but I like little thrills. Since I was a kid I've been like that—putting my toes over the edge of the train platform, leaning forward over a mountain ledge, that kind of thing. It feels powerful, to be so close to making a bad decision and then not make it.

Rob appears quickly when I knock on his windowpane. He's having a good hair day, which happens more often now that I've told him you're not supposed to brush your curls, only comb through them with your fingers for definition. He offers me his hand but I straddle the ledge awkwardly instead, stretching my toes until they touch the floor. "Jesus Christ, you're wet," he says when I finally stumble inside. He leans over my shoulder to poke his head through the frame. "I didn't even know it was raining."

"Lucky you." I untie my shoes and carry them to the bathroom, where I leave them upside down against the radiator. I hang my socks from the shower's curtain rod and droplets fall from their toes to the tub. His washer and dryer are all the way in the basement, and the residents share them.

I untie the plastic bag that fell from my head to my shoulders during the ride like the world's saddest shawl. "You don't have a hair-dryer, do you?"

He appears in the doorway and hands me coffee in one of the paper Starbucks cups he keeps beside his microwave. He hates washing dishes. "Alas, I do not. I could go get you one, though, if you wanted." He steps into the bathroom and opens the cabinet beside the sink, like a hair-dryer might be hiding there. It's not.

I've never regretted telling anyone something more than when I told Rob we were broke. I'm pretty sure he pictures us living in the basement of the Episcopalian church, where they run the soup kitchen and needle exchange. "I have a hair-dryer," I clarify. "Just not one *here*."

"Don't get offended," he says, even though I'm not offended, I'm just talking. What *is* offensive is the uniform he's wearing for tutoring, a green T-shirt so wrinkly it looks like an over-microwaved pea. He has very nice arms from rowing crew in college, but the long sleeves completely hide them. Though I guess it's better for me if he looks like a schlub. Rob tutors at Great Expectations, in the strip mall across from the Village Market where I work. I actually get jealous, when I think about him sitting across from Bethany or Amy or whoever, reminding her to reduce her fractions, to multiply both sides, to make an educated guess. It's sexy, having someone explain things you don't understand.

I smell something burning. He likes his toast so black it turns his tongue dark, and he never listens when I tell him burnt food gives you cancer. "Are you trying to make breakfast or commit arson?" I ask.

He closes the cabinets with a hard snap and something crashes inside that I can't see. "Are you trying to say my toast is ready or just being an asshole?"

"Jesus. I was joking." I focus on peeling off a weak part of my fingernail to avoid looking at him. Eye contact intensifies his moods.

"Sorry I don't think life's one big fucking joke." He slaps his feet against the tile as he walks out of the bathroom, to make sure I know he's mad. I try not to let it bother me. Rob's very sensitive for a teacher.

My wet clothes are making my skin cold and itchy, so I peel off my work uniform and underwear and hang them over the edge of the sink, where a beam of sunlight's falling from the window. I look ugly in the mirror. I'm one long rectangle, no hips or chest, just bones stretching skin, but not in a model way, in a malnourished-teenage-boy-who's-beaten-every-shooter-game way. I wonder if I would be here, if I were a pretty girl. It's harder to hide something everybody wants.

I find a towel in the bathroom closet, below a shelf of body sprays and prescription creams. It's thin and the color of mud and smells like mildew, but at least it's dry against my chest. I use one hand to cinch it closed and the other to hold my coffee.

Rob's still in the kitchen, even though toast only needs to be buttered and placed on a plate.

"Are you okay?" I call down the hallway.

"I'm fine. Why would I be anything other than fine?" he shouts back.

Whatever. I walk into his bedroom and sit on the edge of the mattress, rest my coffee cup on my bare knee so I can feel its heat through the paper bottom. Rob returns with his plate of toast, a napkin tucked into his collar like a little kid. He stops in the doorway. "What are you wearing?" he asks.

"A towel."

"Don't be a smart-ass," he says, but he's smiling now. Our eyes meet and I don't look away, even though part of me wants to. Everything with Rob is an experiment. I learn what I like and what I don't, and I know that he, unlike the boys at school, won't tell a single person.

"Do you love me?" I ask. Not because I think he'll say yes. But because I want to know what he'll say instead.

Something changes in his face. He drops his plate to the dresser and opens its drawers with his back to me. "Here." He tosses a flannel shirt and a pair of boxers onto the bed, face still to the wall. "Put these on."

"I asked you a question." His buttons are on the opposite side of the shirt, and I have trouble getting them closed. The boxers are easier to put on, but they aren't as soft as I think they'll be—the stiff fabric reminds me of a hospital gown.

I watch his knuckles tense as he makes fists with both hands. "Don't play with me, Jane."

"I don't know what you mean."

He turns around and exhales through his nose so heavily that I feel his breath touch the hollow of my neck. "This isn't high school. This is real life." I don't say anything to that. He kneels in front of me and grasps my chin between his thumb and forefinger. "Okay?"

"Okay," I say. A droplet falls from my hair onto his wrist. When I talk, I feel the pressure of his grip on my jaw.

He moves his thumb to my lips and I open my mouth. His skin's salty on my tongue. I could bite down.

We both know I won't.

. . .

WHEN I PULL INTO THE MARKET'S LOT, it's empty except for two crookedly parked sedans and a pack of chattering seagulls. The rain's finally let up, and I stand on my pedals and tip my face toward the weak sun. Rob ended up taking my clothes to the basement laundry room to dry them, and my collar's still warm against my neck, still smells like the jasmine dryer sheets he buys in bulk and scatters across his apartment to keep the mice away. Sometimes I forget how happy small things can make you.

Employees enter through the back, beside the concrete platform where the delivery trucks unload. I lock my bike to the rusted grocery cart corral beside the dumpster, from the Market's original days as a family-owned store and pharmacy half its current size. I heard that the original owners sold after their son overdosed during the closing shift—they found him in the walk-in freezer near the icy boxes of prepackaged meats. Supposedly overdosed, I should say. I don't remember who told me that story, or what they were trying to make me feel by telling it.

Inside, Eric's fleece is already hanging on the coatrack in the back room. He's the closest thing I have to an enemy, because he's too tall and a bad worker. I briefly consider filling his pockets with the stale Twinkies in the expired-goods cart before swiping my time card through the plastic strip on the wall.

"Hey, Liability," Eric says as I slip through the swinging door to the deli. He's called me this ever since I mopped the tiles in front of the cheese display and a middle-aged woman glided across them like they were coated in ice. She was fine, just a bruised wrist from the fall (let it be known that I had displayed not one but two WET FLOOR signs), but our manager, Ricky, had a whole panic attack over it.

I don't bother saying hello, just go to the sink and wash my hands. Eric's also a sophomore in high school, but he goes to Beacon Prep, which is where you're sent if you're rich, male, and scared of public school. He only works at the deli because his father, who owns a local lobster company, wants him to learn how a business operates "from the ground up." His father's very proud of being a Self-Made Man, which apparently means owning a business that's been passed from father to son for decades. When I asked Eric why he wasn't working for his father, he wrinkled his nose and asked if I'd ever smelled a lobster boat.

"Did you take the sandwich temperatures?" I ask.

"No."

"Did you even put the sandwiches out?"

He slumps against the prep counter and opens a box of plastic gloves, stretching one until it breaks. "No."

"Did you do anything?"

"Always the same questions." He tsks his tongue. "You're very predictable, do you know that?"

I take a rag from the cabinet above the counter and go out front to wipe down the customer-facing side of the case. I'm scrubbing at a dried smear of coleslaw when someone's shadow falls across the display meats behind the glass.

"Eric?" our manager says. I twist around, still crouched near the floor. Ricky's scrubbing his hands together so intensely that little bits of rolled skin fall to the speckled linoleum. He recently told us he started a course of Prozac, but he doesn't think it's working.

I return my attention to the coleslaw. Through the fingerprinted case I can see Eric from the waist down: glossy leather belt and lumpy pockets stuffed with a vape pen and the car keys to his mom's Mercedes. "What?" he asks.

"Can I speak to you in private?"

The khakis crease at the thighs as he steps forward. "Am I in trouble? I was just about to put the sandwiches out."

"No, no, nothing like that. I'll meet you in my office."

Eric's hand trembles above a shrink-wrapped maple ham. The case has gone foggy with my breath, and I wipe it with my bent elbow. On the other side, all of his fingers curl toward his palm except for the middle, which he stretches straight and taps once against the glass, just above my nose.

"There you go," Ricky says as Eric exits the deli. Then he turns his attention to me. My knees pop when I stand and Ricky looks left and right, like he's about to tell me something illegal. "Eric's going to be out for the rest of the day, okay?"

"Are you firing him?" When I think about that possibility, I get the same feeling of tingly satisfaction that came with passing a girl on the track.

Ricky looks shocked, but there's a low bar for that. "No, no. A strictly personal matter."

"Is everything okay?"

"You're So Vain" starts playing over the speakers. Ricky lifts his head and raises a hand, like he's swearing on his life. He loves knowing more than you do. "I'm really not at liberty to say."

AFTER WORK, I ride my bike to the beach and smoke by the tide pools. It's one of the few places where I can be alone without being bothered. I used to go to the library, but then one night a woman followed me outside when I went to get my bike. I could hear her flip-flops smacking the sidewalk as I kneeled down to undo my lock, and then her wet breathing as she stood over me. You shouldn't be out alone after dark, she told me when I looked up.

Her ponytail was tied up so tightly it looked like it was taking part of her forehead with it.

I do this all the time, I said.

And what does your mother think about that? A breeze blew through the parking lot and she shoved her hands into the kangaroo pocket of her red sweatshirt. It said *PTA CEO* in ugly block letters across the chest.

She doesn't care, I told her.

Maybe she *says* she doesn't care, but she does.

No, really. She doesn't. I twisted the combination to my lock, and its two halves fell apart in my hand. Can I go now?

You remind me of my daughter. She thinks I give bad advice.

The woman's hands squirmed inside the pocket—it looked like a squirrel was moving around in there.

I don't know your daughter, ma'am. I tossed one leg over my bike seat and stood there with my heels lifted off the ground.

No, the woman said, looking off over my shoulder. I suppose you don't. She was staring at the moon then, a fuzzy crescent above the trees, and I started to pedal away. Be safe, she called after me, like it was something I could control, or that she could, by saying it.

I take off my sneakers and socks and dip my toes into the water, stirring the sandy puddle until a whirlpool appears. The surface reminds me of the marbled paper we'd make in elementary school art class, the reflected smoke of my cigarette rippling through the swirled water. I used to smoke before practice, hiding behind the football shed and finishing as many Parliaments as I could before someone would start looking for me. I ran faster if I smoked—that's just a fact. When I circled the track afterward, light-headed and tight-lunged, I pictured my whole body cleansed from the inside, burned down so I could build it up again. If I just ran fast enough, everything would incinerate. Which meant I could be new.

I don't stay very long at the tide pools. Someone's getting married at one of the rental houses that line the beach, and she keeps shouting about the sand and the smell. When I walk past their porch I see her big netted skirt pushed between the wooden posts and hear her ask why some random girl is out here ruining her shots—doesn't she realize this is practically private property?

I bike through the pharmacy drive-through on my way home and pick up Mom's medicine. Every time I pay I hold my breath because I still use Dad's card, which I stole from his wallet last year when he first started talking about going out West. That was also when he told Mom he'd been putting away so much money in his HSA that she wouldn't have to worry at all while he was gone. That's her weak spot. When someone tells her they've done something good, she so badly wants to believe them.

Obviously he knows I have the card because I charge between five hundred and a thousand dollars' worth of prescriptions to it every month. One possibility is that he feels too guilty to call and ask about it because he hasn't contacted us once since he left. The other possibility is that he thinks he'll be able to pay it back one day because he's delusional like that. Most likely a combination of both. His weak spot is that he believes he can change, despite overwhelming evidence to the contrary.

When I come home, Mom's reading a magazine in my bed with the blinds closed and the lights off. I know she's high because that's the only time she goes into my room without permission. Usually she's very good about asking.

"I see you picked up my poisons," she says, pointing to the paper bag full of pill bottles. "Where else have you been?"

I kick off my sneakers and they bounce against the wall with a soft thud. "Work."

"Work, work, work." She sings it back to herself like it's a song from a musical. "You work too hard, baby."

"I work just enough." There's a paper plate on her lap holding a slice of reheated pizza we ordered last week, orange oil pooling beneath the crust. "Don't get that on my comforter, please."

She stretches open her mouth and eyes and makes her entire face into one shocked O. When she's stoned she acts like a mime. "I would never. I do the laundry, after all." She raises the pizza to her mouth and takes a bite. The edges of her lips shine with grease and the collar of her shirt is speckled with crumbs. "What did you do after work? Weren't you off at six?"

"I went to the library." I climb onto the bed next to her and wriggle underneath the covers. "What have you been up to?"

"Oh, same old, same old."

"Is it bad?" I flip onto my side so that I'm facing her. She doesn't smoke during the day unless the pain makes her want to break her own pelvis and pour her brain through her ears. That's what she says when she's trying to be funny. When she can't be funny, she shuts the bathroom door and lies naked in the empty tub with the faucet pouring hot water over her head and binder clips clamped all over the soft part of her lower stomach. DIY acupuncture.

"Did you eat?" she asks.

"Do you need Advil?" It's not easy to get a prescription for Percocet or OxyContin anymore, at least not around here. And Mom's pain doesn't have a source, according to the doctors, which is a lazy way of putting it, because she points to the same place below her belly button and at the back of her skull whenever they ask. What they mean is that they can't find *evidence* of the source, because apparently being a doctor means second-guessing whatever your patient tells you until a scan or test proves it.

"I can make you a sandwich." She finishes the pizza and places the plate on the carpet. "That was the last slice."

"I'm not hungry."

"You need to eat."

"I will, I will." She clicks her tongue at me. "Later, Mom." I close my eyes and press my thumbs to my lids until I see bright red. "Just let me lie here for a second."

She sighs and picks up her magazine, but I don't hear her flip the pages. She's looking at me. "My sweet Baby Jane," she says softly. "When did you get so old?"

It's the same thing Dad said, when he surprised me at practice back in March. I had just zipped up my duffel when I saw him standing on the other side of the chain-link fence, playing with some dandelions he'd yanked out of the ground. Luckily everyone was talking about prom, so no one paid attention when I waved goodbye and ran over to him. You look like a pedophile, I said.

Nice to see you, too.

Have you been home?

His face told me that no, he hadn't, and no, he wouldn't. How's your mom?

Counting down the days until you come back, I said, even though that wasn't true.

September, he said. I told you, I'll be back before your junior year.

Sure.

Don't "sure" me.

We both had our fingers wrapped around one of the fence's metal diamonds, which were approximately five hundred degrees from the sun. I made a bet with myself that he'd let go before I would. How's Head and Shoulders?

Don't call him that, Jane.

That's what I nicknamed Dad's brother, John, because he's a major flake. The whole reason Dad went out to San Diego in the first place was to help him sell home-security systems—John said that the warm weather and "active West Coast lifestyle" meant plenty of beautiful days for thieves to break into houses while their inhabitants were out surfing or whatever.

I'm trying to do the right thing, he said. His hand fell from the fence.

Out of the corner of my eye, I saw my teammates turn to look at us. I gave them a big wave, like the waves they would give when their boyfriends came to pick them up, like I was another happy girl with no issues and an optimistic view of my future. They went back to talking.

Listen. I could feel the sun shining through the holes in my jersey, burning the skin along my shoulders. You having to prove yourself is getting really fucking old.

He said that I'd understand one day, when I have my own family to take care of.

I already have a family to take care of, I told him.

That's when he asked me when I got so old, and also if he could give me a ride home. I said he could, because if I caught a ride with the other track girls I'd have to talk about stupid things, like whether blow jobs counted as sex.

I'll be back soon, he said when he dropped me off. I promise.

He always promised. I stood on the curb and watched him back out of the driveway and turn down the street, because I wanted him to know I was watching him and that I'd remember what he said, even if he told himself I wouldn't.

"I'm only sixteen," I say to Mom.

"I've never felt older than I did at sixteen." She pulls the covers up to her chest and moves her face so close to mine that our noses touch. Her eyes close.

"Do you want me to turn out the light?"

"I won't be able to sleep if you haven't eaten."

"I'm going now. Hand me your plate?" I check my phone as I walk out of the room—seven thirty. "G'night, Mom."

"Good night, baby." I flick off the light and the room goes gray. She rolls over onto her stomach, bony shoulders like mountain peaks beneath the sheets. I suddenly feel as though I miss her, even though there she is, right in front of me.

In the kitchen, I make a peanut butter and jelly sandwich and go outside to eat it on our front lawn. The summer people are having a party a few streets over, probably to celebrate the start of the season. They use our street for overflow parking when they throw parties—sometimes they even slip a warning note in our mailboxes: *Hi, neighbors, it might get a little loud tonight!* Someone's blocked our driveway with their white BMW, and I walk up and press my head against the driver's side window. Expensive-looking lipsticks sit on a plastic tray behind the gearshift. I try the door just to see if they're as stupid as I think they are, and it swings open into my hip without a sound. I lean over and take one of the lipsticks, open its gold cap. The waxy stick's purple, like the dried prunes we sell in plastic bulk bins at the Market. I try to think of something good to write, something that sticks with you forever because it's that long-lasting combination of meanness and truth, like when my cousin said I wasn't actually that smart, I was just good at making people feel like they'd said something stupid. But in the end all I write is LEAVE, right across the hood in big blocky letters. I drop the open lipstick on the car seat and hope it melts into the leather upholstery.

When I pick up my plate to go back inside, the sound of the party gets louder. I can't see the house or the people but I can hear laughter and the clinking of glasses. Their music pounds through our neighborhood, drowning out the waves and the wind.

THE NEXT DAY ROB AND I are supposed to go to the beach in Rockpoint, a town an hour away where no one will recognize us. I wait by the bottom of the fire escape in my cover-up, holding a picnic basket packed with cucumber sandwiches and a mason jar of homemade lemonade, feeling excited and also embarrassed, which is what happens when I actually put effort into something. The cucumber sandwiches might be too much. I got the idea from the Martha Stewart magazine I stole from the store, which said that "tea sammies" were the ideal beach food.

We're scheduled to meet at noon, but I wait fifteen minutes and Rob doesn't appear. Rob's always on time.

I leave my picnic basket and bike on the grass, climb up to his window, and knock twice. He walks slowly into his room and heaves up the screen and the storm window like they weigh five million pounds. "Are you mad at me?" I ask through the empty frame.

"Why would I be mad at you?" he says from inside.

"I don't know. That's why I'm asking."

I wait for him to say that he's not mad, to do something to make me feel better, like saying I'm beautiful. No one has ever called me beautiful. Mom might have, but she thinks it sends the wrong message to girls, so instead she tells me how perceptive and resilient I am. Who cares about being perceptive and resilient?

Rob does not tell me I'm beautiful. "Do you need something?" is what he says instead, and there's no world in which I would allow myself to say yes.

Wind blows up through the grated floor of the fire escape, tossing my skirt. I press it down with my hands. "Are we still going to the beach?"

"Fuck." He bangs his knuckle against the frame.

"You forgot."

"I've been busy."

"It's Sunday."

He sucks in his lips when I say that. They make a little hissing sound, like a balloon deflating. "Are you fucking with me?" I have no idea what he's talking about, and I tell him so. "Your friends haven't said anything?" He looks over my shoulder like one of them might be standing there.

"What friends?" I ask, because I know it will make him feel bad for me and I'm not one of those people who hates being pitied. Pity is one of the best ways to get what you want. And I want to go to the beach.

But he's not listening. He's looking somewhere else, somewhere beyond me. "Jane?"

"Yeah?"

"You should really lock your bike."

THE FIRST TIME I rode in his car, it smelled like artificial lavender and stale coffee, and his back seat was covered in crushed Diet Coke cans. I thought about whether he was less attractive for drinking all that Diet Coke, which I associated with the poetry

girls who dressed up as Sylvia Plath for Halloween and mixed random herbs into their hand-rolled cigarettes. Ultimately, I decided
no. Because it was one thing I knew about him that no one else did.

He asked if I minded if we stopped for gas. He was giving me a
ride home from Kid2Kid, the middle school tutoring group I'd
been with since freshman year and which he had recently became
the faculty advisor of. I waited until everyone else had left, until
only the two of us were sitting on the sidewalk. I told him my mom
wasn't answering my texts. He touched one finger to his lips and
narrowed his eyes, which made me think he was going to ask who
my emergency contact was or if any of my neighbors were home.
But then he said that he could give me a ride, it wasn't any trouble
at all.

While he stood by the pump, I took one of the cans and placed
it in my backpack. Only later, when I was describing the day back
to myself as I lay in bed, did I realize this was creepy. I don't have
that inherent sense that most people have, that intuition about
what's acceptable and what's not.

On my bed, I pulled the can from my bag and pressed it to my
mouth until it clicked against my front teeth. I closed my eyes and
saw his long pointer finger peeling back the tab, his lips opening
before they sucked against the raised metal edge. I thought it would
taste like him, but it didn't. It was metallic instead, like a penny, or
like blood.

After that day, he always drove me home. We didn't discuss it.
We both just knew.

It was late April when we kissed for the first time. The sky had
been dark all day, and droplets began to slide down his windshield
like beads of sweat. Wait, I said as we drove past the entrance to
Opal Point. Pull in there.

He parked between a set of faded lines near the concrete steps to the beach. I love the ocean during a storm. We leaned against the seawall, cracked from years of hurricanes and blizzards and floods, and watched the whitecaps fizz like soda poured too fast. For a second, I thought the blink of the lighthouse was faraway lightning, a seagull moving through its flash. Then there was a crack and the heavy rain came. I closed my eyes and felt him take my hand. I wondered if this was really happening, and when I opened my eyes, it was.

The entire windshield blurred with water, the rinse section of a car wash. The hood of my sweatshirt had filled with rain, which started to trickle down my back. I took off my shoes and socks and wrung my ponytail over the car mat.

You're shivering, he said, a raindrop quivering at the tip of his nose. He reached into the back seat and dug around until he found a beach towel to wrap around my shoulders. It was printed with girls in coconut bras doing the hula.

He rested his elbow on the armrest between us and cocked his head like he hadn't understood something I'd said. He was waiting, I realized.

I reached across the console and placed one hand on the dip between his shoulders, bending him toward me. I lifted the other to his face. The hinge of his jaw quivered under my thumb. Relax, I whispered. I moved my finger to his lips, which were smooth in the center and flaking like bark at the edges. For a second he was very still. Then I covered his mouth with my own. The only kiss I'd ever initiated.

We pulled away at the same time, our breath whistling over the soft thud of the rain. Well, he finally said. What now?

. . .

AT ROB'S, I stand in the grassy clearing near the dumpsters for a while, staring at my bike. I decide that the only way to salvage this day is to make a little money, so I swing my leg over the seat and pedal toward the Market. This must be what Ricky calls initiative.

I'm rounding the corner of the store, the chain of my bike clicking, when I hear a thump. There on the other side of the wall is Eric, hunched forward like a boxer, one elbow drawn back to a sharp point. I'm snapping my kickstand into place when his fist launches into the brick, scraping against the rough mortar.

"What the fuck are you doing?" I ask from behind. He's in his work polo and sweat's run between his shoulder blades, turning the fabric dark and wet. I have a weird urge to touch it.

He whips around with his fist held high. The knuckles are raw and dripping blood, like the juices that collect at the bottom of our roast beef packaging. He's breathing fast. It occurs to me that I should probably be scared. "Why are you in your swimsuit?" he asks.

I look down at the green bikini peeking through my cover-up, which is a crocheted white dress with tassels at the bottom. "It's a long story."

He grunts and turns to face the wall again, cranks his elbow back. "Have you ever"—he asks, fist crunching against the brick— "been so angry, with nowhere to put it?" The elbow pulls away again; the fist launches forward.

The blood starts to trickle down his wrist but I don't turn away. "Since when is there somewhere to put anger?"

The crackle of his knuckle bones sounds like twigs splintering in two. "Like, you know. There's someone responsible. And you take it out on them." He pauses to put his hands on his hips and pant.

"I've never taken my anger out on someone."

He's bent over now but looks up at me. "Really?"

"Really."

"Well, what do you do then?"

"I don't know." I shrug. "Swallow it. It just turns to disappointment, eventually."

He shakes his head and little specks of sweat fly off his forehead. "That can't work." He's still hunched over, but he waves me toward him. "Come here."

I take a tentative step forward.

"Come here and hit me." He rolls his shoulders as he rises. His cheeks are pink, and the hairs of his eyebrows are angled every which way.

"I can't."

"You can." He gets right up in my face, so close I can feel his breath on my nose. "You hate me, right? All those times I've done jack shit during our shifts. That time I called you a cunt."

Something heats up inside my throat, makes my neck go hot. "When did you call me a cunt?"

He steps backward and leans against the wall, like: What are you going to do about it? "Oh, tons of times. Whenever you try to act like you're in charge. Just because no one in your life's ever listened to you doesn't mean you can force me to."

I've never hit anything, not even a pillow. The tendons in my arm light up like a sparkler and an invisible band tugs my elbow toward my shoulder blade. The air inside my lungs sizzles. And then everything releases, like the powder of a firework. I watch my bent fingers collide with his jaw. My knuckles glide inside his wet mouth, brush against the slippery sharpness of his front teeth, past his mealy gums. I'm looking at my hand and it's crisscrossed with pink spit. I'm walking in small circles. I'm sitting on the ground with my back against the wall. The sun is still shining.

He coughs and spits a little blood onto the pavement. It collects in a small puddle beside the strap of my sandals. He drops down next to me. Our mouths are both open wide for air. "How's your hand?" he asks after a moment. I drop it onto his knee because I can't hold any part of myself upright. My elbows are resting on my own knees, all of me slumped forward.

I turn my head and watch him inspect the gash, which is wide and red. "Touch it," I say.

He laughs a little.

"Do it." The skin's curled away from my knuckles like peeled tape. I angle my fist toward him.

He looks straight at me, like I might flinch. I don't. He runs his finger over the split skin and it stings like antiseptic. One nail dips inside and I hiss through tight teeth. When he's done he rests his hand on his thigh, my blood beneath his fingernails. He presses his head against the wall. "I never called you a cunt," he says. "And I didn't mean any of that."

"I know."

"I just thought it would hurt, is all. Fire you up."

"I know."

"You can't go into work dressed like that."

"I know." My eyelids feel heavy, thick. I let them close. "Fuck Ricky."

Eric laughs. "Yeah, fuck him. Fuck everyone but us."

. . .

MOM'S SITTING AT THE KITCHEN TABLE when I get home. "How was the beach?" she asks. "You didn't swim?"

I touch my dry hair. "The waves were too rough."

She nods and squints at her laptop, which is open in front of her at full brightness. There's an ice pack pressed to the buttons of her jeans, sweating across her lap. "Have you seen this yet?" she asks, tilting the screen toward me.

Dear Nashquitten High families,

It is with great sadness that I inform you of the passing of Lucy Anderson this weekend. Lucy was a vital member of our community, and our thoughts are with her family as they weather this insurmountable loss. We will hold an assembly tomorrow, and Ms. Layla Owens will be available to any students who would like support during this time.

Sincerely,

Janet Cushing, Principal

"Did you know her?" Mom asks.

My hands go cold and the tips of my fingers turn numb. I knew Lucy. At the beginning of the school year, I started cleaning the art room before track so Mrs. Brown could pick up her son from pre-school on time. She paid me thirty bucks a week and Lucy was usually there painting. But I would have known her anyway. Everyone did, because she had a seizure on the school bus a few months ago. Someone had filmed it and sent the video around set to an EDM song whose beat matched the shaking of her body. Our team captain showed it to us while we were stretching one day. I had another girl's foot in my hand and as I raised it toward her hip the cell phone screen was thrust toward us. Well, what do you think? our captain asked when it was over. We all just mumbled noncommittally, because it wasn't clear in which direction we were being tested. Then she walked around us in a circle, making eye contact one by one. If I *ever* catch any of you sharing this shit or making anything like it, I'll kick your ass so hard you won't even be able to get on your knees in front of your boyfriend. She meant it, too. I'd seen her bench 250 pounds.

"I mean, I knew *of* her," I say.

"Well, I'm sorry, it still must be difficult," Mom offers. "I'm sure you saw her in the halls and that sort of thing."

I force myself to nod, to try and stay in the conversation. But in my mind, I'm rounding the corner of the store, hearing Eric's fist smack the brick before I see it. She was the cause, that's clear now. I wonder if they were dating. I never heard about Lucy seeing anyone, but I'm also not exactly in the loop for these things. You'd be fucked up forever, if your high school girlfriend suddenly died. I wonder what Rob would do, if something happened. Would he come to my funeral? "They didn't say how she died?"

"They might not know." Mom's eyes are still on the screen, and her pupils vibrate as she rereads the words. "What do you want for dinner? We have some mac and cheese in the pantry. Or there's that frozen pizza."

"I'll get the mac and cheese started." I hear her laptop click shut as I open the pantry door. I know she's twisting her chair around by the squeak of the tile.

"Jane?" she asks.

"Yes?" I pull the thin chain dangling from the ceiling and light washes over our boxes and cans, bags and jars. When did we let everything get so dusty? I kick an unsprung mousetrap in the corner, but it doesn't pop.

"You know you can tell me anything, don't you?"

I pull the blue Kraft box from the second shelf. "Of course I do," I say before tugging out the light. I make sure I'm smiling when I turn around.

ON MONDAY I RUN INTO ERIC at the Dunkin' Donuts on Main Street. It's eight thirty; we should both be at school. "What are you doing here?" he asks. He's sitting at one of the tiny tables near the window, something red and slushy in his hand, and gets up to meet me in line.

"Same thing you're doing." The woman in front of me walks off with her coffee and I order a dozen donuts, tell the cashier in the brown visor to pick them. While his back is to us, a pink box in one hand, the other carefully selecting, Eric slurps loudly through his thick orange straw. "What's wrong with you?" he asks.

I smooth down my hair. "What do you mean?"

"You look like shit."

"Thank you." The cashier hands me my box and I pay with cash. Eric leads me back to his table, but when I offer him a donut he declines—"this is my calories for the morning," he says, pointing to his drink. I open the box and decide on a strawberry-iced. It leaves a greasy O on the sheet of wax paper beneath. "You look like shit, too," I tell him. "So how did you know her?"

He looks up from scraping something out of his thumbnail, but he doesn't ask what I'm talking about. "She was my cousin."

"I'm sorry," I say automatically. The three stupidest syllables on the planet.

He flattens his straw between his teeth. "Thanks. We were pretty close." He pulls his phone out of his pocket and taps on the screen. His pupils flick up and down as he scrolls. "I don't really have any recent photos of us. She hated having her picture taken."

He sets the phone down on the table and opens Instagram. As he's about to click on his tagged photos, I see a picture of her on his feed. "What's that?" I ask. Lucy in her bedroom, back turned toward the camera as she stands at the foot of her bed, trying to pull on a thin, strappy green dress. But the tight fabric's knotted around her head, leaving her white bra and underwear exposed as both of her hands search for the neckline. Her bent arms shimmer in the low light from the single lamp on her bureau, and there's a beer bottle beside her jewelry box. Looking at the scene feels dirty, like I'm seeing something I shouldn't. Then I realize it's the angle. High up and tilted toward her body, as though from a security camera. The caption reads *05/25 9:49:22 PM.*

"Why haven't I seen this before?"

I lean forward to tap the name of the user who posted it, lucystopsandshoots, but Eric snatches the phone away. "Her photography account was private."

"That didn't really look like her." Lucy wore long, billowy clothes like the women at the mall who try to sell you vitamin subscriptions. And her arms were usually smeared with charcoal or dried paint, not streaked with body glitter.

"It was a project for her art-school portfolio," Eric says. He shoves the phone in his pocket and gives me a look. "And for the record, I didn't show you."

I take a bite of my donut. "I don't even know what you're talking about."

In the art room after school, Lucy worked on a canvas the size of double doors, and she used ocean water to do it. What's that smell? I asked one day, and she looked up like she'd just realized I was there.

When she explained, I asked if I could see. She didn't look so sure about that but said yes anyway. She had this big orange Home Depot bucket that was full of water but also hermit crabs and periwinkles and strands of leathery seaweed. Did you get it from the tide pools? I asked. She nodded.

She'd thin gold paint with the water and dribble it over the canvas, where it pooled in pockets like the bloody gauze from my wisdom teeth removal. The painting smelled like sand-baked beach, salty and rotten, especially when the sun shone through the window on the opposite wall.

What do you do with the extra water? I asked her one day.

Dump it back.

Every day? I asked. She nodded. Can I come?

She swiped her paintbrush against her hand a few times, testing the color. If you carry the bucket.

I went with her one day in October, when fall was turning everything brown and crispy. We both wore sweatshirts, and leaves were starting to collect in the storm gutters on the edge of the beach's parking lot. Big signs that said NO SWIMMING were staked everywhere. Red tide had poisoned the water, and the waves looked like the blood that sloshes in medical bags. Beach seagulls are always aggressive, but that day they dive-bombed on either side of us, snatching the dead cod washed up on the shore. The smell of rot was so thick in the air that I tasted the decay on my tongue. Lucy had handed me Kleenex in the parking lot, and now I knew why: to wipe my eyes and cover my mouth when I coughed. It felt like the world had ended and some stupid person had chosen us as the survivors.

I followed Lucy to a set of pools I didn't know existed. Turns out there's a hollow inside the huge rock everyone likes to sunbathe on, and if you squeeze inside it opens up wide like a grotto. Lucy said it filled up during high tide, but at low tide the ocean drained away to reveal a cluster of carved-out rocks. We hopped carefully from edge to edge, but red washed in from the outside opening, touching the toes of our sneakers. The tide had only been there for a couple days, but the pools were already pinkish. Don't touch it, I said.

I'm not going to. She took the bucket from my hands and poured it into a pool, the clear water rinsing out some of the color.

They're going to die, I said. I was talking about the three hermit crabs inside the bucket.

At least they're free, she said, which seemed like a weak argument to me, but the tide was starting to come in, and we had to go.

Eric finishes his drink and reconsiders the donuts. He pulls a Boston cream from the wax paper and holds his hand under his chin as he prepares to take a bite. By now the bell for first period's rung, which means I haven't walked past the open door of Rob's classroom on my way to Spanish. I check my phone under the table to see if he's texted. He hasn't.

"Hey," I say. "Would you want to go to the beach?"

THE TIDE'S OUT and the wet sand's rippled like a thousand snakes raced over it and into the sea. We sit in front of the ugly Geotube they pushed against the bluff last year to keep it from collapsing. I bury my feet underneath the cold sand while Eric tosses an empty mussel shell between his hands. We're supposed to be underwater in seventy-five years, according to the current rate of erosion. They always mention that kind of stuff in science class, for us to make real-world connections. But they never say what we're actually supposed to do about it, besides answer the question correctly on pop quizzes: What is the name of the force impacting Nashquitten's coastline?

I pick a tiny strand of hair off the back of Eric's neck and look to see if he notices. He doesn't. Flies buzz around the mounds of dried seaweed behind us. No one else is here.

"Would you rather live forever or die tomorrow?" he asks, tracing the lip of the shell.

"Die tomorrow," I tell him without hesitation. "You?"

"Live forever."

"Why?" I ask, trying not to sound judgmental, because of course a boy thinks he could still be useful at age 397.

He lies down on the beach and sweeps his arms back and forth like he's making a snow angel. Looking at him, I picture a version of my life where we fall in love. We'd steal each other muffins from the Market's bakery and make out in the Knights of Columbus changing room and sleep over at each other's houses when our parents weren't home. I feel a little sad then, because I so badly want those things to sound nice. But to me, they seem boring as shit.

"I can't imagine ever being ready," he says. "I'll always want more time."

"With who? They'll all be dead."

"You wouldn't be. If you answered the question correctly."

He does this wiggly thing with his eyebrows that must be how Beacon Prep boys flirt. "You'll never get that sand out of your hair,"

I say. He sits up and shakes his head back and forth like a dog. "Well, what would you do if you *were* dying tomorrow?" I ask.

He's quiet for a moment. "You can't make fun of me, okay?" He pauses until I nod my head. "I'd go to my childhood fort in the backyard and die alone, like a wolf. I don't like the idea of anyone being there." He looks down at his hands. "No one deserves that."

"Damn, you're bleak." I brush a strand of dried seaweed from the back of his head. "And that's not true."

He raises three fingers, like a Boy Scout. "I swear. I've thought about this before."

"No, I mean, animals don't actually like to die alone. It's a myth."

He scratches his nose skeptically. "You sure?"

"One thousand percent."

"I think you're a liar," he says, but he's grinning.

"I'm not!"

He picks up a handful of sand and blows it into my face like glitter. I close my eyes at just the right time.

A FEW HOURS LATER, Eric gives me a ride home, my bike rattling in his trunk. I study the profile of his face while he drives, the bump at the base of his nose and the gummy scar slashing through his eyebrow. His future will be extremely straightforward, as it is for people who generally like the life they have. Four years at UMass, a pretty girl named Christine or Elizabeth, a dozen lobster boats, a golden retriever named Waffles or Nugget or some other childhood food. "I can feel you looking at me," he says.

"I'm not looking at you."

He leans back and catches my eye in the rearview mirror. "Sure."

"Was it surprising? That I asked you to go to the beach?"

"What kind of question is that?" He cracks his window and a breeze blows through the car. "I'm not really thinking about you right now. Sorry."

I cover my cheeks with my hands. I don't want him to see that they're red.

AT HOME, I find a sticky note on the kitchen table: *Someone called for you.* I look at my phone, which I've had on silent, and sure enough: five missed calls, three voicemails. I flick off my shoes and drop the Dunkin' Donuts box on the counter. "Mom, I have donuts!" I walk to her room and crack the door. "Donuts," I whisper.

She sits cross-legged in the middle of the bed with a bowl of cereal in her lap. "I hear you weren't at school today." She pats the empty space to her left but I stay in the doorway.

"Who told you that?" I try to think if there's a way to lie my way out of this. I'd assumed that with everything going on, they wouldn't bother checking attendance.

"Mrs. Beagin. They call if you're absent, you know." She pats the comforter again. "They had an assembly this morning. About that girl."

I walk slowly across the carpet. "She had a name." I perch on the very edge of the bed, and the old mattress dips beneath me.

"Lucy." She lifts her spoon to her lips.

"Yeah."

"There's a message on the machine for you. From someone named Henry." Henry is Rob's middle name. "He said it was urgent."

"I don't know a Henry."

"He was calling for Jane."

"Must be a different Jane."

She looks at me in this way only she can—like my thoughts are written on my forehead and I'm watching her read them. "I talked to your father, by the way. He asked me to apologize to you."

I wipe my palms against the comforter. They're sweating. "What for?"

She raises a hand and runs it through the back of my hair, working out the knots with her fingers. She yanks at one near my neck, and it feels like my scalp might peel right off. "He didn't say."

"Oh. Here, let me take that." I hold out my hand even though there's still cereal in her bowl. She gives it to me anyway, and I can feel her eyes on my back as I stand up and open the door. I shut it so quickly behind me that some of the milk splashes out of the bowl and onto my sock, which I drag along the hallway carpet to dry. When I get to the living room I realize that I've rubbed my ankle completely raw. I touch the clear ooze and think about what my father would say if he ever found out about Rob. Nothing, probably. That's one good thing I can say about him. That he always treated my business as my own. Or maybe he was just scared of what he'd find if he didn't.

"What is that?" Mom asks from her room. Sirens, wailing louder and louder. I yank open the curtains above the couch just in time to see an ambulance pull into our neighbor's driveway. There she is on the side stairs, a little pink dress flapping around her knees, one hand on her huge belly, one pressed into her back. She takes a step and I see that the back of her skirt is wet and stuck to her thighs. The baby's coming.

"What's happening?" Mom calls.

She's wearing green plastic flip-flops, and, for reasons I don't understand, shakes them off when one of the EMTs rushes over to take her hand. He's left a gurney in the driveway, but our neighbor doesn't seem to want any of that. He helps her off the final step but she drops to the pavement instead, knees and hands beneath her, belly hanging low. I'm thinking of the video of the horse giving birth that they played for us in health class, the blood and the membrane and the sticky hay everywhere, but also the way the horse had looked over her shoulder when it was over, like she couldn't believe what she'd done. Our neighbor looks up and our eyes meet through the windowpane. She opens her mouth and her lips quiver like she's going to tell me something important, but then what comes out is a scream. I want to crouch out of view, but I don't let myself. I stay.

"What's wrong?" Mom shouts. The bed frame creaks—she's standing up. Outside, our neighbor slams her eyes shut, but I don't look away. Another EMT comes and sits beside her on the pavement, but this one's a woman. She strokes our neighbor's forehead with the back of her palm and says something I can't hear. It seems like they want to take her back inside—the male EMT's pointing to the house—but our neighbor shakes her head.

"Nothing, Mom."

Her voice shoots out as the door opens. "Jane," she says. "Don't lie to me."

The carpet absorbs her footsteps, so I don't realize she's right behind me until I can smell the mustiness of her unwashed shirt. She grabs my shoulder so tightly I stumble backward a couple steps, and as she pulls me toward her my cell phone rings, our neighbor howls, and a second, tiny voice flies out, tasting its first gulp of air.

NATALIE

MY MOTHER CANNOT FIND HER LIPSTICK.

"Where is it?" she asks, panicked. Her arm sweeps over the rail of her hospital bed and the tubes taped to her arm go taut. I watch the graph of her pulse tighten, like it has for every minor inconvenience today, from a lack of Diet Coke to an itch that couldn't be satisfied, no matter how many times I grated a plastic fork over her neck. The beeping, combined with some staticky noise from the room beside us, reminds me of a dial-up internet trill. I used to spend hours on AIM, but I only ever talked to robots, who I asked questions like *What is your favorite fruit?* and *Do you know you're not real?*

"Mom, stop." I reach for her hand, which, even now, is slick with rose-scented lotion. She's been asking the nurses if any of them do manicures, which is so embarrassing that I excuse myself to the bathroom before I can hear their responses. All of her nails are plum purple except for the thumbnail, where the polish has chipped off in chalky strips. She tucks it beneath her curled fingers like I care. I've never seen her undone, not even at night, when she watches television in her pink silk pajamas and a face painted with the Chantecaille foundation she buys on discount from Nordstrom Rack. I once overheard my father telling his friends that she sleeps in her makeup, draping a towel over her pillowcase so she wouldn't stain it. Should I be worried? he asked, but in a way that made it sound like he was joking.

"Here, have some water." I hand her one of the tiny plastic cups the hospital provides and she takes a dainty sip. I'd forgotten the skilled way in which my mother exhausts me, carving my patience down through a small series of requests and comments, like a sculptor shaving away the sharp edges of their marble. A master artist, one might say.

"I need it," she insists.

It's almost one in the morning. What she needs is a sleeping pill. But I go over to the suitcase anyway, a scraped gray clamshell that belongs to my father, my mother disenchanted with anything strictly practical. There's still a series of tics written in Sharpie on its underside, from the summer I was sent to camp and counted down the days to my release. That was the first time I understood my mother's allegiance to appearance. The other girls had huge trunks with brass locks and quilted paisley bags filled with custom stationery and neon gel pens. My most exciting possession was a tiny handheld fan with foam blades, which I insisted on showing to each of my bunkmates. Maybe ditch that, Mona told me as we walked to the showers the first night, fallen leaves sticking to the sides of our flip-flops.

"Is it there?" My mother smooths the silk handkerchief that hides her naked head. She keeps her scarves knotted to the metal legs of the bedside table, and I untie a new selection for her each morning. Tomorrow she'll have a mastectomy to remove her left breast.

"I don't see it." There's a metallic makeup bag that unzips to reveal an overwhelming number of tiny tubes and fluffy brushes, but no lipstick. "You should get some rest. We'll find it tomorrow."

"No, no." I glance up and see that her pupils have shrunk to seeds, which is what happens when procuring the thing is more important than the thing itself. My mother is one of seven girls, the youngest child of a lobsterman and Catholic-school secretary, and she learned the power of tenacity early on. My aunt likes to tell a story about the time they were playing a game called Grip. Kelly (the oldest) would drive, and the rest of the sisters would sit in the bed of the family truck, reaching for tree branches whenever they came to a stop sign. The challenge was to see who could hold on to their branch for the longest once Kelly started driving again. Usually they didn't last long—a few seconds at most—but my mother was a different story. This particular night was cold, and they'd allowed her to tag along for the first time because she'd recently turned nine. Nine, the sisters had agreed, was the appropriate age to begin playing. They lived near the west end of Nashquitten, which was more heavily wooded back then, and my mother grabbed hold of a hemlock tree at the first stop. You sure about that? Rachel, the middle child, asked, because hemlock branches are spiked with green needles. My mother, wanting to prove herself, nodded and tightened her fingers around the thorns. Kelly took off. The girl had balls, Rachel always says at this point in the story. Balls of steel.

According to the sisters, my mother did a full flip over the side of the truck, never letting go of the branch, which cracked off the trunk as my mother hit the ground. They couldn't find her at first because she'd tumbled behind a holly bush, legs cranked over her head as though she were mid-somersault. Both hands were split wide open, hemlock needles sprinkled over the wounds. We thought she was dead, Kelly claims. I wish I had been, my mother added one year, when the sisters were rehashing the story over Easter brunch with so much excitement you'd think it had happened yesterday. Everyone went quiet.

"It's too late to go." I point toward the window, where the moon's risen above the parking garage. "Nothing's even open."

"Ask your father. There's a twenty-four-hour CVS across the street." My father is currently sitting in our car, nursing a cup of coffee from the vending machine. He allows himself one twenty-minute break a day. Otherwise he sits on a folding chair beside my mother, refusing the armchair because its bulk would add to the distance between them. "He'll go," she says, firmer this time. She's right.

My phone buzzes, vibrating against the radiator where I left it. I already know it's a Slack from the founder. It's only 9:00 p.m. in San Francisco—not that he adheres to any traditional notions of time—which means he's just finished reviewing his youngest son's homework. I once dropped off a laptop for him around this hour, and he insisted I come inside and listen to his daughter's essay on *Mrs. Dalloway*. She was a freshman at Yale and had just wrapped up her first set of final papers.

Maybe *insisted* isn't the right word, as he didn't demand that I enter or attempt to persuade me. Come hear my daughter's paper, was all he said, before turning to walk through the front doors, assuming, like all wealthy people do, that I would follow. And I did.

I trailed him through a marble foyer with a double staircase, trying not to stare at the huge portraits that lined the walls. I had no idea if the faces were family or famous or simply Art, but the golden frames surrounding them looked so heavy that I stepped toward the middle of the room, afraid one would slip and concuss me upon impact. He didn't look back once, and I tried not to focus on anything in the house as he marched forward. The founder already occupied far too much of my mental space, and I knew I would obsess over any details I retained, searching the price of furniture in the living room, googling reviews of books on the shelves, identifying friends in his photos. Like my mother, I have a fascination with unattainable lifestyles, but I'd say my interest is more anthropological than aspirational. The founder's interesting because no matter how many conversations we have, no matter how many of his emails I edit, no matter how many of his house's rooms I enter, I gain no further insight into who he is as a human being. I suppose you sacrifice a significant portion of your inner life to convince yourself you're pursuing Innovation rather than a shamefully massive amount of money.

When we finally arrived in the kitchen, I felt dazed, as though I'd awoken from the deepest realm of sleep. The daughter sat at the kitchen table with her laptop, kicking her heels against the wall behind her.

This is Natalie, the founder announced. She majored in English.

This was not true—I majored in sociology—but to him it was all the same. Just another girl who couldn't code.

I expected the daughter, whom I had never met (though I had booked her travel to and from school and coordinated her academic records) to receive this information with disdain, because teenage girls tend to despise potential allies, particularly if they're identified as such by their parents. But she smiled instead. She'd just turned nineteen—I'd spent months in the family's extensive files over the summer trying to locate her birth certificate for one of many college forms. She looked weary in a way that concerned me but which I knew I'd never be able to do anything about.

The daughter asked me if I'd read Mrs. Dalloway. I told her that I had.

Yes, yes, the founder said impatiently. He opened a refrigerator built into the wall that held only stacked bottles of wine. He poured himself a glass of red and leaned against the counter. Read it to her, won't you? They exchanged a glance that communicated her uneasiness with the situation, but he jerked his head forward in a way I recognized, a gesture that meant: Get the hell on with it.

The daughter cleared her throat and launched into an analysis of gender within the book. (I'd previously overheard the founder lamenting her plan to major in women's studies, which he deemed as "meaningless and hollow" as his niece's attempt to pursue professional influencing.) She discussed the depiction of female consciousness, the significance of Clarissa's social class, the representation of privacy as a source of independence. Normally I would never be able to recall a casual conversation in such detail, but the situation didn't seem casual. It seemed like a test. Which made me wonder: *Who was being tested, me or her?*

That was lovely, I told her when she finished, and then instantly regretted it. The founder didn't do compliments, no matter how warranted. He's of the mind that humans perform best when their competence is in question.

Oh, c'mon. He rolled his knuckle against the kitchen counter until it cracked. His fingers were huge, swollen like boiled hot dogs. He experienced something I'd once seen referred to as full-body bloat on his medical record, and he exercised constantly in an attempt to flush out the source of his bulging. Each doctor he went to claimed they were mystified, which is hilarious, because he's clearly an alcoholic and avid drug user. Once, when we were the last ones leaving the office, he'd drunkenly asked me if he could snort cocaine out of my belly button. It was so pathetic and predictable that I didn't say anything besides no.

Tell her what you really think, Li, he insisted. He calls me that because he thinks it's funny—the joke being that the name sounds Asian, but I'm white.

I'm not lying. I thought it was lovely.

This is the problem with both of you. You don't say what you actually think. He snatched the paper out of his daughter's hands. What does this actually *say*? It's so fucking timid. Make a goddamn point, why don't you. He pressed the trash bin open with his socked toe and dropped the paper into it. He liked dramatically throwing documents away. I'd once seen him do it with a government letter announcing his tax audit.

I wanted to say something to the daughter, but what? I'm sorry this is your father, I'm sorry not everyone you hope will understand you does, I'm sorry I'm standing here thinking about all the ways I feel sorry for you instead of doing anything to help?

The daughter traced her finger along a whorl in the remarkably glossy tabletop. Does it matter, she said after a moment, looking up, that I hate you? And that most of the people who know you do, too?

I flattened my back against the wall where I was standing. No one talked to him like that. My pulse vibrated beneath my tongue.

I'd never seen the founder so completely and nakedly shocked. He's a man who prides himself on examining situations from unknown angles, of thinking in ways so unconventional that he's already considered and rejected any idea presented to him. He swirled his wine with such force that it almost jumped the lip of his glass. I would rather make you uncomfortable in the pursuit of excellence than comfortable in the acceptance of mediocrity, he said.

The daughter stood up and clutched her laptop to her chest. What does that even mean, Dad? Just say that you can't love anything that doesn't match your vision of what it should be.

I could hear my own breath whistling out my nostrils.

She disappeared down the hallway, and he finished his wine in one huge gulp before setting the glass on the counter with a rattle.

We stood in silence, listening to her bare feet bang the stairwell steps.

Her mother and I are divorcing. We both stared straight ahead. It's been difficult for her.

Of course.

She's like me, he said, rubbing his chin. Stubborn. It causes . . . disagreements.

Sure.

And brilliant, too. I mean, you heard the paper.

I did.

He pressed open the trash can. Don't tell anyone at the office that you've been inside my house, he said. He reached inside and extracted the paper, which had a smear of coffee grounds on one corner.

I won't.

You can say you came to my house. For the delivery. That's fine.

Okay.

I'm a very private person.

I understand.

He chuckled in a way I'd never heard before, like he was actually amused. He shook the stained paper at me. You will never understand.

MY MOTHER'S HEAD SWIVELS back and forth. "What's that buzzing?" she asks. "Is that Kathy? I don't want to talk to her."

I swipe open Slack. The founder wants to know if I've ordered new snacks for the staff kitchen yet and if I've spoken with the internet provider about upgrading our service. His final message: *This is not a vacation, correct?* "No, it's nothing," I tell her. "I'll go get your lipstick."

The hospital, like all hospitals, seems to have been designed by a coked-out architecture student determined to trap all visitors within its sanitized walls. I've been here three days, and still the brightly painted directions are meaningless—I walk in the direction of the cafeteria, only to be informed that I've entered Neurology, with Cardiology around the corner and Pediatrics down the hall, Trauma upstairs and the burn unit wherever a diagonal arrow is pointing. "Are you lost?" asks a nurse briskly wheeling a metal cart.

I ask him how to get to the lobby and he looks at me with a combination of pity and exhaustion.

"Quickest way is down two floors and past Emergency." He points to a door and then jabs his finger to the left. "Don't pay any attention to the signs."

I push open the indicated door and descend into the bowels of the hospital, which smell like chemically engineered citrus and bleached-out vomit. My steps echo endlessly, the noise reaching somewhere I can't see. I pass no one.

Before I enter Emergency, I hear it—the barked names slicing through stretched moans and hushed conversations. I step into the corridor beside reception, where a nurse is holding a clipboard as she scans the rows of linked seats. A woman in a bedazzled Dolly Parton shirt looks like she's trying to give herself the Heimlich with one of the chair backs, and a boy in a Red Sox cap is holding a wad of bloody gauze to his forearm. The nurse doesn't seem to notice either of them.

"Can I help you?" she asks. Before I can answer, she's raised a hand above my head. "Sir!" she calls. "Sir!"

A man that seems my father's age stands in front of the revolving door, his mouth wide open, cave-like. Looking at him, something happens to me that's only happened once before in my life: I hear him scream before he actually does.

Six months earlier, I stood in the belly of the Civic Center station waiting for the BART. It was late afternoon, almost three, and I was eating a blueberry granola bar I'd found in the bottom of my purse. The station wasn't busy yet, just me, another woman, and a man pacing up and down the yellow caution line. Twin lights appeared in the distance and the speakers announced that a train was approaching. As I stepped forward, I saw the man press his hands to his chest—in an X, as though he were skydiving—and jump. His 49ers cap, too big for his head, fluttered away like a leaf. But when I turned my head to confirm what had happened, he was still pacing up and down the platform. He's going to jump, I told the other woman, who was now standing beside me. What? she asked. I must have sounded hysterical, because she took several steps in the opposite direction and put on her headphones. He— I tried, shouting after her now. And then it happened.

In the waiting room, I'm not the only one who glimpses the future. Everyone turns, and even though the man's mouth is still a silent O, a mother clamps her hands over her daughter's ear and a man bites his shirt collar and the woman wearing the Dolly Parton shirt pauses, still bent over the chair.

When his wail comes, we feel it in our teeth. It sounds like something splitting open that can never be stitched up again. A scar in the making. We look at each other and think: *I will never see any of you again.*

The man starts to stuff his hand into his mouth, forcing the knuckles until they disappear behind his jutted jaw. He's still trying to scream. Spit dribbles down his wrist and onto the tile.

No one moves.

"Aren't you going to do something?" someone asks. When the nurse stares back at me, I realize that I'm the one who spoke.

"He's probably homeless," she says, but her voice quivers. "Where's security?"

"I don't know," I say. "I don't work here."

"I know you don't," she snaps before leaning toward the receptionist. "Sally, page Nathan." She opens several drawers and claws through their contents. "Where's the Narcan?"

The man pitches forward but doesn't fall. He tugs his hand out of his mouth and dry heaves, gapes like a freshly caught fish. I pull my eyes away.

The room around me has gone watery. The edges of the emergency-exit sign waver; the flecked tile floor undulates; the people's faces streak like paint. I try to focus on the bulletin board beside me, with its *Cancer Patient Support Group* poster and *Pint for Pint* blood drive flyer, but the words seem fake and shallow.

"Are you okay?" I ask the man. My feet shuffle toward him, my untied shoelace jumping across the floor. I feel like a balloon bobbing beside the flesh and blood of my body.

He looks up at me with eyes so glazed they seem to be covered with a film. "Where's Lucy?"

"I don't know," I tell him. His hands are bunched at his chest and he begins to wring the hem of his T-shirt.

"Why don't you know?" He takes a step closer. "Where is she?"

At the edge of my vision, I see the nurse on the phone, her mouth scrambling with the speed of her speech. The man's taken another step toward me when a woman bursts through the revolving entrance doors. She runs toward him, her half-tied ponytail loosening as it slaps against her spine. The elastic drops to the floor and bounces toward me as she comes to a stop, hair spreading across her shoulders. I wonder if I should say something.

"Jesus, Charlie!" She grabs both of his arms and yanks him backward. I touch the elastic with the toe of my sneaker. "What the fuck are you doing?"

"She doesn't know anything," he says, pointing at me. "She's useless."

It's something the founder would say—something he has said—and despite everything, I feel the urge to defend myself. But my mouth is too dry to form words.

A hand locks over my elbow. "You're okay, ma'am, you're okay," whispers a man. He smells like menthol, and when I twist my neck to look at him I see that he's wearing a white shirt with a fabric security badge embroidered on the sleeve.

"I need to go," I tell him.

"Are you okay? You're shaking."

"Keep it together," the woman is saying to the man. "We both know it was probably just a seizure."

"How about some water?" the security guard asks.

"We don't know anything," the man says. A sudden clarity comes into his eyes, like he's just snapped out of a daydream. "She has a camera now; did you know that?"

The woman touches one hand to her neck, clawed fingers searching for the elastic. I try to kick it toward her, but the band only flips over once, no closer than it was before. "No, she doesn't."

"Yes, she does."

"Sit down, at least," the guard says to me.

The double doors on the other side of the room swing open and a new nurse appears. Her black clogs squeak against the floor. "Did you buy it for her?" the woman asks. She's mad. "We need to make these decisions together. I've told you that."

The man holds his empty hands toward her. "I have no idea where she got it."

The nurse comes to a stop in front of the couple. She's holding a clipboard with a pen tethered to the metal clamp by a piece of worn yarn. "Let's talk in private," she suggests, and they rush past me back through the double doors. I smell the woman's perfume and I blow hard through my nostrils, trying to extinguish it. Fake lilies and something musky, like wet wood.

"I need to go," I tell the guard again, who is trying to guide me to a plastic chair near the bulletin board.

"You need to take a deep breath," he says.

"I need you to stop telling me what to do," I say, and because I'm sick of all these directions I rush through Emergency's automatic doors, even though the guard calls after me to say I'm going the wrong way.

IN THE CVS, I calm down by uncapping a Secret Shower Fresh deodorant and breathing in the smell of artificial cotton. I've worn this particular scent since I was ten, when my mother told me I reeked of anxiety after a soccer match.

It's started raining outside, and I can feel water dripping from my bangs to my cheeks. The makeup aisle is deserted. In fact, the entire store is deserted, except for a teenage boy staring at a display of condoms and lube that's been inexplicably positioned beside a shelf of nail polish. His hair's spiked with grease and his chin's swollen with the kind of acne that scars. He reminds me of the boy who walked me to the bus after the BART accident. The police shut down the whole station and called a bus to take us to our destinations. Please move calmly, the loudspeakers told us. I'd sat down on a metal bench and had my head in my hands when the boy tapped my shoulder. I think we have to go, he said. I didn't understand where he'd come from, and I stared at him without saying anything. Like, upstairs, he clarified.

He took my arm and helped me stand, and I remember how soft his sweatshirt sleeve felt against my skin. He made small talk as we climbed the escalator, and I wondered why the station below us was empty, and then I thought: *Oh, right.* He led me to the sidewalk where a white bus knelt against the scraped curb. Aren't you coming? I asked when he didn't step onto the stair behind me. I'm going the other way, he said, hooking his thumb in the opposite direction. Good luck.

And then the doors shut and we rolled away.

I crouch down to look at the lipsticks. I don't wear makeup, something that always disappointed my mother. But you can wear eyeliner now, she told me when I turned thirteen, the age she and my father had decided marked the official entrance into teenagedom and thus real padded bras and the Macy's makeup counter. Let me just show you, she insisted, but I told her eyeliner was one of the fastest spreaders of pink eye, which was going around school at the time. That is *not* true, she said, and then she went on about how makeup was a form of art and self-expression, which I half-listened to.

I pick out a red shade in a gold tube. It's dead center in the display, and there's a yellow tag that says it's on sale.

"Great color," the cashier commends me. She's heavily done up, with painted-on brows and foundation sticking to the tiny hairs clustered at the corner of her lips. "You girls are so lucky," she says.

"What girls?" I ask.

"You know." She hands me my change. "The ones that barely have to try."

. . .

"**WHAT IS THIS?**" my mother asks when I hand her the lipstick. "This is tomato red."

"Shouldn't you be asleep?" I counter.

My father has returned from the car, and he shoots me a look from his chair that says: Be nice.

Mom spins the tube and the lipstick rises like an extended tent pole. My father, without being told, reaches for a compact mirror on the bedside table. He holds it up to her face and she leans forward. Outside the nurse is loitering, her silhouette dark on the door's frosted window. Inside, my mother draws. My father waits. I watch.

BLACK ALL AROUND ME: black like crumbled charcoal, black like pooled ink, black like nothing at all. I blink, trying to bring my surroundings into focus, but my eyes can't find a single gradation in the darkness. I wonder if this is death: constantly searching for familiarity that no longer exists. Suddenly the darkness evaporates; harsh light washes in. The brightness is hostile, like the glare of direct sunlight, and I squint my eyelids shut. When I open them again, I'm staring into the flashlight of my father's phone. "You were talking in your sleep," he whispers. "I thought it was your mom at first, but I didn't want to turn the overhead on."

The shades are drawn over the window, but they're thin, and moonlight streaks through them and onto my mother. She's smeared lipstick across her pillowcase, across her cheek. In the morning she'll be horrified and blame us for allowing it to happen.

You couldn't have wiped it off? she'll say. As though we don't love her if we don't clean up her messes.

"You were saying Lucy over and over." He reaches out and takes my hand. "Who's that?"

I rub my eyes—they sting. My contacts are still in, and they've dried to glass against my eyeballs. "It's nobody."

I went to therapy for the first time after the subway incident— that was how my therapist referred to it, as if using the word *suicide* might trigger a psychological collapse. I was only there because my health insurance covered it and my roommate claimed that my mood was "lowering the vibrational energy" of our apartment. Do you feel disturbed by the incident because of what you saw or what you didn't? she asked. I had no idea what she meant and told her so. You saw a man make the most significant decision of his life, she explained, but you have no context for that decision, and you never will. We're always in the paths of others, but it can be disorienting to reconcile that proximity with the impenetrability of a stranger's choices.

Impenetrability of a Stranger's Choices would be a good band name, is what I said in response.

No, it wouldn't. She wrote something down on the yellow notepad in her lap. But Avoiding Vulnerability to Maintain Emotional Equilibrium would be.

"They're working you too hard at that job," Dad says. "I'd love to have a word or two with that boss of yours."

"I'm an adult. You can't protect me from my own decisions." He grumbles something incomprehensible before performing his signature expression of paternal concern, which involves touching his jaw with one hand while he glances mournfully at you from a slight angle. "I know I can't." He forces a smile. "You're perfectly capable."

It occurs to me that my father doesn't think I'm capable of hurting anyone, myself included. I yawn and he presses the car keys into my hand.

"You should go home, dear," he says. "Be safe."

I'M WALKING THROUGH the parking garage when the founder Slacks me. *are you receiving my msgs?* he wants to know, and though I've trained myself to react to anything he does without emotion, I'm exhausted from my interrupted dream and sore from the hospital chair and cramping from my upcoming period and the man in the lobby might have lost Lucy and the man in the subway deemed this world unlivable and my mother in the pus-colored hospital behind me may or may not be dying. I kick the door of the car but it doesn't leave a mark. *what do you think?* I write back. Which I know I'll regret.

When I wake up in my childhood bedroom the next morning, I feel like someone's knee is pressed to my chest. The feeling gets stronger as I take in the wobbly stacks of college textbooks on the floor, the three-ring binders shoved beneath the dresser, the bookshelf of chronologically organized journals so stuffed with the minutiae of everyday life you'd think the writer assumed herself destined for sainthood. The girl who lived here planned to do something both impressive and impactful—she used words like *purpose-driven* to describe herself. When I think about that girl now, she seems a person so fundamentally different from my current self that she must have preceded me in error.

I get up and stretch, dunk my head under the sink faucet, pinch the thin skin around my collarbone. Nothing helps. I wonder if existential dread can lodge in your throat like a poorly swallowed pill. Will your mind, tired of the endless anxieties swirling within it, eventually outsource such concerns to your physical body, where they can at least root into something tangible, like a knot in your muscle or a swollen knee?

Maybe I'm having caffeine withdrawal.

I go downstairs to put a pot on, and that's when I see Mona standing in front of our open refrigerator. Mona belongs to the previous me, who found her funny and chaotic and just the right amount of mean. I pause in the doorframe and wait for her to turn.

"Oh shit," she says when she finally closes the fridge. "Hello, hi." She looks good—she's wearing a pair of checkered yellow pants that I could never pull off, and I can tell that she's done the thing rich people do to their hair, where the highlights are painted on instead of guided by foil. My mom got it done last year, as a present from my dad. "I was just bringing over lasagna," she says, almost nervously, as if I'd caught her stealing. "We've got your whole fridge stocked." She laughs unnecessarily.

I walk in front of her to start making the coffee. She's unnerved by my presence, but I can't tell why. No one's ever scared of me. It feels nice. "How are you?" I ask.

The last time we talked was the day I decided to take my job— almost two years ago, exactly. I could go to grad school and study opioid use in Massachusetts fishing communities, or I could make just below six figures as a glorified personal assistant. We usually emailed back and forth, but I felt this decision was worthy of a call, despite her phone-induced anxiety, which she talked about as though it were a harrowing disease. I remember sitting at the edge of my twin-XL bed, thumbing an edible one of my roommates had given me and listening to beer bottles clang at a pregame down the hall.

Are you dying? she asked. Because you know what unannounced calls do to my blood pressure.

Will you think I'm a sellout? If I take this?

I heard a wet mashing and knew she was chewing on her bottom lip. She'd do it so bad during our calculus exams that a doctor actually prescribed her a mouthguard. I don't think you can be a sellout at twenty-two, she said. I mean, what can you even sell?

A soul.

Oh, fucking Christ. You're right; you should have joined a convent instead.

Are you drunk? You sound drunk.

No, I'm just enjoying this narrow slice of life where I'm young and hot yet smart enough to quote Walter Benjamin.

I don't know who that is. Footsteps poured into the hall behind me, which meant the pregame had ended. Now the real night could begin.

All human knowledge takes the form of interpretation!

Are you telling me this as advice or just quoting your dead guy? I assume he's dead.

Oh, he is. Something rustled on her end, bounced. She loved to belly flop onto her bed like a theatrical whale. I mean, I don't know what you want me to tell you, Nat. Money's money. Morals are just something you pretend to have until it's too hard to uphold them.

That may be the darkest shit you've ever said.

A door opening, enthusiastic chatter. Nat, I gotta bounce; Alice threw up on her favorite loafers. Go save the world! Someone has to.

And that was the last night of the Old Me.

SHE SITS DOWN at the kitchen table, which is stacked with folded laundry, and plays with the corner of a fitted sheet. "Oh, I'm good. Same old, same old."

According to my mother, who knows everything that happens in this town, Mona's applying to graduate school, something that makes less than zero sense to me. Her English degree left her so jaded that she proposed a practical skill should accompany each book on a class's syllabus. Like: Read *Hamlet*; rewire a ceiling light.

"Do you want coffee?" I ask. "Do you still drink it?" For a long time, she'd been on a caffeine cleanse to combat her anxiety. Then she found a classmate from Manhattan who sold Xanax.

"If you don't mind. I'm a caffeine slut now." She mimes drinking from a cup with one hand and giving a blow job with the other.

I'd forgotten how tiring it is to be around someone who thinks entertaining you and connecting with you are the same thing. I keep my back turned as I measure out the grounds. Anticipation's radiating from her, probably some need for catharsis or maybe for-giveness. A couple weeks after we returned from summer camp, back when we were twelve, she stood by our mailbox wringing her hands. I didn't know you were coming over, I told her.

I just thought I'd stop by, she said, the language of her mother. What's up?

It was so hot that the heat rose off the street in shimmery waves. It'd just be really nice, if, uh . . . . She scratched her head with all five fingers. If you could write my parents a note, she said.

What kind of note? I asked.

Like, ah, a thank-you note.

Mona's parents had paid for me to go to summer camp. Insisted on it, actually—it was "a gift of enrichment" and also a "networking opportunity," if I remember correctly. I didn't even want to go—Mona had told me the bathrooms were in an entirely separate building across the lawn from the cabins—but my parents felt it was a "special opportunity for growth." When I told them I already knew how to braid friendship bracelets, they ignored me.

Did your parents not get the gifts? I asked. After we returned, my parents had agonized over which bottle to buy to accompany their thank-you card and thank-you present, which was a duplicate of a ceramic bowl we owned that Mona's mom had once complimented. We were in the packie for almost an hour, examining dusty red bottle after dusty red bottle—there was some argument over the style of wine that should be purchased. When I asked if we could leave, Mom said I needed to be a better ambassador for the family.

Something from you, Mona squeaked out. Something from you would be nice.

My eyelid twitched like it did when Mom got mad at me for something I didn't understand was wrong, like not wanting to show my room to her friend's daughter or reading at the table when we visited my cousins. I signed the card, I said.

Mona looked behind her like she hoped someone would come relieve her of her gratitude-fetching duties. Yeah, I think they'd just like something from, you know, you specifically. You only.

I felt a primal urge to kick Mona in the crotch of her denim shorts. It would have unfolded perfectly: I knew she was on her third-ever period and that she had just started using tampons for the first time, which meant she'd be terrified my swift kick would lodge the Tampax Pearl in the ceiling of her pelvic floor forever, because she was Mona, with a life so uncomplicated that she fixed her fears on impossible situations of her own invention. She'd kneel to the hot pavement in pain, one hand shoved into her underwear to search for the surely elusive strings, one shaking its fist at my all-powerful Keds.

But of course I couldn't. Mainly because it would get back to her mom, and though I didn't care what Mona's mother thought of me, my mother did. And nothing I did was ever really mine alone, but a reflection of what my mother had or hadn't taught me. Sorry, I said, after breathing through my teeth for a good thirty seconds. I'll make them a cootie catcher.

Now in the kitchen, I pour her coffee into my mother's heat-retaining mug, the one that keeps liquid scalding for hours. "Black?" I ask.

"With a little milk, actually, if you don't mind. I'm off that vegan bullshit." I glance toward the refrigerator and she immediately rises. "I'll get it." It takes her a long while to riffle through the shelves. She's never been good at seeing what's in front of her. "Hey, if you don't mind," she says, the gallon of 2 percent finally in hand, "I think you're blocking me in."

I peer out the kitchen window. I was so tired I'd barely registered her Camry when I pulled in late last night—my father used to be a mechanic and still fixes his buddies' cars if they're in a pinch, so I assumed it belonged to one of them. I did wonder why it was parked diagonally, but I'd pulled to the edge of the driveway to ensure the owner could back out easily. There's more than enough space to pull into the road and speed away. "I'd be happy to move it," I tell her. "Would hate for you to be trapped here."

We sit on the back porch once my father's car has been repositioned parallel the sidewalk. It's still raining, sheets of water gliding off our striped awning, the ocean the color of dull steel in front of us.

"What happened there?" Mona asks, pointing to a section of the seawall that's just a pile of sun-bleached rubble. "Colleen?"

I nodded. Colleen was the name of the blizzard that ripped through town this past winter, stirring the waves to such intensity that they slammed against the wall until the concrete had no choice but to crumble. Freezing water poured into our backyard until the first floor was underwater, our furniture bobbing on the misplaced tide, chairbacks scraping the ceiling. My parents had evacuated to a friend's house inland and told me that everyone in the neighborhood stood bundled in winter jackets at the edges of their driveways, staring eastward, the direction of the coast. They couldn't shake the fear that the water would come for them, too. That it was just a matter of time.

But the water didn't come, at least not to those more than three miles from the shore. I watched videos with the sound off at my desk in San Francisco, red rescue rafts floating above our submerged street. I thought the house was a goner. But for once in our lives, we were lucky. The water didn't reach the second floor, and the insurance money came through more quickly than anticipated, likely thanks to the widespread media coverage of the storm. My father sent me pictures of my mother ripping up moldy carpet beside an industrial-sized dehumidifier, her hair tied back in a perfect bun. *Ur mom is a badass!* said the accompanying text, to which my mother responded: *y would u send her that.*

"Do you remember?" Mona asks, blowing steam from her coffee.

I know what she's talking about. We steadied ourselves against that wall when we both got drunk for the first time at sixteen. We stumbled onto the beach afterward and Mona vomited into the ocean, a yellow film that the tide carried out to sea. How many fish do you think will eat that? she asked, wiping her mouth.

At least three hundred, I said.

Three *hundred?* She meant to stumble backward in shock, but she was so out of it that she actually fell on her ass. I held out a hand to help her up, but she pulled me down with her instead. The sand was cold and slick on the back of my thighs, like a layer of wet mud, and before I could stand a wave broke over our heads and tugged us to shore.

My phone vibrates in my pocket, knocking against the edge of my chair. I don't check it.

"Hey." Mona places her hand awkwardly on mine, the way an obligated but uncomfortable teacher might. "I just wanted to say that I'm sorry. About your mom."

I force my mouth into a smile. "Thank you."

"Is she—"

"Dying?" Mona's face puckers at the word. "The doctors are very confident she'll recover."

Mona glances out to the beach. The rain makes the ocean look covered in tiny dents. "Did you know a girl died last night?"

She says this with a degree of incredulity, like it's news. When we were in high school it seemed like there was a death every month. Drunk driving, mostly, but also overdoses. Mona let me borrow her black dresses so I wouldn't have to wear the same thing to every memorial, and I still associate death with the scent of her lavender detergent. Even leaving the BART station, I smelled the artificial soapiness. The school held an assembly after a girl drove her car off the bridge and into the marsh, and I remember thinking, in my folding auditorium chair with the AC blasting goose bumps down my spine: *I can fix this.* I didn't even listen to what the principal said, or the girl's homeroom teacher, or any of the other people who stood solemnly at the podium, leaning toward the microphone that was too short but that no one bothered to adjust. I thought of the studies I could conduct on my classmates, the workshops I could run for them, the different ways I could turn their habits and opinions into data and actionable findings. Papers I could write, speeches I could give, awards I could win. When tragedy occurs, there's a strange impulse to solidify your position in relation to what's happened. Even the generally unaffected feel compelled to locate some connection to the event, hoping a link to catastrophe will increase the urgency of their own life. At least, that's how I felt, back in the auditorium. Like it meant something that I had walked the same hallways she had. Like that alone justified daydreaming at her assembly, her death fodder for ambitions of my own.

"WHAT HAPPENED?" I ask.

Mona looks back at me and the wind pulls her hair across her face. She picks it away, squinting. "Dunno. Some party gone wrong. I heard about it from my roommate. She taught her."

"How's she doing?"

"Who?"

"Your roommate."

Mona seems surprised at the question. "Oh, fine, I think. Rattled, for sure."

"I'd hate to be remembered that way."

"What way?"

I pick up a rock that's lying beside my chair and hurl it over the porch railing. "Just some high school girl."

AT THE HOSPITAL my mother requests laxatives. "Are you serious?" I ask. She's so thin that the paper of her hospital gown has nothing to cling to, a box that skims over her skeleton. She reaches up and tugs on my sleeve, drawing me closer. "They're fattening me up," she whispers conspiratorially. "Do you see my stomach?" She takes a bunch of the gown in her fist and shakes it. "I'm going to die fat and alone."

"Alone? We're right here."

"Your father's left me." Suddenly, she's near tears. "I knew this would happen, I knew it."

"He just went to the bathroom." I take a few steps backward. "I'll go get him."

"No!" she shouts. "No, stay here. Please. Stay."

I've always been terrible at staying. Change is easy, because it untethers you from who you were before. And I've always liked who I could be better than who I actually am. But here—before the wheezing machines and the small woman tied to them, a woman who I haven't seen in months before this visit, a woman whose calls I ignored, a woman whom I told I was "busy, busy, busy," as though I didn't know how sick she was, or how scared—I need to be different. But I don't know how. "Mom, I'll be right back." I can't look at her as I open the door. "I promise."

I find my father at the vending machine purchasing a package of M&M's. The metal coil holding the pouch retreats and the candy lurches forward. "Mom's freaking out. She wants laxatives."

He sighs. "I think she's just nervous about the surgery tonight—it's making her paranoid." He bends down to retrieve his purchase and his back cracks. "Don't get old, Lala," he says, calling me by the name only he uses. "It's no fun."

"Luckily, being young is inarguably delightful."

He laughs and splits open the pouch, indicates for me to hold out my hand. "It may not seem like it, but it's a gift to have what you have."

I toss the M&M's into my mouth. "And what do I have, exactly?"

"Health. Independence. Stable income."

"Ah, yes. The Holy Trinity." You know what I like about you? the founder asked one night when we were the only ones left in the office. A venture capitalist was visiting the next day, and the founder insisted on going over every detail related to the man's personal and professional life, from podcasts he'd participated in to a series of sketchily written blog posts analyzing the Hypnotically Charismatic Tone of his voice. The founder was drinking a beer, but I'd declined the one he'd offered me. You just cooperate, he went on. I tell you to do something and you do it.

Isn't that what a job is? I asked.

He laughed so hard that beer dribbled out of his nose. God, he said, wiping his face with his hand. If only everyone were so willing to be my bitch.

Dad offers me another pour of M&M's but I shake my head. "Should we get Mom something? Like a tea? It might calm her down."

"She's not supposed to drink or eat. Let's just act normal and hopefully she'll follow suit." I refrain from asking for previous examples where my mother followed suit. We walk back to her room but Dad pauses before opening the door. "I forgot to tell you—the Framinghams are coming to visit today. That will be nice, won't it?"

I'd been looking down at the floor, which is the color of tartar sauce, but I glance up when he says this. "Really?"

"Why do you sound surprised?"

"I actually ran into Mona this morning. She didn't mention it."

Dad turns the knob and shrugs. "Anna said she was coming. Maybe she forgot?"

Mona's always had this habit of keeping pertinent details to herself. Like she believes you can make something more interesting just by withholding it. "Maybe."

"Where'd you see her?" he asks, taking a small step inside.

"Who?"

"Mona."

I pause on the metal strip that separates my mother's room from the public hallway. I can't see past my father's shoulders, but it's quiet. "Just at Dunkin'."

He lifts an eyebrow. "I thought you hated Dunkin' Donuts," he says, whispering now.

"I never said that."

His hand is still on the doorknob. "Yes," he whispers. "You did."

In my pocket, my phone buzzes.

THE FRAMINGHAMS BRING flowers and cards and metallic-dusted truffles that you can only find at the overpriced chocolatier in the harbor. Mona has changed since the morning; no more vibrant pants. She wears a white dress that ties at the waist and a pair of pearl earrings. I have on a white T-shirt with a peanut butter stain on the collar. I try to look happy.

We hug and kiss cheeks and nod our heads when there's no one left to hug or kiss. Everyone keeps tripping over the wires at the foot of Mom's bed, especially Mrs. Framingham, who makes huge startled eyes each time it happens. "Do you have any water?" she asks. It takes me a moment to realize she's talking to me. I uncap one of the miniature water bottles on the bedside table and hand it to her. "Thanks, love," she says, patting my forearm.

A question: Do I hate Mrs. Framingham? It's generally agreed upon that you shouldn't hate anybody, that this implies a disturb-ing lack of generosity from the hater rather than egregious behav-ior by the hated. And it seems somehow anti-feminine as well—in CCD they talked about how women were capable of boundless forgiveness, radical love. But I've never understood the concept of unearned absolution, which just seems like a dressed-up version of practiced passivity. One of many reasons I made a bad Catholic.

Years ago, at Mona's high school graduation party, Mrs. Framingham had gotten drunk on dirty martinis and swayed over to me with an empty coupe glass in her hand. We were on their huge, perfect lawn just across the street from Opal Point, the most popular beach. Their front room was entirely glass; if you sat on the sofa you could see all the way out to the lighthouse on the other side of town. I remember watching her reflection march in my direction.

She came to a shaky halt in front of me. Are you happy, dear? she asked.

About what? I asked. Mona's mother was good at setting traps.

Don't look so nervous! About your impressive accomplishment. She smiled at me and her lips thinned to gummy threads. I'm proud of you, Natalie.

Mona and I shared a top-choice college, but only I had gotten in. Thank you.

Mrs. Framingham placed a hand on my shoulder and leaned toward me with a wobble. Milk it for what you can, she said.

Excuse me? I wanted to pull away, but she was leaning on me too heavily. If I moved, she would fall.

Your story, dear. Because that was Mona's problem, wasn't it? She craned her neck to glance behind us at the empty house. It glowed from within like a giant lantern. She always had it just a touch—here she indicated a tiny amount of space between two fingers—too easy.

I don't have a story, I told her.

She looked me up and down like I was something broken she couldn't figure out how to fix. Yes, you do.

Across the street, waves were breaking against the beach. Somehow the water always sounded calmer here than it did at my house. I wondered where Mona was.

It's better, she said finally. To grow up like you did.

Her hand was getting hot on my shoulder. We're not poor, I said. We're middle-class.

She thought that was the funniest thing in the word. Of course, dear, she said. Of course. She tried to drink from her glass, but it was empty. Just remember when you get there: You earned it. She brushed my earlobe with her finger, then gave my hoop earring a gentle flick. It continued to tremble after she'd walked away.

"Marie, you look beautiful," Mrs. Framingham says. She's dressed up like she's about to attend happy hour at the Yacht Club—a black silk dress that's unremarkable in a way that means it's absurdly expensive and a pair of drop diamond earrings. "Doug," she says to Mr. Framingham, "doesn't she look beautiful?"

Mr. Framingham clears his throat. "You look great, Marie."

We're sitting in a semicircle around my mother's bed, like reporters waiting to hear her deliver an important speech. "Thank you, Anna. Thank you, Doug," Mom says. I continue trying to look happy. It's getting harder.

"Natalie, you're so grown-up." Mrs. Framingham turns to face me. "You haven't been home in quite some time, have you?"

"Not in a few months. Work's been hectic."

"Anna," Mr. Framingham says, gesturing to his own teeth. There's a splotch of red lipstick on his wife's front tooth, bright as blood. Mrs. Framingham flashes him a look so scolding you'd think he'd told the entire room she farted.

"A *napkin*," Mrs. Framingham whispers to her husband. "Get me a napkin."

Mr. Framingham looks frantically around the room before spotting the Kleenex box on the radiator. He jumps up from his chair so quickly that its metal legs rattle against the floor like spilled change. I attempt to catch Mona's eye, but her gaze is fixed somewhere in the distance. I incline my head toward hers, jut my chin up suggestively, but her entire face has a waxy quality, as though someone set and polished it into this particular blank configuration.

"How's Mullaney's?" my father asks Mona. "We got some excellent halibut from you guys last week."

I can't stop myself from asking: "You work at Mullaney's?" I once saw Mona vomit into a trash can because a seagull dropped a headless fish onto the pavement in front of us.

"It's just temporary," her father interjects. He sits back down and hands the tissue to his wife, who bares her teeth as she turns away from us.

"It's fine," she says to my father. Her eyes don't meet his, and I try to determine what exactly it is she's looking at. Mom's various monitors? The HVAC vent? That weird yellow wall stain that looks like Florida? "Can't beat that employee discount, right?"

Mrs. Framingham, recovered from the lipstick fiasco, leans over the foot of Mom's bed. "It's amazing how much a liberal arts degree *won't* get you, isn't it?"

My mother sits up a little straighter. She thinks she has the upper hand. "Well, Natalie's degree certainly paid off. She's working at a start-up."

"Mom," I say.

"Are you?" Mr. Framingham asks with genuine interest. "What kind of company?"

"Ah, just ecommerce stuff."

"What's that like, working in tech?" Mrs. Framingham asks, pulling away from my mother and angling toward me. "Do you think Mona would like it?"

"Bad hours." My father crosses his arms. "Natalie's always working."

If there's one thing I can't stand, it's hearing my parents describe what they see as the key characteristics of my job. I kick back my chair and it screeches against the tile. Everyone turns. "Sorry," I say. "I have to pee."

I'm halfway down the hall when the sound of heels tapping tile interrupts the hum of the hospital's AC system. I turn and there's Mona, waving frantically like she's fighting her way through the knot of a crowd. "Don't leave me!" she calls. "They're going to ask about my ten-year plan!"

"Where should we go?" I ask when she catches up, panting like she just ran a five-minute mile. Definitely smoking again. My phone vibrates in my hand, and when I calculate how long it's been since I opened Slack I feel a little sick.

"Anywhere."

A preview of the founder's message lights up on my screen. *u r putting ur job at risk by not responding.* "Do they sell beer at CVS here?"

Mona laughs. "You've been in California too long, dude."

We ride the elevator to the ground floor, make ourselves small in the corner. Shoulders scrunched, hips tucked, hands shoved into pockets. This is what polite, healthy people do at hospitals—make their good fortune inconspicuous. Usually I look down at my shoes, too, to keep from staring, but today there's just a single man pressed against the opposite wall, and he looks like us. Unsick. And somehow familiar, with the face of someone from my childhood, or a dream. His mouth is what gets me—the curled lips slightly parted, as though he wants to say something but can't find the right time to interject. The man from the emergency room. "Excuse me," I say.

Mona's eyes slide toward the man.

The man's eyes slide toward me.

"Yes?" He's holding a newspaper in one hand and beats it rhythmically against his thigh. I can't recognize the tune.

We're quickly descending to the ground floor. We don't stop at five, at four, at three. My phone vibrates against my hip, and for the first time the admonishing buzz doesn't fill me with anxiety. Because whether or not I open my phone, nothing will change. The founder will continue to get richer, my rent will continue to climb, the ocean will continue to rise until we're standing in our driveways watching the shadow of that final wave fall over us.

"Do you remember me?" I ask.

"Excuse me?" The man holds the newspaper still and Mona touches my elbow.

"From the emergency room, last night."

He presses a finger into the first notch of his throat, like he's trying to check his own pulse. "Oh."

Most moments of our lives fall into the archive of the Past, stored in the neat categories from which we build the stories of ourselves: Childhood Trauma, First Shame, First Love, Teenage Crisis of Self, Young Adult Crisis of Self. But certain ones stay in circulation, resistant to storage and designation. Mine: the single minute in the quiet BART station, the man's sneakers scraping the yellow caution line, my voice in my throat, about to say something. Always, forever, about to. "Is she okay?" I ask. "Are you?"

I understand, the moment the words are out of my mouth, that I've asked two impossible questions. The expression slides off his face like a rock off a cliff. And then his feet are in front of mine, his forehead is on my shoulder, wet and twitchy, brow bones sharp against my shirt. He smells like beer, strong mouthwash, dried sweat. I don't recoil, like I thought I might when he lunged toward me. Instead I feel grateful for my body, whose gifts I often forget: receiving, supporting, remaining. The doors open: level one. He steps back and holds both of my hands with warm fingers. "Thank you," he says. And then he exits the elevator, turning the corner so I can no longer see him.

Mona stretches her neck into the hallway. "The fuck?"

"What was that girl's name?" I ask. "The one who died?"

"Uh, I can't remember." The doors are starting to close and she pulls me through them. "Something with an *L*?"

"Lucy?"

"Yeah, I think that's right." I'm being reoriented now, Mona's hands pointing my shoulders in the correct direction. "So *how* do you know that dude?"

"It's a long story." Mona lets out a sigh of exasperation—she used to complain I hid parts of myself unnecessarily—and steps in front of me. The corridor opens up into Emergency, and I follow her past the connected chairs and into another tiled hallway.

"Where are we going?" I ask.

She swivels her head to make sure I haven't fallen too far behind. "What do you mean?"

We pass through automatic doors that smell like Clorox and lemon zest, and somehow we're there. The lobby. I'd forgotten what had first drawn me to Mona: her ability to navigate byzantine systems as though their inner workings were intuitive. When I was younger, I thought this was a gift. Now I think it's a cultivated confidence, drawn from the knowledge that if she needs to simply circumvent said systems, she can.

We face a gift shop with a window display of stuffed animals giving one another fake flowers and chocolates. A sign above them reads WE LOVE FAMILIES! in glittery bubble letters.

"Where did you think we were going?" Mona asks as we push through the revolving doors to the outside.

"Nowhere," I say, and watch her laugh in her separate compartment.

. . .

WE END UP AT THE CVS, where we buy two creamsicle sodas, a bag of Bugles, and a Nerds Rope. The snacks of our youth. The boy I saw the night before is working the register, and he slides our purchases over the scanner as though they weigh five hundred pounds.

"You work here," I say as I hand him my credit card.

He looks profoundly offended. "Yeah."

"I was in here yesterday," I say, in an attempt to justify myself. "I bought a lipstick."

He blows a purple bubble and pops it with an unfolded paper-clip from his pocket. "Everyone's in here, buying their little necessities, their little treats." He cracks a knuckle. "Receipt?"

Outside, we sit at a picnic table mounted on a small concrete island at the edge of the parking lot. "I don't know if our bodies can physically handle this," Mona says as we sit down on opposite benches.

"Oh, they definitely can't." I rip open the Nerds Rope wrapper and examine the clusters of tiny, sugary pebbles. When I put the thing in my mouth it's as tough as jerky. "I heard you're applying to grad school," I say, my mouth full.

Mona sips impassively from her soda. "Yeah?"

"Well, are you?"

"I already applied. Now I'm just waiting."

"That's exciting."

She sticks one of her fingers into the opening of a Bugle. It sits on her nail like an elf hat. "You don't have to pretend to be supportive. I know you think I'm a bad writer and an ethically questionable person."

I'm so taken aback that I cough in surprise. "I don't think that." Behind us, a red Civic pulls out of a parking spot and almost hits a woman power walking back to her car. She smacks the trunk with her open palm, yells something I can't quite hear. "I thought that *you* decided English was a pointless degree."

"What are you talking about?" Her brows furrow together into one confused line. "That joke I made about practical skills forever ago? You were always bringing that up. You take everything so literally."

"No, I don't." My cheeks go hot and I hate that even now, it takes so little for her to embarrass me. "Why do you want to go?" I ask, trying to recover.

She bites off the Bugle with her front teeth. "It'd be nice for my everyday life to reflect some of the things that are important to me."

I can't help myself. "Studying, books—those things are important to you?"

"You *do* remember competing with me for valedictorian, don't you?" She gives me a thin smile that reminds me of her mother's. "Anyways, I'm allowed to want things that don't make sense to you."

Irritation tingles at the back of my neck. The issue isn't my perception of Mona but Mona's perception of herself. Sure, you can claim to be whoever you want to be, as long as no one holds you to your history. "Do you remember what you said to me?" I ask. "When I called you about my job?"

She laughs. "God, I was so fucked up. What was it—go save the world?"

"Take the money. Essentially."

She rolls her eyes. "I wouldn't have said that."

"No. You did."

She shrugs and takes another Bugle from the bag. "Well, I guess I was operating under the well-supported assumption that you wouldn't listen to me." He laughter's light and crisp, like a dry leaf.

I imagine crushing it beneath my foot. "I would have gone to grad school."

LATER THAT AFTERNOON, I sit by my mother's side while my father runs home to get a fresh suitcase of clothes. Mona's insisted I come to O'Dooley's later, so I can watch her outdrink the old men who call her "sweetheart." When I apologized to my parents for abruptly ditching our hang, my father had waved it off with an airy hand. "Oh, we assumed Mona had just swept you up in one of her schemes."

The sun's just starting to set, and orange light stretches through the window in thick blocks. Soon, the doctors will be here to prep Mom for surgery. "What do you think is my worst quality?" I ask.

Mom laughs. "Is this a trap?"

I groan and throw a hand over my eyes. I'm tired of myself. "No. I don't know. Maybe?"

I'm sitting in my father's chair and she reaches over to knead my arm. "You're like me," she says. "Once you've decided what something is, you can't imagine it any other way."

I shake my arm away from her grasp, but her fingers hover in the air like they're still touching my skin. "That's not true."

"All I'm trying to say is that it's a lot more interesting to change your conclusions than preserve them." She lowers the hand to her bed's guardrail and taps out a rhythm that I don't immediately recognize.

"What song is that?"

She laughs and taps out the beat again. "This? 'Landslide.'"

The doorknob twists and we both turn. A nurse in a blue shower cap tells us she'll be coming to fetch Mom in just a moment. The door closes, only to open again a moment later. My father. He's out of breath and presses a hand to his chest as he stumbles inside. "Oh, good! I was scared they'd already taken you in."

I step outside so they can talk before the nurse returns. The hallway's quiet, and I wander until I find the family lounge near the operating corridor, which is full of scraped plastic chairs and reeks of burnt coffee and scented tissues. I pull my phone from my pocket and squint at the tiny red bubble in the corner of the Slack icon. The number inside reads 27. I open my direct messages with the founder and lift my thumbs. I consider several things to say, such as *fuck your wobbly face* and *go to hell* and *your daughter was right*. I also think of something I've almost said several times, on several occasions. The words that reel through my mind like the world's most seductive ticker tape: *I quit*.

The sound of ungreased wheels squeaks through the hallway. When I look up, my phone in my lap, my mother's waving. She has a plastic cap covering her head and a breathing tube branching into both nostrils. One of the nurses is gently pushing her shoulder into the gurney, telling her to relax. "Natalie," she says. "Don't forget—you can always come home."

The double doors swing open to Surgery and the nurses push her through, hand held high in the air. A hand still marked from that hemlock tree, so that when I gripped it with my own, the scar tissue kissed my palm. I lower my fingers and type.

LAYLA

I **PULL INTO THE FACULTY LOT** just as the stoners are snuffing out their morning blunts on the wall of the school. The bell's ringing inside, extra loud thanks to the PTA, who recently fundraised a new speaker and notification system into existence. My vote was for an actual guidance counselor or an automatic wheelchair ramp, but hey. I only work here.

The students say hello in the hallway, maybe in a more casual way than I'd like. One of the seniors shouts my name as he fires finger guns at his friends, who pretend to die against the row of lockers. Automatically, I smile. According to my evaluations, I'm the following: approachable, nice, chill. What I'd prefer they say: intimidating, exacting, tough. Nobody fucks with someone at the intersection of respect and fear. Me, though: I'm always getting fucked.

I try not to breathe too deeply as I wade through the student sea. They reek of unwashed hair and poorly applied deodorant, their raw teenage musk rising up in a thick cloud of scents the rest of us make sure are never public. The worst thing about high school students is that their bodies have reached adulthood before they have. It's both shocking and disturbing to witness: the breasts pushing out of tank tops, the hair curling from shirt collars, the hips straining below too-tight waistbands. And above it all their concealed brains, gooey and fetal with undercooked cortexes. If I sound old-fashioned, I promise I'm not. I'm only twenty-six.

"You realize this is unacceptable, waltzing in at the last possible moment," Mrs. Johnson declares when I enter our shared office. Mrs. Johnson is old-fashioned. Before her diet, she used to tuck a pressed linen napkin into her shirt while she ate microwaved spaghetti with a real metal fork. "It sets a poor example for the students." She crunches down on a mouthful of almonds, a staple of her current regime, where she consumes only unsalted nuts, full-fat yogurt, and seltzers. She burps at least five times an hour.

"Won't happen again," I lie. But really, has anyone missed something important during the first five minutes of anything?

Mrs. Johnson grunts and tosses more almonds into her mouth. She's the most straightforwardly unpleasant woman I've ever met. I once overheard a student say that she resembled an egg, and now I can't unsee it. Pale, blank face with a strikingly oval body, no curves where the hips or waist should be. When she belts her dress it makes an unnatural indentation in her middle, and I tend to stare when that happens.

"What?" she barks.

Today she's wearing a belt. "Nothing."

I sit down at my desk, which is on the opposite side of the room from hers and constantly draped in darkness. We're in the basement, which means our only source of sunshine is a row of stumpy aboveground windows that touch the popcorn ceiling. Said windows are conveniently located above Mrs. Johnson's desk. When I started last year she claimed the furniture had to be arranged this way for fire safety, and because of my general aversion to conflict, I didn't push back.

Even though I've accepted what's become a year-round affliction of seasonal affective disorder, I'm not trying to bring the kids down with me. I keep my lamp on all hours of the day and burn candles with embarrassing names like *princess primrose* and *goddess of desire* to keep my desk somewhat inviting. When I asked Principal Cushing if we could install an overhead light and check the perpetually damp room for mold, she told me not to get greedy. Principal Cushing is one of those hot, unaccommodating women you get aroused by hating.

I haven't even flicked on my lamp yet when our door scrapes against the linoleum tile. Sophia West appears in the frame, her hair tied in a low bun, her wrist jangling three brass bracelets. She's wearing a lavender jumpsuit and sneakers so white she must dunk them in bleach every evening. When I was in high school, I wore satin dresses over nylon stretchy shirts and routinely swallowed the elastics I looped from my bottom row of braces to the top. If only the internet had taught me how to circumvent my awkward phase.

"Ms. Layla," she says, hustling toward me like I'm a bus she's about to miss, "I need to add another school to my list."

Principal Cushing explicitly told me not to allow this. Sophia's currently at thirteen, and her father is already skeptical due to the quantity of liberal arts colleges. *I mean, do we really need another English major with 50k of debt?* he asked via email. I take a deep breath and transform into the person who embodies the characteristics spelled out in my job description: organized, professional, excellent at juggling multiple responsibilities. She's not me, but I know how to be her.

"You've already got a great list," I say.

Sophia leans over my desk to press the lamp's on switch. "None of them are in New York City though."

"The New York schools are some of the most expensive."

"Yeah, but Lucy says access to cultural institutions is indispensable for people who want to study what we do."

Sophia would follow Lucy into the cone of a spewing volcano if she just said please. "Ah." I twirl a pen around to avoid looking skeptical. "And what is that?"

"Well, I don't know exactly." She drops into the student chair I haven't yet moved from beside my own. "Art, urban planning, creative writing. Something nontraditional."

I refrain from telling her that the nontraditional girls I went to high school with are now peddling CBD from the back of their Priuses. "Not math or engineering? I saw you got a certificate of distinction from the AMC 10 last year."

She groans. "I'm never doing a math competition again. I only took the test because Principal Cushing guilted me about the 'lack of female representation.'"

Cushing is particularly skilled at pushing our girls into male-dominated arenas. I heard her parents didn't even let her wear sneakers as a kid, because they were afraid she'd try to keep up with her brothers' rowdy activities. Women really shouldn't move faster than a light jog, after all. "Let's pause on new schools. How about focusing on your essay instead?"

Sophia thinks her essay is genius. In reality it's a disaster. The pages incorporate recipes from pilgrim women, song lyrics about the sadness of the setting sun over the sea, a quotation from book two of *The Odyssey*, a series of eighteenth-century ruminations on death from an obscure female poet, and a brief explanation of string theory that reads a bit too similarly to its Wikipedia page.

"I'm working on a new draft now," she says. "It's in third person."

"Third person?" She nods. A large part of my job is convincing my students that they came up with ideas I planted in their heads. "Why don't you focus on your brother?" I try. "You said he was a big part of your life. Or your mother."

"I'm not writing about her." She says it in a sharp, unrecognizable way that intrigues me.

"Why? She was on your brainstorm list."

"It's too personal."

"It *is* a personal essay," I counter.

"I don't want to, okay?" She rubs one of her hoop earrings, and I can see that her fingers are quivering. "I barely see her anyway."

If I were myself, and not Ms. Layla, I would tell her: This is exactly what they want. Trauma! Pain! An altered worldview! Anything to show that you're not just another well-behaved white girl from the suburbs.

But at school, I'm not myself.

"Perhaps," I offer, treading carefully, "the fact that this touches a nerve means it's worth writing about."

Her hand drops from the earring. "It's not going to make me feel better. Writing about it."

"The point isn't to feel better." I hear myself getting annoyed and clear my throat. "The point is to show them who you are."

"So I'm my absent mother?"

A moment of silence stretches between us like a taut sheet. "That's not what I'm saying."

Sophia looks me up and down with a gaze that shaves against my skin. "I wish you had the guts to tell me I'm not interesting enough without her." Before I can respond, she's pushed her chair back and crossed the room with a step so heavy it vibrates up the legs of my desk.

"You nailed that one," Mrs. Johnson says as the door rattles against its frame. "Now I see why they're trying to bring in more young folk like you."

I consider staying where I am, at my scratched desk with the lamp emitting a bileish yellow that makes anyone who sits across from me look ill. But that's not what Ms. Layla would do, because Ms. Layla recently received the title of interim counselor in addition to her existing job, due to Mrs. Brown's decision to extend her maternity leave indefinitely. That and she's one of the few people at school who feels the students' well-being is not just a priority, but a responsibility.

"Don't run after her," Mrs. Johnson calls. "They don't like that."

But of course I'm already halfway down the hall by then, headed toward the one place every upset girl is known to go. The women's bathroom.

Olivia Cushing's leaning against the busted sink when I enter, the one with a crack that runs through its basin like a hairline fracture. This is the old side of the school, all stained tile and gritty carpet and exposed pipes trailing down the walls like intestines. "Hey," she says, with the kind of forced friendliness that tells me a cigarette or baggie of pills is dangling from the hand shoved behind her skirt.

But I could care less about that. Before she has the chance to speak again, I put one finger to my lips and gesture to the door with my other hand. "Go," I whisper, and she does, because she's really not half as bad as the faculty make her out to be. I can't imagine being the principal's daughter. The girl skulks through the halls with a back so hunched you'd think she'd only ever been yelled at. But she has that electric undercurrent some kids have, too. Like she could set this whole place on fire if you just said the exact wrong thing to her at the exact right time.

At the other end of the bathroom, I hear someone quietly talking. I squat down and see that beneath the door of the very last stall, there's not one pair of shoes, but two.

"She's just trying to be realistic," says a voice, which is warm but impatient in the way of someone who finds their friend's reaction overly dramatic. Lucy Anderson. "The essay is kind of . . . disjointed."

"I know you're trying to make me feel better, but it's actually making me feel worse."

"I mean, I think the mom angle could be interesting."

"Of course you do."

"What does that mean?"

I press my back against the wall beside the sinks and ride it all the way down to the floor. The tile feels cool through my tights.

"I didn't want to take those photos."

A pause. "Well, why didn't you say something?"

"When could I have said something?"

"You said you were excited."

Something clangs against the wall of the stall. Sophia's back, probably. "I lied."

A foot raises, a leather clog with a frilled sock above it. Lucy's. It disappears and I can hear her heel scratch against her ankle. "The photos are meant to make you uncomfortable, Soph."

"They're meant to make the person looking at them uncomfortable. Not the person in them."

The door swings open behind me so suddenly that my hair swishes against my shoulders. "You're still here?" Olivia asks. It seems to take her a moment to realize I'm on the floor. "Did you have a stroke or something?"

The stall door flings open next. "Ms. Layla?" Sophia asks.

One of the strangest parts of working in a school is how it throws the whole system into question. You realize your teachers never had any real authority—they were just older than you and held a stack of detention slips. But I guess that's how everything is, growing up: The systems you once trusted turn out to be nothing more than poorly constructed fantasies of power and order.

"So sorry!" I burst up and immediately slam my head against the coin-operated tampon dispenser. "I thought this was the faculty bathroom."

"Are you okay?" someone asks, maybe Olivia, maybe Sophia, maybe Lucy.

"I'm fine, girls, I'm fine," I say, hoping that if I call them "girls," it will reestablish that they're children while I'm an Adult Woman, despite possibly sustaining a concussion from a feminine-product dispenser. I blow through the door and hurry down the hall, my cheeks burning so intensely that I imagine them melting off my skull like candle wax. The faculty lounge appears empty through its windowed door. I duck inside to examine my face in the mirror above the sink, which reeks of the various Lean Cuisine scraps clogging its drain. Somehow, I'm still intact.

I SPEND THE REST OF THE MORNING reading essays that alternatively move and depress me with their unselfconscious sincerity. It feels inappropriate, the amount I know about these students' home lives, their personal struggles, their dreams. The only reason they bare their souls is because a door might open if they do it convincingly enough. And if it doesn't open, well—I'm the person who they want to explain why.

The bell rings, signaling the final period before lunch, the period when I meet Rob. His room's up two flights of stairs, in what we call the Mold Belt. We're the newest hires at the school, which means Rob had the least seniority when it came to class-room real estate. If I taught, I'd have the abandoned room next to him filled with canned goods from a food drive that never materialized.

I drop the essay in my hand and rub my temples until they burn. The school brought me in on a Field of Dreams grant they received last year, which was just money for a trained college counselor and access to some fancy people from Boston who come and talk to the kids about how beautiful the Tufts campus is and how Harvard really isn't that cutthroat; it's a community, above all. The students always look at me during these talks—we call them Coffee Chats but we don't serve coffee, just Swiss Miss—like: Really? And then I have to look straight at the speaker to keep my expression profes-sional. Who are these conversations for? The students or the news-letter Cushing sends to their parents?

And Cushing, after all, is the real problem, with her vision for the school straight out of the Upwardly Mobile Suburban Handbook. She wants to compete with Southington's and Wassasit's matriculation lists, put a display next to the trophy case listing overeducated alums and their impressive yet inscrutable jobs: Lydia, *consultant*, James, *product manager*. So far, it's not work-ing. If only this were Texas, I overheard one parent saying at a welcome-back event in September. Then at least the state would pay for private school.

The bell rings again—you better be in class—and I get up to leave before Mrs. Johnson returns from her meeting. On the way out, I kick her yogurt fridge three times, so it really shakes. It makes me feel better.

At the top of the stairwell, I pass a group of exchange students from Italy loitering by the water fountain. Cushing started the swap a few years ago, hoping to encourage "intellectual and cultural cross-pollination." As far as I can tell, the only cross-pollination happening is of a sexual nature. "Where are you supposed to be?" I ask, before realizing my mistake. If you ask them to do anything, they pretend they don't speak English. One of the girls holds up her hands in confusion, but when I use the words *Saturday detention* they hurry down the hallway. And that's when I see Jane Ryder standing behind a trash can, pressed to the wall like she's hiding. She looks so much like her mother, whom I only met once, at a college-introduction night for the gifted underclassmen. The other faculty had warned me that she had a pill problem: Apparently, she used to be a very active member of the PTA. They claimed the husband was the cause—he cheated on her with young women who worked on the docks during the summer, teaching sailing or leading kayak tours. At first I didn't understand why they were so interested in Mrs. Ryder; usually the teachers preferred to gossip about one another. Then I realized that when someone disappears without explanation, you have the power to determine what happened to them. And we don't hold that kind of influence very often. At least not here at school, under the surveillance of Cushing and the board and parents so over-involved they'd reattach their kid's umbilical cord if they could.

She wore her hair in long, thin braids, something you rarely see in older women, and her cheeks were so pale they looked blue in the bright lighting. She came up to me after my talk, as the other parents selected frosted sugar cookies and brownie bites from the snack table. I want you to promise me something, she said. I nodded, probably wearily—parents always think I have more power over the admissions process than I do. Promise that you'll get her out of here? she asked. Of course, this wasn't something I could promise. But the way she took my wrists in her hands and held them to her own heart made me say yes.

"Are you okay?" I ask.

"Oh, I'm fine."

"Do you need Mr. Taylor?" I ask, glancing toward Rob's door. It's open.

"No, no, sorry. I'm good."

I pat her lightly on the shoulder—pure blade, all bone. "He doesn't bite."

"Ha," she says, and the noise echoes through the corridor. "Really, I'm fine. Thanks." I watch her hurry down the stairs, head bowed forward like a scolded dog's, and a queasiness rolls through my stomach. The quiet ones are so hard to look out for. They understand the school's economy of attention; if you never ask for anything, no one will look in your direction.

When I walk into Rob's room, he's leaning so far back in his chair that its plastic spine arches. "What flavor?" he asks.

I sit down at one of the desks and spritz it with hand sanitizer from my pocket, because you wouldn't believe what teenage boys will do in plain sight. Someone's etched *suck my geometric dick* into the surface. "Did you have a meeting with Jane?"

"Jane who?"

"Ryder."

He springs forward, his chair bouncing with the movement. "I don't teach Jane." He pounds on his desk until its drawer rattles open. "Why?"

"She was just standing outside your room. Like she was waiting for something."

He looks suddenly alert. "Waiting for what?"

"I don't know. You, I thought."

"I don't teach sophomores." He reaches his hand so deeply inside the drawer that his arm vanishes up to the elbow. "You know that."

"Do I?"

"Yes, you do." When he finally extracts his palm, it's cradling two vape pens. "Don't worry about things that aren't your problem. I'm sure she's fine. Now—what flavor?"

But Jane is my problem. All of the students are. They find me eating lunch at my desk, washing my hands in the bathroom, buying a Sprite from the vending machine. They ask me not to tell their parents. They make me promise I won't freak out. They show me notebook pages with the calorie counts of their meals, healed-over scars hidden by shirtsleeves, text messages from boyfriends, girlfriends, strangers.

Not that Rob would understand any of that.

"What is there?" I ask.

"Mad mango or mellow mojito."

I choose the pen designated as mojito. He exhales a cloud of tropical-smelling smoke and I get up to bang open the window that was painted shut for months until we took a crowbar to its edges. A hit of honeysuckle breezes into the room as I lift its frame.

Outside, tulips are starting to bloom along the border of the student parking lot. I watch a kid in a soccer jersey pick one and pretend to eat it, stuffing the petals in his mouth to the amusement of his buddies. There's nothing more reliable in this world than a teenage boy's sense of humor.

Rob looks so young that he's frequently mistaken for one of them. Skinny and tall in a way he hasn't figured out how to manage, his limbs frequently swinging in opposite directions. His voice has the nervous quiver of a boy who was reprimanded for being too quiet as a child—speak up, son! I imagine he heard often. Not that I know much about Rob's father. Whenever he talks about him, which he does infrequently, it's in that reverent, unexamined way of men who've tried to twist their fear of their fathers into something resembling admiration.

"How's your Tinder?" I helped him make his account last week, when the two of us hid in the art-supply closet while we were supposed to be on lunch duty. My job was to lend the ever-valuable Female Perspective.

"I'm too scared to do it." He chews on the end of the vape pen. "What if a student sees me?"

"Just set your minimum age range to twenty-five or something. Besides, they don't need to be on there. They have each other to fuck."

He shakes his head. "Too paranoid. When are we going to get yours up and running?"

The chances of finding an interesting woman to date here seems less likely than a bolt of lightning and an earthbound comet simultaneously smiting me. "I hate the apps. They make me feel like a dress in someone's online shopping cart that they can't decide whether or not to buy."

Rob laughs and leans over to spit into his metal trash can, the residual saliva dangling from his lips in thin threads. It occurs to me that I should really find a new work ally. "At least you could have it if you wanted it."

"What does that mean?" I ask, even though I absolutely know.

"Just that, you know, it's easier for women. Especially women *on* women. You're nice to each other."

"Are women not nice to you?" I can't help asking.

He smiles crookedly, the corner of his lip catching on one canine. "Not women my own age."

I roll my eyes. Rob loves the attention he gets from the girls here—they make him feel valuable, whereas I've gleaned that women his own age do not. "Do people still die of lead poisoning?" I ask, trying to change the subject.

"Sad people who spend a lot of time in basements do." He tries to take another drag, but a tiny light on the pen's tip blinks orange.

"So essentially us."

"Essentially."

There's still juice left in my vape, but I set it down on his desk. "I guess I should get back to it." I move to stand too quickly and the edges of my vision evaporate, darkness moving in, my head helium. I stumble backward and Rob's hands press against my back.

"You good?" he asks.

I blink and the room returns to normal: laminated geometry posters, electric pencil sharpener, chalkboard ghosted by erased equations. "I'm fine."

His hands are still on my back. "Good."

"WHERE WERE YOU?" Mrs. Johnson asks when I return to our office. "My email won't open. Do you remember what I changed the password to?"

I settle into my chair and ignore her. This is not a tactic I employ with most people, as I myself hate being ignored, but she'll never learn if I keep helping her. Teach a man to fish and whatnot. "Layla," she says. "Layla. *Layla!*" It's amazing how ugly your name can sound in someone else's mouth. I only cave because I can't stand to hear her say it again.

"Isn't it *corgiwiggle34* or something?" I open my own email. A parent threatens to SEND THE PRINCIPAL SOME THOUGHTS if I don't stop giving her son CRAZY IDEAS ABOUT GAP YEARS! I consider writing back that gap years can be thrillingly enriching experiences, especially for students like Corey, who loves to light rolls of toilet paper on fire and hurl them beneath the stall doors of unsuspecting boys. What I actually say is: *Thank you for your thoughts.*

"Corgiwigglebutt154," Mrs. Johnson mutters. I can hear her spank the enter key with her index finger. "Now, why the hell is someone emailing me about a property in Ethiopia?"

I tell her that the message is a scam.

"It's not a scam. He's offering to waive the down payment."

A new message appears in my inbox with the subject line *chat now—my office.* The note is from Principal Cushing. When I open it, the body's blank.

"Are you listening to me?" Mrs. Johnson asks as I stand up.

"No."

There's a sudden crack—her heel hitting the floor. It's so loud that for a second I think our ceiling tile fell out again. "Is that really the tone you want to use with your superior?" she asks.

Mrs. Johnson is one of those women whose entire sense of self-worth hinges on her ability to wield authority. As far as I can tell, she has no discernible talents and no life outside of school. This isn't a cruel perspective, merely facts. The school secretary told me she goes by Mrs. Johnson because she's so insecure about being unmarried at her age. That alone should probably evoke some sense of empathy, but work with anyone in a mold-soaked office the size of an oversized clothes closet and tell me if you have a shred of compassion for them. Sometimes I fantasize about duct-taping her to a chair, pushing it outside, and leaving her in the blind spot of one of the parked school buses.

I toss my backpack over my shoulder and take a breath so tense my ribs shudder. "Since when are you my superior?"

I can hear her calling my name, but I'm already pushing open the door to the cool, empty hallway.

. . .

ALICIA, OUR SECRETARY, looks surprised to see me when I walk into the office. She's addicted to online shopping and has been trying to recruit female teachers to an essential oils MLM in an attempt to support her habit. I generally avoid her. She puts her call on hold and presses the phone to her shoulder. "You in trouble?" she whispers.

"I hope not."

"If you don't know, you are."

"That's not a comforting thought."

"Comfort's for puppies and orphans."

I nod like that's a normal thing to say.

"Owens?" Cushing barks through her closed door.

"You'd better go," Alicia says. "Waiting makes her volatile." I walk past her as she returns the phone to her ear and asks if they do that new monthly installment thing.

Cushing's office is sparsely decorated, with black metal shelving and a huge walnut desk that must have cost more than my monthly salary. There's a slim glass vase on the windowsill behind her, which overlooks the faculty parking lot and the soccer fields. The vase has water but no flowers.

She gestures for me to sit on a child-sized chair opposite her desk. "As I'm sure you've gathered," she says, "the circumstances for our conversation are not ideal."

I can never tell how old she is. Forty? Fifty? Her facial movements are so minimal that wrinkles haven't had a chance to form. Which means there's nothing friendly to focus on, no crinkled eyelids or rumpled laugh lines. Nothing that suggests she is a woman capable of softening. Needless to say, she scares me shitless. Which is what makes her so hot.

"I received a complaint from Sophia West's father about"—she checks her golden watch—"ten minutes ago." She's wearing a black blazer over a white silk turtleneck, and I wonder how she isn't sweating. "He says you were emotionally inappropriate in her college meeting?"

"Emotionally inappropriate?"

Tortoiseshell reading glasses rest on the slope of her nose, and she tilts her face downward to look at me through them. "That is a quote, yes."

I lean back in my chair, which is low-backed and wooden. It digs beneath my shoulder blades like a dull knife. "What does that even mean?"

She sighs like I've asked her to explain why rain is wet. "We both know your work is sensitive, Layla. But there are still boundaries."

There's something about Cushing that brings out the teenager in me. The *something* is that she reminds me of my mom. "I'm sorry, what are we talking about? I suggested she write about her mother. That was it."

A silence passes between us, a noiseless acknowledgment that I'll be too stubborn to accept whatever explanation she provides and that she'll be too stubborn to accept whatever rationale I provide. She runs an almond-shaped nail across a thin golden chain touching her pronounced collarbone. I imagine undoing the necklace for her, separating the delicate clasp with the tips of my nails. The chain slips across her freckled neck before coiling into my open palm. When I close my fingers over the metal links, the heat gathered from her skin touches mine.

"What would you like?"

The voice isn't Cushing's. It's nasal and simmering with vocal fry, and my Kay Jewelers fantasy dissolves. Alicia. Her veiny neck stretches into the room, one lotion-greasy hand curled over the doorknob. She's opened the door to see if Cushing wants a Caesar salad for lunch or something called the Quinoa Renewal Bowl.

Cushing pounds one fist against her desk like a gavel. "I'm in a meeting." Her tone's so sharp I half expect Alicia to fall into ribbons on the floor. She blurts out a stream of apologies and glares at me before retreating into the main office, as though I'm somehow responsible. In her defense, Cushing's excellent at making you wish there was someone other than yourself to blame for your actions.

"It's a sensitive topic for the family," Cushing says once we're alone again. I can't help staring at her necklace. I wonder if I'd be better at my job if I had more sex. Aren't regular orgasms supposed to have a stabilizing effect on the mind, like jogging or meditating?

"Okay," I answer slowly, because I'm trying very hard to focus. "So what would you like me to do?"

Cushing takes off her glasses and slips them neatly into a leather case on her desk. "Well. This is a symptom of a larger issue, one that I've been meaning to discuss with you for some time."

My stomach drops into my bowels.

"The school will not be renewing your contract at the end of the year. We so appreciate all of your efforts, but we believe the college program needs a more robust leader."

The word *robust* sounds foreign and ugly to me, like my name in Mrs. Johnson's mouth. "When," I ask, "did you come to this conclusion?"

"Please don't take it personally. We just need someone with a bit more experience, we've realized."

"You knew my experience when you hired me."

"Yes, well. We weren't sure how it would all play out. This is new for us, too, remember." She stands up, which means she understands the meeting to be over. But I wrap my ankles around the legs of my chair instead of rising to meet her. It's not right, that so much can change in a single day, and without any indication of the impending alteration! Goose bumps rise to the surface of my skin and spread like a rash. No one warns anyone anymore! We're all just edging toward the drop of a cliff and watching one another do it!

She's about to open the door when I speak. "If this is about Coach, then, please, just say so."

Coach is what our gym teacher insists on being called. Earlier this year, a group of my advisees told me that he sometimes appeared in the locker room while they were changing, always acting surprised, like he'd accidentally wandered in. They also reported that his hands would roam during the scoliosis tests he was in charge of conducting and that they'd once seen him pull a particular girl into his office for further testing. That was two years ago—the girl transferred, and they'd never heard from her again.

Coach has led the boys' basketball team to three state victories since.

My students didn't want to go to Cushing. So I did, promising to keep their names a secret. Cushing said she'd look into it but that I shouldn't expect much if the girls weren't willing to talk themselves. You would think, she said at the time, that they'd want to be known. When I asked her why she thought that, she'd leaned against the wall with a shrug. Everyone wants to be a hero, don't they?

"I told you," she says. Her eyebrow quivers but she doesn't allow it to twitch. "We're looking into it, though I know you don't believe me."

Rob once said that the only thing Cushing cares about is her perceived competence. She's got Smart Girl Syndrome, he explained. The only way she derives self-worth is through maintaining her status as the most capable person in the room. Anything that could offer evidence to the contrary is eliminated. "I think we've established that neither of us believes in the other's efficacy," I say.

Cushing walks toward me and puts one hand on the back of my chair. The frame wobbles when she tightens her grip. "He's been at this school for twenty-five years. I owe him, and the girls, my thoughtfulness." She's just beside me, her face hovering above mine. I've never been this close to her before, and now I see her imperfections. A patch of untweezed hairs between her eyebrows, foundation separating across a dry patch on her chin. "I don't have the luxury of knee-jerk decision-making."

I have a card that I've thought about playing many times before, its use defensible only because it could contribute to the greater good of Nashquitten High girls. But not all stories are yours to share, no matter the change they could enact. At least that's what I'd always told myself. "And what would your daughter think about these excuses?" I ask quietly. "Would they make her feel safe?"

Cushing's breath smells like Altoids, and when it blows across my face, the tiny hairs on my cheeks buzz. Why don't you tell your mother? I remember asking as we sat on the grassy slope that leads to the soccer field. Olivia insisted that we talk outside, and only after the clubs and detention had let out for the day.

She wouldn't believe me.

Why do you think that?

Olivia tied back her hair, which she had recently dyed a harsh, unflattering black. Because something like this couldn't have happened to me while she was in charge.

Cushing pulls back abruptly and begins to busy herself with a notebook on her desk. "You can take all your things on the twelfth. No need to come back for faculty meetings."

"That's it?" I ask, by which I mean about ten different things.

"What do you want, Layla? A parade?" She points to the door with her pen. "Just don't make a scene."

Somehow, I walk out of that room and into the lobby, where I find myself in front of a glass case displaying the senior class's baby pictures. Alicia leans out of the office doorway with wide eyes. "What the hell," she whispers, "was *that?*"

I DON'T GO BACK TO MY DESK. Instead I dry heave over the faded pavement of the faculty parking lot before getting in my car to drive home. Right now I'm so numb my entire body feels pumped with lidocaine, but I know the anxiety will come soon, specifically when I look at my bank account and calculate what that equals after rent, health insurance, groceries, loan repayment, gas, phone, internet, electric, beers to quell anxiety, cream for anxiety rash, prescription for actual anxiety, if that online pharmacy that gave me antidepressants once is still in business.

I try to take deep breaths.

The drive's so automatic that it helps me temporarily empty my brain. My place is on the west side of town, as far from the water as you can get. It's a decent spot—the house is updated, the lawn is large, and it's not my responsibility to maintain either of these things. I live with the owner, Mona, a woman I found on Craigslist when I first moved. The rent is so absurdly cheap that for a while I wondered what percent of the mortgage I was paying, until I finally realized that there wasn't any mortgage. Some rare breed of people lives this way: debt-free.

As I pull into the driveway, I try to think of things a normal person would do right now. Walk inside, eat a snack, drink water. I resolve to do those three things in that exact order. When I get to the steps I see that the front door's ajar, blown open by the wind because Mona has forgotten to lock it yet again. She grew up here and says that I worry too much, no one's dumb enough to commit a crime and think they won't get caught. There's no anonymity, she promised.

Mona's at work, but I see that she got the mail before leaving. The sensation of flipping through thick envelopes seems soothing. And it is: pleas to save the children, to buy expensive cake tins, to apply for a low-interest-rate credit card, all shuffling softly between my fingers. Normal people definitely sort mail for seven minutes, I decide.

Recycle, recycle, recycle. I drop them into our blue bin with satisfaction, and when I take a step forward a paper crunches beneath my foot. My lifted toes reveal a crumpled, unopened envelope with a university's name in the left-hand corner. Mona's applying to graduate school and it's not going well. This envelope is small and thin and almost certainly a rejection. I consider whether or not I should text her to ask if she's seen it. She doesn't handle bad news gracefully, which means it would be better for her to handle it at work than at home with me. I send a picture.

In the kitchen I try not to notice the empty bowl of cereal on the counter, flecks of Chex hardening on its rim, or the knife that's been in the sink for days, its blade matte with something greasy and white. I don't clean up after Mona anymore because I'm trying to draw boundaries. What the scope and shape of these boundaries are is unclear, but acting like my roommate's mom is definitely outside of them.

Looking at the baggies of wilted herbs and stained Tupperware containers in the refrigerator, I decide I don't want a snack. Onto drinking water. Since it's Friday, I update my objective to drink beer instead. To feel better about the mess, I open one of Mona's IPAs—what's mine is yours, she's always saying, because she's inse- cure about being an only child.

I take a swig looking out the window and wonder what transfer- able skills I have. The glass is smeared with dusty pollen, every- thing in full bloom. I can listen and I can pull people's stories out of them, which means I could be a phone sex operator or a priest.

I drink more of Mona's craft beer and go to the farthest corner of the lawn, where the grass is so tall it looks like the reeds that grow along the marsh. My phone buzzes—Mona. *Fuck* is all she writes. I send an obligatory sad face emoji back before dropping my phone to the ground, where it lands on an anthill. The ants swarm across my screen like it's a glob of spilled jam, their anten- nas twitching against the glass. If only I could stay hidden here forever.

A FEW HOURS LATER, Mona comes home from the fish mar- ket where she works. It's started to drizzle, but the canvas sail we draped from the roof to two shaky poles last summer keeps most of the rain out. I'm on the porch with the sliding door open, and I can hear her clump through the house. She does not have a light step.

"Come have a drink with me," I call. I'm on my third.

She appears behind the screen, blonde baby hairs frizzing at her temples, work T-shirt knotted at the waist, one pinky finger raised to her mouth, the nail wedged between her top and bottom teeth. Mona is spoiled and slightly unhinged, with the delicate, sly face of an actress in a French New Wave film. I don't exactly have a crush on her. But she's an easy object of fantasy; she's always around. "What are we celebrating?" she asks, slipping outside.

I'm sitting in a lawn chair so low my ass scrapes the ground if I move, and when I look up she seems to be twice my size. "My freedom."

"Oh? What happened?" She accepts the warm beer I pull from the six-pack at my feet. I watch the ridges of her throat wobble as she drinks.

"I got fired."

Her head whips to attention as she drops into the chair beside me. "What the fuck? Are you joking?"

"Cushing pulled me into her office today and told me."

"But they can't do that, can they? Legally?"

"I mean, yeah. Our contract's only a year long."

"What's the reason, though? They need a reason."

"It's a long story."

She swings her head back and forth, unknotting her bun. I fight the urge to take the dangling rope of hair in my hands. I bet it feels like raw silk. "I've got time."

"Oh, just this . . . misunderstanding." I want to tell her the truth, but it belongs to so many people other than myself. I wonder if Olivia, at this very moment, is realizing I betrayed her. Did Cushing think I was insinuating something legitimate? Or just making a cheap rhetorical move? I take a swig of beer and let the carbonation burn my throat. "At least I'll never have to tell a kid their dream's dead again," I say, trying to make it sound like a joke. But one look at Mona's face tells me it hasn't been taken as such.

"You should be telling them not to have a dream in the first place." She smiles at me hollowly. "Why invite the disappointment?"

Before I can respond, she turns her beer bottle upside down and the brown liquid hits the grass with a splash. Some of it splatters across my ankle, trickles toward my toes. "Oops," she says. "Did I get you?"

I pick my foot up off the ground. "Not at all." I've learned that you shouldn't ask Mona if she wants to talk about things. What's the point of talking? she'll say. What does that change?

Chain saws rev on the other side of the trees. Slowly, the forest is coming down. There's an inn being fixed up there, and supposedly a cul-de-sac development is going in soon. Mona says she never thought the town would be so developed—after all, this was a place you wanted to leave, not return to. When I asked her why she'd come back, she just laughed. Which I guess meant she had no real answer.

My phone dings in my pocket and it takes me a moment to extract it—I'm tipsy. *Rob Taylor* flashes across my screen. I groan.

"What?" Mona says.

"It's that coworker I always tell you about."

"The one who seems like he would do offensive stand-up?"

"The very one."

She cranes her neck to look over my shoulder. "Do you think he knows you're leaving?"

"Let's find out." I tap open the message and the screen's harsh light makes me squint.

I've been thinking about you all day.

"Am I drunk," I ask, holding up the phone, "or does this say what I think it does?"

Mona covers her mouth with her hand. "Oh, fuck." She falls back against her chair, and the metal frame creaks as she laughs. "I always said he liked you!"

Another message appears on the screen.

I never thought I'd look forward to tutoring ten-year-olds, lol. I love seeing you work with the students. Is it weird that it turns me on?

All the blood in my body shoots to my heart. In the distance: the grind of the chainsaw, the heavy thump of a fallen tree, men shouting.

"What's wrong?" Mona asks.

The blue ellipses bubble appears, disappears, appears, disappears. I picture his thumbs hovering above the keyboard, typing and then frantically deleting. *Wrong person! Sorry!* What was it they told us at staff training? De-escalate. Cushing, at my first review: You're reactionary, rather than intentional. Take the time to think. Deliberately.

Who was that intended for? I carefully type back.

"Does he know?" Mona's asking.

Kathy, my contact at the middle school. I'm sorry you saw that. I have a bit of a crush on her, obviously.

I don't know any Kathy at the middle school. *Are you sure?*

I'm sure.

Mona's kneeling in front of me, her pupils wide as the sunlight starts to leave us. "What is it?"

A car starts beyond the trees. Friendly goodbyes. The workers leaving for the weekend. For a second, I think I see headlights between the trunks, but that's impossible. The forest isn't so thin, not yet.

Okay, I write.

We can keep this between us, right? I don't want to make Kathy uncomfortable.

I float my thumbs above the illuminated screen. *Yeah.*

Thanks, Layla. I owe you.

He owes me.

I slip the phone back into my pocket. "Was he being creepy?" Mona wants to know.

She tilts her head expectantly. I feel suddenly closed up, like a house with the doors blown shut. "No, just annoying. Wants to know what happened."

Mona puts a hand on my shoulder. "People love to pry."

"Yeah," I say. "They do."

MONA AND I SPEND the rest of the night drinking scotch her father gifted her—her parents always gift her things. Somewhere in the woods, the kids are having a party. Mona tells me a story about the first time she got high, how she drove afterward and a policeman pulled her over. How she'd never seen her father as angry as he was at the police station, and how he never spoke of it again. I ask her if she still thinks about that night. "I try not to," she says. "I could have killed someone."

"But you didn't."

"Yeah, but you know what's funny? When I got pulled over, I was so fucked up that I thought I had. I literally fell out of the car crying, telling the cop I hadn't meant to, I was so sorry, I would go straight to jail, I deserved it." She says it in this way like it's a funny story that happened to a friend, not to her.

"You got that messed up from weed?"

"I don't know." She presses her lips to the rim of her glass. "Some guy just handed it to me at a party. I do remember him laughing at me, though, after I took a hit." She claps her hands together. "Anyway, I'm a fool! End of story."

I might have asked more questions if the rain hadn't turned into a downpour, if Mona hadn't touched her damp fingers to my cheek, if she hadn't told me I was beautiful, if she hadn't held my gaze in a way that made me believe her.

I don't drink often, and tonight I'm drunk. My perception of the present turns patchy, like a television with poor reception. It's when I trip over the dip in the patio floor that Mona says we should call it a night. The pain comes in strange places—my spine, my ass, the crown of my head. Part of me wonders if I'm making it up, amplifying for pity. I tend to get dramatic when Mona's around. Her attention's like a beam of sun after being stuck in shadow. Somehow, we arrive at the stairs. I feel woozily removed from the timeline of my life, as though it's moved into the future and I've failed to keep up. I make myself climb the steps without her assistance. I don't want her thinking I'm some annoying drunk.

Transitions have dissolved: One thing happens, then another. Mona's hands pull a sheet to my chest. A glass of water appears on my nightstand. A greenish capsule of Advil wobbles between my lips.

Mona asks me something, or maybe I ask her something. I'm tired but I don't want to be. Is the night already over? No, it can't be, not yet. She's sitting on my bed and I want her to stay there forever. I ask her to—you don't have to leave—but the bedroom's dark now, and all I see is the gray outlines of my own belongings. Did I swallow the Advil? I smack my lips together. It's gone.

In the darkness, I try not to think about Mona. I try not to think about Rob. I try not to think about Kathy. I try not to think about the person Rob is calling Kathy.

I breathe through my nose and tell myself I will not throw up.

Kathy is a good old-lady name. When I was a kid, my coach called me Gertrude because it would have been an absurd name for a teenager. Gertie for short. I got a nickname because I was special; that was the story. When he texted me on my flip phone or wrote me to my secret email address or messaged me in the chat room he created just for us, he would go: *Is this Gertie?* And always, I would say: *yes.*

I played soccer. I was very good, better than anyone had ever thought I could be. Usually I was clumsy and awkward, but on the field something changed. I finally understood how to make my body useful.

I played at the state level, and they thought I could make it to nationals if I worked hard enough. That's what my coach said, anyway.

There were stretches he wanted to try with me. Special physical therapy exercises. They were intimate, he told me, but that was what made them effective. You trust me, right? he asked. It was a silly question. We both knew the answer.

I quit soccer a year after he started paying special attention to me. I was a junior and my parents were horrified. How would I pay for college without my soccer scholarship? What was I really good at, anyway? Besides chasing a ball the way my coach told me to?

I've only ever told two people, both back in high school. The second was my best friend, Ben. We were born two weeks apart and grew up in the same duplex, our lives unfolding on either side of the common walls. He wanted to play college basketball, and Notre Dame would eventually recruit him. The two of us ran together before school, taking turns planning new routes on the maps the neighborhood association handed out every year.

But it sounds like you didn't say anything? he asked when I told him, genuinely confused. But why would I have? I thought people were good. Which meant someone had to teach me that they aren't. And that's what had happened when I lay on my friend Amelia's floor one afternoon, a snack plate of carrots and hummus beside us, and described what my coach had done to me. When I looked up, her hand was pressed to her stomach as though staunching a wound. Oh my god, she murmured. Are you okay? She dropped the hand and put it over mine. Yeah, I said. Why?

MY PHONE VIBRATES against my pillow. An unknown number. I turn my head and the whole room swings as I raise my arm to my ear.

"I have bad news," a voice says.

"Who is this?"

"Mrs. Johnson." My stomach contracts. "There's no easy way to say this. A student's died, Layla."

"Oh my god. Who?" It sounds like someone else is talking, someone on the other side of the room.

"Lucy Anderson." Her name pools in my ears like clogged water. "The students will want to talk to you."

The walls rotate around me. I sink deeper into my bed. "What am I supposed to say?"

"You'll know what to do."

But that's the thing. I never know what to do. I sit on the slope of the soccer field, or the floor of the girl's bathroom, or the chair behind my dark desk, and the right words never come. Listening can't possibly be enough—it's just an act of reception. Always, when they leave, I think: *What good have I done?*

"No," I tell her. "I won't."

"Layla?"

"Yes?"

"This is no time for a pity party." Her bluntness sharpens something in me. I'm awake. "Underestimating yourself isn't useful." I hear what sounds like a cigarette lighting on her side of the line, though there's no way she smokes. "Go be with someone. This isn't the time to be alone. I'll let you know if there are any updates. And, Layla?"

"Yes?"

"Call me if you need anything. Really."

Slowly, I stand. I tiptoe down the hall to Mona's room and carefully twist her doorknob. It makes barely any noise. But when I peek inside, she's not there. The bed's a pile of cold sheets and skewed pillows. One step into the hallway and I realize how drunk I still am—the floor rolls beneath me like the wake of a wave. I drop to the ground and lie there, pressing my cheek into the rough carpet. When I hold my phone to my face it informs me that my battery is low. I dial anyway.

"Yes, Mrs. Johnson? Can I talk to you about something?"

MONA

I'M ON MY BREAK WHEN Layla texts asking if I've seen a certain envelope from a certain school I applied to. There's even a photo attached, like my linguistic abilities have regressed so dramatically that I now require a visual cue to accompany all words. *No shit, I'm the one who got the mail*, is what I'm thinking but not what I say. Layla is sensitive even though she thinks she's not. It's difficult to live with a sensitive person, is what I've learned. It can make otherwise mundane processes, like brushing your teeth and eating your morning cereal, tense.

I don't respond right away. Layla is one of those people who always texts back immediately, and with long, unnecessary sentences about feelings and observations that aren't relevant to the message at hand. Economy of language is important. That's something I used to believe but now is just something I say. I said it to Layla way back when, and that's one of the things that made my morning cereal tense. So now I am trying to help her relax, to live a little, even though I am generally anxious and do not enjoy spontaneity.

It's a cool May afternoon—I have a sweater on under my apron—and this makes my cigarette taste fucking delicious. The alley smells like fried fish from the shack next door, which is universally known for making the worst fish and chips in town. However, it was not universally known to me when I moved back and had lunch there with my friend, who also happened to be my high school ex-boyfriend. This is fantastic, I said to the friend and ex-boyfriend. He wasn't eating anything, but he was high on something and kept jiggling his knee, bumping the already-unsteady wooden table. No it's not, he spat, it's shit. He said it in this way that made it sound like he was so embarrassed for me and for himself by association that we should both just slit our throats right then and there with my plastic knife and die a slow death on the ketchup-stained concrete.

I snuff out my Parliament on the dumpster lid. I told everyone I quit, and if I reply to Layla mid-puff she'll know that I'm back in business because that's what happens when you work with kids. Your bullshit meter gets so sensitive that you can tell whether two sophomores had sex in the janitor's closet twenty minutes ago just by the tremble of their lips. That's a true tale. Layla found the milky condom lying there in the mop bucket just like she thought it would be and had to pick it up with a pencil.

Sometimes, she tells good stories.

Fuck, I finally type back, by which I really mean *fuck off* or maybe *fuck that shit*, but Layla sends me a sad face back, which means she has interpreted it as *fuck me*. I look at the photo again. The envelope is normal-sized, letter-sized, not congratulations-sized, not please-pick-us-sized, not packet-full-of-hopes-and-dreams-sized. If only I could look at everything in life and know its interior contents. I would have dated significantly fewer musicians.

Embarrassingly, there are tears in my eyes. I roll my fists over my eyelids until they start to sting. I used to do this as a kid and it totally freaked out my mom—You'll get wrinkles! she would shriek, which was maybe the first thing that made me hate her. Or when she told me that my birth had ruined her career. Or that time she said that she had really, really wanted a boy because girls are more work and damn, had I proven her right. Or when she slapped me for embarrassing her at a party, I always thought I was so fucking funny. You can't deny I'm a gas, I said back, because I was fifteen and had just read The Great Gatsby and that sounded like something Daisy would say. Then she slapped me again. Childhood trauma? I barely know her! My therapist didn't think that was very funny, but I told her not to worry, I mean I didn't have any *real* trauma, it wasn't like I'd been raped or something.

I walk out into the street and glance down the hill toward Main Street. The shops look grayish and the ocean's turned the color of concrete, which means we're in for a storm. Maybe the roads will flood. Maybe the seawall will break again. Maybe I'll drown.

The front door jangles open behind me and Marina appears with a bony wrist cranked at her hip. "You good?" she asks, which means my break is over. Marina's seventeen and plans to work on an organic lavender farm in Spain after she graduates next year. Post-gap year she'll study to become a gynecologist, maybe in China because she believes the United States health care system is too Western-focused. Then she'll return to the States to offer her services at Planned Parenthood—she's been practicing abortions on papayas using a video she found on YouTube. I could probably give you one, she said confidently last week while we were skinning salmon. Why she tells me all this is anybody's guess.

"I'm fine." I toss my spent cigarette to the pavement and it lands in a puddle of yellowish liquid dripping from the dumpster. We watch the paper turn the color of piss.

"You can talk to me, you know," she says earnestly, tucking a piece of copper-colored hair behind her ear. For reasons unknown to me, Marina wants to be my friend. When I was her age I thought people older than me were depressing and unfunny, but I guess female friendships with age gaps are in nowadays. My Netflix account keeps feeding me trailers featuring surly teenage girls with stringy hair mentored by hot, confident women in their twenties who don't seem to have jobs.

"Wow," I say. "Thank you." She nods like a gracious sage. The only reason I don't hate her is because I, too, was once a teenager with embarrassing opinions and a desire to do something Deeply Meaningful. Which means I understand the rough road to reality that follows a person with such beliefs.

Marina steps aside as though it's a privilege to open the seagull-shit-streaked door. I kick it with my foot, but the plastic carpet on the other side bunches up in resistance. When we close I'll spray the fish guts out this door with the garden hose and watch them drip down the sloped alley toward the road. It looks biblical, the watery blood running to the street, the bits of flesh sticking to the pavement. The most satisfying part of my day.

Marina bumps into me from behind. "Sorry," she says. "I thought you were moving."

Inside, I clean the fish case while Marina leans against the cash register, pushing back her cuticles with a debit card. The cod, shoved into a mound of shaved ice, stare back at me with marble-like pupils. Beside them sit the swordfish steaks, their edges turned to pale putty because Marina didn't pack them properly. I try not to care about these things, but a laissez-faire attitude can degrade into all-encompassing nihilism if you're not careful. "What are you doing tonight?" she asks me from above.

"What do you mean?"

"It's Friday. Aren't you going out?"

I rise, pushing on the case for support, and my knees pop. "It's very nice of you to assume that."

Marina laughs like this is an inside joke between us. "There's a huge party happening. You should come."

"I can legally drink. Like, at a bar. You know that, right?"

"I know. But it sounds like you don't have anywhere to be." She smiles with the innocent menace teenage girls have been perfecting for centuries. What an age! To be so convinced of your allure and so ignorant of its consequences.

She comes around the side of the counter to stand beside me. "I'll text you the address," she says.

"You don't have my number."

She reaches into the front pocket of my apron and I feel her hand graze my stomach. When she pulls away, my phone's in the grip of her fingers. She enters my name on the passcode screen, six six six two, and it unlocks. She tilts her head at me. "Now I do."

AFTER MY SHIFT I WALK AROUND the harbor aimlessly. I know Layla will be at home editing college essays, reading some of them aloud to hear what's wrong, asking my advice on the trickiest ones, since didn't I study writing, forever ago? It makes my jaw ache to listen, they're so openly earnest. Like hearing a friend read you their poetry or talking to a Jehovah's Witness.

I'm kicking a rock in the general direction of O'Dooley's when my mother texts me. I sit on one of the little benches the beautification committee put in last year, because texts from my mother are usually best read sitting down. Luckily this one is not a fire starter. *Can you stop by the Laurels place?* she asks, referring to the family of my best friend from childhood, Natalie. *Your father thinks he forgot to lock the front door.*

Lately, my father has become obsessed with stacking the Laurels' fridge with casseroles while Mrs. Laurel's in the hospital, delivering a fresh one every day even though none of them, as far as I can tell, have been consumed. My personal take is that they had an affair when we were younger, but Natalie got beyond pissed when I brought this up years ago, both of us home from college. You're always making up these little stories about everyone, she said. Are you really that bored?

In retrospect it doesn't sound all that mean. But when I thought she was done, she said the thing that I think about every few days, sometimes more: Stop inventing traumas to explain how fucked up you are.

Why did she say that to you? my therapist asked. What was the context?

The context was that she'd recently found out I'd fucked her high school boyfriend that she was still kind of in love with, but I didn't say that. Instead I shouted: She's a cunt! Then I started laughing, because I think *cunt* sounds funny, like one of those fruit hybrids, a plumcot or an Ugli.

I forget where I was going with any of this.

Sure, I text back, but my mother doesn't reply and I know she won't. It's expected that I'll obey.

I finish kicking the rock all the way to O'Dooley's. The cliff that used to buttress the sidewalk began to crumble when I was a kid, and the cheap wooden stilts they drilled in as reinforcements are already rotting where they meet the ocean. Which means that on nights like this, when the tide churns instead of laps, the sidewalk and its guardrail sway with the waves.

The pub's front door opens just as I punt my rock too hard. Rae glares at me from the patchy welcome mat, the neck of a Bud Light strangled between her fingers. I watch my rock skitter over the pavement's edge like a frightened hermit crab, hear it plunk into the dark water below.

"Buy this!" She shakes the beer at me.

"No," I say, even though I don't know why she's asking and a cold beer sounds amazing.

"You look like a pedophile out here, kicking rocks." Exasperation pinches everything from her lips to her temples. I threw up into not one but two of the O'Dooley's toilets a few years ago, and she's never forgiven me.

"Oh, I'm sorry for scaring all the *children* away from your bar."

"Just come inside."

"Really *you're* the pedophile," I say, following her through the doorway. "You're the one who was watching me like a little creep."

"A little creep?"

"God, it sounds so filthy coming out of your mouth."

We pull aside the curtain of puka shells that Freddie, the owner, hung up a few months ago to "spruce the place up." Rae leads us to the bar, a laminate counter that runs the entire back wall and which Freddie covered with peel-and-stick woodgrain during the puka-shell phase. Not one stool is occupied. I run my fingers over the pleather seats as we walk by, and they're so chilled from the AC that they must've been ass-less for days. Whenever I ask Rae how business is going, she says they're getting by. Which is Nashquitten for "barely making it." We used to say it all the time back in high school, when she was a senior and I was a freshman. We were paired together for some mentorship program that didn't last beyond its inaugural year, and whenever I passed her in the halls I'd ask how it was going, to which she would reply, I'm getting by, Squint—my glasses prescription was too low but I refused to go to the optometrist. It was the first time I thought anyone sounded sexy, by which I guess I mean world-weary.

Rae pops open my beer with her bar key and it foams like crazy from all her shaking. "I told you," Freddie says, coming out from the back room. "That shipment of Buds is cursed." Then he sees me and shakes a sausagey hand in disgust. "Oh, Pinkeye is here."

"I have an actual name."

"What is it," he asks, "Feces McGee?" (Perhaps it's relevant to note that I also once visited O'Dooley's on a Friday night with what I thought was allergies but actually ended up being a case of pink eye that I gave to three-quarters of the pub.) "I could sue you for damages." He adjusts the tilted dartboard on the opposite wall. "You should see what people wrote on our Google reviews."

"Don't worry. No one reads Google reviews."

"It's all about Yelp," Rae agrees.

"Fuck Yelp!" Freddie steps back and cranks his arm, shoots it forward. The dart spears a vintage Celtics jersey that I'm pretty sure is fake. He turns around and points at me with a thick finger. "You're bad luck, girl."

"Believe me, I know." I sip my beer and turn back to Rae. "Wanna go to a high school party tonight?"

She raises an eyebrow and pours herself a glass of water from the soda gun. Suddenly the music switches on, and "Have Yourself a Merry Little Christmas" floats through the air. "Some of us have to host the Knights of Columbus adult spelling bee. But I'm glad you're staying in touch with your inner child."

"My coworker invited me."

"The little gynecologist brat?"

"The very one!"

"Kids are too bold these days."

"It's the internet," I tell her. "They know everything and they get to know it privately, shamelessly! If we wanted to know how a blow job worked we at least had to ask a friend."

"Stop talking about blow jobs!" Freddie shouts from somewhere behind me, maybe the men's bathroom.

"Long gone are the days of Phone a Friend." Rae reaches over to take a sip of my beer. She does it in this lingering, protracted way that indicates we're shifting the conversational tone. I gulp my spit since she has my beer. "How's the school stuff going?" she finally asks.

"I've decided to take a page from your book! I'm going to become an actress!" I straighten my spine and tip an imaginary hat. "Bonsoir, madame."

She sets the beer back on the bar. "Who are you?"

"I dunno." I shrug and slump back to my normal posture. "Someone French."

She reaches both of her hands back and leans against the shelf behind her, the one that holds the bottles of cheap liquor. (There is no shelf that holds the bottles of expensive liquor.) She has that exasperated expression again. "I'm being serious, Mo. How are you?"

The beer is so cold and slick in my hand that I half expect to look down and see that it's melted through my fingers. "I'm seriously fantastic." I'm suddenly aware of the smell of the place—all the sweat and spilled drinks and stubbed cigarette butts soaked into the carpet. God, being sober here is so fucking depressing. "Probably, I feel like you felt."

She gives me a good up-and-down but still takes the bait. "Felt when?"

"When you realized you weren't good enough to make it in LA." I drain the last of my beer. "God, that must have been so embarrassing."

Something crashes behind us—Freddie messing around with the lights or the sinks or the tables, who knows. Rae sticks out her bottom lip and nods her head slowly, one finger pressed to the slope of skin beneath her nose. Do I feel bad? No. And that's my problem—I love to fuck myself over.

"Hey, Mo," Rae says. I lean in her direction but only an inch. The finger drops from her face and lands on the hollow of my neck. She presses into the bony pit, and I feel my heart beat against her. "I'm getting tired of feeling sorry for you." Then she spins around so that I'm practically eating the ends of her ponytail. "I'll see you."

"How much is it?" I peel my thighs off the stool and the pleather crackles like cocktail ice.

She looks at me over her shoulder. "Oh, fuck off. I'll never charge you."

OUTSIDE, IT'S STARTING TO DRIZZLE, but the rain is practically invisible—you can only see it if you tilt your head at just the right angle. The docks behind O'Dooley's are busy with men heaving up chains and tying complicated knots. The stationary boats rock against their moorings like impatient children. When I was little I begged my parents to get a boat, going so far as to write them a three-page letter detailing the undeniable positive effects it would have on my development as a nine-year-old. My mom looked at it a little sadly, which was unlike her. Then she tightened my ponytail and patted me on the shoulder. Where, she asked, would we even go?

I find my keys in my pocket and start the trudge back up the hill to my car, which is parked beside Mullaney's. I should probably make it clear that I was lying before, about Rae. I actually feel very bad. But, God, the shame. I'm addicted to it.

AT HOME I DRINK BEER with Layla and smoke out the first-floor bathroom window when I go to piss. Apparently, she got fired. I say *apparently* because it wasn't in writing and I don't think they'd go through with it anyway—Layla's one of two people there under fifty-five. Plus, she's pretty good at her job, from my perspective. But all I say is "I'm sorry" because you really shouldn't contradict someone when they're trying to wallow.

We finish the beer quickly and I bring out the scotch my father gifted me when I graduated college. After a few heavy pours and no dinner besides a bag of tortilla chips, we're really cruising. I grab Layla's face with my hands and tell her she's a beautiful person with one of the most genuine hearts I've ever known. I'm not sure if I really believe that, but there it is coming out of my mouth. It makes Layla smile and also cry. She tells me that I'm hilarious and uncompromising, which is a pretty big word to use when you're drunk. I'm almost hazy enough not to wonder what she means by it.

We're outside on the porch when Layla says she needs to go to bed. She's slumped so deeply into her lawn chair that I can't imagine her standing up, but she does it, wobbly as she is. "It's late!" she shouts, even though it's only midnight.

"Go upstairs," I tell her, standing. "I'll bring you some water."

"Water!" She pantomimes drinking a glass and then mumbles something about how good my hair smells. Layla's had a crush on me forever and it's particularly obvious when she's drunk. *Let's not do this,* is something I've almost had to say, but not yet. It's all fine because she never remembers anything in the morning. I once let her kiss my open mouth the night of her birthday party. We had just gotten home from the bar and took turns holding on to the other's arm as we kicked off our shoes. We were both lonely and did not want to be. It's very rare. To be feeling something as deeply as someone else at the exact same time. Rarer still for you both to know it.

"You're so nice to me," she says.

"I'm really not." I don't like it when she gets this way, making me into whoever she needs in order for her desire to be worthwhile. After all, if you can't have something, it should at least be worth wanting.

She takes a shaky step toward the door. "You're going to get into school, Mo."

"No, I'm not. That was the last school. You know that."

Shouts ring up from the woods and we both turn our heads. A party's been happening on the other side of the trees for about an hour now. Probably the construction workers who've been fixing up the inn over there. Sometimes I'll go for a run through the woods after work and they'll invite me to have a beer on the half-built porch, or they'll request my presence at a late-night gathering if I'm really lucky. The shouts dissolve and the music turns up to the kind of volume that makes your eardrums feel swollen. They must have something to celebrate.

"It'll work out," Layla says. Her head is nodding and I wonder how many times she has to say those three unfounded words to students delirious with failure. Why do people feel the need to lie in the face of undeniable evidence? It hasn't worked out, and it won't work out. Do I appear so fragile and delusional to Layla that she needs to appease me like one of her advisees? Always, I'm a child: to my parents, to Rae, and almost certainly to Marina—that must be why she's drawn to me.

My phone buzzes. It's not until I unlock my fingers to retrieve it that I realize my entire body's tensed up like a curled fist. *About to go to bed. Please tell me you checked the door and forgot to text.*

Layla's head swings over my shoulder. "Who's texting you?"

"No one."

"A lover?" she teases. All the booze is draining from my head, and Layla's getting closer and closer. "Hey," she asks, "are you okay?"

I sense that she wants to touch me, and every nerve ending in my body withers at this prospect. I've only been reliably touched in moments of distress or despair, like a part of me had to break in order to warrant being held. And that's the ugliest kind of touch. All obligation, no tenderness. I'd rather be slapped.

"It doesn't concern you," I tell her, which is exactly what my mother would say, but Layla's that level of drunk where tone is indecipherable. Then her hot mouth is at my ear. She's trying to say something comforting and encouraging and kind, her unsteady hand reaching for my shoulder, the fingers outstretched like an animal about to strike. But she loses her balance. Her whole body is about to press against mine, soft and sweat-sticky and dripping with the desire to give me something I don't want. I see what I am about to do and then I do it. The sounds of my arms slicing through the air rings in my ears before I even move them. I push her.

Hard.

Too hard. She thumps against the glass door like a confused bird and then sits in a heap on the concrete patio. Her hair covers her face.

My whole body is hot like a coal. At some point I stuffed my thumb in my mouth, and when I draw it out there's blood on the knuckle. I lick it off and kneel in front of her. She groans and I part her hair. Her eyes are half-open.

"Can you help me?" she asks.

"What do you—"

"Up," she says. "Just help me up."

Inside, she insists on walking up the stairs without assistance, which maybe means that she knows, even though nothing is broken or bleeding and she's confused about what happened. Exactly, verbatim, she asks: "What happened?" I tell her she tripped. As I'm telling her this I'm imagining it myself—her clumsy feet, the cheap flip-flops, that weird slope on the patio. When I wake up tomorrow morning, this is what I'll believe happened. Memory is one of the easiest places to hide.

Once she's finally fallen onto her bed, Layla says her head hurts. I pull back the comforter and make her swallow an Advil once she's crawled beneath her sheets. She still has on her jeans, a single button undone before she gave up, and her contacts are in. "What would you do?" she asks sleepily. "If you were me?"

"About what?"

Her eyes close. "Sure."

I'm sitting on the edge of her mattress and I rub the corner of her comforter between my fingers. "You need to sleep, Layla."

"I'm not an angry person." The end of her speech trails off like a dream's about to take over. She flips onto her side, away from me. "I'm not . . . what's the word? With the *v*?"

"*Vindictive?*"

"Yeah, that one."

I turn off the light on my way out. The rain sounds like quarters bouncing off the roof. Through the hallway window I can see where we were sitting just seconds ago: empty lawn chairs, tipped-over beer bottles, concrete patio gone dark and wet. I'm thinking of the phrase *capable of.* Why do we assume there are certain things that we aren't *capable of?* Like there's an invisible boundary all sane people are guaranteed to brush against? I have always felt *capable of* everything. I'm not sure what could stop me if I wanted something bad enough.

My phone vibrates in my pocket. *Mona?*

I'M STANDING IN MY DRIVEWAY with my rain jacket on trying to figure out how you know if you're too drunk to drive. Probably the question itself is the answer. A coyote howls somewhere in the distance, which seems like a bad omen. It's exactly twelve minutes to Natalie's house on town roads so familiar I could drive them blindfolded. But could I drive them under the influence of two beers and two glasses of scotch, which may be more like three beers and three glasses of scotch, given my less-than-sober calculations?

The rain abruptly stops when a pack of teenage boys comes pushing through the woods beside the house. "Hey!" I yell. "Private property!" I expect them to laugh, maybe shout at me to fuck off. But they say nothing. They barely look at one another before running off in different directions, some toward the road, others into neighboring yards, all wary of the streetlights, ducking into darkness.

I hear what sounds like someone vomiting. When I walk toward the yard's periphery with my phone's flashlight on maximum brightness, I can see that it's a girl in a pink velvet slip dress. That girl is Marina.

She's sitting on the lawn, staring up at the moon. When she sees me coming she tries to hide the pile of yellow bile by covering it with some nearby leaves. Wet hair sticks to her face in thick rib-bons and her naked feet are caked in dirt. "Really?" I ask.

"Mona?" Her voice is somehow both childlike and weathered. "Can we have some water?" She shifts and the dress rises up so I can see her underwear, which is white with a tiny pink bow on the waistband. I look away.

"Who's 'we'?" Another girl, this one with dark hair, peeks up from behind a holly bush. She stands and I can see that her blue shift dress is splattered with something dark across the stomach, something I tell myself is definitely not blood but dirt, or ketchup, or even just water, it's been raining, after all. She walks toward me, feet smacking against the damp grass. She, too, is barefoot.

"I'm fine," the girl says, sensing my question. "Really." She comes so close that I can taste her smell: sweat curdled with anxiety, cherry-blossom body spray, something musky and thick, like dead animal. She reaches for my hand with icy fingers and presses it to her waist. I close my eyes, preparing to graze a warm wound, but the fabric is cold, untorn.

Sirens echo in the distance. "What happened?" I let my hand drop away.

"We'll tell you if you let us inside," the girl says. She passes me and gestures for Marina to follow.

But Marina doesn't follow. "Am I a bad person?" she asks from the ground.

"It's locked," I shout at the girl, who's almost to the front stairs. It's a lie, but she sits down on a step anyway.

"Marina," I say, "what did you do?"

Red and blue light splashes up the yards at the front of the cul-de-sac. The sirens are close now, shrieking from what seems like all directions. The girl sprints back up the lawn and starts to lift Marina to her feet. "We have to keep moving," she says, shielding her mouth with her hand like that will make their conversation private. Then she turns to me. "Don't tell them you saw us. Please."

As she bends to hook her hands beneath Marina's armpits, house lights begin to turn on. This isn't the kind of place where a person hears an ambulance at one in the morning and pulls their pillow over their head. My neighbor's floodlight falls across the lawn, and that's when there's no denying it. The blood across her belly. "I don't even know you."

Her face crowds together, like a string's pulled all of her features to its center. "I thought you were Marina's friend."

"No," I say. "We just work together."

The girl shakes her head and pulls Marina toward the dark bushes, the soles of her feet flashing white with each step. She looks so small and frail, which is the danger of girls. They look like deer when, really, they're wolves.

"Marina," I start, but she's whispering something in the girl's ear. I watch them press together and then slink off into the shadows. I wonder vaguely if I should try to contact their parents. Which makes me think of my mother.

I decide I'm feeling sober enough to drive.

I FOLLOW THE CONES of my headlights through the town's narrow streets, some lit by streetlamps, some opaque. The sky opens up again and droplets smack my windshield. Rain makes me existential. I'm considering all the life I haven't lived and all the life that I have, and how unfair it is that the only person I can be is myself, this Mona from Nashquitten, and that I unknowingly committed to being her, forever, the second I slipped into this world.

I've stopped looking at the road—I'm staring at my own dim reflection in the rearview mirror. My eyes lock with their duplicate, and that's when I feel the car glide beneath me. My chest presses the taut seat belt, my head swings forward, the wheels fail to find pavement. I can't see the yellow line, but I sense that I'm skating over it. I've always thought that I'd be cool with death, but it turns out that I'm actually not at all ready to die. I scream like my voice can save me.

The rain lets up for the briefest moment. I can see. With a plastic picket fence feet in front of me, I right the wheel and reenter my lane.

I breathe, barely. Air scrapes along my throat like stale bread crumbs.

When Natalie and I were sophomores, one of our classmates drove his mom's Subaru right into the brick wall of the old gym. He made it but never walked again, and the school didn't have any wheelchair ramps, so his friends had to take turns carrying him up the stairs. A few months later this other kid crashed on 5A at the Murder Merge and he was fine, but his best friend in the passenger seat died. Then summer came. The girl that everyone had pretty much written off because she sold Oxy drove her car right off the road that winds up Third Cliff. There was no safety railing then and she was gone upon impact. The beach below was closed for a long time, and we all complained because it was easier to act like we'd had something taken away from us, too. I remember getting ready with Natalie for prom and this big sigh she let out while she put on her lipstick. Can people just stop dying? she asked. Exhaustion was the better choice over fear—focus on the tragedies you'd already endured, rather than wondering if you'd be the victim of one.

I take a right onto Grove Street with my still-shaking hands and pass the turn that leads to my parents' house. It would have been so easy for my mother to walk (not even drive!) to the Laurels', but of course that was out of the question. I pull into their empty driveway, which is made of crushed white seashells that sound like broken glass beneath my tires. The rain pours into the car when I open my door, and I wonder why, exactly, I still listen to my mother. My body appears in the glass door's reflection as I run up the concrete pavers to the front steps, and I get the distinct feeling that I'm fourteen again, holding a secret in my throat that only my best friend will fully appreciate.

My father has, in fact, left the door unlocked. I gently push it open, and everything's wrong. The smell has changed from citrus to sandalwood, there's no longer a thick red rug beside the shoe rack, and there's no music drifting through the hallway. Natalie's mom used to play classical music whenever I came over, I think because she once overheard my father listening to Bach in his study. She's such a wannabe, Natalie whispered one time, shutting off the stereo. A wannabe what? I asked. She arched her eyebrows like I was an idiot. A wannabe you.

A huge crack of thunder splits the sky and the lights go out. I feel my way up the stairs, to the place I've found a hundred times in the dark and will always be able to: Natalie's room. Her door's wide open and when I step inside the lights flicker on like they know I'm there. There's a banner above her bed displaying the name of the college I wanted to go to, and her diploma from that college is propped against her bookshelf. It's crazy that I'm still fucking jealous.

I open Natalie's drawers, rifle through her closet, unbutton all of her child-sized shirts and dresses so they're almost falling off their hangers, but not quite. I wonder if there's a correlation between being skinny and uptight. Maybe all that internal clenching makes your metabolism speed up.

I'm looking for something, but I'm not sure what it is. I find her diaries—there are four of them—in a shoebox underneath her bed. I've never had any ethical hang-ups about snooping. If something's there, why shouldn't you have the right to look at it? And it's not like we hold ourselves to such standards of privacy once the person's dead.

But, anyway, I open the diaries. I search for my name but there's nothing exciting, just boring shit that reaffirms my opinion that I squandered my high school years. I flip through the pages so quickly some corners tear. Finally, something in an entry from our graduation month, purple pen smeared from the side of her hand: *Mona lacks conviction and I think always will.* The sentence makes my chest go watery.

Something about Natalie is that she could look at a person and see what they didn't know about themselves. She used to shock me with revelations about our classmates or their parents that I recognized as blatantly true once she spoke them. About my own mother, she once said: She feels like she wasted her life. What? I said, laughing. We were sixteen, seventeen. Don't you think? Natalie asked. She followed the same suburban blueprint as everyone around her and now she has nothing to show for it. She has a family, I said. She has me. That's true, Natalie allowed. But those things don't belong to her.

It was a very disorienting experience, hearing her insights. It made you feel like there was some secret language of behavioral meaning that only a select group of humans could understand, without any clear way to gain proficiency. And that meant that you would only ever live on the surface of things, like a water beetle skimming the skin of a pond while the real life pulsed beneath it. Most people can make peace with this. But I wanted to write.

I decided I would be a writer when I entered high school and had no discernable talent besides studying, which was less a talent and more a frenzied quest for validation whose success I could guarantee through a steady diet of flash cards and insecurity. The two other things I excelled at were reading an insane number of books and writing fake doctors' notes, and one was more lucrative than the other. I wrote notes for the burnouts, who paid me ten dollars to convince their homeroom teachers that they weren't fucked up, only sick. I'm not a good liar, but I'm a great mimic. In college, I once convinced a fraternity brother to Venmo me five hundred dollars by writing him an email as the newly instated Greek Life Social Chair to help fund a Librarians and Barbarians party that would *attract the most pussy this campus has ever seen* with the stipulation that *as we all know, good pussy has a high price.*

So I went to college and took a bunch of English classes that I told my parents were econ classes. Natalie was the only one who knew the truth. My junior year, the English department procured a fancy young writer for a visiting professorship, which meant he taught one class a semester and occasionally roped in his friends for university-sponsored readings. I took his course, which he canceled half the meetings of due to "literary obligations." What he didn't cancel were the required conferences about our final portfolio.

When I entered his office, he was fiddling with an automatic espresso machine on a table below his window. Would you like? he asked, gesturing to it, and when I shook my head he abandoned the machine in a dramatic way that implied I'd insulted him.

So, your work, he said abruptly. He produced one of my stories from a blue folder sitting on his desk and flicked through the pages briefly. It is . . . fine, he said eventually, and I could already tell where the whole conversation was going. Off a cliff.

It's . . . what's the word I'm looking for . . . .

He leaned back in his chair and kicked his feet up on the desk, inches from my face. He wore leather sneakers with soles that had been imprinted with tiny triangles, and the tiny triangles had filled with crumbled leaves and dirt. I stared at the dirt and tried to convince myself that whatever came out of his mouth next, I wouldn't care.

Glib. He turned his chair and swept his feet from the desk in one motion.

Glib? I repeated.

He nodded and began to pick at his eyebrows, which were enormous and the texture of steel wool.

It's like peering into a puddle, he said.

What does that mean? I managed to ask, despite the fact that I had a pretty good idea.

It means I don't believe you.

Me, or the stories?

They're the same thing.

Are they?

He closed my folder and raised a finger like I had interrupted him. You just need more texture in your life. He swiveled his neck to look out the window behind him. This place certainly isn't helping.

What if I don't want more texture?

God, did he think that was hilarious. I could see every single one of his teeth when he laughed. Mona, Mona, Mona, he said after catching his breath. I'll remember you.

No, you won't, is what I wanted to say.

I went straight to the library afterward and sat on one of the old benches in the lobby that had the name of a dead donor on its back. I looked up *glib* on my phone, and then and there I decided that I was done. I'd thought my writing was the sincerest part of me. Turns out it was the shallowest.

Then I walked to the row of public computers and emailed Natalie, because I told Natalie everything. While I waited for her to respond, I watched videos of old women grooming small dogs on YouTube, which was what I did when I was sad. I waited three, four hours.

M,

Don't take this the wrong way, but do you think he's right,
maybe? That you just have some growing up to do? It seems like
he was trying to help, after all.

N

P.S. Still your biggest fan. Always.

Her words made the palms of my hands go hot and itchy like I'd touched poison ivy. I immediately forwarded her the portfolio that I'd emailed my professor a week ago, with just one sentence: *You decide.*

She never did. Either she didn't read it at all or she found the pages so offensive that she'd rather pretend I'd never sent them in the first place. I didn't bring it up because that felt like asking someone if you were pretty after they'd had sex with you. The deed was done, so why ask for clarification?

I close the diary and put it back in the shoebox beneath the bed. The rain raps against her window like hundreds of tapping fingernails, and I decide that I won't be driving home tonight. In the morning I'll text Layla something casual and inquiring, like, *how are you feeling? I haven't been that drunk in a looooong time.* Maybe I'll bring her a donut.

Downstairs on the couch, I fall asleep quickly but shallowly, waking up every so often and forgetting where I am. Natalie and I used to do this thing called Whispers at sleepovers, where we'd whisper a story in the other one's ear while she was falling asleep and see if she could remember it in the morning. Natalie told the same one over and over. A little girl fell out of a truck because she grabbed a roadside branch, but I never heard the ending. I always forgot to ask her in the morning—was the moral to avoid wanting something too much, or too little?

Later, the front door pushes open and Natalie's shadow drifts through. My mother had mentioned something about her coming home, but I rarely retain the details of our conversations. I hold my breath as she unties her shoes.

She doesn't see me. *I missed you* is what I'm trying to decide if I truly feel, or only wish I did.

WHEN I OPEN MY EYES in the morning, the house is silent and the sun slashes through the window like sharpened teeth. My stomach growls, and on a hangover scale of bushy-tailed to walking dead I haven't quite approached zombie, but I'm close. I go into the kitchen with the idea of taking one of my dad's many casseroles home, and as I'm riffling through shelves of tinfoil-wrapped pans and icy bags of peas, I hear someone clear their throat behind me. Natalie's looking at me like: Really? I knock my head into the open refrigerator turning toward her.

"What are you doing?" she asks.

"The casseroles." I gesture toward the fridge. "My dad made you casseroles."

She moves past me to open a mason jar of coffee grounds sitting on the counter. "I see."

I'm suddenly aware of the bleach-stained yellow pants I'm still wearing from work, their ambient fish smell. "How long have you been back?" I look around for something to subtly douse myself with—air spray, maybe even hand sanitizer—but no luck.

"Just a few days." She gestures to the coffee pot. "Do you drink it now?"

Drinking coffee makes me feel like my heart is going to tunnel through my sternum. "Sure."

She pours two more scoops into the plastic filter she's holding and asks me what I'm up to. I try to say same old, same old, but my lips are suddenly parched and it sounds like I'm doing an offensive Russian accent.

"Am I blocking you in?" Natalie asks, turning to look out the kitchen window. "I'll move."

I tell her it's fine, but she insists. Anything to get away from me, it seems. She walks so quickly out of the kitchen that she trips on the hallway runner.

I'm searching for the closest donut shop on my phone when it starts to buzz. Layla. I walk to the back of the house, where their porch faces the ocean. It's still raining, and I duck under the same striped awning that's been there since we were kids. I once accidentally set it on fire with a sparkler, which made Natalie's mom beyond mad. I don't know why they never replaced it. The right side's still black and frayed, like a shredded strip of tire.

Layla's breathing heavy when I raise the phone to my ear. "Is your hangover that bad?" I ask with a laugh, trying to sound fun and lighthearted and warm, and then she begins to wail, a word I've never used for a grown adult's sobbing until now. Her crying comes high-pitched and shivery and congested over the line. I hear her yank a tissue from the box and blow. "Hey, hey now," I say. It sounds like I'm trying to soothe a horse. "We were both really fucked up. I didn't mean to—"

"I'm sorry, can I talk first?" She takes a mucusy inhale. "One of my students died, and it's kind of just hitting me."

"Oh my god." I sit down on one of the porch chairs. "What the fuck?"

"It happened next door, Mona. The kids took over the inn after the workers left."

"What?" A hollow feeling moves through my chest, like my lungs have dissolved.

"They haven't told us what happened yet. Her name was Lucy—I think I told you about her? The artsy girl?"

I have no recollection of an artsy girl.

The line beeps. "Shit, I have to go, it's school. I'll see you at home."

My phone's burning when I pull it away from my ear, like a sun-baked rock from the shore. I have the sudden urge to throw it over the thin wire fencing that separates the Laurels' property from the public beach, but then a shadow drops across my arm and Natalie sits down on the chair beside me. "You good?" She hands me a mug that's too hot to hold, but I hold it anyway. "I moved the car."

"Great, thank you."

She looks at me with narrow eyes. "You're making your Don't Panic face."

"No, I'm not." My pulse buzzes in my earlobes and the tips of my fingers like electric current, and there's also something trapped at the bottom of my throat that I am trying my hardest to shove down, shove down. "How's your mom doing?" I ask, grasping for topics of conversation.

"Oh, you know." Natalie shrugs. "Sick."

A gull cries overhead and we watch it glide through the rain with tattered wings stretched wide. I feel sickeningly present, as though both my past and future have evaporated, history and possibility eliminated.

"Tell me," Natalie says.

"Tell you what?"

"Whatever it is you're obsessing over." She sets her mug on the arm of her chair and shifts her body to face mine. "I see you, Mo."

What makes you so sure? is something I don't say. But I speak to fill the silence: "A girl died, is all. My roommate was her college advisor."

"Shit." Natalie runs her short fingernails along her bottom lip. The cuticles are brown with dried blood, and it's nice to know that despite her various accomplishments, she still peels her hangnails. "Did you know her?"

"Not exactly, no."

"What happened? Overdose? Drunk driving?"

"That," I say, "is the million-dollar question."

Natalie pulls her knees to her chest and rests her chin on them. "This place is as much a shithole as ever, isn't it?"

I feel the same defensiveness that someone else's critique of your particular family dynamics can incite. "I wouldn't call it a shithole."

She laughs. "You literally wrote *here's to getting out of this shithole* in my yearbook."

"I don't remember that."

"I didn't mean to offend you."

"I'm not offended."

Her phone buzzes in her pocket and she grimaces when she holds the screen up to her face. Beyond the porch, something flutters across the sand and lands on the tall blades of beach grass. For a second I think it's some kind of small bird, maybe a plover, but then it glints metallically in the weak sunlight. Nothing more than an abandoned chip bag.

"Do you think I lack conviction?" I ask.

"What?" she says, not looking up. "What are you talking about?"

"Nothing, I guess."

She raises an eyebrow as she tucks the phone back into her pocket. "You're funny, Mona, you know that?"

"I've been told once or twice."

She pulls back the sleeve of her sweater to check the pearlescent face of her watch. "I should really get to the hospital."

"Of course. Don't let me keep you."

On my drive home I call Marina, but she doesn't pick up and her mailbox is full.

I CAN'T FIND MY KEY, so I swipe my credit card in the thin space between doorframe and door, something Natalie taught me forever ago, back when she thought she might pursue a rebellious phase. Layla isn't there, and I've taken exactly three steps into the living room when my mother calls me. "We're going to visit Mrs. Laurel today," she says when I pick up, no greeting. "Can you be there at one?"

I look around the empty house, at the fan beating silently above me and the unworn shoes kicked near the door and the pile of mail on the coffee table that's one breeze away from a landslide. "I don't see why not."

Upstairs, I search for something to change into that my mother won't deem "aesthetically offensive." After locating a boring white dress she'll approve of because it was once hers, I open my desk drawers and look for the pills I bought from a Village Market cashier when I first moved back. John or Aaron or something else Christian and forgettable. All I find are old receipts and used-up ballpoint pens, which is probably a good thing because I'm not the kind of person who flourishes on drugs.

I sit on my bed and press my head between my knees. Something I know about myself: Deep down, I'm a coward. Always, my impulse for self-preservation devours whatever selflessness I have left. A brave person would have insisted that Marina stay, would have asked the girl about her bloodstained dress, would have invited them inside and dried their wet hair with warm towels. Not even a brave person. A normal one.

I call Marina again. Nothing.

MY PARENTS ARE ALREADY in the lobby when I arrive. My mother's wearing a black dress that I've never seen before, knee-length with bell sleeves and golden embroidery circling the neckline. She is of the better-overdressed-than-under variety.

"You look nice," my father says. He's dressed normally, in a blue checkered button-down and belted jeans.

"Shall we?" My mother reaches out to smooth my hair. "Do you have a hairbrush?" she asks as we walk to the elevator. When I tell her no, she nods and presses the circular button with a determined finger. But she doesn't say anything more. I think she's trying to loosen up these days. Or maybe she finally got a Xanax prescription.

We stand in silence in the elevator, watching the light for each floor turn yellow as we rise. There's a hunched-over woman pressed into the opposite corner, her hand on a metal pole hold-ing a yellow bag of liquid. A thick plastic tube runs from the bag to somewhere beneath her thin gown, and goose bumps sting my arms, which is what happens when I look at sick people. Logically, I know that my body will break one day. I just don't need to see the proof.

My dad says he needs to use the bathroom, so my mother and I wait in the hallway. There's an empty room beside us with the door open, and the smell coming out of it is far too human for my liking—musky and sour, like the unwashed armpits of someone very nervous.

"Don't let her get in your head," my mother says abruptly, look-ing over my shoulder and down the hall.

I look down the hall, too, to see if she's referring to someone specific—my mother has many enemies. There's no one but a nurse slapping a clipboard against her hip. "Who?"

Her eyes snap to mine so suddenly and intensely that I almost expect the movement to make a noise. "Natalie."

"Natalie doesn't get in my head." No more than anyone else, anyway. My head is full of people.

"She thinks she's better than you," my mother says matter-of-factly. "Always has."

Because she *is* better. "All right."

"You know you have incredible potential, don't you?"

When I think of a twenty-six-year-old woman who spends her days handling dead fish before coming home to a house filled with rejection letters and the belongings of another grown woman she lives with, I think Potential. "Where is this coming from?" I glance back toward the bathroom door and pray for it to open.

"You look lost," she says.

I glance frantically to my left, then my right. "Yeah, how'd we end up in this hospital?"

She smiles at me in a pained, soft way that's outside her usual repertoire of judgmental expressions. Which means she has news. The last thing I need today is more news. "Don't be fresh."

"Who?" I ask, "me?"

"I have something to tell you, Mona." She flattens her hand against the wallpaper, which is a series of thin gray lines surrounded by abstract shapes. "We're going to move. I can't stay here any longer."

The surprise coats me like a thick film, preventing the actual news from absorbing. "What?"

"I'm not happy here and I haven't been for a very long time. But that doesn't matter. I want to know if you'll be okay? With us gone?"

Do you think I'm okay now? is something I almost say. "Where are you going?" I manage to ask instead.

"Florida? Texas? Somewhere with no income tax."

"And Dad's fine with this?"

She winks at me, which I find far too playful a gesture for the situation. "He does what I tell him to."

"Should *I* move?" is what my mind is thinking and also what I end up saying out loud.

"Well, we got you that house," she says, as though I'd forgotten. One of my biggest regrets: allowing them to buy me an "investment property" as a way to lure me home. "And anyway, it doesn't matter where you go. That's what everyone thinks in their twenties: Oh, if only I were somewhere else, everything would be different. No it wouldn't. Then it'd just be you, somewhere else."

"So I should just kill myself is what you're saying?"

She stiffens. "There are some things you shouldn't joke about, Mona."

The bathroom door swings open behind us and my father emerges, shaking his wet hands: "No paper towels."

"I know you better than anyone," my mother says. I don't argue. It's easier to graph the earlier version of someone onto their present self than to admit your understanding of their character has eroded.

"You ladies ready?" My father steps in front of us.

"Mona," my mother says, "you're seriously not going to do anything about that hair?"

WE TALK ABOUT MANY THINGS in Mrs. Laurel's small, bleached room, but I don't digest any of them. As a kid I perfected the art of what I call Absent Presence. I'm able to interact with others at only the outermost layer of consciousness, which is nothing more than a polite shell for my interior world. As in nature, shells are successful because they seem like a natural extension of the animal. I look nothing but normal.

I widen my eyes and nod my head at appropriate moments. I smile. Never am I not smiling. But really I'm huddled deep in the core of myself, contemplating whether I have wasted my entire life in moving back to this town that I never liked to begin with, this town that never offered me much besides sunburn or frostbite depending on the season, this town that was never what I wanted it to be (because nothing ever is), this town that will be underwater in seventy-five years or less, this town that made me and then took me back, this town where I told Natalie that I thought there was a monster inside of me and she said me too, this town where my mother called her twin sister who lived in California every night until she died suddenly of a heart attack, this town where I almost drowned and my father pressed the seawater out of me, this town where things are beautiful though I'll never admit it, this town where my classmates died so young, this town that my parents told me was paradise, to trick me into believing.

This town where I told Layla: You won't last long. She thought I was joking.

A shuffling of positions. Movement. The conversation's just a din in my ears, like I'm listening to it through a seashell, but I start to surface. Natalie stands. She pushes in her chair politely and walks toward the door, which she pulls open with a graceful yank of the wrist. *Take me with you*, I think, pulling myself out of my hiding place.

I follow her outside without explaining myself to the group— someone asks where I'm going but the question slides off of me like oil. In the hallway, I shout Natalie's name a few times before she turns around. She looks surprised to see me. "Do you want a snack?" she asks.

In the elevator, something strange happens. Natalie and I are standing in the corner, just minding our business, when she starts talking to the person across from us. I'm not really listening, as my mind is currently stuffed with its maximum number of anxieties, but I snap back to reality when I hear crying. The man's flung him-self at Natalie, his chin shoved into her chest, and I'm ready to shove him out whatever door opens next when Natalie's hand wraps around to touch his shoulder. I watch their reflection in the mirror: Natalie holding this strange man, their heads bowed together like two swans, the lights of the floor buttons flickering behind them. *She's giving him the exact thing he needs* is something I don't know how I know, but I promise, I do.

When I ask her who he is, she can't explain.

AT HOME, Layla's waiting for me on the steps, a bright-pink cardigan pulled around her shoulders and bare feet tapping the ground. She walks over to the car before I've even opened my door and talks to me through the open window. "Marina Nowak is here for you," she says.

Blood whooshes in my ears. Part of me wonders if I summoned her. "You know Marina?" I manage to ask.

"Yeah, I advise her. It was fucking weird. I gave her tea."

"That's Marina from Mullaney's," I explain.

"Who?"

"Pinkface." I call her that because she's always using too much blush.

Layla tips her head back and moans. "Why the fuck is this town so small?"

INSIDE, MARINA SITS at the kitchen table with her head slumped on its surface. I wish I had a cigarette more than anything else in the world, and then I realize I'm an adult, so I can. Layla goes upstairs to shower and Marina lifts her head as she disappears through the doorframe. "I hate tea," she says. "And I didn't know you lived with Ms. Layla."

I find my pack in its secret place, at the very end of the knife drawer. "Adults live together when they're poor."

Marina rolls her eyes. "You're not poor."

"You know how much we make at Mullaney's." I sit down beside her. "Do you have a lighter?"

"I'm seventeen and this is your house."

"So? Teenagers think it's cool to smoke." The unlit cigarette wobbles between my shaking fingers. I suck on the rolled paper, try to focus on her face. It's impassive, inaccessible.

But she makes it easy for me. "Aren't you going to ask me why I'm here?"

The filter's growing soggy on my tongue. "Why," I ask, "are you here?"

She takes a deep breath and the air shudders through her flared nostrils. She opens her mouth to speak, but all that comes out is a strangled gasp, like some invisible hand has closed over her throat. She pushes the heels of both hands into the edge of the table and braces against it. "I can't say it. I'm not kidding. It's like I'm physically incapable."

She drops her forehead to the table and starts to cry. I touch her shoulder blade and watch my fingers fall with each shaky exhale, then rise again. Behind us, the steps creak. I don't turn my head, but I know Layla's at the turn in the staircase, her hair twisted in a towel, listening. Light falls through the kitchen window and onto the part in Marina's hair, illuminating the teenage grease at the roots, the flakes of dandruff. One hand lies beside the mug, fingers spread. Her nails are cut short and practical, but their crescents are stuffed with dirt, other dark matter. *You'll survive this* is something I can't quite figure out how to say.

I slide my thumb beneath her chin and gently lift it toward me. "You're going to tell me what happened. And I'll help you figure out what to do. Okay?"

She pulls herself up now, leans back into the chair with a creak. Her head swings in something approximating a nod. "Are you ready?" I ask.

"No." She wipes her eyes with the sleeve of her T-shirt. "But I'll tell you anyway."

MARINA

IF YOU WANT TO KNOW WHAT HAPPENED, I have to start
with the story.

> Once upon a time, there were two sisters, Rebecca and Abigail,
> who lived with their father at the edge of Nashquitten. He was the
> town's lighthouse keeper and made sure that all boats navigated
> the harbor and beyond safely. One day he had to go into town for
> provisions and left Rebecca and Abigail in charge.

My mom first told it to me and my sister when I was seven or
eight. She said that we had to listen very carefully because it was a
True Story. But it sounded fake to me, so I kept interrupting to say
so. When we finally got to *and they lived happily ever after*, I mumbled that they'd never lived at all, and my little sister, Helen, looked
over at me with her eyes all squinty: Don't ruin it!

Shut up, idiot, I told her, and she started to cry. Mom told me
not to talk to my sister like that, and I told her I wouldn't if Helen
wasn't such an idiot, and then Helen wailed *I'm not an idiot*, and I

said, Sounds like something an idiot would say, which made Mom
give me her warning face, so I went, What, you think she's *smart?*
and then I had to go sit in the bathroom by myself for being exces-
sively unkind. *Fake!* I shouted before I slammed the door, which
made one of the towels hanging on its rack fall over my head.

Why does that matter? my mom asked later, when I was allowed
to leave the bathroom and lie on her bed. She sat beside me and
smoothed my hair with her fingers, which smelled like the garlic
she'd chopped for dinner.

Why does what matter?

Whether it's fake or not?

Because you said it was true!

And if I was lying? How does that change the story?

I had the feeling that I was being tricked, so I slapped her hand
away. It just does, I said.

Tygrysku, she whispered, which means *little tiger* and is what my
grandmother used to call me. There isn't as much truth in the
world as you think there is.

Well, how much is there?

She smiled. Depends on who you're asking.

Rebecca and Abigail were preparing to carry whale oil up to the
light when they heard distant noises. They walked to the end of the
jetty and squinted past the waves at the hazy horizon. There,
emerging from the grayish film, was the silhouette of a warship.

I don't even like parties, especially ones held at half-built houses
with nails sticking out of the walls. I drink too much to get comfortable, and once I'm comfortable I always end up talking to the
nerds. This is how I end up upstairs, standing beside Lucy near one
of the empty window frames. We're in AP Calculus together, but

she's always raising her hand and asking unnecessary questions to prove just how deeply she understands a particular topic. We get it. You want to be taken seriously. "Why are you here?" I shout over the music, because this seems like her literal nightmare.

"I'm trying something new," she shouts back. "Tonight, I'm not Lucy."

So you're someone who goes to parties alone? "Where's Sophia?" I ask, looking around. Not that I'd even be able to spot her—everywhere I look is a knot of grinding groins and tangled tongues. I've been in a dry spell ever since I hooked up with a Knights of Columbus lifeguard last summer, but this could be my chance to change that. Everyone's out tonight. Why wouldn't they be, when school's almost over and crop top weather's arrived and Johnny's Liquor finally started accepting our fake IDs again after they got busted last summer? Even the ghosts are here, those pale girls that wear all black and can't stop giggling at whatever meme shit they have pulled up on their laptops or phone screens. In a bizarre turn of events, Emma Clark, their ring leader, is wearing full-on red lipstick. And does it actually look good? Am I the only one who might not get fucked tonight?

"She's visiting her cousins this weekend." Lucy stoops down and picks up a half-full Solo cup that I'm pretty sure was abandoned by one of the football players.

"Should you be drinking that?" I ask. "With your medication?"

I'll remember the look she gives me for the rest of my life. Like she's going to incinerate any single thought I have about what she should or shouldn't do by beaming straight electricity through my eye sockets and into the soft mush of my brain.

"What medication?" she asks.

"Ay, look at this champion!" Olivia slides up behind me and knocks her shoulder into mine. "Drink, drink, drink!" she shouts while Lucy chugs, and I think about how much more useful she'd be if she ever knew when to shut the fuck up.

"Have you seen Marco?" Olivia whispers in my ear. "Look."

Tonight's the last hurrah for the exchange students, who are flying back to Rome tomorrow. I follow Olivia's gaze to the other side of the room, where Marco's jerking his limbs in something that can only loosely be called a dance, while the soccer boys egg him on and spray shaken PBR cans at his face. He has no idea that he's been the butt of their jokes for the last month. I'd feel worse about it if he weren't such a piece of shit. "Ha ha," I say, looking at Lucy out of the corner of my eye. She's turned away so that her back's facing him. I don't blame her, after that video he made.

Someone turns up the music. The beat's heavy and fast, and I can feel it under my feet like the vibrations of a train. Lucy swings her arms over her head and sloshes her hips from side to side like they're made of water. "Don't you think she should say something to him?" Olivia asks, talking about Lucy and Marco. She drapes her sticky arm over my shoulder and I want to shake it off. "I mean, it's her last chance."

"Don't start anything, Liv."

"I'm not starting anything. He started it."

Lucy glides past us so smoothly that I actually look down to make sure her feet are touching the floor—it's like her body doesn't have a single bone. "Hey," I shout, but she doesn't turn. She drifts out from under the roof and onto the unfinished deck, and, I swear, the minute she steps outside, it begins to rain. She dips her head back and closes her eyes like she's facing the warm stream of a shower.

"I don't want to get wet," I say to Olivia, but she's not listening to me. No one's ever listening to me.

"I should say something to her," she insists. "Just so she knows she has the choice."

I go, "What the fuck?" but Olivia's already walking onto the deck's unsanded planks with that straight-as-hell posture she puts on when she thinks she's being helpful.

The air's thick with everyone's breath and sweat, so I lean out the empty window to catch some of the spring breeze. Outside, the trees huddle together so tightly you'd never know a neighborhood was a quarter of a mile away. There's nowhere like this left in town anymore, nowhere you can go and feel like the rest of the world's blocked out. And soon these trees will be gone, too—there's already a row of stumps where they've shaved them to nothing. Thinking about the destruction of nature depresses me, so I dip back through the frame. Olivia isn't back. Through the weave of my classmate's limbs I can see her hand on Lucy's bare shoulder, water flattening their dresses to their chests, Lucy shaking her head, her hair spraying them both with rain.

The thin straps of my heels tighten against my ankles as I try to hurry toward them. Olivia can talk you into crazy shit—she once convinced me to let her tattoo an M across my hip bone with a sewing needle. She knows exactly what to say, is the thing. No one can take this away from you, she told me. Once you make the decision, it's yours, forever.

"What did you say?" I ask. Out on the deck, the floor points toward the forest like the bow of a ship. The pieces that will protect it are stacked by the empty doorway—wooden railing slats, sheets of screen—but for now it feels stupidly open. Which it is. The floor's also slick as shit in the rain, and I feel myself start to glide across the wood like it's a fresh sheet of ice, smacking right into Lucy's side, taking her with me. We skid toward the drop-off that I now understand to be a fucked-up amount of feet off the ground. I see the lawn spreading before us as our feet flail, the empty swimming pool below widening, our hands grasping for safety that doesn't exist. What's funny is that I don't think about memories, or dreams, or my family as we coast toward the edge. I think about the white flags near the Murder Merge and how I know literally nothing about any of the people they represent. I think about how the defining characteristic of my life will be dying too young. I think about how I would never have chosen to go this way, and how I can't choose how they'll remember me, either.

I've already closed my eyes when Lucy throws her weight against me. Her shoulder tunnels into my chest like I'm one of the football team's practice dummies, and after the longest stretch of seconds in my life, we come to a stop. The breeze blows pine needles across our toes and then over the floor's sharp edges. I'm so drenched in rain and sweat that I can feel my underwear sticking to my thighs and my dress suctioned to my stomach. "Holy shit," I breathe, but Lucy doesn't look scared at all. She looks excited.

"Is this what it feels like?" she says.

"What do you mean?" I ask, but then Olivia shouts, "Holy fuck!" and the moment's passed. She starts to run toward us, then rethinks it and waddles like a penguin instead, the way our parents taught us to do when our driveways freeze. The light bounces off her body glitter, and when she gets close I smell chemical sweetness, like artificial strawberries. She always has to try so fucking hard. "Did anyone else see that?"

We all turn around, but no one's noticed us. A couple's making out in the porch's empty doorframe, their bodies sealed together like the teeth of a zipper, and I watch their tongues dart in and out of each other's mouths with the kind of speed that looks painful.

"Let's go back inside," I say, because I, too, would like to be just another dry, clueless body someone wants to make out with.

"Are you hurt?" Olivia asks. Whenever drama happens, she has to feel like she's participated in it. She takes one of my hands and examines it like I almost broke my wrist, not like I almost flew off the side of a house. I tell her I'm fine, but she keeps pressing at my bones like they'll reveal they're actually broken.

"Stop," I say, too harshly. She lowers her head like I've hit her. "Liv," I try, but she's already turned to Lucy.

"Are *you* hurt?" she asks. I can't deal with her attitude right now, so I step away from the edge and catch my breath. It's still tight in my throat, like I'm gasping for air as I tread water. And as I lean over to suck in everything my lungs will hold, I hear it. A kind of scraping behind me, like a dog with long toenails skidding across hardwood. The girl in the doorframe pushes her partner away to shout, "Grab her!" and heads turn, including mine. The girl's pointing past me. My head follows her finger like it's illuminated.

The rain crystallizes, the music fades, sweat blurs my vision. Olivia screams. In the second that I blink, Lucy's gone.

> The sisters turned to each other, unsure of what to do. The ship grew crisper, closer. We need to tell them, Abigail said. She was younger, only by a year, but that year made a difference. People tended to ignore her. Tell who? Rebecca asked, already sounding defeated. Rebecca had a certain confidence to her, but it dissolved quickly under pressure. She was not a leader.

We've all got our necks craned forward like maybe we didn't see what we saw, like maybe she's actually standing there with her toes curled over the edge, like maybe our lives don't have to change tonight. "Holy shit," someone says. You can feel the bass from the music shaking all the way up your skeleton.

"Don't look down," I tell Olivia.

We all move at once.

I don't remember how I get downstairs, how I push open the door, how I climb down to her, but there she is and her chest is covered in blood so thick it looks black. She's fallen onto the floor of the unfinished pool, a small puddle of rainwater collecting around her. Pine needles in her hair. I understand what I'm seeing; I smell the fresh concrete and the metallic blood. But the horror pours over me slowly, like honey.

When I look up everyone's gathered on the ledge above us, a ring of drenched faces that can't decide whether they want to see what's happened or save themselves from seeing. The rain pings off the pool's floor, the sound mixing with the hiss of a hundred people shallowly breathing. The air's too thick now, too hot. When I inhale it feels like the steam off a pot of boiling water.

I start yelling Olivia's name, and it's my voice that spooks them. The first person runs. Then the second. Kids sprint left and right like deer splitting through a forest, their feet spraying water across one another's ankles. It's dark except for a strobe light and a broken projector someone brought to throw kaleidoscopes across the trees. I keep catching half-lit glimpses of people I know in the turning colors. From the bottom of the pool I scream for them to help her, "Please get help, please!" And I actually believe that's where they're going, as they disappear into the woods—to save us.

It's when I pull Lucy into my arms that I begin to tell her about Abigail and Rebecca. She feels so heavy and warm, like when my babcia was sick. She asked me to lie in the hospital bed with her because she said she forgot she had a body unless someone was there to remind her. My mother sat in a little chair in the corner when she died, but I stayed curled on the sheets with my arm over hers until the nurse asked if I wouldn't mind getting up. Możesz opowiedzieć mi historię? were her last words, but I couldn't think of anything to say besides Kocham cię. Maybe that's enough of a story for most of us, though. She seemed satisfied.

Abigail had an idea. Follow me, she said, and the sisters raced back to the lighthouse. In the common room of their living area was a fife and a drum they sometimes entertained themselves with after dinner. They ran back to the edge of the jetty with instruments in hand, both of them breathing heavily. What now? Rebecca asked. Play, Abigail said.

Time passes, but I don't know how much. The belly of the pool's filling with rain, enough to cover our ankles now. I try not to look at the color of the water. Soon I'll need to take us both somewhere dry. Soon I'll need to stop waiting.

Lucy starts to go slack against me. It feels like something essential is draining out of her, something more than blood from the wound. I can hear the sheets of insulation flapping in the wind, the beer bottles rolling across the ground above us. How much time does it take to call fucking 911? My phone's in Olivia's pocket— my dress doesn't have any. "*Help!*" I shout. "*Help us!*" My voice echoes against the pool's walls and bounces back at me.

"Hey, hey." I slap Lucy's cheeks a couple times, until they turn pink. Her eyes are closed and I try to pry them open with my fingernails. "I need you to listen, okay? The story's not over yet. Don't you want to know how it ends?"

I feel crazy keyed up, like the one time I took coke at homecoming, and I swear my heart is running into different parts of my body, running everywhere except my chest, where I feel an empty and open aching that sucks at my ribs like a whirlpool.

I shout Olivia's name. I shout it over and over until I hear a crackling somewhere in the woods, branches being broken. The rain must have finally killed the projector, because when I look up all I see is a puddle of black. Until a tiny light glows at the pool's edge, and I slowly make sense of Olivia behind it, holding her phone.

She slides down the sloped wall in her tiny pink dress and no shoes, pressing her hand into the side. "Fuck," she says when she's standing beside us. "We're fucked."

Abigail struck the drum and Rebecca raised the fife to her mouth. At home they'd always been conscious of making too much noise, but in this moment they were free. They played more loudly than they ever had in their life, so loudly that when the noise reached the approaching warship, the British soldiers froze. They know we're here! one shouted, and panic rippled through the deck. What do we do? the second-in-command asked the captain. The captain tugged at his beard and squinted into the distance—his telescope showed only fog and water. It sounds like an army, doesn't it? The second-in-command nodded. It does, sir.

A breeze blows through that makes me suddenly aware of how cold the water is beneath my knees and how stiff Lucy is on my lap and how alone we are. "Marina," Olivia says. "We need to go."

I hover my hand above Lucy's nose. "She's breathing," I say. "Barely."

"She doesn't want to be here," Olivia says sharply.

"You know that for a fact?"

"I was there."

"So was I."

An ambulance wails in the distance. Olivia grabs my ponytail and yanks it so that I'm looking up at her. "We need to go."

"No." I whip my head so hard that she stumbles backward. "I have a story to finish."

The shadow of the ship seemed to be growing smaller. Did it work? Abigail shouted over her drum. Rebecca removed the fife from her lips to ask, Can we stop? No, Abigail cried. Keep playing!

I start to braid Lucy's hair, which is what my little sister does if we're watching a movie and my eyes start to close. "What do you think will happen to them?" I ask, quietly, to keep Olivia from hearing. We're so wet that when I try to weave the strands together they tangle instead, wrapping around my fingers like that time I got caught in my dad's fishing wire.

Olivia's walking circles around us now, pulling her dress away from her stomach and then letting it snap back. That's her problem: She never fucking *does* anything. "Help me pull her up."

She stops walking. "What?"

"It's too wet down here. And the EMTs will just have to get her if we don't."

"That'll take forever. You don't want to be here when the police arrive. We're trespassing."

"We can't leave," I say, and that's when things change between us. Because this isn't something I should have to say to her. She should just know. And now I'm wondering: What else do I think she understands that she doesn't?

"I can't have an *arrest* on my record. And there's nothing else we can do for her anyway."

"Then go."

"I'm not leaving you here."

I don't say anything to that.

She stops pacing. "What, you think I'm lying?" When I still don't speak, she tosses her head up to the sky and lets out this horrible laugh before crouching down in front of us. "You know what? Fuck you, Marina."

I don't watch Olivia disappear. That's what she's always after; a reaction to confirm her influence isn't imaginary. "It's just you and me," I tell Lucy. When I pull my hand away from her head, hair sticks to my wrist like the strands of a broken spiderweb.

The ship continued to get smaller and smaller until it was nothing but a faraway speck, a speck that could have been a seagull or a rock or even a very distant lighthouse shepherding the opposite side of the coast. Abigail put her drum down. Did we do it? Rebecca asked, the fife still raised near her lips. I think we did, Abigail said, and they hugged so tightly they couldn't even feel the wind whipping off the water.

The sky has turned clear and hard-looking except for a single blanket of clouds that hide the moon. I'm not superstitious, but I somehow know that if the moon moves out from beneath them, Lucy will die. The siren is loud now, and the ambulance lights turn the lawn red. I hear vehicles pulling up on the other side of the inn, people talking. "We're here!" I yell, but my voice is thin from all the other shouting I've been doing, and the pool's acoustics swallow my words.

"You won't even notice I'm gone," I tell Lucy before I slip out from underneath her. "I promise we'll finish the story." Wind swipes at my back as I pull her to the wall and rest her back against the smooth incline. Before I leave, I reach down and squeeze her hand. I swear I'm not crazy. She squeezes back.

The shallowest part of the pool is three feet, and I realize I have to run up the rain-covered concrete as fast as I humanly can in order to make it to the grass. It takes me a few tries, but I finally fall onto the ground and manage to shout: "*Right here!*" I know it's loud enough because someone on the other side of the inn asks, "What the hell was that?"

And that's when something drags me backward.

It's got me by the shoulders—I can't snap my head back enough to look—and my heels grind into the ground, carving tracks in the mud. I'm about to scream when I finally twist my face around and dark hair falls over my eyes.

"Jesus Christ, you're heavier than you look." Rain drips off Olivia's chin and onto my nose. "Just stay still."

"Let me go," I start to say, but Olivia shoves a sweaty hand over my mouth, her thumb breaking through my lips. It tastes like sand and salt.

"Shut the fuck up. I'm helping you." She pulls me into the woods and props me against a tree with thin branches that brush the tips of my ears. She leans down to wipe her fingers across my cheeks, and that's when I realize I'm crying. "Shh," she says, and then more desperately: "*Shh.*" I can't see anything through the braid of trees in front of us, but I hear footsteps, hear EMTs shouting into walkie-talkies, hear: "female adolescent, not moving, undetermined wound."

"See?" Olivia says. "They found her."

My brain's buzzing like flies are feeding on it. Just because you're found doesn't mean you're safe.

"Switch with me," Olivia's saying. She's holding my arms above my head, peeling my dress up and over them, tugging her own dress off, standing pale and milky in the moonlight. "A little help?" she asks, but I don't answer because I'm watching the clouds. The cold air needles the skin below my bra. I'm still watching. Olivia shoves me through fabric, pulls my arms through the holes. I'm still watching. She tries to pull the skirt over my thighs, but it's too tight, my hips are too wide. I'm still watching. The moon slides slowly away, growing bright as a pearl. The clouds dissolve.

When I finally turn, Olivia's in my blue dress, and it's dark with blood. "What did you say to her?" I ask.

"To who?"

"Lucy."

She doesn't have any shoes on, so she traces her big toe through the dirt. "I just told her it wasn't her fault. The video."

"Why would it be her fault?"

"Sometimes it's easy to blame yourself for things that happen to you."

She sounds honest when she says it, but I'm not sure I believe her.

When their father returned home, he listened to their story in open-mouthed amazement—he and some other men had seen the ship from town but assumed its retreat meant a confused navigator at the helm. He brought the girls to the pub to tell their story, and the townspeople bought them pints of beer and plates of brown bread.

When I get home two hours later, my parents are asleep. They think I went to see a movie with Olivia—they knew not to wait up. But when I climb the stairs, pulling the dress down with each step, I see a light on in the hallway. When I pass my sister's door, it squeaks open.

"What happened?" she asks. Her hair's in two long braids over her shoulders, the only way she'll wear it for bed. She's eleven but small for her age, and she still wears nightgowns with lace trim. She won't have an easy time in middle school.

"What do you mean?"

She just looks at me.

"Don't worry," I tell her. "Nothing happened."

She closes the door an inch. "Why's your hair wet?"

"I took a shower at Olivia's."

"But you shower in the morning."

"No, you shower in the morning. I shower whenever I want." She gives me a skeptical look but doesn't say anything else. "Good night, kapustka," I say, using grandma's word for her.

She closes the door, but just as I'm about to walk away, it opens. "Will you sleep with me?" she asks. "I don't like the thunder." Mom says she's way too old to be scared of sleeping alone and that we shouldn't encourage it.

"Sure," I tell her. If Mom asks, I'll say the thunder scared me, too.

The girls lived as heroes for the rest of their lives, and to this day we still celebrate their courage on May 25. Which is to say they lived happily ever after.

Here's what happened: I was there. So was she.

I came home.

She didn't.

POST

OLIVIA

INSTEAD OF BEING A NORMAL human being, Mom tells me
I'm running late by clicking the garage door open, which makes
this side of the house rumble like an avalanche is incoming. "Just
tell me!" I shout down the hallway. "*Tell* me we're leaving!" She's the
one who asked me to find Lila's Seesaw in the first place! I toss
some of her frilly pillows aside—Lila loves girly shit—and discover
the rabbit flopped against the headboard. Mom's been threatening
to get rid of the thing for years, since Lila still sucks on his ears
when she isn't looking, but she's never followed through. Figures. If
that were me, Seesaw would have been shredded in the trash can
before I even noticed he was gone.

Dad's calling my name now because according to what Mom
says in therapy, I "respond to him better." "I'm *coming*! Jesus Christ!"
I grab the rabbit and run down the stairs, slamming down on each
step as hard as I can because fuck Mom and her schedule and mandated family time.

"There she is," Dad says with his nervous smile that means Mom
is about to lose her shit. Also in therapy, Mom says that Dad and I

"team up against her." Dad doesn't go to therapy because Mom doesn't want him there.

He opens the door into the garage and I can see that Mom's already backed the minivan into the driveway. "Does she think she gets a prize if we're the first ones to summer camp?"

"Be nice," Dad says through gritted teeth. "Please, *please* be nice." Why everyone always acts like I'm the instigator is beyond me.

Mom honks the horn like we're not right there, like we're not fucking looking at her hanging out of the driver's side window, and Dad, the most whipped man in Massachusetts, gives his please-Lord-release-me-from-this-life wave. He actually jogs to the car, but I keep my pace slow and even, staring into Mom's sunglasses the whole time. Even though I can't see her eyes, I can still tell what she's thinking: We're going to have a talk later. We're always having talks. She doesn't seem to understand that talks don't accomplish anything if they only consist of reviewing the events that led to the talk in the first place.

I slide open the back seat door and dangle Seesaw toward Lila, who's strapped into her seat with her Mad Libs like the well-behaved daughter she is. "Yay!" Lila grabs the rabbit and hugs him to her chest, shoving her chin between the ears, which are stiff and gray from her spit. "Thank you, Livy."

I buckle my seat belt and close the door. "You're welcome."

"Are we ready?" Dad asks, trying to sound excited and ignoring the fact that Mom's backing into the road at approximately seventy miles per hour. "You're going to make so many friends, Lila."

Lila pops one of the ears into her mouth and Dad glances toward Mom, checking if she sees. But she's hell-bent on getting to the highway and doesn't even glance in the rearview mirror. "I'm nervous," Lila says. Her voice sounds wet and thick as she moves her mouth around the ear. Gross.

"You're nine!" Dad shouts, like this is new and exciting news. "Nine-year-olds don't get nervous."

Mom's listening now, because she wants Lila to have a life free of insecurities and doubts, the perfect angel daughter that will be the shining legacy of our family. "Don't be scared," she says, looking straight ahead. "They're going to love you." Lila doesn't say anything, and that's when Mom looks over her shoulder and sees. "Get that out of her mouth, Liv."

"She can hear you." I brush Lila's wrist, which is still the slightest, smallest thing I've ever touched. "Can I hold Seesaw?"

"Are you nervous?" Lila asks, her spit dribbling down the fabric.

"Yes."

"Why?"

"Because I'm going to be here without you."

She pulls the rabbit out of her mouth and looks down at it. "I'm going to miss you."

"No, you're going to forget about me. And you'll have so many stories to tell when you're back!" I try to sound excited because the truth is that I'm actually dreading three weeks alone with Mom and Dad. When Lila's around, Mom at least focuses on how amazing she is, rather than what a dumpster fire I am.

"Here you go," she says, handing Seesaw to me. "He'll keep you safe." I wipe the spit off his ears with the edge of my sleeve and say thank you.

"Where are we going, Will?" Mom asks impatiently. We're approaching the ramp to the highway and she starts to speed up. "I don't know where I'm going."

Dad taps on the dashboard screen and plugs in our destination: Camp Wawona for Girls in Newbury, Vermont. When I was a kid I was sent to Aunt Gerri's ranch in Wyoming to learn some "grit," except I only lasted four days because I got kicked in the face by a horse and fractured my jaw. Of course, Mom was pissed at *me* for getting my face split in two. I just wish you were more careful, she'd say when she'd bring my bowls of chicken broth, and I couldn't even say anything back because my mouth was wired shut!

But now Ms. Lila gets to go to "the premier girl's camp in the Northeast," with warm showers and a petting zoo and gourmet meals. When Mom and Dad were about to leave to get her, they both put their hands on my shoulders—Mrs. Henry, the neighbor who was staying with me, clunking around in the kitchen behind us—and said: This isn't going to change anything. We're going to love you both exactly the same. Even when I was eight, I remember thinking: Yeah, right. When Mrs. Henry showed me the pictures from Guangzhou a few days later, I knew it wasn't going to be the same. They'd never looked at me the way they looked at her. Still haven't.

"Do you want the iPad?" Dad asks, passing the screen to Lila. It's already preloaded with some show she loves about horseback riding babysitters.

"What am I supposed to do?" I ask.

"Read," Mom says. "Better yourself."

"I get carsick if I read."

"Listen to some music," Dad suggests, trying to keep the peace.

"My headphones aren't working, remember?"

"Here, use mine." He starts to dig around in the backpack he has at his feet, and Mom looks to the left to adjust her mirror.

"You could just use this time to reflect," she says.

"Reflect on what?" I ask, because I know exactly what she's talking about, but she's too chicken to say it.

"Whatever's on your mind."

"Here we go!" Dad extracts the headphones and tosses me the tangled black wires. "That should do the trick."

"What's on my mind, Mom?"

Dad's eyes shift from me to the driver's seat. "Hey—" he starts, but Mom interrupts him.

"I don't know," she says. "God knows I have no idea what you're thinking."

He leans over to her and whispers like it's possible to keep a secret in a minivan. "Not now," is what he says.

I jam the headphones into my ears because even if I had something to say, my mother would be the last person to listen.

WE STOP AT A CAFÉ in New Hampshire for lunch. It's just a little stand with some picnic tables on the lawn, but Dad gets all worked up saying how quaint this part of the country is, how crisp the air is, how adorable the houses are. He and Lila go to order for us while Mom takes a work call and paces around the little wooden bathroom shack. I text Marina and ask her if she wants to go to the movies when I get home, but she doesn't answer. Now that school's out she's been full-on avoiding me, even though I'm the one who made sure she didn't do something stupid that night. I saved her.

We have reports of you and Marina Nowak present at the scene of the crime, Officer Donelson said, who I wasn't scared of because he'd been our DARE officer, and you don't get assigned DARE unless your coworkers think you're too stupid to be helpful at the actual police station.

You have reports of a hundred people present at the scene of the crime.

Don't be a wiseass. We also have an eyewitness that said it was you who pushed her.

That was a surprise to me, and I sucked my tongue into my teeth to keep from looking freaked. Who said that?

You know I can't tell you.

They're lying, I said. Obviously. I tried to keep very calm because what gets people in trouble is the anxiety and the overexplaining. I had no reason to be scared. I didn't do anything.

He snapped his gum, which smelled like artificial grapes. This is a serious accusation. I need you to be honest with me, Olivia.

I tried to *help* her. It's not my fault that she slipped or had a seizure or jumped or whatever. Everyone knew she hated it here.

Do you hate it here?

I don't see how that's relevant, I said. And then he opened the metal door and let my mom come in to take me away.

"We're eating hot dogs!" Lila says, rushing toward me. She doesn't slow down in time and thumps right into my stomach, knocking us both over. She laughs when she hits the grass, and I try to feel light and happy like she does instead of annoyed and sore like I actually do.

"What are you most excited for at camp?" I ask from the ground.

She sits up and pulls a bunch of flowering weeds out of the grass. Her fingers move like a sailor's as she knits them into a neat daisy chain. Guaranteed queen of friendship bracelets. "Swimming, I guess."

"But you can swim at home."

"Yeah, that's how I know I like it. I don't know if I'll like any of the new stuff yet."

"You'll like it all."

She looks up at me skeptically. "You sound like Dad."

"No, Dad would say you'll *love* it all."

She jams her fingernail through a rubbery dandelion stem. "I'd rather just stay home with you."

I run a hand through her hair, which is soft and warm from the sun. I would stay home with Lila all day if I could, because she's the only person who thinks I have something important to say. I've never figured out how to talk in a way that makes other people want to listen. In second grade, Mrs. Marks took me aside and said I should practice speaking more softly, so my voice wouldn't *startle* anyone, like we were a room full of baby rabbits instead of sugar-high eight-year-olds. But I listened to her because she was a scary bitch in the way people who work with kids sometimes are. Which meant that when I got to third grade, I was too quiet. So Mrs. Wilson took me aside and explained how important it was for a woman to use her voice, mainly because we'd just learned about Fannie Lou Hamer and she wanted us to understand that history lives on in the minds of the people, or whatever. This cycle repeated every school year, too loud, too quiet, rinse and repeat, until I got to high school and finally decided I didn't give a fuck what a rando with a degree that qualified them to give detention slips and check girls' skirt lengths thought about my voice.

But I am kind of paranoid. About Lila, I mean. What if she only listens because she's my baby sister, and whenever I leave the room she thinks: *Thank God she's gone?*

It's like she knows I'm thinking about her because she pokes me in the band of my bra, which is what she does when she really wants my attention. "Do you think my mom ever went to summer camp?"

"Doubt it. She would've gotten kicked out for making everyone in her cabin cry."

She shakes her head like an adult dealing with a much stupider adult. "No, not that mom. *My* mom."

"Uh," I say, because we really shouldn't be talking about that here.

Before Lila came home, I found a manila folder full of adop-
tion papers in Mom's file cabinet. Toward the back of all the
forms and pamphlets and write-ups was a tiny photograph paper-
clipped to a pink sheet of paper. It didn't seem like anyone would
miss it—all the sheet had typed on it was the name of her birth
mother and the mother's birthday. So I slipped it out of the folder
and hid it in the drawer of my desk, waiting to see if anyone
noticed. No one did.

I gave it to Lila last year, after she asked where she came from.
They were doing family trees in social studies, and as Lila sifted
through all of our Irish ancestors on the genealogy website, one of
her friends had leaned over, pointed at the screen and asked: But
where's your real family? And Lila didn't know.

I'd asked my parents before when they were planning to tell her.
Soon, when I first asked; At the right time, when I asked again;
Someday, when I asked a third time. We promise, they repeated,
and Mom always told me not to break my promises. I should've
known that when adults say "someday," what they really mean is
"never." And that when they tell you not to break something, it's
because they already have.

"Look at these!" Dad says, walking toward us with a red tray in
each hand. "The most beautiful hot dogs I've ever seen!"

Lila knots her final stem and asks me to lean forward. The dandelion puffs tickle the tips of my ears like a hundred tiny insect
legs, but I try not to squirm. "Perfect," she whispers.

"C'mon, girls." Dad places the tray on the nearby picnic table
while Mom walks back with her phone dangling out of her pocket.

I take Lila's hand and tug her toward me. "You know there are
some things that only we can talk about, right?" I raise my eyebrows to help her get my drift.

"I know," she says, in an unconcerned way that suggests she has not gotten my drift. But before I can try something less subtle, she's taken off for the picnic table.

"Liv," Dad calls. He waves a plastic fork at me, and maybe it's the way he says my name or the way Lila skips around the table or the way my mother leans over to kiss the part of her hair but I feel about ten universes away and I know there's no way of getting back to them, not after what I've done. The smell of the Listerine strips melted on his tongue, the blood that rubbed off the dress and onto my stomach, the sound of Ms. Layla's voice asking, How did it start?, the way Marina thought I would leave her there, and I did.

"Coming," I shout back from the grass. I try to make myself feel better by thinking about the Plan. Once Lila gets back from summer camp, I'll run away. My parents will be so obsessed with hearing about her transformational adventures that it'll be easy for me to sneak out. I'll take the train from Boston to Brunswick, then get one of the college kids sticking around to give me a ride up to Bar Harbor. Bar Harbor's full of summer people, and I've already found a resort that gives their employees free housing, so I'll make bank. I'll dye my hair blue so no one recognizes me. I'll be an entirely new person. Dana, maybe, or Tess.

But I don't feel better thinking about all that because the Plan has a shit ton of issues. Such as how to get a new phone so my parents can't track the old one, how to make it so they can't freeze my debit card, where to stay before I convince the resort to hire me, what happens when the summer ends, what to tell Lila. The person who could solve them is Marina because she hates surprises and loves plans. But she's not talking to me. And even if she were, her response would be: you fucking idiot.

"Olivia, come on," Mom shouts. "We need to get back on the road." Dad gives her a look and whispers something in her ear, probably a weak *ease up* or *it's fine, Janet.* Such a simp.

I push up off the ground and wipe the dirt on my jeans. It's hot and the sun's so strong it feels like there's electric coils under my skin. When I sit down beside Lila, she hands me a puckered pink hot dog that's dripping water from whatever pot it was boiled in, and I could spew up my cereal just looking at it. "I'm good," I say, handing it back to her.

"What do you mean, you're *good?*" Mom asks. She's eating her hot dog so fast you'd think she was trying to go professional. "You need to eat something."

"I think you'll like it," Lila says, because of course she loves downing sweaty hot dogs at a roadside stand in the middle of live-free-or-die New Hampshire.

"Really, I'm fine." I push my checkered paper boat to the middle of the table and a fly immediately lands on the relish.

Dad turns back toward the little trailer where two teenage boys are taking orders. "Do you want something else? They had sandwiches."

"No, it's just too hot to eat."

"Too hot to eat!" Mom hoots. "I'm so sorry, I didn't know we were in the presence of a duchess!"

Lila looks at me with crinkled-up eyebrows. She never gets the joke. "That's normal, Janet," Dad murmurs at his hot dog. "It is quite warm."

"Quite warm!" Mom begins, but I don't hear her punch line because I'm already walking across the lawn to the car, already biting my lip so it splits open beneath my teeth, already sucking in the part of my stomach he traced before finding what he wanted, already saying nothing, already more ashamed of myself than she

could ever make me. I know why I was chosen. He saw the rotten-
ness inside of me, just like she does.

I don't realize I've punched the side mirror until I'm crouched
to the pavement pulling glass out of my knuckle. My heart's beating so fast it makes the roof of my mouth tremble, but I feel the
empty kind of calm that comes after running until you almost
throw up. I touch a sliced knuckle. The skin's shredded around
the cut like the frayed hem of my distressed jeans. Mom and Dad
are going to flip.

"What's this?" I hear Dad's voice say behind me. "Oh, God, are
you okay?"

"Are you kidding me? Olivia, what the hell?" I flick some of the
bloody glass shards to the ground. For a high school principal in a
Catholic town with a drinking and drug problem, she sure acts like
she hasn't seen shit.

All I can make out is white sunlight where their faces should be,
but I feel Lila's hand land on my shoulder. "Livy?" she asks. I swat
her fingers away—she's too close. "Not now," I say. "Not now."

When the clouds finally cover the sun, she's looking at me like I
slapped her.

"Fucking hell." Mom shakes her phone at Dad, at me, at everyone but Lila. "We need to move." She points one skeleton finger at
me. "We'll talk about this after Lila's settled. This is coming out of
your babysitting money. Lila, are you okay?"

"I'm fine," Lila says, and I think she sounds like me.

NO ONE SAYS ANYTHING for the last two hours of the drive,
not even Dad. He just turns on Bruce Springsteen and hums along
like maybe we can all pretend that the mirror isn't busted and

Mom isn't pissed and Coach didn't touch me and a girl didn't die and Lila was always, only, one of us.

Mom watches me in the rearview mirror with squinted eyes. I stare right back. "Don't make that face," she says.

"What face?" I ask, but she doesn't have an answer.

"WE'RE HERE!" Dad turns past a pink sign hand-painted with the camp's motto: *Girls today, leaders tomorrow.* "Lila, we made it!"

Two blonde girls with thick braids and fanny packs materialize outside the car, waving signs that say WE'RE SO HAPPY YOU'RE HERE! and WAWONA FOREVER & THEN SOME! I hate them.

Another blonde girl appears out of nowhere with a clipboard and a walkie-talkie strapped to her belt loop. Dad rolls down his window and she shouts, "Welcome to Wawona!" so aggressively that I swear her spittle lands on my arms. "Who's Miss Lila Cushing?" She looks at me and I immediately point to my right. This girl practically forces her torso through the window, trying to make eye contact with Lila. "You're a Wawona Woman now! Congratulations!" Mom claps in the front seat. "Now, Daddy," she says, and I feel more nauseated than I did staring down that damp hot dog, "let me give you the directions to the cabin."

The camp's located at the end of a long dirt road that borders a lake, and we bump along the path behind three other minivans. They've set up two posts, one at the beginning of the road and one at the end of it, and tied wire from the first to the second. Hanging from the wire are hole-punched greetings from alumni that say original things like: *Go get 'em!* and *You're in for the best weeks of your life!* I bet at least 75 percent of the writers are still virgins.

"Look at these." Mom points at the cheap pieces of poster board like they're the eighth wonder of the world. "You'll write one of these someday." That's when I look over at Lila and see that she looks straight-up terrified to be heading toward three weeks of sloppy joes and skinny-dipping and whatever else they do at camp that went unmentioned in *The Parent Trap*.

"Hey," I whisper. "You're going to be fine."

I swear there's a visible lump in her throat when she swallows.

Dad tells another girl—this one in high-waisted shorts and a tank top that definitely doesn't have a bra under it—Lila's name, and she directs us to drive over the grass to a clearing in front of three cabins. "You'll be in the Daisy cabin," she informs us, and Lila opens her eyes so wide that I could pluck them out of their sockets.

We back into a spray-painted rectangle and Dad pops the trunk. Little girls with braids are everywhere: French braids, fishtail braids, Swedish-looking braids that wrap around their heads like crowns. I wonder if this is to guard against lice, which apparently runs rampant at summer camps. "Should I braid your hair?" I ask Lila.

Her hand jumps to the back of her head. "No!"

"Aren't you so excited?" Mom asks, oblivious as ever.

Her counselor turns out to be a freshman at the University of Vermont who's thinking about taking a year off to focus on her gluten-free granola business, which has really taken off at her dorm and the local co-op. She's able to do it all without renting a commercial kitchen because of cottage law. Have I heard of cottage law?

"No," I say, dropping Lila's human-sized duffel bag in front of her bunk bed. "You really want the bottom? You get a bird's-eye view from the top."

"Do I need a bird's-eye view?" she asks, panicked. "Are there things I should see?"

"Only if you don't want to get pranked," the counselor says.

"I don't!" Lila cries.

"Oh, well." The counselor scratches the side of her head, which is covered in three different braids that twist into one giant bun. "The top then, maybe."

I can see another car through the screen windows, and the counselor rushes out to greet them. Lila's the third one here, but the earlier arrivals left to complete their swim tests. Mom and Dad are outside, arguing about the best way to unpack the roof carrier. I sit down next to Lila on the plastic-coated mattress, which smells like campfire and piss. "Are you okay?"

"I want to go home."

"You just got here."

She shakes her head miserably, the way I used to when Mom would drop me off at mandated piano lessons. "This is even worse than school."

"I'm sure they'll be nice. Everyone here seems so . . . nice."

"Everyone's always *nice*." She reaches for the window behind the bunk and cranks it open. A breeze blows in that smells like grass and twenty different types of Bath & Body Works lotion. "Mom's nice, and Dad's nice, and you're nice." The tips of her ears are turning red, which means she's pissed.

"What's wrong with nice?" I wouldn't mind someone being nice to me every once in a while. But clearly I've said something wrong, because Lila stares into my eyes without a single blink, runs her tongue over her teeth so intensely it forces her lips apart, and jerks back an arm to slap me.

I don't let her. It's hard to follow through, the first time. Easy to think too much about what you're doing, to block the adrenaline instead of surrendering to it. I close my hand over her wrist while it's still hovering beside her jaw.

"Why?" I ask. She wiggles her fingers but I don't let go.

"You're hurting me," she says to her knees.

Outside, a new family is unloading their car. I can hear the parents debating whose job it was to pack the health forms and whether it's too much to ask someone named Katie to scan them. "What have I ever done to you?"

Lila tries to twist her arm from my fingers, but I'm stronger. "Stop, Olivia," she says. I can't remember the last time she used my full name. For some reason it makes me tighten my grip instead of loosen it.

She raises her eyes to look at me, like that might make me let go. When it doesn't, she drops her elbow to her side, my hand falling with it. "It's not about doing anything to *me*. It's what you do to everyone else. I have to make Mom and Dad happy to make up for you. And I have to make you happy to make up for Mom and Dad."

My fingers slip from her wrist, which is warm and pink from my touch. "You don't have to make me happy."

"Yes, I do," she says. "I'm your sister."

A burst of air blows through the cabin, raising the dust on the floor. The new family stands in the doorway, looking lame as hell. The dad's wearing those shoes that are the actual shape of your foot, the mom has on transition sunglasses that make her look blind, and the girl's clutching a stuffed squirrel missing one eye. "I'm Anne," she says, coming up to Lila. Anne clearly can't read a room.

Lila glances up at the bunk above us, and when she brings her chin down, she's smiling. "I'm Lila. Nice to meet you."

Anne holds out her hand to me. There's some sort of sticky liquid webbed between her fingers. "My religion's opposed to handshaking," I explain.

Lila stands up and starts to unpack her backpack. "That's Olivia. She and my parents were just heading to the mess hall."

"For family snacks?" Anne's parents ask from behind us. They're rubbing sunscreen on each other's noses that looks like Wite-Out.

"Yep," I say. "For family snacks."

"Don't eat the blackberries," the father says. "They aren't organic."

"You sure you don't want a Fruit Roll-Up or something?" I ask Lila, whose back is to me.

"Those things are pure white sugar, you know," the mother says. Lila doesn't even turn around. "I'm good."

"Fine," I say.

"Very nice to meet you," Anne tells me as I pull open the screen door.

Mom and Dad have finally unearthed Lila's bedding from the rooftop carrier, and now they're slumped against the car with the goods like they've finished five rounds of CrossFit. Mom holds the Arctic-weather sleeping bag that cost more than the prom dress I wanted and Dad clutches a stack of four down pillows that are supposed to support juvenile neck development. "Who's ready for L.L.Bean's finest?" he asks.

"Lila wants to set up herself," I say. "There's food at the mess hall."

Dad raises a skeptical eyebrow before setting the pillows down in the open trunk. "Is she sure? You know how great I am at hospital corners."

I nod. "She's sure."

"Well, if that's what she wants. The whole point of this is to let her strike out on her own." Mom tosses the sleeping bag into the back seat. "It's fine to leave the car unlocked, right?"

"I don't know," I say. "It's kind of a rough area."

They ignore me and Dad claps Mom on the shoulder. "Our independent women. May we know them, may we be them, may we raise them!"

"Oh, shut up," Mom says, but she's smiling.

It's crazy how they never have any idea what's happening. I could slit my arms from wrist to shoulder and as long as I wore a sweater, they wouldn't have a clue.

"Are you coming?" Mom asks as she turns in the opposite direction of the cabins. "We don't want to crowd her."

She acts like I'm a mile behind her instead of a step. "Yes," I say. "I'm right here."

LILA MEETS US ON THE PORCH of the mess hall an hour later, after we've eaten tiny grilled cheeses and drank secret-family-recipe punch that's definitely just powdered Kool-Aid. "I'm all set," she says. "Thanks for everything."

"Thanks for everything? What are we, strangers?" Dad wraps an arm around her shoulders and squashes Lila to his side. In my head I know that nothing has actually changed since I saw her in the cabin, but I can't help thinking that her face looks hollower, like someone suctioned out the baby fat that I loved to pinch between my fingers. Has she always looked this tired? "You must be pretty eager to get going, huh?"

"Uh-huh," she says into his armpit.

Mom holds out her hands. "Come here." I watch Dad pass Lila to Mom and wonder how parents can pretend not to have favorites. Everything depends on us loving certain things more than others. Otherwise everyone would just be stuck in a whirlpool of indecision with about a million equal options. Otherwise nothing could be beautiful, if nothing was ugly. "We're going to miss you so much."

I wait for Lila to say, Me too, but she doesn't.

"Okay, well," Mom goes. She had crouched down so that their heads were at the same height, but now she straightens up, steps back to get a good luck at her. I wonder what she sees. "You're probably ready to be rid of us. You got your phone card, right?"

"Right."

"Give us a ring when they let you, okay?"

"Okay," she says. Then she waves at me. "Bye."

Really? I want to say. A fucking wave? She crosses her arms over her striped tank top and stares at me like she doesn't understand why I haven't started walking away. Maybe if I hadn't already had a mini-breakdown today, I'd have more fight left in me. But I don't. I raise my hand and say, "Bye, Lila." The words taste like chalk in my mouth.

IN THE CAR, the dirt road feels bumpier than before. Maybe the braided witches cast a spell over it to keep people from leaving once they realize how lame Wawona is. "Jesus Christ," Mom says. "We're going to pop a tire."

"No, we won't." Dad taps the screen and clicks on navigation. I watch him confirm the first address that pops up: home.

"Do you think three weeks is too long?" Mom asks. "That seems kind of long, doesn't it? But that's what the director recommended."

"I trust the director," Dad says.

"What do you think, Liv?" She turns around to look at me. "You know her best."

The lake splashes beside the road like what I imagine is happening in my stomach. Three whole weeks with just the two of them: We'll kill each other. "She'll be fine."

"See?" Dad says. "She'll be fine."

I reach down for his headphones, which I dropped onto the floor when we were first getting out of the car. My hand brushes against something soft and damp, and that's when I look down and see two wrinkled velvet ears. Seesaw. Crumpled into a ball like a piece of trash.

"I guess you're right," Mom says.

I pick up his floppy arm and tuck him under my seat so they won't see. No matter what they say, I know Mom and Dad aren't ready for Lila to grow up. I know because I'm not, either.

WE GET BACK TO NASHQUITTEN around six, a full half hour before the GPS ETA because Mom drives like the PTA's chasing her with a new prom proposal in hand. While she and Dad stand on the front steps discussing dinner options, I tuck Seesaw into my backpack.

I try to sneak into the house through the side door, but no dice. "You!" Mom points her phone's flashlight at me even though it's not dark out at all. "You come with me."

"I have math to do," I say, because she's making me do algebra workbooks all summer. My B-minus was not an accurate assessment of my knowledge, according to her. She doesn't like for me to be bad at things because it reflects poorly on her own parenting.

She's read approximately three thousand books about raising secure and motivated children, which means, theoretically, I should be a valedictorian with unshakeable body confidence and my own charity for child leukemia.

"Math can wait." She starts walking toward the driveway, which is my cue to follow. I drop my backpack on the lawn with a loud sigh and grumble about how many problem sets I have to work on, but she just pauses for a second at the side mirror, which lost more shards on our drive home. "Let's go for a walk."

We live in a cul-de-sac at almost exactly the center of town, halfway between the ocean and the west side. Mom grew up in this house, and she and Dad have been renovating it since they got married right out of college, which is when my grandparents moved to Florida. Almost none of the original parts are left, except for the kitchen doorframe where Grandpa used to mark Mom's and Aunt Sally's heights. When I was little, I liked to stand by the tiny ticks and measure myself by their age. I'm six-year-old-Mom tall, or nine-year-old-Sally high. I'm way past the marks now, but Lila still fits.

r u free, I text Marina, because I don't want to be alone with my parents their first night without my sister.

"Put your phone away," Mom says, even though she's looking straight ahead. "And hurry up."

I jog to catch up with her at the mailbox, because this woman wouldn't slow down if I were rolling behind her in a wheelchair. "Happy?" I ask when we're side by side.

She turns onto the street and starts to pump her arms like she's at one of the Y's step classes. "I have a proposition for you."

"A proposition?"

"A proposed plan of action."

"I know what a proposition is."

"Private school." She stops walking and I pause at the last second, just an inch from her shoulder blades. "What do you think?"

My nose is practically touching her spine. "I thought private education was obscene."

"I mean, the question of whether I *personally* believe in it is a separate conversation. We're talking about your future. God, I can feel your breath on my back. Come around so I can see your face."

"It seems like the same conversation to me." When I step up to join her, I notice tiny droplets of sweat along her hairline. She never sweats—that's her thing.

"That's because you're young. You can't live every single belief you have."

"You can just say it's easier," I tell her.

"What's easier?"

"Being at school without me."

The Monday after it happened, we had a mandatory assembly instead of first period. Marina was absent, so I sat in the back row of seats with the stoner kids and put in earbuds that are easy to hide behind my hair. I didn't want to listen to my mom talk about how tragedy can ultimately bring us together as a community, or Ms. Layla explain the importance of expressing our feelings, or the PTA president remind us that our parents are here to help. All the bullshit you say when you don't understand why something happened and so you don't know how to prevent it from happening again. The best thing to do in these circumstances is to end the meeting by playing some lame folksy song and then sending us on our way, like they did when Carrie Matthews got too fucked up on a boat one weekend and fell in and drowned. (The cops say she was in the water for a full five minutes before her friends noticed.)

But they screwed up this time. This time, they left time for a Q and A.

I took out my earbuds because one of the stoner kids slapped my arm with his clammy hand and squealed, Oh shit! before jumping to his feet and clapping.

One of the freakishly pious Catholic girls, Sally, was standing in the aisle between the front-row seats, her chest puffed up like a pelican's beneath her ruffly white peasant top as she shouted at my mother, who was standing at the podium with absolutely no expression on her face: Why won't you tell us what actually happened? Was it a suicide? A medical emergency? Foul play? We deserve to know!

Normally no one listens to Sally—she talks too much about how we're all going to hell for our various sins. But there was something in the air that morning, in that assembly hall with broken AC that smelled like skin and breath and sweat. I'm still not sure if it was fear or anger or maybe both. But either way, when Sally started walking up and down the aisle, raising her fist in the air as she chanted, We deserve to know, people joined her. And she eventually made her way to the very back row of seats, where she pointed at me as she turned her head to the stage. I heard your daughter was there, she yelled. If you don't know what happened, why don't you ask her?

I couldn't say what went down next, because I pushed past the stoner kid sitting beside me, shoved Sally's devout ass into an armrest, and ran into the bathroom, where I vomited into an unlined trash can.

Mom runs her hands over her face, tugging down her eyelids so I can see their slimy pink rims. "Why do you willfully misinterpret what I say? I'm trying to help you."

She starts walking again, but this time I keep up. "I'm not going."

"I don't want to fight. Just think about it, will you?" Even though she's looking straight ahead, she manages to find my hand and squeeze it. "You could start over, Liv."

But there's no such thing as starting over, not when you've done what I have. And I think that's how it should be. Your choices have to mean something, even if they mean something terrible.

At the party that night, I dared Lucy to push Marco off the upper deck. And I wasn't joking when I said it. He would have deserved it—I still believe that. I thought maybe he'd break a leg, a couple ribs. And that wouldn't have been anything close to what he did to her. Boys don't understand how painful it is to have someone steal the parts of you that should remain private. Pain means bones and blood to them. Something they can point to. Something someone else can see.

Of course she didn't do it. But the way she looked over at the ground while I was talking: I'm the one who put the idea in her head.

Marina told me I screamed when it happened, but I don't think that's true. She's the one who screamed. I was looking through the doorway to the framed part of the second floor, to where Marco was leaning against a wooden post with a beer in one hand, laughing at a joke I couldn't hear. I was thinking: I could kill him. When I turned to tell Lucy, she wasn't there. And the next thing I remember is holding Marina close as we fought our way down the stairs, everyone packed so close that I couldn't breathe without inhaling the strands of someone else's hair.

In the end I tried to be logical. It's what Mom had begged me to be over and over again: You're too emotional, too hotheaded, too sensitive. So I examined the facts. Three girls, two alive, one dying. One smart, smart enough to take her out of this town, if she plays her cards right. One already dead, even if she's still breathing, even if we'd like to think there's something we can do. One who knows it doesn't matter how smart you are if the cops catch you somewhere you never should have been with someone else's blood on your dress. I couldn't save Lucy, but I'd saved Marina, hadn't I?

"Do you think I'm going to hell?" I ask.

"What?" She stops walking. "Of course not, no." She pulls me to her chest, so that my ear's right beside her heart. I don't remember the last time I was this close to her. Everything starts slipping, like I'm on the deck of a boat tipping to one side, and I can't help it. I'm crying.

"Shh, shh." She lowers us to the ground and we sit on the edge of the sidewalk, in front of the new house that's been for sale forever. The back door's unlocked, and before everything Lila and I would sneak in and lie in the empty Jacuzzi tub. I don't take risks like that now.

"Sometimes I worry I gave you the worst parts of myself," she says after we sit there for what seems like a very long time. I pull my head off her shoulder. "I don't want you to be scared like me."

That actually makes me feel better—I laugh. "You're scared of literally nothing."

She looks across the street and shakes her head. "I'm scared of many things. What could happen to you, mainly."

My heart speeds up. "What do you mean?"

"I've had nine overdoses, four rapes, five bomb threats, three suicide attempts, and six deaths in the past five years. And that's just what got reported." She brings her thumb to her mouth and chews on the knuckle. "Every year I think I'll get better at protecting them. And I don't."

"You can't control that, though."

"Tell that to my conscience."

We never talk like this, and I wonder, not for the first time, if she knows. Ms. Layla promised she wouldn't use my name, but adults always sell you out in the end. It wouldn't be the worst thing if she knew. Maybe it could be good. Maybe it could be really good.

I'm about to open my mouth when our neighbor Ted jogs by with his golden retriever. Mom loves him because he went to Williams. I hate him because he wears a CamelBak and compression socks for mile-long runs. He slows down and pulls one earbud out. "You ladies all good?"

"We're great," Mom says with this huge fake smile. "Just having some girl talk."

"All righty then." He puts the earbud back in and jogs away. And just like that, the moment's over.

"Did you know he went to Williams?"

"I know, Mom."

She slaps her thighs once and stands up. "Well, we should get back. Your father undersalts everything unless I'm there to watch him."

I glance back at the empty house. When they were still building it, Lila and I would stand in between the beams holding up the walls and take bets on how it would look when they finished. A sink over there, a tub by the pipes, a fridge in that corner. We were wrong about everything.

"Coming?" she asks.

I nod. The sun's started to drop toward the treetops, and it burns through the clouds like the beam of a flashlight. I hear someone's sprinkler turn on in the distance.

"What's up with Marina?" Mom asks as we walk back. "Haven't seen much of her lately."

"She's really busy at Mullaney's."

"Ah." She pulls her sunglasses out of her pocket and polishes them with her shirtsleeve. "Is she doing okay? With everything?"

What's everything?

Being left alone in the bottom of an empty swimming pool because your friend's gut told her to run with the crowd instead of stay with you? Or maybe holding a dying girl for thirty minutes because no one called 911, not until that friend heard your voice through the woods and knew she had to? Or it could be watching said friend reappear a thousand lifetimes too late, not to help but to talk you into leaving. Maybe it's being dragged away from the girl you tried to save. Maybe it's not saving her.

"Yeah," I say. "She's all right."

AFTER DINNER, I sneak Seesaw upstairs and hide him under Lila's comforter. I'm sitting on the edge of her bed when my phone finally vibrates. Marina.

hey, sry for the delay. i'm actually going to go stay with my aunt in oregon for a little while.

ok, I type back. *when will u be back?*

i don't kno. ill txt u.

i might not be going back 2 school, I tell her, and wait.

She's typing. And then she's not.

i miss u.

Nothing.

How do people without best friends live? Half of life is just waiting to tell something to the person who knows you best. And if you don't have that person, you wait forever.

My face is planted in Lila's pillow when I hear the bedroom door swing open. I roll over and there's Mom in the doorway, her cell phone pressed to her neck. "What are you doing in here?" she asks.

I wave away the question and press the pillow into my closed eyes.

"It's Lila."

I immediately sit up. "Is she okay?"

"Yes, she's fine. But she's really freaked out. Something about a photo?" She shrugs like Lila said something much crazier than *photo*. "I don't know. She wants to talk to you."

She hands me the phone and for a second I think it's going to slip out of my hand, my palm's so sweaty. *Probably just nerves*, Mom mouths.

"Uh, hey." Mom tips her head against the doorframe and I realize she's planning to stay and listen.

"What'd you do with it?" Lila demands, immediately at my throat. "Where is it?"

"I didn't do anything with it," I say slowly. "I didn't touch it."

Touch what? Mom mouths and I ignore her.

"It's gone! I put it in my folder with all the envelopes and stamps and it's not there!"

"Okay, slow down, slow down. Did you check everywhere? What about the bottom of your backpack? Did it fall out?"

"Of course it didn't fall out!" She's crying now, and I cover the phone with both hands to keep Mom from hearing.

"Hey," I say quietly. "We can get you a new one."

A new what? Mom wants to know.

"It's not the same," Lila sputters out. "I'm such an idiot! I should have just left it at home. Dumb, dumb, dumb!" It sounds like she's hitting her head against something.

"It was an easy mistake. Just don't . . . hurt yourself."

What! Mom spreads out both of her hands and shakes them at me.

I can hear her catching her breath. "Okay. Okay." Air whistles through her wet nose. "Let me talk to Mom," she says suddenly, in a tone I've never heard before. It's cold and dull, like metal.

"Why?" My throat's so tight it hurts to swallow.

"Let me talk to her, Olivia."

"Lila."

"Put her on, please."

"What?" Mom says, out loud this time. "What are you two talking about?"

I press the phone to my chest. It rattles with my heartbeat. "Hey," I say. "I have something to tell you." I point to the bed so she'll sit down, and that's when Marina texts me, saying she misses me, too.

RAE

THE POET VISITS ME AT WORK, so I know something's up. Freddie and I both turn when the security system chimes, as it does when any of the doors open. We used to have a classic bell, but that was before a group of Oxyheads smashed the front window with their bare hands during Valentine's Day. We were pretty upset about it, but then one of them wrote Freddie a long apologetic letter that outlined his mommy issues, daddy issues, general depression, etc., and we caved. By "caved" I mean we didn't make them pay for it and by "we" I mean Freddie. But it's all water under the bridge ever since Freddie discovered he can use the security system to watch the racoon that carries fish home from the docks. He calls him Lockland.

I can already feel myself getting annoyed when the poet runs his fingers through his hair as he walks in. Those oily fingers tracing streaks of grease through his roots, those fingernails loosening flakes of dandruff. It's amazing how much someone can annoy you when you're supposed to love them.

He ducks as he passes from the dining area into the bar, where the ceiling drops abruptly. The story I've been told is that the height was meant to weed out drunken sailors back in the day—if they were too blitzed to lower their heads, they smacked them on the wooden beam and knew it was time to go home. I only mention this because the poet is five foot seven and the ceiling is five foot ten at its lowest, which we all know leaves a three-inch difference. He perceives himself as a much taller man, like a Yorkie who tries to roughhouse with rottweilers.

"Ho, ho, ho," Freddie says as the poet straightens up. Freddie's not fond of the poet because he originally moved to town with the intention of helping his cousin flip run-down beach houses, an enterprise Freddie finds fucking parasitic. Do I disagree with Freddie? No. Do I enjoy being served oysters on the half shell? Yes. I've never pretended not to be a sellout.

The lifestyle of oysters on the half shell is not the kind of lifestyle embodied by O'Dooley's and its patrons, which is why the poet generally avoids the bar. He says it lacks atmosphere. I made the mistake of disclosing this to Freddie around three o'clock one morning, after we'd worked the bar's thirtieth-anniversary party (total shit show: I watched a woman try to grab a seagull's foot so she could fly) and the poet hadn't made an appearance. What's wrong with the "atmosphere"? Freddie asked, making very dramatic air quotes, and when I said that was the thing, the poet didn't think the bar *had* atmosphere, he nearly gasped. Is he the one who wrote that Yelp review?

"What's up?" the poet asks, leaning against the bar's counter. He looks good, even with the greasy hair. That's the thing about artsy types—they don't look authentic if they're not dirty. From the corner of my peripheral vision, I can see Freddie eyeing his shirt, which says *Supreme* in bright-red font. We're both behind the bar pretending to work. I've polished the same beer mug five times, and Freddie's been spraying the soda gun on and off, on and off.

"Supreme what?" Freddie asks.

"Hmm?" The poet lifts his ear ever so slightly.

"Like *the* Supremes? Or are you *the* supreme poet?"

"Sorry?" the poet says, with the lilt he adopts when he's not actually trying to understand. I've been on the receiving end of this lilt many a time. It once made me throw an orange at him, which turned the poet on. You're so feisty, he said, and I threw another one at him.

Freddie tosses his towel over his shoulder, his sign that he's given up on the interaction. "Sit wherever you'd like."

Not so long ago we used to be packed out at 5:00 p.m. on a Friday, with everyone from sunburned fishermen to weary-eyed teachers, all eager to get fucked up and finally start their weekend. We weren't exactly strict, either, so we'd get some high schoolers with their fake IDs taped to the side of Village Market reward cards. No more of that after Lucy, though. The cops watch these kids so hard now that I saw one get a ticket for jaywalking across Main Street.

I pick up the empty tip jar and drop two of my own dollars in. "Murphy's still public enemy number one?" the poet asks, and I glance over at Freddie, who practically shoots flames out of his eyes whenever they're mentioned.

"We don't even think about Murphy's." He opens his mouth, scrunches up one cheek, and spits a wad of saliva onto the carpet. "That's what I have to say about Murphy's."

The rival bar opened up six months earlier, with IPAs and organic beef hot dogs and cocktails on draft. We weren't worried at the time, not until our crowd started thinning and we sent Charlie over there on a reconnaissance mission. I'm gonna be honest with

you, he said when he returned, cheeks pink from the cold weather.
It's awesome.

"Guess what," the poet says. He turns his head toward me so
sharply his neck pops. He's one of those people who likes to extend
intense focus to the person they're talking to. Generally, he likes it
when people call him *intense*. He seems to think it means the same
thing as *smart*.

"What?" I ask, my stomach already tensing up like a closed fist.
I hate surprises.

"I got you a script! Or—what do they call it in the business?
Sides! I got you *sides*."

"What, you mean a play?" Freddie asks.

The poet ignores him. "So, it's this independent film—"

"I watched them film part of *The Departed* in Southie," Freddie
interrupts. "I even snagged a bagel from craft services when they
weren't looking."

"What kind?" I ask.

"Cinnamon sugar."

"Nice."

The poet taps his fingers against the bar impatiently. I can see
the swirled smudges they leave on the varnish, tiny maps of grease.
"It's a great opportunity for you, Rae."

On our first date, I told him that I'd once wanted to become an
actress. Neither of us had used a dating app before, and I felt off-
balance, watching the face I'd stared at on-screen materialize in
reality. So I started sharing. I'd never even acted in school plays as
a kid, but I liked the idea of getting to live out other lives. It's
always seemed strange to me—that we've not only agreed to a single
narrative but that we aspire to disrupt it as little as possible.
Divorce, career change, tragedy: all generally undesirable aberra-
tions. I wanted something different.

So, two months after graduation, I bought a ticket to LA with no place to live, no agent, no plan. My mom had just died, and the move gave me a sense of control—like I was overpowering that unforeseen anomaly with an improbable choice of my own. I stayed on a friend of a friend's couch for a week before moving in with a girl I found on Craigslist who called herself a healer. She put me in touch with an agent who made me pay five hundred dollars for representation and a series of headshots that we took in his mold-splattered garage. I put the headshots, which we printed at OfficeMax, in my seatback pocket and drove around the city auditioning for the murdered mistress or the raped girlfriend or whore number four, and when I wasn't pretending to be a battered woman I cleaned apartment complexes. I wish I could help you, my roommate told me when I came home one night, a mug of kava in her hand. But I have, like, no idea how.

Why I told him all these things during the first date is beyond me.

"What do you mean you 'got a script'?" I ask. "Like you bought one online?"

"No, no, no." He reaches over the bar and grabs my hands, like he can sense my trust is waning. "One of my buddies in Cambridge is directing his first feature, and he sent me the screenplay. He does super interesting things with narrative temporality."

"*Time*," I tell him. "Just say *time*." And Harvard. Just say Harvard.

The poet blinks at me in a don't-be-rude way, and for a second I think we might fight right there in front of Freddie. I hate watching couples fight in public—it's like when men come into the bar with their waistband unknowingly exposing their ass crack. You have to pretend you don't see anything when, really, it's all hanging out.

"Anyway." The poet lets go of my hands. "He wants you to read for it."

"Me? Why?" I haven't so much as read a casting call since I came home seven years ago. My father had called asking what he should do with my mother's clothes—save or donate them? I'd left him alone to empty our house. I still feel guilty about it.

The poet checks his watch. "Are you almost done here? I can tell you everything on the way home."

Behind me, I know Freddie's wringing out the dirty towels before carrying them to the laundry machine in the back. He's sniffing each one to decide whether it needs bleach or just regular detergent. We've worked together so long we can sense each other's shadows. "I still have some stuff to finish up," I tell him.

"Get out of here, Rae." Freddie appears at my side, a bin of towels pressed to his stomach. "I've got the rest."

Lately, Freddie's insisted on working Friday nights himself—go have a life, he tells me—but I like to linger because I have this crazy, uncrushable hope that our customers will reappear and it'll be busy just like old times. That they'll be so drowned in Catholic guilt they'll tip 40 percent and promise to never visit Murphy's again.

For someone without a lot of luck, you sure have a lot of hope, an ex-boyfriend once told me. Is that hot? I asked. No, he said after thinking for a moment. It's kind of sad. "You positive?"

"I think I can handle this crowd." Freddie winks and gives me a firm clap on the shoulder. I can hear the poet impatiently tapping his foot on the other side of the bar, the toe of his leather shoe striking the vinyl siding.

"You don't have to be so rude," I tell him outside on the sidewalk.

"Rude?" the poet repeats, indignant. The poet believes himself to be so self-aware that all outside opinions are rendered moot—if he'd behaved a certain way, he would know it already. "I was trying to save *your* Friday night. You're too generous with your time. He takes advantage of you."

"Advantage of me?" I hiss, but the poet's already started walking and doesn't hear me. I jog to catch up, my work clogs slapping against the sidewalk. I'm lucky that, despite his artistic ambitions, the poet is a generally unobservant man. If this were not the case, he'd see my fists ball. My jaw tighten. My shoulders tense.

Luckily, he doesn't see anything at all.

"NATHAN'S REALLY COOL; you'll love him," the poet says, opening his laptop. "He was easily the best in our writing workshop. Just, like, reams of talent."

"Reams," I repeat.

"I think he did a Sundance lab or something last year. Everyone thinks he's going to explode."

"Who's everyone?"

He ignores me and opens an email thread called *Untitled Project Casting.* I sit beside him at the kitchen table and stare at his screen, where a woman is serving a beer with one hand and pouring a vodka shot with the other. Her face is flushed from doing too many things at once and there are damp half-moons darkening her gray T-shirt below the armpits. She's serving a man with cheeks turned permanently red from too many years of drinking and a bald spot that glows white in the camera flash. They're smiling at each other conspiratorially, the way friends do when they feel close and untouchable.

On his screen it's May 25th, roughly nine o'clock. We've packed the pub with three times our legal capacity thanks to the K of C fundraiser, and in an hour the fire chief will show up, demanding we split the crowd or pay a steep fine, but then Freddie will hand him a Long Island iced tea and soon enough he'll have forgotten why he even showed up in the first place. In two hours I'll have sweated so completely though my shirt that a drunk woman offers me hers in the bathroom and proceeds to walk through the bar in just her bra. In three hours some of the men from the dock tug the decorative fishing net from the ceiling and start wrapping it around anyone close to them, demanding a kiss for their freedom. In four hours Charlie gets a call on his cell phone and swivels his barstool around with a finger in one ear to listen. He twists his face in confusion and I mouth, *What?* while a woman grabs my elbow because I'm not pouring her gin fast enough. His eyes go so wide that I see every pink vein trembling at their edges, and out loud I go, What, what? The woman starts pinching me for her gin. Charlie shoves the phone into his pocket and slaps the bar so frantically that it makes the shot glass for the gin rattle. I have to go, I have to go, is what he starts shouting, and I leave without asking any more questions, and the woman yells after us: My gin! and Freddie asks if we're okay as we rush out. I drive so fast to the emergency room that to this day I don't remember doing it. I only remember Brynn's face when I pull up to the revolving doors, her body hunched small to sit on the sidewalk, her mouth opening as Charlie scrambles out of my car: Where were you?

"What's wrong?" the poet asks. "I thought it was better than a traditional headshot. Authentic."

On the other side of the screen, it's October 10. I roll the date over in my head, try to believe it: You are here, I tell myself. Here is now. When my mother died, time advanced and retreated like the tide. I would finally find myself in the present, only to be tugged back into my memories without the realization that my footing was shifting. And that's the thing, about tides: It's impossible to tell which way they're moving when you're standing in the middle of the ocean.

"Where did you find that?" I hear myself asking.

The poet has minimized the photo now, sensing that he's done something wrong without understanding why. "Facebook. You were tagged."

I stand up and retrieve a glass from the cabinets above the sink. Physical objects help, I find—anything you can grasp. I press the glass into the stainless steel fridge, and filtered water pours into the cylinder, turns it cold.

"Are you good?" the poet asks from the table.

"Yeah," I say. "One second." I drift through the glass doors that lead to the balcony—they seem to open on their own. Outside, the harbor is dark, the streetlights along the water turning it an ugly grayish color, like bad milk. Buoys clink against one another in the distance, as do the beer bottles of teens that sneak into the docked boats at night. Somewhere, people are laughing. I can feel my memories from May going cloudy, like the sand-stirred waves of a storm. I grasp the balcony's metal railing, and it seems to wobble beneath my fingers, but when I lift my hands the bar is still. In my pocket, I reach for my phone and search her name. I hold it to my ear and listen to it ring, and ring, and ring.

Hi, this is Lucy. I can't come to the phone right now, but leave me a message and I'll be sure to get back to you ASAP.

The doors slide open behind me. "Who're you calling?" the poet asks, his voice tight in the way that means he doesn't know whether to be concerned or jealous.

"No one." Salt-heavy wind blows against my face, clears my sinuses. I haven't hung up. My fingers open and my phone falls from them like something much heavier than an envelope of metal and wire. I hear it crackle against the sidewalk below, feel the poet's hand on my shoulder as he peers over the balcony.

"What the fuck?" he's saying. "You could have hit someone!"

"It slipped."

He tells me to go inside, and I sit on his plush gray sectional with my knees to my chest while I wait for him to retrieve the phone. He walks back into the condo shaking his head. "Miraculously, this is all that happened."

He drops the phone beside me, which now has a jagged scar running diagonally across the screen. When I tap it to life, the pixels along the gash blur into a smeared rainbow.

"You need to tell me what's going on up there," the poet says after a moment. He's sitting on the coffee table facing me, chin resting in one hand.

"You know what happened."

"No," he says. "Not from you, I don't. Not really." He always acts like I was there, but I wasn't. I was as far away from her as he was.

I look around the room, searching for a way to change the subject. "What's the script about?" I ask.

He rests his chin on his fists in a way that seems to mean: You can't get off that easy.

"Really," I insist. "I want to know."

The poet's narrowed eyes make it clear that he's weighing the options. Attempt to prod me (likely unsuccessfully) into a difficult, lengthy conversation, or concede and allow the evening to lift into a lighter note, one that could possibly end in sex, if he plays his cards right. "I've only seen a synopsis," he finally says. "But it's brilliant."

I sink into the couch, note how the cushion molds to my spine, press my fingers into the soft upholstery. It feels real enough. "Can I have a glass of wine?" Somewhere along the way I lost my water.

"Sure," he says, standing up, and I sense the past lapping away from us, receding to that faraway place where everyone tells me memories should reside.

THE NEXT MORNING I MEET CHARLIE at his house for coffee. I've had coffee on his front porch every Saturday since I came back from Los Angeles and he tricked me into it. *Your mother would have wanted it* was what he texted, which isn't exactly a lie but also isn't the truth. Who knows what that woman wanted.

Charlie thinks he knows. He and my mother were best friends since the womb—their mothers were also best friends, and they were born on the same day two hours apart. Irish twins, as Charlie incorrectly puts it. Technically, he's my godfather, though I don't think any of us believe in that stuff anymore. Even my father stopped going to Mass years ago.

He's waiting on the front steps when I pull into the driveway. "Rae-Ban!" He locks me in an embrace that smells like smoke and toothpaste. He gave up booze after Lucy, but life isn't worth living without a vice, as he likes to say. He doesn't hide the cigarettes now that Brynn's not around. We sit at the metal café table on the back side of the porch, the side that faces the ocean, and he taps open a box of Parliaments.

"How's that boy of yours?" he asks, shielding his lighter from the wind. Charlie's vibe has gotten even more paternal since my dad moved upstate last year, an act that Charlie unfairly interpreted as an act of fatherly abandonment. *I'm not deserting you, am I?* my father asked after I'd tugged down the door of his U-Haul, the last box finally Tetris-ed into a corner. *You're three hours away*, I told him with a laugh. But I'd be lying if I said I didn't feel differently when the truck finally disappeared over a hill. It felt like whatever had happened with my mother was finally over, and the only way we'd gotten there was by separating.

"I'm thirty. He's not a boy."

"He sure sounds like one, the way you talk about him." He holds the cigarette between his lips so he can press down on the plunger of the French press. Even now, he doesn't know how to use it without Brynn. He's overfilled it, and grounds float through the murky liquid like potting soil. "You don't have to pretend you're happy, not here."

He pours me a mug of coffee, and the surface shines like oil in the sun. I sip it slowly, trying to catch the grounds on my lips before they can filter into my mouth. "We're going to break up," I say, startling myself. I hadn't realized I believed this, but now that I've spoken it, I know it's true. Sometimes I think that we already know what our futures hold—we're just waiting for the right moment to stop hiding from ourselves.

Charlie's halfway through his cigarette, burning fast. I fan the smoke away from my face. "Well, I'm sorry to hear that," he says. "You'll be breaking his heart, then? Just like Corrine with all the Baskin boys."

I don't understand the reference to my mother, so I just smile at him through tight lips. I have thought, more than once, whether it makes sense for me to keep coming here. Charlie likes to dangle my mother's past over my head like a carrot I should beg him for. Only I'm not hungry and never have been. "How's Brynn?" I ask.

He extinguishes his cigarette on the porch railing and it makes a hiss—there's still dew on the wood. "Oh, you know her." He turns to look out at the beach. It's low tide and a field of wet rocks are exposed, waiting to be blanketed. "She's always trying to reinvent herself."

"I like Brynn," I offer.

"Did I say I didn't?" He takes the first sip of his coffee and grimaces through it. "I'm the one who married her."

He did, but everyone—even Brynn—knew he really wanted my mother. That's the thing about living in a small town. Everyone sees through what you say you desire and knows what you actually do.

"When are you gonna get out of O'Dooley's?" he asks, changing the subject. "You know you're too good for that place."

"I think I'm just good enough for it."

"But you must," he says, reaching for another cigarette, "have aspirations."

Beyond the porch, the tide is starting to finger its way back toward the house. The waves unfurl in frothy sheets, the noise echoing up to us. For so long, people have begged me to want things. What does Rae want? my therapist asked when I finally agreed to counseling after years of refusal. What's on Rae's horizon? When I said, Nothing, she blinked and then scribbled something on her clipboard. By "nothing," she said, do you mean inner peace? No, I said, I mean nothing. She popped the cap of her golden pen into her mouth. Explain that to me.

What was there to explain? I'd lived more than enough life by the time I was nineteen. All I wanted was for things to be still. My favorite thing in the world is floating on the ocean's surface during the summer. The water fills your ears with white noise and your body's weightless and the sun warms your face and it's impossible to want anything other than what you have in that moment. If I could do that forever, I would.

"What aspirations do *you* have?" I ask, which makes Charlie laugh so hard that he can't properly block his lighter from the wind.

"Aspirations are dead to me," he says once the flame licks the rolled paper.

"They're dead to me, too," I say, and when we look at each other's eyes, I think he might be the only person in the world who I have a chance of convincing this is true.

THAT NIGHT THE POET TAKES ME into Boston for a dinner party. He'd first suggested the train, which had made sweat prick every one of my pores. You seem like someone who would love the train, he said when I suggested we drive instead. I do love trains, I said, just not tonight, and then I kissed his neck, trying to remember what girlfriends do to ease these small tensions, trying to remember what a girlfriend is at all.

As we leave Nashquitten, we come to a series of tracks just as the warning arms lower. There are two stops in town, one on the west side and one on the east, just before Nashquitten becomes Walden Landing. I avoid the crossings when I drive, but there's no way to tell the poet that without telling him everything else. I dig my fingernails into the sides of the leather seat as the train approaches, its front lights sending tunnels of white toward us. The warning bell begins to ding over and over, a continuously struck triangle. The horn rushes toward us like it's moving through a funnel, siloed and then blaring. The wheels scream against the track. I don't realize I've shut my eyes until the poet asks me why they're closed. The heavy rush of the train shudders through our seats as its tethered cars snap by.

And then, like that, nothing. I open my eyes to the arms rising, the tracks clear. The poet has turned on the visor light to look at me. "What was that all about?" His voice is more annoyed than concerned, because this behavior indicates that I may not be an exemplary dinner guest, which indicates his taste in women may be questioned by his friends.

"It was nothing." I flick off the tiny light. "I felt nauseous."

"Do we need to go home?" he asks, in a tone that makes it clear going home is not an option.

"Really," I tell him. "I'm fine." I press my nose to the window, but it's so dark that all I see is my own ghostly reflection. My mind feels soft like taffy, and as we bump over the tracks I try to convince myself that there's nothing to see, that her body isn't lying there, that that was years ago.

THE PARTY'S IN THE SOUTH END, a part of Boston I've never visited because someone once told me it was all bulimic women in stilettos and inbred toy poodles. The poet turns onto a leafy street with side-by-side brownstones and streetlights made of lanterns burning with actual fire. "So this is your friend's house?" I ask as he parks. The friend, whose name I can't remember, is an ex-banker who does stick-and-poke tattoos at pop-up markets.

"It's ours, technically," the poet says. He steps out of the car and goes around the hood to open my door.

"Technically?"

"Yeah, my parents wanted to have something downtown." He flicks his hand when he says *downtown*, and I can't tell if that means downtown is over, or downtown is on the rise, or downtown is where it's at and always will be. "He's staying in it until he decides about graduate school." I met this friend once, at a bar halfway between Nashquitten and Boston. He kept going on and on about the death of DIY shows. "You're good," he says as we follow a path of bricks to the front steps. "Right?"

Luckily I don't have to answer, because the house's iron door heaves open above us and the friend peers out with his hand held over his eyes. "I knew I heard voices!" he declares. "I thought I was going fucking crazy there for a second, like really losing my shit but not in a fun way, you know?"

"Nope, not crazy, just us," the poet says, and I follow him up the stairs to the front door. I'm about to step inside when the friend grabs me by the shoulder. "You've seen some shit, haven't you?" he asks.

"Excuse me?"

He pulls me in close, kisses my forehead. His hands jitter with whatever he's taken, and I can feel his ribs vibrating against mine. "Trauma's fantastic on you."

DINNER IS ROWDY and elegant and insufferable. I can't keep track of the inside jokes, the names, the references. The perfume from the woman beside me—Elise? Ella? Esadora?—is so strong that I can taste it, soapy and musky like old bathwater. The dining table is large enough to fit twelve and we've smashed sixteen around it, our elbows rubbing each other's plates, our hair grazing each other's shoulders, our crumbs spilling across each other's sleeves. Someone's speaking Portuguese even though it's established that no one else does, only Spanish, and then someone's practicing their Catalan and some French is thrown into the mix and the whole time I'm trying to figure out if I'm having a stroke or if it's just that no one's speaking English. I'm almost square in the middle of the table, the eye of the storm, and more than once I think I might pass out from the body heat and the wine and the air being sucked into everyone's mouth but mine. Two hours pass and I want nothing more than to go home. But when I pull the poet aside as he goes to retrieve yet another bottle of red, he squeezes my arm and says: The director will be here soon. You have to meet the director. Think of all the doors that could open, if you'd just talk to the director.

"Want some?" my overperfumed neighbor asks. She's drunk and cutting cocaine on her dirty dinner plate. I watch the powder disintegrate into a smear of melted butter.

"No, thank you."

"You guys"—she gestures toward something in the distance, maybe the fireplace—"make zero sense."

I know what she's talking about. "Why's that?"

Her eyebrows rise in offense, or maybe confusion. "He's like"—she makes an erratic whirl of her hands—"and you're like"—the hands turn to fists and pound each other—"you know?"

"Totally," I say, and I rub one hand against her back because she's now collapsed onto the table.

"I don't feel good," she murmurs. "I think I'm going to be sick." And that's when I jump up to search for my purse in the hallway.

Outside, the air is crisp and clean like a bleached sheet. I'm so busy breathing it in that at first I don't see the friend who lives here, pressed against the stairs' railing like a wife watching her sailor depart from his dock. "Too much party for you?" he asks.

"I have a migraine."

"Sure." He eyes me up and down before producing a flask from his pocket. I expect whiskey, but the taste is herbal, bitter. "Fernet," he says when I hand it back. "Drink of the gods."

"Of course," I say, and he laughs like I've said something much funnier. "Hey, do you know when that director guy will be getting here?"

The friend tips his head back. "What director guy?"

"I dunno. One of your college buddies, I thought."

He doesn't seem to hear me. "We don't deserve this glorious night." He swings his face back down. "But you do. You deserve it."

I let out a little laugh. "Why do I deserve it?"

He looks up at the sky again and doesn't answer but moves his lips silently, like a fish. I step in front of him in an attempt to hold his attention. "The director," I ask again. "You don't know a director?" I gently tug his chin toward me.

"This is my party, is it not?"

"It is."

"Don't you think I would have known if a director was coming?" He blows air through his mouth like a horse. "I specifically said in the evite: no randos. I fucking hate people I don't know in my house."

And then, suddenly, I get it. The poet's always tried to motivate me—with group exercise schedules, class catalogs from the local art center, forwarded emails from the community college—but he's never been this creative. I let go of the friend's chin. "I think I've been played."

"What?" He fans his hands on either side of his jaw. "No! I don't want anyone to play you *ever*."

"I appreciate that." I open my phone and try to navigate my home screen while working around the rainbow-tinged gash, which has only grown in the past few days. "If you were me, how would you get home?"

. . .

AN HOUR AND A HALF LATER, Charlie picks me up at a late-night café where the friend and I have been eating eclairs and drinking sparkling water flavored with rosemary. He keeps telling me his high is over and then asks why the birds on the wallpaper are moving or what that crazy man is saying. (*He* is that crazy man and he is saying: "What's that crazy man saying?") I request that he walk home before I get in the car, so I stand outside on the sidewalk and watch him cancan the half block back to the house and shout the nickname he's given me: Baby Tiger Warrior.

"Who the fuck was that?" Charlie asks when I slide into the passenger seat.

"The nicest guy at the dinner party, if you can believe it." Charlie shakes his head and pulls onto the main street, which is now clogged with Saturday-night traffic. "Thanks for coming out all this way to get me. It's just the train—"

"I know." He raises one hand, eyes still on the brake lights in front of us. "I know, Rae."

I fall asleep against the window, and when I wake up everything around me is familiar again. Charlie's about to turn onto my street when I ask if it'd be okay if I came over. "You can say no if it's weird. I'd just rather not be at home." I don't remember the last night I spent at my place instead of the poet's. My landlord, Maureen, always wants to talk about Lucy. When she wants to "chat," as she puts it, she taps the handle of her broom to the floor (my ceiling), which is the signal to meet her on the rickety back stairs. It must have been an accident, right? she asks every single time, like I'll have a different answer than *I don't know*. That's how it is with tragedies—the people untouched by them look for any excuse to get involved. But you two were close, she said to me one night, when she offered me a glass of bourbon I didn't know how to refuse. Her daughter and son were asleep inside, so we sat on the lawn in her beach chairs. I mean, you must know her psychology, she insisted. I don't know anything, I told her, because that's the thing about people. You only ever see your interpretation of them—not who they actually are.

"Okay," he says, coasting past the turn. "You can stay in Lucy's room, if you want."

I can't tell if this is a request or some strange challenge. "Are you sure?"

He nods, head trained on the road. "I like the idea of her not being the last one who slept there."

EVER SINCE THE ACCIDENT, I've avoided the third floor of Charlie's house. The low-ceilinged attic used to be storage, but they redid it to be Lucy's wing when she turned fourteen. I remember her showing me around when they'd just revealed it would be entirely hers—she had color samples taped to all but one wall, which she planned to paint a mural on. I'm not sure if she ever finished it.

"You want to go up?" Charlie asks. We're standing at the foot of the staircase. It looks steep and treacherous in the hazy light of the hallway lamp.

"When was the last time you went up there?"

He shakes his head. "Only Brynn," he says, and I wonder if he understands how unfair that is. When I was in high school I was over here every week, babysitting so Brynn could work without interruption. Who knows where Charlie was. He had a bad fall on the docks and had broken his hip, I knew that. I could hear my parents whispering about him at night after they thought I'd fallen

asleep—the walls in our house were so thin you could hear someone taking a piss from your bedroom. I kept a mental catalog of the
words they used most frequently: *intervention, irresponsible, imma-
ture.* Then there was the month he disappeared; my parents told
me he was visiting family in California. This happened again a few
years later, only then I'd seen enough at school to understand that
he was probably only a town over, at the pale brick building that
housed Sunrise Rehab.

Never have I heard an adult (besides the DARE cop) talk about
the pills running through town. It's common knowledge that you
can get them from the teenagers at the Village Market or Cassandra
at the Wash-a-Whirl if you know the right things to say. After
Mom, I thought about it. My friend Jennifer brought me a tiny
baggie full of them at the funeral, which in retrospective was one
of the more thoughtful gestures. But I was too scared. There are
people like Charlie who disappear and come back. But there are
more people who just vanish.

I once asked my mom outright if Charlie was an addict, and she
got mad in a way she almost never did. You think you know things?
she said. I made sure you don't have to know any of this shit! She
was shouting then, and Dad had to come in and calm her down.
You're living the dream! she yelled as he held her arms back. I've
never told him what I found the night after it happened. A pill
bottle hidden under some socks in her dresser drawer, several years
expired and prescribed to Charles Anderson.

"Come on." He places one foot on the first stair. "There's nothing to be scared of, right?"

There's everything for us to be scared of. But I follow him anyway as he climbs. "Right."

On the second-floor landing he reaches up to tug the string
attached to Lucy's ladder. I've never seen it lower before, and I'm

surprised by the slowness of the descent. It'd always already been unfolded.

In my pocket, my phone buzzes. The poet. *where r u? zach says u left?!* I click the button that makes my screen go dark.

"You ready?" I ask Charlie.

"As I'll ever be."

Upstairs, the wing is clean and spare and huge—I'm shocked by its size without Lucy's clothes flung over her desk chair and mirror, without the art supplies scattered across the ground, without her. The window below the pitched roof seems perfectly aligned with the moon, and glowing light dribbles onto the glossed hardwood floors. Things are crisp, unadorned: Brynn has emptied the bookshelves and the closet and replaced Lucy's electric-blue sheets with white ones. It could be the room of a model home, if not for the mural on the wall facing the bed.

It's a swirl of ocean colors: the deep sapphire of night water, the translucent green of tide pools, the diluted turquoise of everyday waves. They're marbled together like the papers from Florence Lucy so admired, a box of which she once secretly blew all of her confirmation checks on. (That was a secret Charlie and Brynn did discover, when they requested she put the money in a savings account weeks later—too late.)

I'm walking toward the wall, and yet the paint, so thick in some areas it protrudes like mountain peaks, seems to pull me into the distance. I want to follow it. My peripheral vision fades as I move closer; the wall goes liquid. Pure, runny color. Slick, loose, thawed. Blue and green and somehow purple, too, like fat on broth, oil on puddle, light on soap bubble. *Is melting an action,* I wonder, *or just a consequence?* My head swims with the hues. I'm afraid to look down, to see my body. Bodies are stiff; bodies are straight. Bodies ruin everything, Lucy once told me. She was being funny, I think, or maybe I told myself she was so I'd feel better. When did she say that? There's so much I don't remember. I wish I could capture what I witness and trap it in an overturned jar, a specimen that's never allowed to leave me.

It's May 25, but I haven't gone to work yet. I've just gotten out of the shower and my hand is wet when I reach for my ringing phone, which I've left on the lip of the sink. Lucy's name flashes on the screen. She wants me to pick her up—she can't remember if she took her medication or not. I don't ask why she's calling me instead of Charlie or Brynn.

When I pull into the school parking lot, she's already waiting on the sidewalk. "Thanks," she says when she gets in, her voice heavy with the kind of exasperation that suggests you could never understand what led to the exasperation in the first place.

I ask her how her day's going anyway, and she cranks back her seat all the way and closes her eyes. "Shitty."

"That bad? It's only eleven."

"I have a ton to do and not enough time to do it." She sits up suddenly, like she's had a bolt of an idea. "Do you have a dress I could borrow? Like, something kind of slutty?"

"Is this for your portfolio?"

She nods. "I'm tired of doing self-portraits. I want to be someone else."

The truth is that I find Lucy's photos disturbing. Her bare back in the shower, hands pushing shampoo through her hair, dark with water. Her huge sleeping shirt skimming her thighs as she bends to twist the dial on the baby monitor her parents make her use in case of a nighttime seizure. Even the bumps of her spine against her striped sweater as she sits hunched on a kitchen stool with a white pill raised to her lips. Always shot from behind. As though she's trying to one-up the video by exposing her own private moments. As though the camera is a leering stranger about to devour her. "I don't know if I have anything that would fit the bill."

She places two fingers on her neck, which means she's counting her pulse. The seizures have made her extraordinarily anxious, a sense of dread following her like a shadow. Her heart beats so loudly that she hears it when she tries to fall asleep, and her chest aches, it's so full of tension. She makes me promise not to tell anyone, especially not her parents. It's a promise I keep.

"Have you been practicing your breathing exercises?" I ask.

"That's such a grown-up thing to say," she complains. Her eyes are still closed. "*Try this one patented method and all of your problems will disappear!*"

"You can't just do nothing."

That gets her attention. "I'm doing many things, actually."

I take this as my cue to be quiet. I've only seen Lucy have a seizure once, when we were swimming. This was before they got her medication dosage right, and the doctor didn't think her case was particularly serious—just go live your normal life, they told her. With one caveat: Make sure you're supervised, just in case.

I'd been floating on my back, and when I righted myself Lucy was thrashing in the waves. I thought it was a joke at first, just a bit, but then her head surfaced and I saw her eyes had rolled completely back, two white globes beneath her eyelids. I started screaming. I have no idea what I screamed, but my throat has never burned with so much noise. I pulled her against me and wrestled her mouth open with my fingers, trying to purge the water collecting in her throat, and at some point a lifeguard appeared beside me, he was telling me to please let go, we were rushing toward the beach, he was laying her down and compressing her chest, she was spitting out seawater, I was kneeling in the sand—I didn't realize how hot it was from the sun, not until later, when the skin on my legs began to peel—I was thinking, The Diastat, I need the Diastat. The medicine was in my tote bag, and my sprint to it felt miles long, my search through the bag endless, my fingers so slippery from ocean, sunscreen, sweat. I scrambled back, losing my footing in the sand, and handed it to the lifeguard, who said he knew how to use it. He lowered her bikini bottoms and pressed down on the plunger. I watched the whitish liquid in the tube go down. Only now did I realize that a crowd had gathered around us, moms with stricken leathery faces and their oblivious kids in bucket hats. Give us some space, the lifeguard shouted, but they didn't.

The seizure stopped. I had my eyes on her sandy feet, because I couldn't look at those white eyes. Her toes stilled. Space, the lifeguard repeated, and now that the drama was over some of the watchers began to disperse. Lucy came to a few minutes later, glazed and disoriented, her forehead scrunched. She said a name, the words thick with confusion, and I realized that it was the lifeguard's—they knew each other. Of course they did. He couldn't have been more than sixteen. Where was I? she asked.

I explained that she'd had a seizure.

She sat up slowly, the lifeguard's hand on her back. I'm fine, she said, slapping it away. Her eyes went to the Diastat injector beside her. Who? she asked, pointing to it. Neither the lifeguard nor I spoke for a moment.

It's totally normal, he finally said. It's a medical thing.

Her whole face cracked when he said that, and I could see that she was going to cry. Let's go home, I said, helping her to her feet. I told the lifeguard thank you, and he gave us a small wave.

She started sobbing as we hurried down the boardwalk, reeds scraping our ankles from between the slats of the wood. He's going to tell everyone! she shouted in between shaky breaths. Everyone!

He wouldn't do that, I said, and she stopped walking.

She turned, tightened her towel around her shoulders, and shook her head like I'd disappointed her in a way she could never articulate. You have no fucking idea what people would or wouldn't do.

WE PULL INTO HER DRIVEWAY and she tells me to wait in the car. While I fiddle with the radio, I picture her peering into the a.m. compartment of her green pillbox, noting the Keppra or its absence. It seems like a task for a much older person. "Fuck me," she says when she returns. "I'd taken it after all." She closes the door with a slam and starts to tug at the hairs of one eyebrow. The skin above her lid turns pink as she plucks.

"You know you can talk to me, right?" I say as we drive back to school. "It'll make you feel better."

"Who even cares about feeling better," she says. "It'd be nice to just, you know, control my own body." She opens the window, a rush of air filling the car. But before I can suggest turning the AC on, she's clicked it closed.

I don't tell Charlie or Brynn that I picked up Lucy that day. And as I watch her make her way up the concrete steps of the school, her spine hunched over like it's carrying an enormous backpack, I don't realize it's the last time I'll see her. In fact, as she heaves open one of the double doors, I'm thinking that what we really need is a girl's night, a longer time to chat alone, just the two of us. I'm thinking pizza and maybe a little bit of beer for Lucy, just a single bottle. I'm thinking that I'll text Charlie about it when I get home. Only I forget and never do.

Something blurs my vision, something flesh-colored. It's a pair of fingers, and they belong to Charlie, and he's snapping them right in front of my eyes. "Jesus," he says when I blink. "Where'd you go?"

I shake my head and he doesn't press me. "When did she finish it?" I point to the mural. "She told me she was still working on it."

"She was always saying that—it's not done, it's not done! But it looks done to me." He sits on her bed and the mattress squeaks with his weight.

I reach out and touch one of the peaks, which is glossy and smooth, plastic-like. Occasionally my fingers brush something grainy, and when I peer down to examine the paint I see that something else is ribboned through it, glitter, maybe, or sand.

"What should I do with it?" Charlie asks from behind me.

I'm only half listening, dipping my head up and down to track the way the grit catches the light. "With what?"

"I mean, I can't just leave it there. But I can't get rid of it, either." When I turn he has his head in his hands, the bald spot at the root of his skull shining in the lamplight, his chest rising toward his shoulders, then dropping. Over and over. He's crying.

In situations such as these, people like to ask: "What would *x* want?" X being, supposedly, your dead loved one, when really *x* is you, because the question is only ever poised to justify what you need to do to move on: donate their jewelry, recycle their notepads, give away their cat. I don't mean that people shouldn't heal. I just mean that we shouldn't hide our own desires under the imagined ones of the dead—I think we owe them that. Their freedom.

The bed's box springs sigh when I sit down beside Charlie. His shoulders are so broad that when I wrap my arm around them, I only barely touch his opposite side. "You don't have to decide right now."

He wipes his eyes with his knuckles. "I don't like putting things off."

I'm not sure how to tell him that this is what his life is now: the great procrastination. All you want to do is push the forgetting as far away from you as possible. Which means you have to let some of your life linger in the past.

"Here," I say, tugging him up. "Let's do this, for now." I strip the top sheet off the bed and drape it over the wall, tying one corner to the slats of the nearby closet door and letting the rest skim over the mural's crags and valleys. You can still see the colors through the sheet, but only barely. "A temporary fix," I offer. I know he'll never take it down.

Suddenly Charlie looks very tired, like his skin's stuck to every hollow of his skeleton. The dips under his eyes are so pronounced they look like spoon rests. "I feel old," he says as I walk him down the stairs, the thin plywood shivering with our steps. "I mean, I don't give a shit what I look like. But inside"—he taps his chest—"I feel like an artifact."

"It's been a long day," I assure him. "It's normal."

He leans against the doorframe to his bedroom and rubs his bald spot with one thumb. "You know what's crazy? I don't think I ever believed that I'd actually get old."

"Maybe that's healthy."

"No. Just delusional, like most of my beliefs." He reaches a hand out to rumple my hair. "Good night, kiddo," he whispers, and when he looks at me I know he's looking at her. So I kiss him on the forehead like I saw Lucy do so many times before, and I head upstairs.

In the morning there will be a text from the poet asking me to call him, and I'll do it, but only to say that I'm breaking up with him. He'll get angry because he thinks he's done nothing wrong, he was just trying to help. You needed a win, is what he'll tell me. I won't be able to convince him that has nothing to do with it. I just don't like him.

I'll go to O'Dooley's even though it's Sunday and I don't really need to be there. Freddie will already have a percolator of burnt-smelling coffee going, and he'll pour me a cup without asking. He'll say we're going to kick these Murphy's fools to the curb, and I'll put my faith in him because I love a good rally.

I'll go out to the docks after I clock out and call my father, who will be dropping a tea bag into an empty mug, the kettle whistling in the background. He'll tell me he misses me as I walk up and down the wooden slats, tapping my free hand against the metal poles that pierce the water, tunneling down into the eventual promise of solid ground. I'll tell him I miss him, too, and it will be true. You've really built a life there, he'll say, haven't you? I've always had a life here, I'll reply, and he'll clarify: a life of your own. I'll look out at the water, which is empty and the exact color of the black sky above, and I'll feel the past and the present knitting together in a way that—for once—doesn't make me dizzy. Yes, I'll say, I have. And without grasping at anything, I'll feel steady.

MAUREEN

IT'S ALMOST FIVE PAST SIX, but Cushing still hasn't shown up, and lord knows we can't start without her. I pull back my seat and the legs squeal against the freshly waxed floor. I'm sitting directly beneath the basketball hoop because I can't trust Loretta to book an appropriate room, not even for our first meeting of the year. She thought the gym "had character." Not only that, but the four tables she set up are askew, like the rectangle got a little drunk and couldn't remember what a ninety-degree angle was. And of course Diane didn't bring the snickerdoodles she promised and Peggy claimed Office Depot was out of notepads "for the foreseeable future." This is why I tried to initiate an application process for the PTA. How the fuck does this bag of morons even bother to get dressed in the morning?

I consider asking Loretta to turn on the projector attached to my laptop, but think better of it and press the button myself. The agenda appears on the vinyl screen covering the opposite wall, blurry and gray because my colleagues thought a DJ for the

post-prom lockdown was more important than smartboard tech-
nology. *17:50: Mingle. 18:00: Opening Remarks. 18:03: Homecoming.*
18:13: Coach's Retirement Party. 18:18: Robert Taylor. 18:45: Anderson
memorial monument. 19:15: Closing.

"Janet's not gonna like that," Diane murmurs in between mouth-
fuls of assorted tree nuts. When she realized she forgot the cookies
she ran outside to retrieve the jumbo container she keeps in her
minivan, which is so smeared with fingerprints the plastic's practically opaque. Not that these goons care. "You should really run
this stuff by us."

I ask Diane if she bothered reading our weekly email, to which
the agenda was attached, and she waves a cashew at me. "I get a lot
of emails."

The double doors beside the bleachers open. At first I think it's
Cushing, but, no, it's someone much better: Layla Owens. Our
teacher representative for the year and my only real ally. Turns out
most parents join the PTA to gossip rather than advocate for educational advancement.

"How are you?" she asks, pulling out the chair next to me.

"Sifting through the bullshit." I make *Robert Taylor* and *memorial*
bold so everyone knows that's our main focus. They're going to try
to make the dance and retirement party overpower everything—we
once had a thirty-minute discussion about linen versus disposable
tablecloths. "You?"

"Oh, you know. Surviving." I can tell—she looks like shit. They
tried to can Layla at the end of last year, but the investigation into
Robert made that look like a pretty piss-poor move. The only good
thing to come out of all of this.

She twists in her chair. "Where is everyone?"

More than half of the other parents left at the end of last year,
all for various reasons, according to the exit surveys I distributed

(Too busy with soccer season! Starting yoga teacher training!). But you don't have to be a genius to see the truth. After Lucy, they thought we might actually be tasked with making real shit happen. And if I have anything to say about it, that's exactly what we'll do.

The doors beside the bleachers open for a second time, and I swear the room's temperature drops five degrees. Janet Cushing, the biggest cunt I've ever met, has arrived. She's wearing high-heeled boots and a wrap sweater dress belted at the waist, and I sure hope that outfit keeps her warm in hell. She walks to the empty chair beside me and pulls a folded Kleenex from her dress pocket. After a few aggressive strokes of the plastic seat she sits down. "Well," she says. "Shall we begin?"

As expected, Loretta, Diane, and Peggy try to linger on the logistics of the dance, which isn't for two months and which will follow the exact format used for every homecoming since the dawn of institutionalized learning. I shut them up by saying that Lisa's on Main, a bottle shop in the harbor, has agreed to provide an array of charcuterie and nonalcoholic sparkling ciders.

"Really?" Cushing asks, like it makes sense for a struggling wine store to sponsor a school dance. But anything that saves money piques her interest. It's no secret that she's in budgetary hot water for the college-prep program, a passion project that's better at burning cash than getting kids into top schools.

"Really. So that takes care of that." Before anyone can protest I'm onto my next slide, which says ACCOUNTABILITY in thick red letters. This is not a group that responds well to subtlety. "We don't think the Robert Taylor situation has been adequately, or thoughtfully, dealt with," I begin. "Nor do we feel that way about Lucy Anderson's death."

"I'm not sure *we* is appropriate here," Diane interjects. "This is more of a *you* situation, no?" She looks around the room for backup, but Loretta and Peggy have dropped their gaze to the brown plastic table in front of them.

"I agree with Maureen," Layla says.

"Well, of course you do." Diane drops her hand into the jug of nuts and roots around like some treasure is buried within the macadamias and pecans. Just looking at her makes me feel the grit of flavored salt beneath my fingernails. "But you have a biased perspective."

"How is my perspective biased?" Layla asks. "I work here. I see what happens every day." Her voice catches, the sign of frustration churning to tears. "I'm *here*," she repeats. I feel so deeply for her that my own throat starts to swell, but I can't have her crying. Sobs will undo any credibility we have.

"Listen," Cushing says, in the clipped way of someone who doesn't tolerate emotional discourse. "We all want the same thing. We want to establish a level of normalcy for our students again. We want them to feel that school is a safe environment. We want them to thrive."

"Is Rob coming back?" Layla manages to ask. Her voice wobbles but doesn't break.

Cushing interlaces her hands and rests them on the table. "We are not discussing the terms of Mr. Taylor's suspension publicly. And certainly not before the internal investigation is complete."

Loretta raises her head so suddenly I wouldn't be surprised if she gave herself whiplash. "It's innocent until proven guilty in this country," she says with a passion that can only be stirred by perceived wrongs against Her Boys, three towheaded idiots who use their pocketknives to terrorize the local squirrel population and skin the pleather of school bus seats. "And I, for one, would love to see us retain our male role models."

Now Peggy raises her head because she believes any opinion said loudly is worth supporting. "With Coach retiring, who are they supposed to look up to? Dale?" Dale's AP Bio students got the most fives in Nashquitten High history last year, but he's unmarried at fifty-three and plays in a punk band called Murder Toast, so the parents don't trust him.

"A beloved mentor." Cushing tries to smile, but it's more like she's baring both rows of teeth. "He'll be sent off well."

"I heard he's being pushed out," Diane says.

"And why would that be?" Cushing asks sweetly.

Diane shrugs. "I don't know. Just like I *don't know* why the Taylor investigation hasn't wrapped yet. Are you digging around until you can find something to bury that poor man with?"

"'Inappropriate contact with a student,'" Loretta says, quoting the email Cushing sent before school let out in June. "What'd he do, text a girl about her homework? That's how this generation of teachers connects with their classes. They're seen more as a friend than an authority figure."

"I wish Mrs. Miller would text Max about pre-calc," Diane snorts.

Cushing cracks her knuckles—she knows she's losing her grip on the conversation. "Like you said, Loretta. Innocent until proven guilty." She glances up at the projected agenda. "Are we done here?"

"We still have the memorial to discuss." I highlight the words on my laptop so that they glow yellow on the screen.

Diane shakes her head as she screws the lid back onto her nut jar. "The kids don't need a reminder of that, Maureen. They're trying to move forward, not backward, you know?"

Unsurprisingly, Peggy agrees. "They have college to think about."

"Everyone already feels so bad about the whole thing. They deserve to just be kids again." Loretta points at my laptop. "Maybe we can do a fundraiser for suicide prevention or something. What do they call that charity website? The one people were using after the blizzard?"

"GoFundMe," Peggy offers.

Loretta snaps her fingers. "There you go! We can do a GoFundMe."

Cushing leans over and closes my laptop with one extended pointer finger. The screen turns white in front of us. "Well, sounds like that's settled."

Peggy starts a dainty clap, and the other two women join in. "I love a productive meeting," she says.

"What just happened?" Layla asks as the women pick their handbags up off the floor and discuss what group exercise class to attend in the morning. "Did we get played?"

"We got fucking steamrolled." They push open the gymnasium doors, and I picture myself strangling each of their sun-wrinkled necks with a pink resistance band. Diane would be the only one I'd really have to wrestle with. The other two have the physique of a noodle.

A blunt clang echoes through the gym and we both turn. Cushing's got a table on its side, her toe poised above its metal skeleton. She kicks it until the bar finally folds.

"We've got that," Layla says. The two of us exchange a glance. "Don't worry about it."

"You have to kick them in just the right spot, or they don't collapse." She tilts another table to the ground, punts it with a metallic peal, and then goes to straighten the stack of blue gymnastic mats leaning against the wall.

Layla leaves to retrieve the dolly and I tip my own table over. I drive my toe into the metal hinge once, twice, three times, but nothing moves. "Motherfucker," I murmur.

Cushing appears beside me. "Let me do it," she says, and the legs fold with a single strike. We lower the tabletop to the ground together, each of our hands on a plastic corner. "I wish you had the tiniest shred of faith in me, Maureen."

"It's not a question of faith. It's a question of trust."

"There's a difference?"

Of course this godless woman couldn't understand. "Faith doesn't require proof. Trust does."

"And what haven't I given you proof of?"

"Your ability to keep these kids safe."

Cushing looks at me for a moment like I might say more. When I don't, she chuckles to herself and grinds the heel of one hand into an eyebrow. "You're a tough fucking customer, you know that?"

"I'm a mom."

"What, and I'm not?" I watch her heels dull the waxed floor as she crosses the room to tug the projector screen up. Then she drops to the floor with a sigh, her back against the wall. She takes off one boot and uses its rounded toe to massage the socked sole of her foot. "I'm on your side, you know." She pats the wall beside her and waits for me to join her. The brick's rough against my spine as I slide to the ground. "I know he did it. Rob." I open my mouth, but she raises her hand before I can speak. "The issue is the girl. She's begging me to just drop the whole thing. She doesn't think she can stay anonymous if we fire him." She plucks a piece of lint from her dress. "And she's probably right. The school newspaper's already threatening to launch their own investigation."

"Gossip dies down eventually," I say.

Cushing rolls her eyes. "Sure it does. But the funny thing is that it's not even the kids she's afraid of."

"Who, then?"

"Who do you think?" She looks at me but I just shrug. "Her mom. She thinks the news will kill her."

I press my head back into the wall and stare at the ceiling. The basketball-championship banners flap like sails as the AC kicks on. "She's probably right."

"Yeah," Cushing says. "She probably is." We're silent for a moment, and I can hear the electric buzz of the vending machines plugged into the other side of the wall. She turns her cheek toward me. "Emma will be just fine, you know."

God, what I wouldn't give to believe that. "Olivia will be, too."

Cushing's eyes turn hard and glassy like marbles. "She wants to murder me for sending her to this new school."

Perhaps that's one thing Cushing and I both understand: what it's like to have a daughter who hates you for helping her. "It doesn't matter what she wants. You're her mother."

A beam of light falls across our foreheads, and I turn to see Layla standing in the doorway, the dolly beside her. "What're you guys doing?" she asks.

"Nothing." Cushing jams on her boot and rises to her feet. "I should really be going."

"What was that all about?" Layla asks when she's gone. "It looked like a heart-to-heart." We carry the tables together to the dolly.

"Just her attempt at placation."

"Did it work?"

"Get the fuck out of here. *Did it work.*" We retrieve the final table and slot it into the row, which looks like a line of tipped dominoes.

"So, no." Layla pushes the cart forward.

"No."

Outside in the hallway, past the trophy case and cage of basketballs and framed photo of Coach's face, a woman is sitting on the stairs that lead to the top row of bleachers. The student council's holding a spirit day for the first football game on Friday, and the railing is already strung with metallic tassels in the school colors, blue and white. The string near her elbow is bare, and a little pile of plastic shreds sits at her feet. She grinds one black boot into the heap as she stands. "Hey, are you guys with the PTA?"

She looks vaguely familiar, but then again so does everyone in town. "Yes," I say cautiously, because sometimes the buttoned-up moms like to come and yell at us about the after-school (optional!) sex-ed workshop I fought tooth and nail for last year. You think it'd been called Bring on the Sluts! for all the brouhaha it caused.

"I'm Lucy Anderson's mom." She says this hesitantly, like she's not sure if this is a card she wants to reveal. "I saw that the memorial was on the agenda for today, and I was hoping I could listen in."

Of course. I've never seen her in person, only a grainy newspaper photo.

"You saw it on the Google site?" Layla asks proudly, sending a glance my way while she says it. She insisted we needed a website so that the larger school population could see what we were up to. I didn't have the heart to tell her that the larger school population doesn't give a single fuck about what we're up to unless it involves sex or drugs.

The woman nods. "I'm Brynn." She extends her hand, and we both shake. I'm surprised by the solid grip of her fingers.

"Unfortunately, the meeting ended early," I say. "We didn't quite get to the memorial."

Brynn's wearing a plaid jacket about three sizes too big for her—I guess that's the style now—and shoves her hands into its wide pockets. "Maybe that's for the best. Her father and I would prefer there's no physical memorial on the school grounds."

I can't hide my surprise. "That's the least they could do, after everything that happened." I feel my neck turkeying and straighten my posture. "Or didn't happen, I should say."

Layla looks at me with those eyes that mean: Don't get fired up. She tells us she needs to get home to review essays, but is there anything else I need from her? She's been a nutcase about work ever since they tried to fire her. "No, no. Get yourself home." I put my hand over Brynn's, and she only flinches a little. "Hey, what about you and I grab a drink?"

MURPHY'S IS CLOSED ON MONDAYS, so we go to O'Dooley's instead. Not my first choice—it smells like basement carpet and toenail clippings—but where else are we going to go, that stuck-up wine bar that opened across the street?

"My husband used to be a frequent flyer here," Brynn says as I push open the front door, and I know what that means: alkie. It's a good sign, that she's told me this. She trusts me.

Rae's working and tells us to pick whatever booth we like, which is no surprise because they're all empty. "How are you?" she asks Brynn as we're about to walk away.

"I'm great." Her smile's so forced I half expect her lips to tear. "Oh, and thanks for keeping Charlie company. He gets lonely so easily."

Rae twists a pen that's stabbed through her bun. "I'm really not over there very often. But, yeah. You're welcome. He's actually doing pretty good."

"Sure," Brynn says airily, and then she tilts her head in a way that means I should lead us to our seats.

I choose the one that has the least tears in the leather cushions. It's a shame that Freddie doesn't take any pride in the appearance of the place. It's not enough to have cheap beer these days. People want atmosphere.

"You've got history with Rae?" I ask.

"You could say that." Brynn slides into the seat across from me. "She was kind of like family, once upon a time."

"Once upon a time," I echo, but she doesn't elaborate, so I offer an interpretation of my own. "She's fucking your husband?" I ask, though Rae's never seemed like a husband fucker to me.

"I highly doubt it. We're separated anyway." She shrugs off her enormous coat and pushes it into a pile beside her. "We were having issues even before all of this."

"Because of the drinking."

She raises her eyebrows delicately. I'm being too forward. "Partially, yeah." Rae brings us both a water, and Brynn takes a long sip from hers. "So what about you? Are you married?"

"We got divorced ages ago. He lives in Nevada now. But I've got a girl in Lucy's class, actually."

For a second I regret saying that—it feels like I'm bragging: Look at me! My kid's still alive and well! But Brynn doesn't seem to mind. "How's her year going?"

"Oh, fine. I mean, she's gotten mixed up in some shit, but what kid hasn't?"

Brynn looks out the window beside us, where you can see the docks and then the lighthouse if you really squint. But Freddie's gotten so lazy that the glass is covered with a thick smear of dust and beer-stained fingerprints. "What'd she get mixed up in, if you don't mind my asking?"

"Of course I don't mind," I say, but my stomach's got that wobbly feeling. I flick my straw aside and take a big gulp of water directly from the glass. "Ah, just shit on the internet."

Brynn's face inclines toward mine. She is a very graceful person, I'm realizing—every time she moves it's poised and elegant, like a ballerina. "That's a very large category, shit on the internet."

That refined face of hers is making me nervous. I feel huge and sweaty and graceless, an ape at the table. "I mean, just sending weird things, specifically." I get that twitch in my chin that comes on when I kneel in the confessional booth, staring at the thin, grated partition between me and Father Paul. I'd think the whole ceremony was bullshit if not for the real and total relief that floods in when he tells me that the Lord forgives me. It feels unspeakably good to know someone else does, because I sure as hell can't.

Rae returns to our table to take our orders. Brynn goes first, and I say I'll have whatever she's having, which is something I don't hear because I'm focusing on the soggy coaster beneath my water glass, the scratched varnish on the table, the dried piece of gum stuck to the napkin holder, anything to keep my mind on what's happening instead of what's happened.

"What weird things?" Brynn presses.

I see myself at Emma's desk while she's in the shower. I'm sitting down on her pink rolling chair, I'm opening her laptop, I'm flicking the crumbs from her keyboard. I'm entering her password, which she thinks I don't know: *knot4U2cb!tch.* I'm looking for the email about SAT prep she "forgot" to forward me, the one with her practice-test scores. I'm clicking her text messages closed, barely registering the action because I so badly want to see how she did. I'm ignoring the text messages continuing to stream in, *ping ping ping ping ping.* I'm exhaling through my nose because I can't concentrate on her inbox with all of this chaos. I'm clicking open the messages to see what all the fuss is about. I'm reading the texting version of laughter: *hahaha lmao lololol HA rofl.* I'm picking the first text and scrolling up for context. I'm playing a video that I don't understand at first: just a blurry walkway between the seats of a school bus. But then I'm watching it pan to the ground. I'm watching a figure shake. I'm hearing someone shout. I'm hearing pulsing dance music that drowns out the shout. I'm hearing my own shaky breath. I'm watching the figure thrash, and I see now that it's a girl, and that the music is meant as a soundtrack to her seizure. I'm digesting all of this, my fingernails scraping half-moons into Emma's desk, my head shaking *no, no, no,* when her door opens and she's standing there in her towel, water dribbling from the ends of her hair to the floor. She looks young and stupid and responsible. *What the fuck?* she's shrieking, rushing to the laptop. *What, I'm asking, did you do?*

"I said: 'What weird things?'" Brynn repeats.

"You know." I feel drunk and high and everything else that frizzles your senses. "Inappropriate chats. That kind of thing."

Brynn nods. "It's so dangerous out there, isn't it?"

"It really is," I manage to say.

Rae comes back with two white wines that I know are warm just by looking at them. "Chardonnay for my ladies." She places the glasses in front of us and gives the table a little pat before walking away. If Rae knew she'd never let me step foot in this bar again.

"Are you okay?" Brynn asks.

"I'm fine. So, the memorial," I say, straightening up, trying to imitate her posture. "What's the issue?"

"To be completely honest with you, school wasn't the happiest place for Lucy." She places the glass's stem between the slit of two fingers and raises it to her mouth. "I don't think a statue, a sign—whatever other bullshit Cushing comes up with—would be appropriate."

"But don't you want something to sustain her memory? Something you have control over?"

"I don't have control over anything," she says. "If I did, my daughter would still be here."

I'm flailing. "But what about her friends?" I try.

"Her friends don't need an ugly plaque and a bunch of dying flowers to remember Lucy." I'm losing her fast. She taps her pink nails against the tabletop; she looks out the window again.

"What about something to do with her art?" I'm striving, reaching. All of the articles mentioned her paintings.

"Those were an escape from everything. It seems almost, I don't know, *violent* to trap them at school." She smiles and takes a sip of her wine. "I don't mean to sound rude, but . . . why do you care?"

I'm telling Emma to wait in the living room. After the divorce, I turned the bottom level into a separate apartment to boost our finances—lord knows Kevin's child support wouldn't be reliable—and I'm wishing we had a downstairs I could banish her to. I don't want to be near her. I'm hearing Lloyd peek his head out of his room and ask what's going on. I'm hearing Emma say, Shut up, none of your business. I'm scrolling through the texts, I'm trying to calculate how many people have seen the video, I'm realizing that I should multiply every pasted freeze-frame by two or three or four, I'm realizing that the number will only grow with each second that passes, I'm realizing that what I thought my daughter did at this desk is extremely different from reality. But what I don't realize yet, what is only slowly dawning on me, is that nothing dies on the internet. Everything, immediately: eternal.

Brynn's looking at me expectantly. The wine is spewing its rotten scent across the table. The sweat on my palms is dripping into the cut on my pinky. My ribs are tightening around my guts like a corset. "I'm the PTA president," I tell her. "It's my job to care."

AT HOME, LLOYD'S EATING a Fruit Roll-Up on the couch. I drop my purse on the floor and ask him if he remembers what

I said about Fruit Roll-Ups before dinner, to which he goes, "What dinner?" and raises his hand above his eyes, searching the room like a sailor. Eight's turned out to be a particularly sassy age.

"Don't be a smart-ass," I tell him. "It's unbecoming. Where's your sister?"

He shrugs and points to the closed door of her room. "In there, I think."

"You think or you know? Did she vanish after walking you home?"

He squints his eyes at me. "Why is nobody allowed to be rude except for you?"

Any other day I would actually entertain this conversation. But not today. "Go to your room."

"No," he says. He picks up the remote and turns on the television and Jesus Christ my blood just might boil out of my veins. I carried you for nine months in my very body! I wiped your ass and sucked out your snot and sang you to sleep and this, *this* is how you repay me? For all the shit I hid you from, including your fuckup of a father, who, may I remind you, requested *not* to see you? Do you know how goddamn lucky you are to have me?

"Well don't explode about it," he says, eyeing my face. "Geez, I'm going, I'm going."

I take the deepest breath I've had in weeks and walk to Emma's door. "It's me," I say.

"What?"

"Can I come in?"

A pause. Hurried shuffling behind the door, rearranging. "Fine."

All the blinds are pulled shut and the space heater she insisted on is pumping away in the corner, making the room at least eighty degrees. She's hunched in her pink desk chair, wearing only boxer shorts (who knows from where) and a thin white tank top. I sit on her bed, which is still covered with stuffed dogs, despite her saying every Christmas that she's going to donate them. I fluff the ears of the oldest one, Snowflake. "You know, if you wore normal clothes, you wouldn't need that heater."

"What are normal clothes?" she asks, not looking up from her laptop. "The potato sacks you wear?"

"Ouch."

"It's not a lie."

"I didn't say it was." She ignores me. The only sounds are the clacking of her keys and the hiss of the heater. "What are you working on?"

"Homework."

"Did you have a good day at school?"

"It was fine."

"Any news?"

She stops typing and swivels around in her seat. "If you want intel, just ask me for intel. Which I have none of, for the record. I don't know about Mr. Taylor, and no one's even talked about Lucy since school started." She whips back around and starts typing again.

What a liar she is. Where did she learn it from? I sometimes wonder. "I met Lucy's mom today."

Her shoulders raise an inch but she keeps typing. "Yeah?"

"Mm-hmm."

She doesn't turn around, but I feel a question formulating. You can always tell when your kid is trying to figure out how to talk to you. "Was it weird?" she asks finally. Her hands pull away from the keyboard. I'm in.

"A little, yeah."

Em drops a bare foot to the floor and slowly rotates toward me. "Did you tell her I was sorry?"

"She doesn't know it was you, hon."

"You always say that, but I just have this feeling she does."

I give her a good, long look, which I rarely have the privilege of doing, what with all the closed doors and hoodies and hair in the eyes. Her milky, undefined face, all soft curves and baby fat, just begging to be shaped. Her curled body like an unsprouted seed. By the time I was her age, I'd crashed a car without a license, caught my mother with a man who wasn't my father, had an abortion, tripped on acid, hitchhiked up the California coast, watched my grandmother die, broken my ankle skiing down a mountain, swum naked in the January ocean. Whenever she comes home from school, this is exactly where she wants to be: sitting in the blue glow of her computer, alone.

"Why are you looking at me like that?" she asks.

When I asked her why, this is what she told me: I wanted them to see me. What are you talking about? I asked. Sure, Em wasn't queen bee Ms. Popular, but she had friends—other pale skinny girls that held their screens too close to their faces. They don't count, she said, talking about Jessica and Louise and Holly. Everyone *counts*, I protested, and she actually got mad, lit up with this hot ball of anger whose lineage I knew all too well. No! she shouted, so loudly that I told her to quiet down, she would wake up Lloyd. No, she said again, softer. No one knows you exist until you give them something. My mouth went a little dry when she said that. And what did you give them? I asked. She didn't even look ashamed when she said it: Something to laugh at.

"I *am* sorry," she says. "I mean, you know that, right?" She looks suddenly shaken, and I feel like I'm much farther from her than the other side of the room.

"I know you are, Em. I know." I stand up and go to pat her head, but she grabs my wrist when it starts to descend.

"I don't know what you want me to do," she says. "You look at me like I'm this disgusting little alien."

"Em, let go."

"Are you going to hate me forever?" Her whole body starts to shake. "I only did what you told me to!"

I jerk my wrist away, and her hand slaps against her own chest. I mean to say *I don't hate you*, but what comes out is: "That's enough."

"I wanted to tell Lucy," she says softly. "Now I can't even apologize."

Is that what would have eventually happened, I wonder, if I hadn't been there? Shouting at Em to put on her pajamas, to get dressed and explain what the hell I'm looking at. Her shouting back at me that it's just a joke while she lobs sweatpants at the floor, screaming that I don't understand anything, then crying, sobbing, exploding: Stop making me feel bad! Stop, stop, stop. In the middle of it all, Lloyd cracking open the door, asking if we're okay. It's March and he's just turned eight and I'm thinking: *Please don't turn out like your sister.* We're fine, I'm saying, and then Em shuts the door in his face. When the door closes, a wave of clarity rushes through me, like I've huffed smelling salts. I see exactly how the next month plays out: The girl's parents will go to the school, who will attempt to sniff out the source, given the pledge we signed to fight cyberbullying just six months ago. The other kids will sell out Em, given her lack of social capital. She's weak under pressure: She'll cave. The moms in the PTA will blindside me at a meeting, handing out their own agenda unexpectedly. The first item will be: *Petition to elect new president.*

Her only words accompanying the video were: *lol look at this.* Say someone else sent it to you, I'm telling her. She's still in her towel, every soft item of clothing she owns heaped on the floor. Blame it on one of the exchange students. Say they have a different sense of humor.

She sits down on the bed and doesn't say anything. Is that what you want to be remembered for? I'm asking, and there she goes. She's crying again.

I'm picking up the laptop and dropping it on her damp lap. Who's the weird one? I'm asking. Marco?

Every spring we host a group of exchange students from outside of Rome, who don't do much besides terrify their host parents by sneaking out to get fucked up on the beach at midnight. It's something Cushing started years ago—cultural exchange, my ass.

She nods without looking up at me. I think he's on the spectrum, she says quietly.

He'll be gone in a week. I'm leaning forward to open the laptop now; I'm tapping the screen to life. It doesn't matter what he does here.

I'm standing by the door as she types out her messages. I know Lloyd is sitting on the other side with his ear pressed to the wood, trying to piece together a story from slices of our words. I couldn't sleep! he'll exclaim when I finally open the door.

Later that night, I'll feel so nauseated that I'll dangle my head over the toilet for hours, waiting to purge something that never rises up out of me, of course not, because I'm not sick in the body. I'm sick in the spirit. I'm a liar and a traitor and a snake and everything else I tell my daughter not to be. But, God, I've spent my whole life getting screwed. When I was nine my dad dropped me off at my grandparents', this time for good, and that man really told me: You're on your own now. And you know what? He was right. My ex tried to trick me into thinking we were all in this together, kumbaya, peace and love, but no! Never! The only person you know will be by your side is the one fucker you can't get rid of even if you wanted to. And she stared right back at me in the toilet water.

"I need to do my homework," Em says. She swivels back to her desk, sniffling and pulling at her eyelid like she does when her contact's been in too long. "Can you just leave me alone?"

"Em—" I try, but she raises up one hand.

"All I want," she says slowly, "is to be as far away from you as possible."

She still believes she can wound me. Let her think so.

I push open her door, but it bumps against something in the hallway. I take a step forward and there's Lloyd, full deer-in-the-headlights pupils. "Listen," he says, crawling backward. "My room was really boring."

I sigh and wave him forward. "Let's just get dinner going, shall we?"

We move to the kitchen, and Lloyd sits at the counter while I search the refrigerator for a vegetable. The crisper drawer's empty except for a few shriveled-up carrots and a crown of molding broccoli. I wish Em would get her driver's license so she can do the shopping, but she refuses. Driving makes her anxious, of all things. Since when did freedom worry anyone?

"Why aren't you like that with me?" he asks.

"Like what?"

"Like how you are with Em."

"How am I with Em?" I close the fridge and turn around. Lloyd's sitting at full attention, hands crossed neatly in front of him. He's such a little weirdo—a tiny man in kid's clothing. Not like us at all.

"It's kind of like you're"—he presses his pointer finger to his lip, considering—"scared of her?"

I can't help laughing. "Why would I be scared of my own daughter?"

"That's what I thought," he says. "I thought you weren't scared of anything."

I'm a sucker—I melt when he says that, my chest going warm with affection. I lean across the counter to kiss him on the forehead, which he receives with a scrunched face. "Your mom's pretty tough, isn't she?"

Lloyd's no fool. He never agrees to something without thinking about it. He chews on his bottom lip while he considers, and I can see the gummy hole where his tooth fell out last week. For some reason, those are the only things he doesn't question—the tooth fairy, Easter Bunny, Santa Claus. "Em's tougher," he finally says.

I'm so taken aback that for a second I don't know what to say. "I didn't realize it was a competition."

"You're always competing," Lloyd says, in this startled tone that implies I've forgotten a very obvious and crucial piece of information. A tone that says: You know who you are, don't you?

THE NEXT DAY I GO to confession after work. I work at the Lighthouse Cinema downtown doing their finances, which get bleaker every day. We've only got two screens and they can't even pack those out on a regular basis. Everyone wants the reclining seats and the drink service at the new theater two towns over, which just shows you how soft we're getting. I like the stiff red chairs at Lighthouse that make your back ache. It helps you pay attention, since the programming staff insists on only showing indie films where skinny people in linen lament how empty their huge modern houses are.

The Lighthouse is right in the heart of the harbor, which makes it easy to walk to St. Mary's. I cross over Main and follow the sidewalk to the church's property, which is sandwiched between the two roads leading out of town, 5A and West Avenue. I dip my fingers into the holy water at the top of the stone stairs and get in line, which is only two people deep. Based on the number of people I see here—and by that I mean the *lack* thereof—you'd think this town was populated exclusively by archangels and the twelve disciples themselves.

I'm trying not to fidget with my hands too much (I get twitchy without a task) when who do I see but Janet Cushing leaving the confessional. "I didn't know you were Catholic," I can't help saying as she walks by.

She turns in surprise. "I don't make it to Mass as much as I'd like." She's wearing a leather skirt with her white blouse, which seems inappropriate for both school and church, and I know my eyes are lingering on it. She smooths the black fabric.

"It's good for us," I tell her.

"I know," she says, overenunciating the words like I'm slow on the uptake. "It's church."

The old lady in front of me shuffles forward, and I move closer to the nave's domed doorway, which Em called the gumdrop when she was little. Now she won't step foot in here. "How do you feel?" I ask Cushing. She hasn't moved, so there's a good four feet between us. "Absolved?"

She crosses her arms (unsurprising, given that thin little blouse she has on). "I don't believe in exoneration," she says. "Only accountability."

"Wow, you really are a principal."

She cracks a smile at that! I'm stunned. The ice queen melts before me. "A bad one, many would say." She raises a combed eyebrow. "You, for example."

"No, no. Haven't you heard? I'm a Catholic. I don't talk shit about anyone." The old lady glares over her shoulder when I cuss.

Cushing walks toward me then, her pin-thin heels striking the tile floor. She looks suddenly very serious, like she did when she first walked into the PTA meeting. "I want you to hear this from me first," she says, dropping her voice to a whisper. "Rob's going to take a sabbatical until the spring semester."

I would be surprised, if only my ability to be shocked at such things hadn't been drained out of my body long ago. "And then he'll be back?"

"I think that, with some time away, he probably won't *want* to come back." She raises her palms. "It's the best I could do. The parents and kids love him. And without the girl coming publicly forward, the accusations seem a bit . . . abstract. But I tried, Maureen. Really, I did."

"Yes, that much seems apparent."

She looks up at the ceiling, which is a mural of the Virgin Mary. She's visible from the waist up, the rest of her body covered in clouds, wearing a pink robe and blue headscarf. You know a man painted her because she has this empty, faux-serene expression on her face that conveys absolutely nothing besides: I am here to sacrifice. A miserable image.

"Can I give you some advice?" she asks, gaze still trained upward, like we're in a planetarium. "Just worry about your own daughter. If it's not your job to worry about the other students, then don't."

Normally, I would fight this. But sometimes you see another human and sense what shaped them, like looking at a painting and discerning the brushstrokes. No one protected her. And this is something our own daughters will never understand. That we were never girls, not really. For a moment we were children, yes. But a girl and a child are not the same. A child is a pet. A girl is prey.

"Next," a soft voice calls. I look ahead of me and the old lady is gone—all the entryway frames is an empty line of pews. The damp air that hangs in stone buildings blows through the lobby, and Cushing presses her hands together, blows on them. It's difficult to hate a person once you start to understand their origins. Look at what we've made, from a set of circumstances we had no hand in choosing.

"That's you. I don't think your sins get forgiven if you make the priest wait."

"Stay safe out there," I tell her.

"Same to you." She heaves the huge wooden door open, the fall air lifting her hair to her ears. I can hear her heels click down the outside stairs even after it closes. Father John is calling my name now, because I'm the only one that would hold up confession. The narthex smells like smoked incense and wet rocks, and when I take my place beside the latticed grate I have trouble remembering what exactly it is that I wanted to say.

WHEN I GET HOME, the couch is empty and the television is off. "Children?" I call. "Offspring?"

I pick some of Lloyd's Legos up off the carpet and slip my heels into my hand. In the hallway I can hear the muffled murmuring of closed-door conversation, probably Em FaceTiming one of her nervous friends—I swear all they talk about is their never-ending apprehensions. I kneel down and press my ear into the wood just below the doorknob. In a single-parent household, you only have so many sources of information.

"And then he got so busy, he had to take a private plane to New York City," I hear Em's high, trembly voice say. "And he really wanted to take us, but there was only one open seat on the plane."

"How fast did the plane go?" asks Lloyd, eager and hurried, his words rushing into one another.

"Five hundred miles per hour."

"Woah."

"Yeah. And you were too little to remember, but one time he flew back this huge cake that had an *E* and an *L* on it and sprinkles everywhere."

"Was it vanilla?"

"It was."

"Does he take lots of private planes?"

"*Only* private planes, Lloyd. You see, he's actually very scared of flying, and so the only way he feels comfortable doing it is if he's completely alone and they turn out the lights and close the shades." A pause. "That's why he can't visit us right now, you know. There's a private-plane shortage."

My knees press deeper into the floor. Don't tell Lloyd, Em had said at the beginning of the school year, when I told her their father wouldn't be making his yearly visit. Let me break it to him.

"I thought you said he was busy running the zoo." I can feel my eyebrows pull together. Kevin works in animal control. At least, he did a year ago.

"Well, that, too, of course. But that's only half of it, Lloyd. He wouldn't just let *work* keep him away. Do you know he actually tried to ride a horse to us? But the horse got too tired, and Dad had to turn back around."

Is Lloyd buying this? I scrape my ear against the door. Maybe Em offers what the tooth fairy and Santa Claus do—magic worth believing in.

"So he's just scared?" Lloyd asks. "Scared of planes?"

"Yep, just a little spooked. But you know what it's like to be scared, don't you?"

"Yes," Lloyd says quietly.

"Dad just needs a little courage. And he'll find it, eventually."

For a few moments all I can hear is the hissing of her space heater. Lloyd's thinking those words over. "You promise?"

Em doesn't even hesitate. "I promise."

I pull my ear away and press my back against the door. My heels are still in my hand, and I fling them down the hallway toward my room. One of them slaps against the wall thanks to my shit aim, and I can hear their bodies shifting in the bedroom.

"Mom?" Em calls. "Are you home?"

For a second I don't say anything. I just lower my head to the ground and lie there on the cool hardwood, tension leaving my body like a balloon releasing air. The door pops open and hits me lightly on the hip. "What are you doing?" Em asks. Lloyd peeks out at me from behind her shoulder, chewing on his thumbnail.

"I wanted to listen to your story." She searches my eyes with tiny pupils, trying to figure out if she's in trouble. "I like your version," I say. "It's much better than mine."

She shifts her bare feet. "Are you sure?"

"Yes. Tell me how it ends."

"It can't *end*, Mom. It's us." Lloyd steps out from behind her and crouches beside my stomach. "C'mon, Em. Keep going."

I look over Lloyd and up at my daughter, who, for the first time in recent memory, holds my gaze. Don't spoil this for him, she seems to be saying. But I'm not thinking about Lloyd. I'm thinking: When did you grow up? How?

"Okay, Mom," Lloyd says, taking my hand. "The only rule is we have to listen. You can't make your little comments."

"Shh," Em says. And I close my eyes, ready to go wherever she takes us.

SOPHIA

I'M IN THE BATH AISLE at Walgreens when I see Mr. Taylor. It's eight o'clock on a Friday night and I'm looking for my special Aveeno soap they always sell out of, the one that smells like figs. I watch him out of the corner of my eye and wonder if he knows about the signs posted around school, the ones that say *Justice for Mr. Taylor!* in straight-up calligraphy, which is how you know a mom made them. There weren't any signs like that for Lucy. Just whispers behind closed bathroom stalls, offensive conspiracy theories published anonymously in the student newspaper, and endless taps on my shoulder. When I bent down to drink from the water fountain, when I took notes in class, when I pushed my plastic tray along the cafeteria's metal railing: tap, tap, tap. I couldn't believe they felt confident enough to touch me. But their questions were even bolder, which always began with some variation of How are you holding up? before moving to what they really wanted to know, which was: So, what do you think happened? That's when it all started to make sense to me. Of course these people had left her there. Because their sense of responsibility was so nonexistent that they didn't even feel shame about the party—instead they felt comfortable asking a dead girl's best friend if she thought she'd killed herself.

He tugs down an ugly beanie he's wearing so it covers the tops of his saucer ears. I don't know why everyone finds him so attractive—he's just another pale dude with messy hair and a tattoo on his bicep. I guess it has to be the tattoo. A sketched sword that you can barely see the tip of when he rolls up his sleeves to solve a problem on the whiteboard. Hints of things are always hotter than the things themselves, like the V of a pelvis above a waistband or a bra beneath a sheer shirt.

His eyes lift from the row of dandruff shampoos. What are you supposed to do when you see a sexual offender? Say hello? I do end up saying it: "Hello." And he gives this little robot-jerk of his arm: "Hi." I guess the thing about bad people is that they have to keep on living their lives until we decide what to do with them.

We both turn our attention back to our respective shelves. I stare at the salicylic acid body washes and salt scrubs for ingrown hairs until I hear his footsteps patter away. At the self-checkout machine, I pass my Aveeno soap over the red lines of the barcode scanner and pray that he's already crossed the street when I get outside. But then I move through the automatic doors and see that he's rounding the corner for the back parking lot instead. I try to keep my distance, but he picks up his pace and it occurs to me that he might think I'm following him. Should I say something? Just shout: I'm being normal! Not stalking you! But then why am I thinking about *his* anxieties? He should be thinking about *my* anxieties as a member of his apparently target sexual demographic!

Even though it's only November, it's started to snow, and I hurry along to my car, blinking wet flakes out of my eyelashes. I crouch behind the hood and watch Mr. Taylor get in his Subaru from across the lot, and it's when he pulls himself into the driver's seat, the interior lights illuminating his face, that I feel my fists clench. Because he doesn't look just tired or resigned or bored but actually sad. And how dare he? How dare he feel bad for himself when he nearly ruined Jane's life? When he didn't even get fired? I'd never even heard of a sabbatical until Principal Cushing wrote it in her email.

The inside of his car goes dark and the headlights flick on. I stay squatted beneath my side mirror as he backs out and exits the lot, his tires leaving melted streaks in the light snow. I wish Jane would let me take my revenge, which involves stalking him to his apartment and covering his front step with the dead frogs they keep in the bio fridge for dissection labs. Imagine coming out of your house to see a dozen pink amphibian bellies strewn across your welcome mat and red paint on the floor that says WE'RE WATCHING. You'd be scared shitless!

But Jane doesn't want to scare him shitless, is the problem. Jane doesn't think he did anything wrong.

I drive home with my box of soap on the passenger seat and think about what I should do if Brynn calls me. My dad's on a golfing trip for the weekend, so I'm home alone until Sunday, which means I've technically got forty-eight hours of freedom stretching in front of me. But lately I've been thinking it's not particularly healthy to spend multiple nights a week with my dead best friend's mom, especially since Lucy's death has turned Brynn into a kid. She was always one of those uptight, overly responsible parents—when we were in middle school, she'd check both Lucy's homework and mine before we could watch TV. But now she wants to drink pinot grigio and smoke joints and play this game she calls "Bazinga!," which involves throwing darts at her wall without a dart board. Plus, her apartment is one of the most depressing places I've been in my entire life, though of course I wouldn't tell her that. It's this huge concrete block that's supposed to be what Brynn calls Organic Modern but actually just looks like a fancy prison, one for old white guys who got caught insider trading.

The snow starts coming down thicker, and I turn up the speed of my windshield wipers. It's not impossible to see, but it's not exactly easy, and a trickle of sweat moves down my ribs. I always get a little nervous driving Graham's car, because when he gave it to me he said, Keep it safe, Blinkie, and I take those kinds of things seriously. He calls me Blinkie not because I blink a lot but because of "blink and you'll miss it." When I was in middle school, I got all hysterical when no one asked me to the winter dance, and Graham said that they were all idiots, that soon enough I'd be in such high demand that if a boy so much as blinked, I'd already be taken. Graham's good at making you feel better, even if he's lying. He lives in New York now, trying to be a director, and I miss him like crazy. Even when Graham was at UMass he'd drive down every other weekend to see me. Sometimes I wonder if I did something wrong, to lose him and Lucy in the same year. But Brynn says that's an unproductive way of thinking. According to her, the universe is an Etch A Sketch: a bunch of random powder we try to make into pretty shapes to avoid feeling dead inside.

I finally see my turn up in the distance and blow out a sigh of relief. Since everything happened, I get nervous doing things alone. I used to think that everyone was on the same page, that we agreed being human meant taking care of one another. But now I under-stand that a lot of people—maybe most people—think that being human just means taking care of yourself and those you've already decided have value. Which is why it seems likely that if I hit a patch of black ice and skidded into the maple tree across the road, no one would stop to help me.

I pull into our driveway and press the garage opener clipped to the visor. I wonder if Mr. Taylor's entering the parking lot behind his apartment building at the same time. I wonder if he's about to have a date over, because why purchase dandruff shampoo unless you're trying to make a good impression? I wonder if she looks like Jane. I wonder if she knows what he did, because it's not like you're legally obligated to disclose all the ways you're sketchy on a first date. I wonder if she fucks on the first date. I wonder if she rolls up his sleeve with her white teeth, very slowly, so you see the point, the blade, the grip.

Am *I* attracted to Mr. Taylor? No, I don't think so. I'm just bored.

The garage clicks shut behind me, and I push open the door to our front hallway, which is warm and bright. Dad's left me a note— *pasta in the fridge*—and I eat it on the couch without bothering to warm it up first. I consider whether it's too late to text Jane, but Jane's never doing anything (no offense to her), so I go for it. It'll be helpful to have a legitimate alibi when Brynn inevitably texts me in an hour—I'm no good at lying, says everyone.

Jane tells me she'll be over in thirty and asks if this is a sleepover situation, to which I say sure. We never hung out before Lucy. I'm only being honest when I say that I didn't really know she existed. Well, I knew she *existed*, but she was so quiet that I just assumed she was on drugs like the other silent girls in the back of my classrooms. I mean, do whatever you want to do—it's just not for me. I took Molly before the carnival sophomore year and projectile vomited all over the Tilt-a-Whirl, and when I thought I was finally done I stepped off the ride and yakked all over some woman's miniature border collie. Then I felt so bad for the dog that I tried to kiss its black rubbery lips. Ah-ha! its owner kept shouting. Ah!

Just when I think you can't possibly surprise me, there you go, Lucy said. She sat me down at a picnic table near the Ferris wheel and held a Coke to my lips.

Graham said it would be fun to do it together, I explained.

She shook her head. And where's Graham now?

I looked around at the candy-colored lights and steaming food stands and swinging rides. The bathroom, I said. He's probably in the bathroom.

Sure he is. She made me sip more soda through the straw. I hate that he does this to you.

My stomach should have been empty, but I felt its contents creeping toward my throat. Does what? I asked.

Includes you for just long enough to figure out what he'd rather be doing.

I think I'm gonna be sick.

She picked up an empty popcorn bucket off the ground and held it in front of me. I don't think casual drug use is your thing.

I WATCH A DOCUMENTARY about cults until Jane arrives. I can't understand why you'd follow someone who calls you a whore and drops your phone in a swimming pool when you try to call your family, but there are a lot of things I don't understand. The appeal of sporting events, people's obsession with lobster, thermo-dynamics. Why Lucy said she'd never do anything major without me, and then did exactly that.

The headlights of Jane's car are shining through the front window when I get the text from Brynn: *what r u up 2*. I write her back that I'm sorry, I'm busy tonight, and watch her speech bubble appear, disappear on the screen. Finally she says: *no worries, enjoy your evening*, and I try to swallow down the guilt that makes my throat feel swollen. I haven't figured out the right way to tell her that I can't be her daughter and she can't be my mom. So for now, we'll pretend.

Jane rings the doorbell and I carry her sleeping bag inside, which is covered in dusty snow. "It's like a blizzard out there," she says. "I could barely find your driveway." She pulls off her boots and jacket and I make sure her shoes go to the shoe rack, her coat to the coat closet. Even when Dad isn't here, I get the sense that he's still watching over everything, like an OCD Santa Claus.

I make us hot chocolate with peppermint schnapps from Graham's secret stash in his closet. He has a little board beneath his shoes where he used to hide all his liquor when he was in high school. Dad doesn't drink and is a little weird about it, so Graham still keeps some stuff up there, for emergencies. "Guess who I saw at Walgreens?" I ask when we've settled onto the couch with our mugs. I love Jane, but she's not very talkative, which means I have to lead the conversation. But she can go on about Mr. Taylor forever.

"Who?"

I raise my eyebrows and curl my lips suggestively, the facial equivalent of: Oh, you *know*.

"No," she says, leaning toward me. "Really?"

"He was buying dandruff shampoo." I feel warm and weirdly capable from dolling out my secret knowledge, like I could jump up and break our coffee table in two with my bare hand. Maybe it's just the schnapps.

"He didn't use to have dandruff," she says authoritatively. "I bet that's a stress thing."

"Is he still texting you?" I ask.

Now it's her turn to raise her eyebrows, which, combined with a head tilt, is the facial equivalent of: Do I have something to show you. She pulls her phone out of her pocket, taps open her messages, and holds it up to my face. An unknown number has sent her several messages, such as: *I need u 2 kno how sorry I am.* Or: *please please forgive me. i'm not a bad person.* Or: *y the fuck am I risking this if u won't even write me back.*

"Woof." I hand it back to her. "Why don't you block him?"

She looks at the phone so tenderly you'd think it was a golden-doodle puppy. "Oh, I don't know. That just seems unnecessarily cruel."

So here's the thing about Jane and Mr. Taylor. Even though I hate him, Jane wishes I didn't. She once talked over an entire three-hour marathon of *Buffy the Vampire Slayer* explaining why he's not a bad guy, not at all, and I guess as her friend, I should believe her. But the problem is that I want two things. The story where Jane's fine and the story where she gets justice, even if she doesn't believe that she needs it.

At school, no one knows she's the girl. The current running theories are Esther Lundiman, our school slut (not my designation, just an accepted superlative), Chiara Ricci, hottest exchange student (again, not my personal designation but an accepted superlative), or Olivia Cushing, because she's unhinged enough to fuck a teacher just to get on her mom's nerves. Olivia's probably the most popular opinion, because she switched schools and Principal Cushing's been keeping the whole thing super hush-hush. I practically piss my pants whenever she passes me in the hallway, but Jane says she's actually really nice. Not that I trust Jane's character judgments.

"Do you think you'll ever see him again?" I ask.

Jane puts the phone down and considers this. "I don't know. It'd have to be in, like, New York City or something. Somewhere totally anonymous."

"I want to lose my virginity in New York City," I hear myself telling her. This was actually Lucy's idea, right before everything happened. We'd been secretly going to the after-school safe-sex workshop, and we were walking home after having successfully unrolled condoms on two spotted bananas. We know the first time's going to be shit, she said. So why don't we just go somewhere fun and get drunk and meet some random guys we'll never see again? That's why I hate this place, she said, her face going hard. Anything you do becomes this stain that sticks to you forever.

Jane looks more interested than she's been all night. "Really?"

"Yeah," I say. "Go somewhere fun and get drunk and meet some random guys I'll never see again."

"*Guys?*" she says, all scandalized.

"Guy. I meant guy."

"Okay, wait." We're sitting on opposite sides of the couch facing each other, our legs pretzeled, and she presses her hands into my knees. "I know this sounds crazy, but what if we went to New York this weekend?"

It occurs to me that you have to be crazy to date a teacher. "What, are you serious?"

"Yes!" She bounces up and down, and a little of my hot chocolate dribbles over the rim. "Your Dad's not home, and my mom never knows where I am anyway."

I don't want to seem as lame as I am, so I point to the window. "But it's snowing."

"Who cares? Do you melt?" She laughs. "And your brother's there, too, right? It's perfect!"

One of the ways Jane and I are different: When she wants something, she'll blow through every single roadblock to get it. Me? I hit a roadblock and try to stop wanting the thing that brought me to it. "How would we even get there though?"

She presses more heavily into my knees. It hurts. "The train! Go to South Station and take Amtrak. It's a straight shot." She picks up her phone. "I'm going to buy our tickets now. I have money from the Market; you can pay me back whenever."

"Uh-uh," I'm saying.

She taps a button and grins. "Done!" I don't think of Jane as a squealer, but there she is, squealing; there I am, following her lead; there we are, holding each other's arms and jumping up and down on the couch like we've never, *ever* been more excited for anything in our entire lives.

AT SOUTH STATION we join the crowd of people staring up at the automatic timetable hanging from the ceiling. Dad and I don't come into town very often, and when we do, we drive. A man in a tan overcoat pushes me into one of the metal café tables they have all over the concourse, a woman with a Yorkie shoved under her arm jostles past me to get to the Starbucks line, a weirdly confident kindergartener tries to sell me a Twix from his pocket. There are little kiosks with green roofs everywhere—a magazine stand stacked with covers so glossy they reflect the station's fluorescent lighting, a coffee shop counter lined with pour-over sets the shape of hour-glasses, a bakery with chocolate chip cookies the size of dinner plates. I hold my duffel bag tight to my ribs because Dad says the city is full of pickpockets. I'm sure he's exaggerating, but it does seem pretty easy to take whatever you want in this sea of people. I try to take a deep breath, but everything smells like burning bagels and exhaust from the trains outside. Jane seems unfazed by it all, even though she's never been anywhere besides Connecticut and New Hampshire, to visit her cousins. I wonder what would faze her. Ever since we've become friends, I've never once seen her shaken.

"Track five," she says, taking my arm. "Let's go!" All she has is her backpack, the one she brought for the sleepover, and it's much easier for her to run than me. Why are we running, anyway? Are we late? Are we going to miss it?

"We're just having fun!" She shoves open the huge doors that lead to the tracks. "Come on!"

It's not snowing anymore, but the air still has a bite to it. I bury my chin in my scarf and think: *Fun! We're just having fun!* Because my stomach is rolling like I might throw up.

Outside, there are loud whistles and chugging engines and people who are actually late sprinting down the long narrow plat-forms. A low, automated voice announces last calls, and conductors lean out open doors shouting the same thing. They actually do wear those little caps with the puffy tops. Apparently I stare too long at the caps because Jane grabs my wrist and shouts, "Hurry up!"

Our train's sprayed with dirt, and someone's traced *love lies!* on it with their finger. Jane has our tickets on her phone, so we go straight inside, only I notice that she's not leading us to Car E, which is where our seats are. "Hey," I ask, "where are we going?"

She presses a button and the doors to the next compartment open automatically. "To the café car."

The train ride to New York is four hours long, and we spend it all in the café car. It's only ten in the morning and I'm already exhausted from our day, which involved packing my bag, locking the house, double-checking that I'd locked the house, driving to the train station, lying to my dad when he texted *good morning!*, riding the commuter rail into South Station, weaving through all the bodies at South Station, and finally plopping into this little metal booth with sweat all over my side from scrunching my duffel against my coat.

I fall asleep for a couple hours. When I wake up, Jane's handing me a coffee in a small paper cup that says *Amtrak* on the sleeve. "You should call your brother," she says. "So you have somewhere to sleep."

"So both of us do, yeah?" I rub the grit out of my eyes. Graham's rarely up before noon, but he'll be awake now, probably smoking a CBD cigarette with his coffee. He's very into CBD now—he says it's pot's straight-edge sister. I slide my phone out of my pocket and so does Jane.

"I'll be with Rob," she says, extremely casually. "It's not like anyone's keeping tabs on him during the sabbatical."

"What?" I try not to sound too startled as I look up from my coffee.

"Isn't that the whole plan?" she says. "We'll both lose our virginity in New York!" She whispers this last part, leaning across the wobbly table.

I feel like I did that time on the Tilt-a-Whirl, right before I spewed my Molly-laced vomit across its spinning metal sides. Like my mind had been diced into tiny pieces and I could only hold on to the smallest shreds of comprehension. "What?" I say again.

Jane falls back into her seat. "Who knows what will happen. But I just need closure, you know?"

In my personal opinion, no one *needs* closure; they need to accept that whatever they wish still existed is actually dead in the water. But if you go around telling people harsh truths, they tend to get offended, so I just go, "Uh-huh," and try to pull the confetti pieces of my thoughts back together. "Let me call Graham."

He picks up on the first ring. "Blinkie!" He sings my name a couple of times, going high and then low, like he's doing scales.

"Listen, I did something a little crazy."

"What, you forget to return a library book?"

"Ha ha." Jane's texting, and I raise my head to try and get a look at her screen, but then she pulls the phone into her lap. "I'm actually on a train to New York right now. Dad doesn't know."

He's silent for a moment, and then pretends to cry. "Blinkie," he says through fake tears, "I've never been more proud of you."

"Yeah, thanks." I roll my eyes. "Can I stay with you, just for a night? It's me and my friend Jane."

His voice goes all faux serious now. "It would be an honor to host you and your compatriot."

Jane looks up and mouths *not me*, waving her hands, but I ignore her. "Thanks, Graham."

"Where are you getting in? Penn Station?"

I mouth *Penn Station* at her, and she shrugs. "I think so?"

"You're on the train, not the bus?" I confirm this. "Okay, Penn Station it is. What time?"

I try to get Jane's attention, but she's too busy texting. "Uh, I'm not sure."

"Blinkie! This city's going to eat you alive."

"I'll text you. I'm not in charge of the . . . itinerary."

"Hey, just—" his voice shifts into something that's actually serious. He sounds like Dad. "Just be careful, okay?"

"I'm fine, Graham. I always am." I try to sound upbeat, but it just makes my voice turn more bitter.

I hear him swallow over the line. "I know, Soph. I'll see you soon."

. . .

WE PULL INTO PENN STATION at 2:09 p.m., exactly eleven minutes earlier than what I ended up telling Graham. Everyone lined up to exit twenty minutes before we even got there—I thought they were all using the bathroom—and so Jane and I are pressed up against the café car's counter waiting to leave. It's taking so long that I start getting worried the train's going to back up toward Boston and we'll be stuck on the return trip, a useless, stupid loop of a day, but then Jane touches my shoulder.

"We made it!" All it takes is her fingers on my sleeve and that excitement flows from her hand to my bloodstream. Just like with Lucy—I felt whatever she did. I don't know if that's one of my worst qualities or my best. Everyone talks about easily influenced people like they're weak, but I think clinging to your own thoughts and feelings is a different kind of weakness. I like being pulled into someone else's world.

We're finally at the little door with the porthole, and Jane easily steps onto the yellow caution line.

"Come on," she says from the other side. "Aren't you coming?"

I know there's only an inch between the train and the platform, but it feels wider and dangerous, like a whirlpool's swirling there, threatening to suck me down to the tracks.

Jane holds out her hand. "It's just a step," she says.

I know. I close my eyes, clutch my duffel, and jump.

GRAHAM'S WAITING FOR US like he said he'd be, which is a relief. He waves from a silver pole in the corner, wearing a crinkly leather jacket that looks way too light for this weather. I glance over at Jane because she seems like someone who would freak over older men in leather jackets, but she's twirling in circles looking at all the people crammed into this tiny hallway.

I haven't seen Graham since the funeral, which is the only time I've ever seen him cry. He loved Lucy. The three of us would hang out all the time—he never shooed us away like most brothers would have. I know his friends thought it was weird, and my dad, too, who once pulled him aside and said: I don't know about you spending all this time with the girls.

But I never cared. The second I step off the escalator, I run to him.

He smells like cologne sprayed over sweat and dirty clothes. After we're done hugging, I look up at his face, and I'm not sure if he hasn't slept or I haven't seen him in a while, or this is just what New York does to you, sucks out whatever brightness you once had. The excitement that Jane pumped to me fizzles out like soda water gone flat.

"You look great, a real woman about town!" He spins me around, my duffel slapping against my hip. "And who's your partner in crime?"

Jane introduces herself and then stretches out her hand, which Graham kisses. It's a little embarrassing, but she just giggles. Graham has the kind of personality that makes it difficult to tell if he's fucked up or just feeling himself.

"Let's get out of here." I like this station even less than the one in Boston—the ceilings seem freakishly low to the ground, like we're in a bomb shelter.

Graham pumps his arm into the air. "Onward!" he says, turning back toward the escalators.

"Where are you going?" I call after him. I've decided that moving underground is for rodents, not humans, and I would very

much like to be in the actual city, with trees and grass and air. I see
a set of stairs to my left, but I have no idea if they lead outside.

He's already boarded the escalator and starts to shrink away.
"You need the subway, Blinkie!" And then he's gone from our
view.

Jane touches my shoulder, but this time all it does it make me
aware of how sore my arm is from holding my stupid duffel bag.
"Why does he call you that?"

"It's a long story," I tell her, and then we move toward the sink-
ing belt of stairs because where would we go without him?

I KNOW GRAHAM LIVES IN BROOKLYN, but that's all I
know. He lived in the Bronx and Queens for a little while, too, but
I never saw those places—he said they weren't fit for company, whatever that meant. He'd even made his current place sound temporary, but the way he's talking about it now doesn't sound temporary
at all. "I can't wait for you to meet my girlfriend," he's telling me. I
think it's kind of fucked up that I didn't know he had a girlfriend,
but I'm trying to be a good sport so Jane doesn't think our family
is a dysfunctional cluster of weirdos. I ask him what she does, trying to convince myself I should be happy for him. But then he tells
me she's a model-actress and I'm pissed all over again. I don't trust
pretty people.

It takes a half hour to get to Prospect Heights, and while we ride
I watch a man at the end of the train touch himself, a woman
across from us clip her fingernails (the little shreds landing *very*
close to my sneakers), and a tiny dog let out a thin stream of piss
before his owner yanks him through the closing doors. Jane nods

off on my shoulder and her head's so heavy you'd think her skull was filled with concrete. I watch the electronic map above the door tick closer to our stop, and I feel myself getting mad, but it's not at Jane, or Graham, or even myself for agreeing to this Objectively Bad Idea. It's at Lucy. She's the one who sold me on this place.

You can be whoever you want, she said. You can walk everywhere without ever having to get in a car. You can drink at all the bars because no one IDs, and you can eat pizza for one dollar at midnight. You can wear short dresses and low-cut shirts and no one cares; it's normal. You don't have to go to church—you won't even know anyone who goes to church! And you'll be my plus-one to all the gallery openings and film screenings. Oh yeah? I interrupted. You're getting invited to those? Of course, she said, and she wasn't even joking; she was dead serious. She knew she was special. It was like she already knew how her life would unfold, and the rest of us would just have to wait and see.

Graham's sitting behind me and taps my elbow to let me know our stop's next. I shake Jane awake and she groans, slaps her cheeks a few times. We all stand up and grab the metal railing above our heads, but as we pull into the station I lose my footing for a second, sliding across the scraped floor. My shoe glides underneath the seat I was in a second ago, and when I finally pull it away, Graham's hands on my back, a long string of purple gum flaps from my heel.

"Ah, shit," Graham says. "That happened to me last week."

"These are my favorite shoes." I wait for him to respond, but he's too focused on looking over the sweaty heads of all the people in front of us.

"We'll get it off." Jane squeezes my arm and I wish she would stop touching me.

I shake my foot back and forth and scrape it along the floor but the gum doesn't budge. My special sneakers, the ones Lucy gave to me last Christmas, with the seashells she'd embroidered along the tongue in blue thread. I feel a throb in my throat and a prickly burn behind my eyes. The doors open. Graham gently pushes me off the train, says, "Excuse me, excuse me." He starts to mumble something about a paint scraper he has at home, about hot soapy water. He hurries ahead of us to lead the way, and Jane turns around to look at me with an encouraging smile. Then the smile falls right off her face.

"What's wrong?" she asks.

People bump our sides with their scratchy winter coats and sharp elbows and they're moving with such determination that I'm pretty sure I could stand still and they'd crowd-surf me to the sur-face without noticing. I pause for a second in front of the turnstile, and a woman behind me yells to hurry the fuck up. Jane's already cleared the one beside me and holds out a hand to help tug me through. "I'm fine," I tell her. But I can't help it—hot tears are slip-ping down my cheeks.

We're on the stairs now, and my shoe sticks to every step. "It's not just the sneakers, is it?" she asks. She raises her eyebrows in the facial equivalent of *tell me*, because I'm the only one she's ever told about Mr. Taylor, and that's a secret of such magnitude that I'll be owing her mine forever. Above us, I can see the light from the city dripping down, and we're almost out, almost free. "She lied to me," I manage to say. "This place isn't like she said at all."

"How do you know?" Jane asks. "We just got here." She wipes my eyes with a tissue from her pocket. I don't turn my head away, even though part of me wants to.

The opening above us widens, and now I can see the top of the stairs, the sidewalk and its rush of shoes. When we finally get to the street, I feel like we've broken through the crest of a wave.

Graham's waiting for us, bouncing from foot to foot in the cold. "You two are *not* New York walkers," he says. He rubs the arms of his coat like he's trying to start a fire. "Let's get inside."

Give it a chance, Jane mouths to me as we follow him around the corner. I grind my shoe into the sidewalk, and when I lift it up to examine the underside, there's still a glob of purple stuck to the sole. It looks like a scab.

"Hurry up!" Graham yells from the crosswalk. "The light's turning!"

Of course it is. Can nothing here fucking wait? I run to catch up, but by the time I get there he and Jane are on the other side of the street, and I've been left behind.

GRAHAM'S APARTMENT IS NOT NICE. It smells like the sauerkraut our grandmother used to make, and it's *maybe* the size of our two bedrooms back home pushed together, if I squint my eyes to make the floor look wider. All of the doors are open when we walk down the hallway (which is pretty much the exact width of Graham's shoulders), and I can see that one room is just a twin bed and a dresser missing two drawers. The other one's not much different—a double bed that fills the room wall to wall, so you'd only be able to crawl in by climbing up the bottom edge of the mattress. "Very efficient," he explains. At the end of the hallway is the kind of kitchen I imagine they have in a camper van, with one counter that can barely fit a cutting board, plus an oven the size of a throw pillow. Over the top of the kitchen is a shaky-looking loft that's so close to the ceiling you wouldn't be able to do anything except lie flat down on the bed, which is what I guess that particular roommate does. Graham gestures for us to sit on two nearby stools with glittery plastic seats. "Yeah," he says, leaning back against the tiny counter. "We really love it here."

I look over at Jane with a scrunched mouth that is the facial equivalent of *Jesus Christ*, but she's got these pinned-open eyes and this hanging mouth that are the facial equivalent of *I want this*. Snap out if it! I want to shout at her, because it makes me feel very alone. Not wanting what everyone else does.

We soon learn that not only does Graham have a girlfriend, but he lives with her. He tells me the girlfriend's name but I refuse to learn it—she'll be gone soon enough, just like all the others. She appears from the bathroom and swirls around the apartment in a black jumpsuit, mopping the dirty floors with the soles of her socks. I can't decide if she's pretty or just skinny. Her face is freakishly symmetrical, with cheekbones so high that the rest of her face looks semi-collapsed, and her hair's that unnatural dark red that comes from bricks of henna dye. It's no wonder why Graham picked her. She looks like Mom.

Beyond the girlfriend, there are two more roommates who are somewhere called Hudson for the weekend. "Can I get you some tea?" the girlfriend offers, tugging out a little golden cart from beneath the counter. There's a wooden box full of tea bags on it, along with a tiny milk frother, a miniature strainer, and several bottles of liquors with unfamiliar names.

"Or something stronger?" she asks with a wink. I don't appreciate the wink and look away so she knows it.

"Water's fine," I say before Jane can cut in and ask for a shot of Everclear or whatever else is aging on that cart.

"Do you mind if I make a call?" Jane asks.

The girlfriend flutters her hand toward the open window, which leads to the fire escape. "Be our guest."

Jane climbs through the window frame and I spin around on my stool, which is facing an alcove scooped out of the wall beside the kitchen. It has a small couch the color of wasabi, where Graham's girlfriend has perched beside him, stroking his arm like it's covered in velvet.

"So Soph." The girlfriend shakes off my brother's arm to lean toward me. I think she's pretty bold, shortening my name like that. "Where will college be?" She raises her eyebrows in this awful, expectant way, like we have an inside joke. "New York, maybe?"

"Oh, don't ask her that," Graham groans. "Literally the last thing any high schooler on the planet wants to discuss."

Her question does make my stomach flip, because I'm seriously behind on my applications. I can't get my essay right, and my first application's due next month. I have this half-baked piece from last spring, but even Ms. Layla thinks it's shit because she not-so-gently suggested I try "going in a new direction." But the issue now is that she won't tell me what new direction to go in, ever since I got a little testy when she suggested my mom as a topic. I shouldn't have told Dad about it, that's for sure. He always makes a mess of things when it comes to Mom. Last week I suggested exploring my journey from hating mayo to tolerating it, and Ms. Layla didn't even laugh.

Jane pulls herself back in through the window and her cheeks are as pink as apples, but I know it's not from the cold. "He's on his way," she tells me, so excited she doesn't even whisper.

"Ooh," the girlfriend says from the couch. "Who?"

Jane slides onto the stool beside me and tents her hands over her face, trying to hide her smile.

"Jane's got a boyfriend," Graham teases. "What about you, Blinkie?"

"No," I say sharply, because it's a stupid question. When would I have been thinking about boys? Before or after my best friend's funeral?

Graham must hear in my voice that he's misstepped, because he steers the conversation back to Jane. "He's in New York?" he asks. "How'd you meet him?"

I turn toward Jane, very interested to see how she answers this question.

"He's from back home," she says carefully. "We met at school. He's taking the bus here."

"Oh, how fun. We should have a special dinner tonight," the girlfriend says. "To celebrate new beginnings!" She claps at her own suggestion, and Graham pulls back her hair to kiss just behind the curve of her ear. I drift toward the open window, which is sucking cold, heavy air into the apartment. It doesn't feel like something's beginning to me—it feels like it's ending. I look over at Jane to see if she feels it, too, but she's got her phone screen held up to her face like a mirror. I don't know how she doesn't get it. He isn't coming. He never was.

THERE'S NO DINING TABLE, so we crowd onto the couch for dinner, with Graham and his girlfriend melted against each other on the floor—the girlfriend says sitting on hardwood is better for digestion. I think about how much this would drive Dad crazy, no real table, no real napkins, and I realize that's why we've never been here. I don't care what Dad thinks, Graham's told me about a million and one times. Like it's the most embarrassing thing in the world to want your parent to accept your life.

Graham and his girlfriend serve us several different types of pasta that they made by hand over the course of the past three hours, shouting at each other to get the damn water boiling and flour the countertop before making up with kisses by the sink with way too much tongue. Graham never used to be a PDA person, but maybe he doesn't consider his apartment public. When I asked him if he wanted any help, he gritted his teeth and said that the most helpful thing I could do was just enjoy myself.

For whatever reason they have brass candlesticks, and the girl-friend lights two tall blue candles with a rainbow Bic she pulls out of her sock. Graham gets up to pull a bottle of red wine off the top of the refrigerator and pours it into four coffee mugs. "Liberté, égalité, fraternité!" he shouts for his toast, which I know Jane will eat up. I slide my eyes over to her while I take my first sip, and her cheeks are scrunched up to her eyes with happiness.

Half of the plates are in the dirty dishwasher, so Jane and I share one that's shaped like a rooster. We sit crossed-legged and lay it across our touching knees, being careful not to shift too much when we reach for bread and salad and more wine. Everything tastes good, but not as good as I thought it'd be. Real life's never as good as the stuff in my head, Lucy used to say.

She said it when she was taking my photos for her art portfolio, the two of us lying on my bed while she clicked through the view-finder on her Canon.

Do I look ugly? I asked. Her head dangled off the foot of the bed, the camera held below her chin, but I was on my side, curled away from her. I didn't want to see the pictures.

Of course you don't look ugly. You're incapable of looking ugly.

I stared at my carpet, which was covered in dirty clothes: mismatched socks, wrinkled shirts, piled-up jeans. What's the problem then?

I don't know. I think it's the lighting.

Just a few minutes ago, Lucy had stood on top of my dresser and raised the camera over her head so that it touched the angle where the two walls intercepted the ceiling. Just act normal, she'd said, like it was normal for me to try on the dresses I'd stolen from my mother's closet before she'd come back to pack everything she owned into cardboard boxes. When I asked Lucy to come down and help me with a zipper, she said she couldn't. You have to pretend I'm not here, she said. That's the only way this works.

You don't need to use them if they look bad.

I'm *going* to use them. They just need some editing.

Well I can help you, if you want. I flipped over so that I was facing her. I took that Photoshop class in the fall.

That's okay. Even though she was staring down at the camera, I could tell from her voice that she was making a face. Whenever it came to her art, she held me at a distance. I'm not sure if it was because she only wanted to make things that were fully hers, or if she thought I would make the things worse.

When I rolled off the bed, her thumb still clicking through the frames, I felt like something had been taken from me that I couldn't get back. Which I guess is how she must have felt after I texted her the bus video and asked: *have you seen this?*

The girlfriend drops her plate to the coffee table with a clatter. "When's your lover coming?" she asks Jane, who practically chokes on her grass-fed meatball.

"Soon." She checks her phone beneath the plate. It's almost eight and Mr. Taylor supposedly left Boston at two. I don't say anything.

We practically lick our plates clean because Jane and I under-stand the cooks will be offended if we don't. The girlfriend gets up to do the dishes, insisting there's nothing Jane or I can do to help, and she ties her hair up with a cloth napkin like a sexy milkmaid. I feel so full that I crawl onto the floor to lie down beside Graham, who's rubbing his stomach like he's pregnant. He lowers himself down next to me, and the second his head touches the floor, my phone buzzes in my pocket. "Uh-oh," he says, because we both know. I slide the phone up to my ear and clear my throat before I say hello.

"How's the evening going?" Dad asks. I can hear the chatter of his golf buddies—one of them, probably Mr. Brown, shouts, "Hiya, Soph!"

"Oh, fine." I look around the room for details I can use to round out my story. "Jane's sleeping over. I hope that's okay."

"That's fine. I wouldn't want to be alone in that house either." Dad likes Jane because she's quiet, which in his mind implies level-headedness. If only he knew.

"What time will you be back tomorrow?"

"My flight gets in at six, so I should be home around seven. Hey—is it really fifteen degrees there? I was just looking at my weather app."

My face must have gone white, because Graham starts mouthing What? Over and over. I shoo him away with my hand and sit up. "Oh, yeah. It's pretty cold. I don't know the exact temperature; we haven't gone outside."

"Well, do me a favor, will you?"

Graham slides himself up one arm and tries to lean in toward the phone, but I jerk my head away from him. "Sure, what?"

"Just leave the faucets on so the pipes don't freeze like last win-ter. All you need is a little trickle of warm water, that's it."

"Okay," I tell him. My cheekbones feel tingly, like someone's rubbed Icy Hot on them. "I'll do that."

"Thanks, sweetheart. I'll let you get back to Jane. Love you."

"Love you, too," I hear myself saying. The call ends and I drop my phone to the ground. "Did I sound weird?" I ask Graham. "I feel like I sounded weird."

"You sounded fine. What happened?"

Now that I'm not focused on pretending to be normal, I can feel a full-on freak-out rising in my chest. "He wants me to drip the faucets!" My words spew out like the water I imagine will burst through our frozen-ass pipes. "How the fuck am I supposed to drip the faucets? I'm here!"

"What?" Jane says from the couch. "What's wrong?"

Graham laughs and claps my back like everything is status quo. "Your first time getting in trouble! This is a milestone!"

"It's not funny."

"Oh, whatever." He rolls his eyes and pokes my chest like I'm some little kid. "You'll be fine. You're Dad's favorite."

He's always saying this like I campaigned for Dad's affections, like I shouted "Me, me, me!" and kissed the bottoms of his feet when really Graham made things exponentially harder while I at least tried to help. I was a kid, too, when she left. More a kid than he was. And look at him now! Far away from us like he always wanted, with a hipster girlfriend and train tracks and a million strangers between us. "You decided to be reckless like her. That was your choice."

"Don't talk about stuff you don't remember," Graham says, his voice low and rumbly now, like it's being ground through gears.

"Why do you do that? Why do you act like I wasn't there?"

Jane's rising up off the couch now, and I become aware that the sink is off—the girlfriend slinks toward us with her head held low. "Why don't you guys talk outside?" she whispers. "More privacy."

I think Graham's going to do what he always does, which is say, "Fuck that shit," but instead he walks to the window and smacks it with his open palm, shoves it up. Once he's on the fire escape, he turns around and looks at me like I'm the biggest moron he's ever encountered in his twenty-three years of life. "Are you coming or what?"

I climb outside and he brings the window frame back down behind me with a slam. "Calm down," I tell him. "Jesus."

"I fucking hate when people say that." He grabs hold of the railing and looks down at the street. His breath swirls around him like cigarette smoke. "Do you know Dad told me that, when she first left? I was crying and he told me: 'Calm down, calm down. This is normal.'" He twists his head to look back at me. "It wasn't normal."

Graham's problem is that he can never get out of his own head. He only sees what Graham sees; he's incapable of widening his perspective. "Dad was just trying to make you feel better. I mean, what would you have wanted him to do? Say she wasn't coming back?"

"Something that wasn't a lie." He drops down to one of the rusted steps leading to the upstairs apartment and it shakes with his sudden weight. "What did he say to you?"

Our only rule, up until now, apparently, was that we didn't talk about that night. I think we always knew that we had different ideas about what had happened, and that it could be dangerous to compare them.

"Nothing. He said nothing." Across the street, a couple's waving their arms at each other so dramatically you'd think they were in a silent movie. They're fighting about something—all I hear is *mother-fucker*. "He was too busy with you."

"That's not right."

"It is. I promise you."

"Well who told you then? He must have said *something*."

"No. You guys were upstairs when the phone rang, the one we used to have in the kitchen. I picked it up and talked to her. She said, 'I love you, but I can't do this anymore. I'm so sorry.' She was crying. And then she hung up." The wind blows a balloon of freezing air into our faces, and it's only then that I realize we're outside in thirty-degree weather with no coats.

"You never told me that," he says.

"I didn't tell you or Dad. When he came down the stairs, I just said, 'I know,' and that was it."

"What were you, eleven?" Graham asks.

"Nine," I say. "I was nine." I try to smile at him and it makes my face feel like it's cracking in two.

The sounds of the couple fighting and an ambulance whirring its siren and doors slamming open and shut all clash together below us. "I hate this place," I tell him, after we've been silent for what feels like a very long time.

"I know."

"Lucy told me I'd love it."

Graham lets out a white puff of air when I say that. He taps his knee with one hand and gestures to his chest with the other. "Come here, Blinkie."

I go over to the stairs and sit on the step below him, my back resting against his shins. He leans forward and wraps his arms around my shoulders. "I miss her, too," he says.

Because we've just finished fighting, and because we don't talk like this anymore, and because I won't see him for who knows how long, I don't say what I'm thinking. Which is: *You don't miss her like I do. No one does and no one ever will.*

"She thought you were going to do big things," he says. "And you will."

For some reason, everyone thinks I'll feel better if they put words in her mouth. "She never said that."

"She did." One of his arms drops away from me and I can feel him digging around in his pocket. His hand falls in front of me with his phone screen tilted toward my face. "See?"

It takes me a second to understand what I'm looking at, like squinting at one of Lucy's canvases. The stack of blue and gray speech bubbles, the names attached to them. I can feel my eyes buzz in their sockets, moving back and forth so quickly that all I catch is flecks of the sentences. *haha* and *college* and *painting* and *lol* and *fuck* and *what!* and *noooo* and *nyc* and *omg* and *soph.*

I look straight through the grate below me, which means all I see is a bunch of other grates. "Why were you texting her?" is something I seem to say.

"We were friends," he says, and I wait a beat to see if that's a joke, if this is some elaborate attempt to make me feel better, like all the shitty short films he makes about moms and sons instead of going to therapy. "We had a lot in common."

All the spit sucks out of my mouth. "Don't say you were both artists. Please, don't say that." I can feel his legs shift against my shoulder blades. "You're not an artist."

"And you are?" he asks after a moment.

"No," I say. "Of course I'm not." I stand up and rest my arms on the railing. I can't look at him. "Grow up."

"She was right. You can really be a cold bitch." Behind me, I hear him open the window and crash into the apartment.

"I'm not anything," I say, and even though I'm alone, it feels like I'm talking to her.

"Is everything okay?" the girlfriend's asking. The smells of the kitchen leak out, Bolognese and fried onions and toasted bread, and I think I might hurl. I'm dangling my head toward the ground, dropping spit to the sidewalk, when someone taps my back. I turn to see Jane standing behind me.

"Do you want to talk about it?"

"No."

"Okay."

We stand there in silence for a while, until Jane steps behind me and belts her arms around my waist. I try to remind myself that I've felt my life was over before, but it never was.

"He's not coming," she says. "I guess I never thought he was, deep down." She lifts one hand and runs her fingers through the hair tucked behind my ear. Immediately, she finds a knot. "Why do I always want things I know I can't have?"

"What did he say?" I ask, because I'm not really in a state of mind to be answering loaded questions.

"Nothing. He just stopped responding." She tries to pry the knot apart with her fingernails, and the tension zips right up to my scalp.

"Typical."

"I'll say."

"Did he hurt you?" I ask after a moment, because I've always wondered but never asked. And it seems like I'm saying all sorts of things I never thought I would tonight.

She laughs and the sound tinkles against my ear. "I never would have let him." I try to laugh, too, even though my question didn't ask what she would or wouldn't have let him do. I don't even know if I believe in choice anymore. So much seems to just happen to you.

Something wet touches my forehead, and when I look up I see that it's starting to snow.

"Just like back home," Jane says. She forces her fingers through my tangled hair and I feel something rip. "Ah-ha!" She holds out her palm so I can see the knot, which looks like a mouse nest, all matted and brown. And then she holds her hand over the railing and uncurls her fingers. My hair drops much slower than I thought it would, floating on the wind like a feather. Across the street, a man carries a wrapped sandwich out of the bodega, a cat darts across the sidewalk, and the lights of a brownstone flick on, glowing like jack-o'-lantern teeth. The voice of an unknown woman drifts toward us: "I mean really, who does he think he is?" The cold air makes everything sharper, like when the optometrist slides a new lens over your eye.

"You're right." Jane moves beside me now and stacks her arms on the railing, rests her chin on her wrists.

"Right about what?"

"She wouldn't have left this." Jane's looking up at the sky, and I have to admit there are more stars than I thought there would be in the city. They look like rhinestones sewn to black velvet. "She wouldn't have left you."

"I hope not." But that was the thing about Lucy. Just when you thought you could see her clearly, something blurred. And she knew that; she liked it—hiding behind different versions of herself. That's what I think the photos were about, after all. Who you become when your body doesn't belong to you, but the people monitoring it. The second I put on my mother's dress my back straightened, the tips of my shoulders pinched together. Like I was back in the ballet class she used to teach, one hand pushing my chest open, the other pressing at the root of my spine.

"Hey." Jane looks deep in my eyes, like: Come back to me. "We could seriously fuck Olivia up, if we wanted to."

For a long time, I *had* wanted to. But mostly because I wanted to blame something that wasn't a wet floor, or a drunken misstep, or a part of my best friend that she'd never shown me. The first day back at school in September, I pushed Marina Nowak into the handicapped bathroom stall and pressed my thumb into the hollow of her throat until she started to choke. I'd heard that Olivia had dared Lucy to jump, that she'd walked her right to the edge and then given her a push. But Olivia had transferred schools, so Marina was my next best option. My whole summer had been spent watching: pictures of dollar bouquets my classmates placed on her grave and posted to Instagram; security footage the police played for me, pausing on grainy figures they hoped I recognized; neat brown boxes at the foot of Lucy's bed that slowly filled up with the objects of her life, objects Brynn held to my face and asked: Do you want this? I was tired of watching. I wanted to act.

We didn't do anything! Marina gasped in the bathroom.

I pressed harder. She made a retching noise and her throat vibrated against my fingers. I felt suddenly repulsed by her fragility. God, I said, you're so fucking pointless.

I released my grip and she fell against the wall of the stall, grabbing her neck with both hands. She opened her mouth and a tangle of spit fell into the toilet.

Don't tell anyone, I said before I opened the stall door. As far as I know, she didn't.

School seems as distant as the moon right now, with the plastic barriers on the second-floor balcony and the suicide-hotline stickers on every teacher's door. They decided on suicide because doctors didn't find evidence of a seizure, the police couldn't get anyone to talk, and while accidents are unpreventable you can at least *try* to stop kids from killing themselves. But Lucy had so many plans. Do suicidal people have ambitions? Besides trying to leave this world? I guess wanting to die and wanting to live aren't mutually exclusive. Though one wins out in the end.

"Nah. Olivia's nothing but a stack of mommy issues in a trench coat."

That makes Jane laugh. She softly punches my arm. "You know, we still have time to lose our virginity."

"Oh, Jesus." I roll my eyes and lean into Jane's side, where I can feel her ribs expanding with laughter. "Yeah, let's pop our cherries after eating five plates of pasta in Prospect Heights's smallest apartment." That makes her really lose it, and she fans her face while she gasps for air. "So you really didn't do it with him?" I ask, because her laughter makes me confident.

She shakes her head back and forth. "He was *way* too chicken," she says between hiccups. Her face stills after a few moments and she wipes her eyes on her sleeve. "I would have, though. For sure." She slides her chin into the crook of my neck. "Who would you pick? I have no idea what your type even is."

I feel a weight press down on my chest and consider whether it's best left there. "Oh, I'm not a virgin. I just said that to Lucy to make her feel better."

Jane doesn't say anything for a second, and I can feel her opinion of me shifting. "Really?"

"Just—you know how it is. No one wants to be left behind."

"Yeah."

We're pressed close together, but I feel like there's this wall between us. And I can't figure out what will take it down. "Don't you want to know who it was?" I finally ask.

She pulls away, her eyes looking at me from their very corners. "It was nobody," she says. "Right?"

"Right." I had forgotten that Jane understands something Lucy didn't. You don't have to possess a person's every secret to understand them.

Jane and I sleep on the couch together, underneath a scratchy Moroccan blanket that the girlfriend retrieves from her closet. Graham doesn't say anything else besides asking if I have a toothbrush, to which I say yes.

In the morning we eat yogurt the girlfriend fermented herself in an Instant Pot, and it tastes how I imagine the sludge beneath your toenails would. Jane eats it all because she's polite, and I pour mine into the tiny compost bin when no one's looking. As the girlfriend washes our empty mason jars, she asks if we need help getting to the train station. I reply that we can get there fine by ourselves, thanks. Graham doesn't even come out of his room to say goodbye.

"Should you talk to him?" Jane asks when we're out in the hallway, about to step onto the stairs.

"No. I'm always the one making things right."

I BEAT DAD HOME by a few hours. When we finally get off the train in Nashquitten, the car's so cold that we have to chip ice off the front doors with our keys just to get inside. I'm afraid it's not going to start, but Jane says she believes. And she's right. We huddle there shivering, hugging each other over the console for warmth, and the lights come on just like they always have. "Look how lucky we've been!" she says, which makes me wonder how she's going to tell the story of our weekend.

Back at home, Jane backs her mom's car out of the driveway and honks the horn the whole way down the street, trying to play some song I don't recognize. That's how we first became friends. The funeral was over and we'd all moved to the Painted Pearl for the reception, where everyone ate lasagna and garlic bread out of metal heating trays. It was insane to me, that anyone was able to eat. So I went outside and walked away from the harbor, toward the little parking lot down the street that people use for hiking around the marshes. The lot was empty except for a single beat-up Prius that was banging out some unfamiliar melody on its ugly-sounding horn. As I was walking by, Jane rolled down the driver's side window. I know you from English class, she said.

What are you doing? I asked.

I feel less sad when there's music.

You call that music?

She laughed. I don't have the best instrument to work with. Do you recognize the song?

No.

"Where Have All the Flowers Gone." Get in and I'll play you the real version.

So that's what we did for the rest of the day—Jane drove us around while she played me her music, which seemed like a Sad Dad playlist, but I didn't say that. You know what's weird? she said at one point. What? I asked. I didn't know anyone who died before this. Besides, like, my grandma. I pressed my head against the window and watched my breath fog the glass. Yeah, I said. Me neither.

Inside, I run around the house turning on all the faucets, and when not a single one refuses to flow I praise God for the first time in seven years. Then I go around making it look like I never left: I stomp through the yard leaving footprints in the snow, I put two bowls and three plates in the dishwasher, I hang a towel on the rack in my bathroom.

That evening I watch Dad's car take our street slow, careful of the black ice. Mom used to whip down our road so fast that the neighbors actually slipped a note under our door one day, calling her a danger to the Elm Street community. The speed bumps came a year later, and Mom cursed whenever we bumped over them because of course she didn't actually slow down. Woo-hoo! Lucy would shout if she was in the car, and Mom would turn to me and go, I like this girl.

Three weeks after it happened, Mom called me. Ever since she left, she's sent me cards for every holiday, always signing off with *I hope we can talk soon*, but I never respond. She thought it was because of some moral hang-up that I had, about the affair and the lying and of course the leaving. I mean, sure, I would have had plenty of ground to stand on. But it wasn't because of that. It was because I thought she was a coward. She was too scared to ask for what she wanted. So she waited until she was so desperate for what she needed that she had to hurt all of us to get it.

She called my cell phone while I was doing calculus at the kitchen table. Dad wasn't home yet, and I had all the windows open so I could smell the honeysuckle blooming outside. I heard, was what she said, to which I didn't respond. Graham must have told her.

Then: What if you came here? You can have your own bedroom. It's almost summer.

She lives in a town in California called San Luis Obispo, which I know nothing about. Graham visited her last year and loved it, but of course he did. Her boyfriend's a professor at the college there and Graham thinks they'll get engaged soon.

You know you didn't do anything wrong, honey, she said.

Of course I hadn't done anything wrong. I'd been in Connecticut the night of the party, celebrating my little cousin's twelfth birthday. The next morning, I'd woken up on the couch beside a pile of unwrapped presents, and my phone, which was on the floor near a forgotten paper plate crusted with frosting, had nine missed calls and three voicemails.

I almost hung up on her, and she must have sensed that because she squeaked out: Wait! I just wanted to say that I love you.

Okay, I said.

That's it?

That's it.

Lucy thought I was too harsh on her. You realize she's going to be your mom forever, right? she asked me the night of my fifteenth birthday. My mom had tried calling, but I'd let it go to voicemail. We'd just ridden our bikes to the beach and were wiping sweat off our foreheads as we rushed into the ocean, throwing off our shorts and shirts as we ran. That doesn't end just because you don't talk to her, she said, right before the sand dropped off beneath us and the water rose to our chests. I dunked my head under so that I wouldn't have to answer. Lucy thought she understood the world better than most people. But really, there was a lot she didn't understand.

The garage door screeches open and soon my father's in the hallway, tapping his snowy boots against the doorframe. I take his coat and hang it up in the closet, smoothing the collar so it's unwrinkled. "What the hell happened to the car?" he asks. I adjust the box of baking soda that's on the closet shelf, to ward away the mildewy smell of damp winter jackets. "It's covered in ice. Did you leave it outside?" I can hear his routine: the boots dropping onto the rubber mat near the shoe rack; the socks scratching against his ankles as he pulls them up. "Sophia? Did you hear me?" I say nothing. "Sophia?" he asks again. "Soph?"

I close the closet door and turn around. "I went to New York to see Graham."

He pauses, bent over one foot. "What?"

"Don't worry, I learned my lesson, it was a shit show."

He straightens up slowly, like I'm a wild animal that might pounce. "I'm not really sure what to say."

"Would it bother you," I ask, "if I called Mom right now?"

He walks over to me and cups my cheeks in his hands. They're swollen from the sudden heat of the house. "Is everything okay?"

I nod. "It will be."

BRYNN

BEFORE I DECIDED TO SEARCH for men on the internet, I tried the old-fashioned way of doing things. I read my book at dimly lit bars and drank foamy lattes at busy cafés and sat at rickety patio tables with an open face—that kind of thing. I tried to look intriguing, which I did by wearing colorful costume jewelry or reading books whose covers had gold stickers advertising the prizes they'd won. The costume jewelry was unbearably heavy—I had a nightmare that I was standing on all fours like a cow, a pendant strung around my neck like a yoke—and the books all seemed to be hinting at some subterranean emotion I could never quite discern. A character would say: Do you ever miss a life you never had? And the other character would reply: Only when I forget I'm living in this one. And I would wonder if people were now writing novels to enhance the mystery around the human condition rather than illuminate it.

The waitress at Bar Hola agreed with my literary assessments. I started going there every Tuesday, Wednesday, and Thursday, and I would make her listen to passages that I read aloud from whatever brick I'd recently acquired. If you're wondering why I continued to read them, despite my obvious disappointment, I'll tell you that I was trying to improve myself and that reading books seemed more appealing than going to Pilates or attempting to shift my overall worldview.

You should try those romance paperbacks they sell in the checkout line at the grocery store, the waitress told me. You know, the ones that feel like they'll fall apart in your hands? In the little metal carousel? I knew exactly the ones. They'll probably be more stimulating, she said. You need to be stimulated. I agreed.

This suggestion came after I shared, as a digression from our book talk, that I had only had sex with one man in my life, a man who also happened to be my ex-husband. I was trying to say something meaningful about life and opportunity and missed chances, but apparently that didn't come through because the waitress told me I needed to get laid, or at least get a vibrator. I was offended that she thought I was the kind of woman who didn't own a vibrator.

What about the apps? the waitress said as she handed me my check in the little plastic holder.

Ha! I shouted, because I'd had too much white wine. A young person's game!

No, the waitress said very seriously. It's the new frontier for women of any age. As though wading through pudgy men in the throes of midlife malaise was equivalent to discovering a matriarchal society full of braless and fairly paid citizens.

Which brings me to this very moment, on my couch in my condo with a seventeen-year-old sitting beside me. Sophia's figured out how to link my phone to the television via some application that she insisted was legitimate, and now we're staring at a slack-jawed man whose swirl of hair is so thin it looks like he's glued a dust bunny to his head. "Do they start with the unattractive ones?" I ask. "To keep your expectations reasonable?"

"Mrs. Anderson!" Sophia exclaims, because she still doesn't feel comfortable calling me Brynn even though I no longer consider myself a Mrs. or an Anderson. She was always more traditional than Lucy, and I wouldn't have minded some of that rubbing off on my daughter. But Lucy was never particularly susceptible to outside forces. When she was diagnosed with a peanut allergy at age six, she snuck handfuls of peanuts for a month, convincing herself she could undo the diagnosis through sheer determination. (I hope no mother ever has to go through as many EpiPens as I did that August.) Sophia, however—Sophia was susceptible. Lucy had turned her from a math whiz to an aspiring writer, to Sophia's father's dismay. She even accompanied Lucy to a twenty-four-hour marathon at the local movie theater that both myself and her father refused to watch. It was a full day of experimental films that promised to be "disturbing, enlightening, and soul-shaking." No, thank you. And now, this girl doing the bizarre work of guiding a divorced, grieving mother through the labyrinth of dating apps—this isn't Sophia behavior. It's pure Lucy.

"He's not *that* bad," she says.

"I want someone younger." I reach over the couch arm for the pinot grigio on the side table. "I think I'd be a good cougar."

"How much younger?" Sophia's still holding my phone and taps open the dating app's settings, which appear on the television. "Like, forty?"

"Sophia, *I'm* forty." She tries to keep the shock off her face, but it shows in her eyebrows anyway. "Put it to twenty-five." She looks up at me with eyes that clearly ask, Are you serious? "Do it!"

There's a line for age preference on the television screen, and I watch the dot slide from one end of it to the other. I pour the wine into my glass and give it a satisfied swirl.

"Just be careful." Sophia navigates back to the bachelors. "Young men like to take advantage of older women. It makes them feel powerful."

"I'll keep that in mind."

This new batch is instantly superior—toned and bright-eyed like all they do is powerlift and sleep an uninterrupted eight hours. "Swipe yes," I say. "Yes. Yes."

"You mean swipe *right*."

"Sure," I tell her, too mesmerized by the landslide of youthful, unblemished faces. Their skin is so taut and smooth it looks more like poured plastic than flesh. "Why do they look so perfect?"

"Filters," Sophia says matter-of-factly, and I have no idea what she's talking about.

We swipe yes on approximately fifty-two men over the course of a half hour, at which point Sophia wonders if we've exceeded what constitutes a "healthy" amount of swiping. The answer to that is: absolutely. But it's the first time my attention has fully turned from Lucy, like my mind's blinkered anything but these unknown men from recognition. I suppose it's the only truly novel experience I've had since her death. "Just one more," I say, and Sophia gives me a look but scrolls to the next man all the same. Cole Emerson. His face looks familiar and yet unplaceable, like an actor who appears on popular commercials but doesn't have enough charisma for film.

"Oh, shit." She leans toward the television. "It's Mr. Taylor."

When she says his name, the individual pixels seem to rearrange themselves into something coherent, like the twisting of a camera lens into focus. Waiting in the parking lot of the little strip mall outside the harbor, Lucy's shadow appearing behind the tutoring center's frosted glass doors. The door jolting open, Robert waving, Lucy's bright-red coat emerging, the one she loved more than anything, the one with the canvas collar she embroidered, thin loops of flowers native to this coast. Robert leaning down to say something, her mouth widening into a laugh.

Me, when the passenger door opens: What were you two laughing about?

Lucy, sliding into the seat, balancing her backpack on her knees: Oh, nothing. Stupid stuff.

Me: It's going well then?

Lucy: Yeah, my math's up 120 points.

Me, leaning over to kiss her on the cheek, which she begrudgingly allows: That's great, honey.

Lucy: Rob says I should apply to Amherst. He says it has a great art program.

Me, fiddling with the windshield wipers, even though it isn't raining: Rob? I thought you called him Mr. Taylor.

Lucy: Not when he's my tutor.

Me: (Silence while I weigh how much I trust my daughter against how much I trust this man.)

Lucy: He had a couple seizures when he was a kid.

Me (skeptical, but attempting to fight my skepticism with a belief in the greater good): Really?

Lucy: Yeah. They went away on their own. I guess he grew out of them or something.

Me: The doctors say that could still happen.

Lucy: I know what the doctors say. (Silence while she looks out the windshield at the strip mall, which is in desperate need of a renovation and reeks from the dump down the street.) Why aren't you driving?

Sophia gets up from the couch and walks right in front of the television, like she doesn't believe what she's seeing.

"That's a pretty ballsy move." I take a gulp of wine so large that I can feel its burn flaring in my nostrils.

"Maybe for Rob Taylor it is." Sophia touches one finger to the screen before returning to the couch. "But not for Cole Emerson." She takes a picture of his profile with her phone and texts it to her friend Jane.

"Be careful with that," I say, though I'm not sure why. The man needs no protecting.

"Don't worry. Jane won't tell anyone. Did you hear that he's coming back?"

"No. I don't get those emails anymore."

Sophia sucks her lips into her mouth and I realize I've said something wrong, which I seem to be doing frequently these days. For a second I think she's going to say "I'm sorry." But of course she doesn't, because so many people have said those words to her, too. Though I rarely feel anything besides the urgency of a shit or the faint grumble of hunger these days, something warm stirs in my chest. Tenderness, it takes me a moment to realize. For Sophia, who stayed.

"It's late," she says. "I should get home before my dad calls."

"Okay. You're good to drive?"

She laughs at that, though I'm not sure why. "Yes. I'll text you when I'm home." I watch her pull on the red jacket that was once Lucy's. If you flip up one point of the collar, *LA* is stitched on the underside. If you flip up the other: *SW*. My mother couldn't believe I gave it to her. Like it wasn't always Sophia's.

When she leaves, the condo seems to expand into something dark and sharp, full of right angles and shadows. It's true that I haven't exactly decorated since I moved in during July, but I never saw this place as permanent, anyway. The minute I buy a real couch (currently it's two love seats pushed together) or a plant, I'll be acknowledging that this is in fact my life. And I have a bad habit of believing that refusing to accept something is the same as inciting change.

I bring the bottle of wine into the bedroom and scroll through my phone, where I get a lot of ads that ask me if I'm sober-curious. As I'm about to open the apps one last time, just to see if there's anyone new on the roster, I hear my front door rattle. A block of light falls through my cracked bedroom door, accompanied by the clomp of heavy male boots. Something creaks, crashes. A yell of: "Oh, god damn it!"

Finally, the bedroom door swings open and Charlie hops through it, one foot pressed to his knee as he attempts to untie his shoe. "Your lock's sticky," he tells me. "And why's your floor lamp so close to the door?"

"Did you break it?"

"What, the lamp?" The shoe pops off and flies across the room, thudding against the wall. "It's fine. I, however, am not."

"No?"

The other shoe comes off, though with less bravado: a simple drop to the floor. "No! I swear, your apartment's always trying to attack me."

"My condo."

"Your *condo* is always trying to attack me." He flops onto the bed like the exhausted teenager I met at seventeen. Charlie was about to graduate, and I was finishing up my junior year. Our shop teacher had left unexpectedly—some family drama—and with only three weeks until summer, the faculty decided to put Charlie in charge. He was known as a talented woodworker with grades that could easily tip toward a diploma or away from it, depending on any particular test score, but if he finished out the class without any major hitches, his degree would be guaranteed. Plus, he was charismatic enough to have become senior-class president on a ticket that promised nothing besides Hot Dog Fridays. The teachers thought we would listen to him far more readily than Mr. Rogan, and they were right.

"Did you sign the divorce papers?" I ask.

"I would have told you if I had." He wiggles up the comforter so that he's lying beside me with those puppy-dog eyes that haven't worked in years. "You're really that sure?"

I've been sure since he came home so drunk he vomited over my freshly planted rosebush. I've been sure since Lucy asked me, Where's Dad? and I didn't have an answer. I've been sure since I had no idea where he was that night, and didn't until Rae dropped him off at the emergency room, reeking of beer and guilt. They don't tell you how easy it is. To wake up beside someone, their heavy arm draped over your shoulder, and realize: Oh, it's gone.

"I'm sure." And then I turn toward him, because unlike Charlie, I can fuck someone and have not a single drop of feeling toward them change.

THE NEXT DAY I RIDE the train into Boston and back without ever getting off, a frequent pastime of mine. I like watching the world around me smear into streaks of color—it reminds me of the paintings Lucy made after her diagnosis sophomore year. This is what it's like, she said, showing me the canvas that she'd propped against the foot of her bed. What what's like, I asked. She drew her finger through the paint, which I hadn't realized was still wet. It feels like I'm trapped inside a soap bubble, she said, not seeming to hear me. Everything sounds muffled, and when I look out, all I see are these warped, blurred shapes. And I don't really understand the shapes, so I see them for what they actually are. Which is what? I asked. She leaned over and wiped the paint from her hand to my wrist. Color, she said. We're all just color, in the end.

The train pulls up to a concrete platform in front of a parking lot. Winter's coming and the sky's the purplish blue of a fresh bruise. Maybe I'll go back to work next month—things are slower with the holidays. I've been on a mental health break since everything happened, whatever that means. They insisted I take off "as much time as I need" and then seemed surprised when that turned out to be quite a long time. Every few weeks, Patty, the president's assistant, reaches out to ask how I'm doing, which I know means: When are you returning? I sold one of the estates by the cliff early last year, which means that, financially at least, I'm fine. And, God, not a single bone in my body misses that office. Pretending to care about Cora's hip replacement and Daniel's bratty son-in-law and Paul's chihuahua, who frequently ate and subsequently vomited up small items like dimes or bottlecaps, which Paul would photograph once regurgitated and share "in case something similar ever happened to us."

"Mommy, why aren't we moving?" a little girl in the seat behind me asks. We have been stalled for longer than normal. I'm sitting in the very last car, and when the doors beside the stairs slide open I realize that I've timed my ride poorly: the Catholic boy's school in Weymouth has just let out.

A herd of musty, sweating young men swarm the aisle, ties askew, collars wrinkled. They're shouting and hooting like a freed family of monkeys, slapping one another everywhere: shoulders, heads, asses. I keep my head down so they won't ask if they can sit beside me. But before I know it, a pair of gray trousers with grass stains on the knees is sliding in next to me.

"What's up, Auntie Brynn?" the owner of the trousers asks, and when I look up I see that my nephew Eric is rummaging through his backpack beside me. He smells like teenage boy, which is to say he smells like insecurity and the attempt to cover it with Axe body spray.

"Oh, just waiting to shuffle off this mortal coil."

"You're funny," he says. At least someone thinks so.

"I thought you drove yourself to school now, no?"

"I dinged Mom's fender and now my driving privileges are indefinitely suspended."

Sounds like my sister. I once got a speck of dirt on a skirt she let me borrow when we were kids, and I wasn't allowed to get dressed *near* her for two months. "Hopefully it's on the shorter end of indefinite."

"Were you visiting the MFA?" He continues to dig through the dark cavern of his bag, which contains so many books, notebooks, and granola bars that it must tip him backward when he carries it.

"Not today." Lucy and I used to visit the Museum of Fine Arts almost every week, and when he was younger Eric would often tag along. He and Lucy were born two days apart and had a freakish, near-telepathic connection—I once watched them silently touch fingers and then move in tandem to retrieve baby carrots from the refrigerator.

This was before Nashquitten had access to any sort of public transit. I would drive us forty-five minutes to Braintree, where we could catch the very end of the red line and ride it into town before switching to the green line (the kids were always amazed that I had the route memorized—Do you need a map? they would ask skeptically). It was one of these days that we saw a woman attempt to jump onto the tracks.

We were waiting for the E line at Park Street, having just hustled up the stairs from the station's lower platforms. The trolleys screeched against their tracks so loudly that Lucy and Eric had their thumbs in their ears, and I held their wrists as we jostled through the stern-faced young professionals and clueless tourists. I noticed the woman as I directed the children to a metal bench. She had the fluttery hands of someone who wants to make a big decision but can't quite commit to it, and her eyes were tumbling back and forth in their sockets. I assumed she was high and stood to the left of the children so that she wasn't in view. Hooray! Lucy said when the headlights of the trolley appeared, pulling her fingers out of her ears to clap.

What's she doing? Eric strained his neck to look over my shoulder.

What's who doing? I'd crouched down to the children's height, but at that moment I stood. The woman had inched up to the rusted edge of the tracks and was peering over them as though she'd seen a mouse crossing the metal slats. I turned around, hoping someone was about to do something. But no one was. The headlights grew larger as they approached the opening of the tunnel, and I heard Lucy go, Oh no, behind me.

I don't remember moving, but the kids told me afterward that I was faster than a cheetah. The train had entered the station and ground toward us, sending a scattering of sparks into the air. The woman's face scrunched in concentration and I knew she was building up the courage to jump, which is not all that much courage, when you think about it—maybe a millisecond's worth. As she leaned forward I grabbed her from behind, digging into the soft fleece of her sweatshirt. People were waving at the train now, shouting for it to stop. Someone was yelling about an emergency brake. One of my hands found the woman's hood and I used it to drag her behind the spray-painted yellow line, where we both collapsed to the filthy ground. I would like to say that I did the following next: asked her if she was okay, helped her to her feet, gave her my phone number in case she ever wanted to talk.

But I didn't.

I jumped up and pulled Lucy and Eric away from the horseshoe-shaped crowd that had formed around us. The children had migrated toward a friendly looking woman with a leashed dachshund, and I pressed them so tightly to my chest that they must have felt my blood pulsing against their necks. You're okay, I kept telling them—it wasn't a question. You're okay, you're okay. When I finally looked up, the crowd had dispersed, the train had left, and the woman was nowhere to be seen. Maybe she knew what had really happened: that I'd saved her not because I felt some higher moral obligation, but because I didn't want my daughter and my nephew to watch her die.

"Are you okay?" Eric says. "Your cheeks are a little red."

"Do you remember that woman?" I ask him. "The one at the train station, when you were little? When the three of us were in Boston?"

He extracts a half-eaten candy bar from his backpack, which has melted chocolate smeared across the pulled-back wrapper. "What woman?" He takes a bite. "Someone we knew?"

"No, just—" I try to think of a better way to describe her but realize that I have no idea what she looked like. "Just a woman."

"Nope." He cocks his head like he's trying to figure out if I've fully lost it or am simply behaving normally for someone whose child died seven months ago. I can already hear him telling my sister: Auntie Brynn seemed a little out of it; do you know if she's doing okay? And then my sister, trying to balance her sympathy for my situation with the obligatory irritation she feels for the baby sister who got everything: Oh, that's just Brynn for you.

"How's school going?" I ask, desperate to change the subject.

His lip curls like his father's does when he takes out the trash—a little rolled-up cold cut. Why my sister married that man is a mystery to me. Well, it was for the money. You can't blame someone for wanting an easy life, I suppose. I used to feel so high and mighty for being the breadwinner, but now I understand that I *had* to feel that way in order to convince myself all that exhaustion was worth it. There's no real empowerment in this life. Just the people you commit yourself to and the ways in which you love and hurt one another.

"It sucks," he says. "When am I ever going to use calculus or European history? I'll forget everything in a year."

"That's true. You should ditch."

He finishes his candy bar and tosses the dirty wrapper into his chasm of a backpack. "You need a partner to really pull off a ditch."

"What are you suggesting?" I ask.

"Nothing. But you *have* always been the cool aunt." He gives me this mischievous look that reminds me of his mother before her most prized possession was a robotic vacuum.

"Listen," I tell him, leaning toward his ear. "I'm in. But there's only one rule."

"Don't tell my mom?" he interrupts.

"Boy genius." I give him a kiss on the cheek. "I knew you were my favorite for a reason."

. . .

THERE ARE NO OTHER CARS when I pull into my allotted space in the complex's parking lot. I moved in two months after the accident and haven't seen a soul since. There are only a dozen units, and though the spot isn't the most popular—the bare stretch of land between the harbor and the lighthouse, home to a handful of ill-placed takeout spots and not much else—it's cheap. I make my way up the concrete staircase that straddles the side of the building, each floor split into three units, the levels stacked neatly on top of one another like a concrete layer cake.

Inside, I lie on the couch and swipe through milky-faced men who look more suited to fix your wireless router than make you cum. The quality has gone down significantly since my initial foray into the meat market. The succession of contextless faces soothes me, neither drawing my thoughts into the past nor launching them into the future because I'll never meet any of these men. I'll simply use them as a mental white noise machine. Their flat pancake faces, their favorite movies, their gripped beer cozies—it all means nothing to me, just as I mean nothing to them, our interests and images a wave of curated static.

But you can only count on anonymous static for so long, especially in a small town. I'm on a different app—Sophia's set me up on three—when the name Cole Emerson appears again. I scroll through his pictures, which show him engaged in various tasks that men believe reinforce their sexual virility: mixing a cocktail in a silver shaker, playing the piano with one bare foot pumping the pedal, walking a rescued dog. He looks entirely different from the man that walked up to my car in early May, idling at the curb while I waited for Lucy.

Robert (swiping a hand through his hair nervously): Hi, Mrs. Anderson! Can I ask you something?

Me: Is everything all right?

Robert: Oh, yes, everything's fine. I just wanted to check something with you.

Me (warily, in that such statements never end well): Okay.

Robert: Lucy asked me to pose for her. For a portrait, I mean. And I just wanted to make sure that it was okay with you.

Me (confused, skeptical, still wary): Lucy asked *you?*

Robert: Yes. We'd do it at school, of course. Nowhere private. But I just wanted to ask you.

Me: Why?

Robert: Why what?

Me: Why did you want to ask me?

Robert (his forehead beginning to grow damp): Oh, I just . . . didn't want you to get the wrong idea.

Me (smiling): What's the wrong idea?

Robert (crinkling his eyebrows together, laughing nervously, taking a step backward): There's no wrong idea, of course! I just like to be transparent with parents, when possible. You know, in case there are any concerns.

Me: Since Lucy asked you, I have no concerns.

Robert (still walking backward): Excellent, great, okay!

Lucy (appearing from the frosted doors): Hi, Mom.

Robert (retreating behind the frosted doors): Have a great day, you two.

. . .

IT'S DIFFICULT TO SEE WHAT'S shaping a kid when you're in the process of raising her, in the same way that you don't sense the design of a place when you're standing in it. My first time on a plane, I was shocked to look down and see the ground's uniform patchwork of carefully plotted tracts and roads, all stitched together like a quilt. After Lucy's diagnosis, I knew something was different. I just couldn't tell exactly what, or why. Epilepsy wasn't the answer, or at least not the whole one. It was the first domino that knocked down several others.

In the upper right corner of Robert's profile, there's a glowing red heart. I quickly switch out my photos for three of my sister and change my name to my maiden one: Brynn Brady. The heart seems to glow with even more force once I've done this. When I finally lower my finger to the confirm button, it explodes into pixels of confetti. A premature celebration—I still don't know if he likes me back.

LATER THAT NIGHT, Charlie calls me. I'm in the bath, supposedly reading my book but really nodding off against the tiled wall. I dry my hand on the shower curtain and reach for my phone, which is sitting on the closed toilet seat. "Did you see the email?" he asks.

"What email?"

"The one from Officer Donelson."

My stomach acid curdles when Charlie says that name. The two of us at the station, seated at the tiny metal table. Donelson coming in with his arms crossed, his teeth crunching down on a mint. I'm so sorry for your loss, he said, which you could tell was not an infrequent phrase based on how easily it slid out of his mouth.

The message appears at the top of my inbox: *Anderson Case Closed.*

"Are you reading it?" Charlie asks.

"No."

"Are you going to?"

"No."

I never wanted an investigation to begin with, but Charlie insisted. When it first happened, I thought he might actually hurt someone. He knocked on the door of every kid who was at that party, idled outside the school when the final bell rang, walked the beach at night looking for bonfires. He was convinced someone did it, and he was convinced that someone was another child. The idea of an accident, of a simple slip and fall—that was impossible to him. It was too ugly, too nakedly unfair, even though we've all been warned since childhood that none of us should expect to receive what we deserve in life.

But that's what had happened. Lucy wanted to let loose, as stressed as she was compiling her art portfolio for applications, and she got a little drunk and stepped off into what she didn't realize was thin air. There wasn't a push from a classmate, the tests showed no seizure, and she certainly didn't jump willingly. It was simply a horrible, unalterable miscalculation. I know my child. This is how she died.

But Charlie didn't see it that way. How can you just do nothing! he shouted at me in the old house, while we sat on the bed we had stopped sharing months earlier.

There's nothing to do, I told him. By which I didn't mean: We can't bring her back. More like: The world is empty now.

I hang up and toss the phone to the bath mat, which is so thick that the screen disappears within the loops of yarn. As I'm about to slip under the water, my phone dings, a specific, bell-like note that only means one thing. He likes me.

TWO DAYS LATER, I arrive at the restaurant's parking lot five minutes before our reservation. We've agreed to meet for lunch, which makes me slightly insulted on my sister's behalf, given its decidedly lower standing than dinner. He chose the Mill Cove for our rendezvous, a wide-windowed restaurant facing the water that still has some elements of the original mill. I was surprised that he suggested a restaurant in town, but I suppose Cole Emerson has nothing to hide. Kids, parents, colleagues: They all want him back. Even with the car windows closed, I can smell low tide churning just beyond the lot.

I don't really have a plan, per se, for this confrontation. I just need a simple answer to two questions: (1) Why did Lucy choose you for a portrait? And (2) Where is it? Probably some outside advice would have been wise, but I don't talk to many people—never have. I've lived a deeply internal life, which I didn't identify as such until a friend in high school asked me what I did at home while my parents were gone. They were both nurses and worked odd hours—if one of them was home, they were most likely sleeping. Oh, I don't know, I said. Read or think. By the look on her face you would have thought I'd said I skinned cats in my free time. What do you think about? she asked, which I thought was a bizarre question. Everything, I said. What do you think about? She squinted up at the sky like she was having trouble remembering.

Who likes me or who doesn't. That's kind of depressing, I replied.
Yeah, she said. It is.

I've never craved companionship like so many people seem to.
Before Charlie, I'd never even had a boyfriend. But during that
shop class, he came up to me one day with what looked like a little
hinged box. This is for you, he said. I saw you playing out on the
picnic tables. I undid the hinge and saw that it wasn't a box at all,
but a mancala board. There were bright, gem-colored marbles sitting in the hollowed-out pockets that reminded me of the striped
hard candies our grandmother put out at Christmas. Did you make
this? I asked. Yeah, he said, of course. The tone of his voice made
it clear that I'd asked a stupid question.

I ran my fingers over the divots, taken aback at having received
such a thoughtful gift. I was also thinking about what he'd said,
about seeing me. It was true that my sister and I would often play
at the picnic tables after school ended, to kill some time before
going back to our quiet house. But I'd had no idea someone had
been watching us. I felt at once violated and flattered. And that's a
very dangerous combination—vulnerability and ego.

I'm about to open the car door when I see him. The curly hair
that he used to keep trimmed to his ears is now at his shoulders,
tamped down by an unflattering green beanie. He looks extra thin
in his black skinny jeans, though he was always a frail-looking
thing. I slide down my seat as he pulls his unzipped corduroy jacket
together, face braced against the wind. He hurries up the wooden
steps to the entrance and then the hostess stand—the huge glass
windows mean I can see everything. He takes off his jacket but not
his hat, and then the hostess leads him to a table and he's gone.

Well. It's now or never. I think of what my sister would say: Why
do you put yourself in these situations? Is it so bad to behave like a

normal human? Or Charlie: You're a real nut, sometimes, honey, you know that? Or Sophia: Ha ha—you're not serious, right?

Luckily, I rarely listen to anyone. Which means by the time I consider their opinions, I've already walked up to the hostess stand, already said, "I'm meeting a Cole Emerson, please." And the hostess is smiling, she's saying: "Right this way."

Robert's seated at a table positioned near the far corner of the dining room, directly facing the huge windows that overlook the inlet bobbing with lobster boats and buoys. In the summer the windows are cranked completely open, so that it feels as though you're sitting on the deck of a huge boat, the sea right below you. I'm considering what to open with—Not who you thought, eh, *Cole?*—when Robert rises and turns to me with a completely calm and expectant smile.

"Mrs. Anderson, hello." He holds out his hand for a shake, which I don't take, then gestures to the chair opposite him. "Sit down."

"So—" I begin as I pull out my chair.

"I knew it was you, yeah." He holds up his phone, which is open to my profile. "You didn't change the last two photos. And you don't come across many Brynns from Nashquitten—not many girls from Nashquitten in general."

"Women," I say. "Women from Nashquitten."

His face goes splotchy when I say that. "Of course, that's what I meant."

"So, what did you want to say to me?"

"Me? You're the one who messaged me under a pseudonym. I assumed you had questions. Accusations, maybe. I don't know."

I take a sip of my water, which is mercifully cold. "Should I have accusations?"

He places both arms on the table and shakes his head. "No. I just want you to know—and I realize there's no reason for you to believe me—that whatever you've heard is completely false. I haven't had any inappropriate relations with a student, ever. And that includes Lucy."

I understand why he was so popular with the kids. There's an openness to his freckled face, a looseness in the features you so rarely see in those who work with the public. Is it the face of an innocent man? It might have been, if he hadn't spoken. I know the lilt of a lie when I hear it. Maybe this is the real reason I came: to hear him undo himself.

He leans toward me, the tablecloth going taut beneath his elbows. "How are you holding up?"

What a question. The more I hear it, the less it makes sense. Have you put yourself back together? it seems to ask, as though falling apart were ever a real option.

"I'm just fine."

He looks toward my hand as though he might grasp it but then raises his eyes to my face. "That's wonderful to hear."

"Is it true?" I ask. "That you had epilepsy as a kid?"

He seems surprised by the direction I've steered us in. "Oh, that. Yes. I was never officially diagnosed, but I had two seizures. Scary stuff."

"Scary stuff," I repeat. "What did it feel like?"

"Excuse me?"

"What did it feel like? When you had the seizures?"

He turns his head to look toward the table dining beside us, like they might suddenly demand he help them finish their order of mozzarella sticks. "Oh, ah, it's difficult to describe. Sort of like a massive headache? A massive migraine, I guess you could say?"

"Interesting." I pull my napkin from the table to give my sweating fingers something to play with. "I've never heard it described that way before."

"It's a very unique experience. That's what I told Lucy, you know. She felt so isolated and trapped."

"Did she?" The napkin's smooth yet stiff, like cheap satin.

"I think that's why she wanted to photograph me for her series. To have a record of someone who'd recovered."

"Series?" After the accident, we went looking for the camera Charlie claimed he'd once seen on her bureau. We found it under her bed, but the memory card had been removed, and we never located it. I concluded it must have been for some school project, though Charlie wasn't sold. She'd never been drawn to photography and had always despised having her picture taken. After the video, she became almost paranoid about it, darting away if someone so much as raised a lens toward her. "Lucy wasn't a photographer."

"I think it was something new she was working on. She told me she was posting the photos on Instagram."

And that's where he's wrong, because I know Lucy's Instagram well, and she did nothing of the sort. Two months or so before the accident, she became increasingly frustrated with me. Anything I did was interpreted as a personal assault: the tone of my voice, the meals I prepared, the clothes I suggested she try on. She accused me of trying to shape her into someone she was not, of fundamentally misunderstanding her identity. I wasn't particularly bothered—I felt these were normal teenage complaints. A phase we would pass through like so many others.

But then she stopped talking to me. She had left her printed-out college essay on the dining room table, and I had done the natural thing, which was sit down and read it. I'd only gotten through the first three sentences (which were nothing but throat-clearing, if I'm being honest) when she appeared in the room with a glass of water and a look so horrified you'd think I was flipping through the pages of her diary. In a matter of seconds, she'd snatched the stapled pages from the table and started shouting at me. Did I have no respect for her privacy? Did I think that, just because I'd given birth to her, everything she did belonged to me?

Maybe if she was a little less self-centered, she'd be able to realize that not everyone was out to get her, I said. Unbeknownst to me at the time, the video of her seizure had circulated just a week earlier. Cushing had kept it hush-hush for fear that it would threaten her beloved exchange program, but Sophia showed it to me when I dropped them off at school one morning, running back to the car pretending to have forgotten her phone. She climbed into the passenger seat and looked out the window to confirm Lucy had entered the building. I think you should see this, she said.

Strangely, the video didn't upset me. I think it triggered some mental defense mechanism that prevented my mind from fully absorbing what was happening on the screen in front of me. Because I knew the second Lucy's body came into view that nothing good would come from remembering those shaky frames. But I did think: Charlie can never know.

Lucy's silence lasted a month afterward, until she suddenly asked me to pass her the orange juice one morning and all normalcy was restored. But at the beginning of those wordless days, it seemed she could freeze me out forever. So I did what any reasonable parent would do: I kept tabs. And the only place you can do that without detection is the internet.

My name was seashell20475, and my profile was empty besides a short bio: *aspiring artist.* Lucy added me on Instagram immediately. Which was when the madness began.

I checked my phone incessantly, the device constantly warm from my inability to let the screen go dark for long. Though Lucy only posted once every few days, I visited her profile as though she churned out new content every hour. I scrolled backward in time, returning to a girl who had once talked to me, who had even thought me worthy of her secrets, such admissions unthinkable now. Frequently, I was tempted to message her one of the old photos: *do you remember this?*

The day she finally spoke, I was so relieved that my elbow buckled as I handed her the jug of Tropicana. I knew any mention of the video had the potential to trigger another exile, so I did something that was much easier than I thought it would be: I pretended the fifteen-second recording had never happened. And Lucy seemed to do the same.

In the accident's aftermath, Charlie did one good thing: take down her various accounts before the funeral, exporting the photos to a blue folder on his desktop. Someday we'll want these, I remember him saying. It sounded like he was trying to convince both of us it was true. We'd gotten her phone from the police, and for a few days Charlie attempted to respond to all the comments, something I didn't have the stomach for. But then I'd found him on the porch one night, pinching back tears with one set of fingers as he typed replies with the other. No more, I'd said, taking her phone from his hand.

"I'm not on social media," is what I tell Robert.

"Well, they were really good," he says, as though this will comfort me. "She showed me some at tutoring."

"What were they of? Other teachers?"

"No." His eyebrows tie together in confusion. "Mostly her."

No, they weren't. Lucy would have jumped into the January ocean before she got in front of a camera. This stringy-haired, damp-foreheaded man might think he knew her, but he didn't. I don't care if he'd had the exact same grand mal seizures as Lucy, or been on horse-pill-sized Keppra, or survived sleep deprivation for an hours-long EKG. He was a perverted hack who thrived on the fantasies of needy teenage girls. I was her mother.

"I've got to go." I push my chair out with a scratch so loud the entire restaurant looks up. "Best of luck to you. With whatever you end up doing."

He jumps as though there's more to say. "Hey, just so you know. Lucy never ended up doing that portrait of me."

"Oh?" I regret having put on my scarf and jacket—I'm swimming in heat.

"Yeah," he says. "I guess she just lost interest."

ON THE DRIVE HOME, I open all my windows and let the cold air prickle my face until I feel more wide-awake than I have in weeks. I'm jittery, buzzing, cracked open. When I come to a stop sign, I text Charlie: *I want to see the photos.* Rob has to be lying, fucking with me, playing some sick game because I played one with him. But that needling at the back of my mind: *What if he isn't? What if we missed something?*

If Charlie's at work like he should be, I might not hear back for hours. My fingers bounce against the screen when I'm done typing, like they've been shocked with electricity. It seems that if I don't use this energy, I'll never have it again. So I text Eric: *ditch?*

He writes back immediately: *! fuck yeah.* Then again, a few seconds later: *sry, shouldn't have sweared.*

I tell him I'm coming. The air swipes through the car as I swing toward the highway. I wonder if this is what Charlie used to feel like, when he was using. Like a lightning bolt bouncing inside a corked bottle.

. . .

ERIC'S WAITING UNDER A TREE near the entrance when I arrive, his jacket hood tightened over his face so that you can only see his eyes. He jogs toward me with his head down when I pull up to the curb, looking over his shoulder every few seconds.

"I thought for sure I was gonna get caught," he says. "They found two kids smoking pot near the football field a few weeks ago and we've essentially been on lockdown ever since." He pulls his seat belt over his chest and taps the dashboard nervously. "Uh, can you start driving, please?"

I tap the gas and we peel out of the parking lot at much more than the recommended fifteen miles per hour. Eric gives a yip like a cowboy and leans his head out the open window, letting the wind pull back his lips.

"Where are we going?" he asks when he ducks back into the car.

I tell him wherever feels right, and he drums his fingers against his thighs with enthusiasm. "Hey, did Lucy ever tell you about a new art project she was working on?" Out of the corner of my eye, I watch him turn his head.

"What, a new painting?"

"No, something else. Photography." He scratches his head and a flake of dandruff floats toward the seat. "Well, she never really liked to talk about something until it was finished."

"I suppose you're right."

"Did you find something?"

"No, I'm just thinking out loud."

"Okay," he says, in a way that makes it clear he doesn't believe me.

I navigate back toward Nashquitten, and when we enter the town limits I hand him a quarter. "Heads is right, tails is left." We pull up to a red light and wait for it to turn. "All right, master of the universe. Tell me which way I'm going."

He flips the coin and smacks it down on the back of his palm. "Right," he says, and so that is the direction in which we turn.

We zig and zag our way through town this way, passing the reedy marshlands and the dump's garbage mountains and the general store where my sister and I used to buy popsicles on our way home from school, flicking the melted juices at each other.

"Does it look different to you?" Eric asks. "Now that she's gone?"

"Yeah," I say. "It does."

He nods and rubs the quarter between his thumb and forefinger. "I'm glad it's not just me."

I take his hand. It's cold and calloused, like Lucy's used to be from gripping her paintbrushes and charcoal pencils too tightly. I wish there was something I could say to make him feel better. But if I knew what that was, I would have told it to myself long ago.

We end up at Opal Point, the sole car in the parking lot. The sky's slate gray above us, blurry with thick clouds, and the overgrown saw grass scissors at our elbows as we walk down the boardwalk to the beach. It's low tide, the wet sand stretching toward the horizon, pockmarked with washed pebbles and crab shells. I lead us to the tide pools, which were always Lucy's favorites. We pick our way over the slick rocks and squat near a narrow basin, which is full of skittering hermit crabs and suctioned periwinkles.

"Look." Eric dips a finger beneath the water. "A starfish." There it is in the corner, fanned across the rock with puffed orange tendrils. Soon it'll be cold enough for these shallow pockets of water to freeze. I wonder if it will survive.

"Should I pick it up?" Eric asks, his hand already moving. I grab his wrist.

"No, leave it be."

He looks up at me in surprise. "You don't want to touch it?"

"I don't think it wants to be touched."

"That's something she would say." He smiles and I realize that he's right.

He withdraws his hand, shakes the water off. "You know you only annoyed her because she cared about what you thought."

"No, she cared what Charlie thought." Whenever she won something for her art, she'd race through the door and ask me where Dad was. Usually I didn't know, and I'd tell her as much. *But you can tell me*, I'd say, practically begging. She'd just shake her head. *That's okay, I'll wait.*

Eric laughs. "Uncle Charlie's not exactly hard to win over. No offense to him."

"Yes, well." I drop to the ground, the rock cold and wet beneath my ass. "He certainly made her feel more appreciated." When Lucy turned eight, he crafted her a mancala board like the one he'd made me so many years ago. She became obsessed with it, tucking the wooden rectangle into her armpit like a clutch and taking it with her wherever she went. Once, she lost one of the marbles at day camp and had a meltdown of such scale that I was called to pick her up. When I tried to tell her we could buy another marble as we walked to the car, she became even more hysterical. It turned out she was under the impression Charlie had made the marbles as well as the board and that they could never be replicated. And even after I explained, that was how it continued to be between them. She saw Charlie as a god of sorts, someone who made magnificent things with nothing but his mind and hands and could teach her to do the same. I was just the woman who did her laundry and cooked her food.

Eric sits down beside me. "I don't know if that's it. She told me she was scared that she'd get on the bus one morning and they'd pass him sleeping on the bench outside O'Dooley's. Or she'd wake up and find him gone, like that one time." I remember that intervention. We'd told Lucy that Charlie was at a fly-fishing retreat in Colorado. "But you." He pokes me lightly in the arm. "You're reliable."

"Reliability's pretty boring, isn't it?"

He shrugs. "Most things that make you feel safe are."

WE'RE WALKING BACK across the beach when we hear someone shouting Eric's name. "Who is that?" I ask.

He extends his neck with trepidation. "I don't know."

The figure's sprinting across the sand now, which makes me feel like we should run, too, but in the opposite direction. I'm about to suggest we hightail it when I hear the voice scream, "*Eric Oliver Walsh!*" and that's when I know it's my sister.

"Shit," Eric mumbles.

I suck on my thumbnail as I try to come up with a plausible explanation for why we're on the beach in the middle of a school day. Nothing logical arises. "If it makes you feel any better, I'm probably in more trouble than you are."

She slows to a jog and throws her hands up in the air to make it clear how exasperated she is. "What the hell, Eric," she says, panting in between words despite the Pilates and interval training and TRX she's always talking about doing. "The school called me totally freaking out."

Eric looks to his mother, then to me, then back to her again.

"It was my idea," I offer. "It's my fault."

My sister stomps her impractical little leather boot into the sand. "Jesus, Brynn. What were you thinking?"

The clouds thicken and her face looks even more menacing in the dark. There's no way to make her understand. "I don't know. I don't know what I was thinking."

She lets out this cruel little laugh that raises the hairs on my arms. "Of course, of course," she mutters, more to herself than anyone. "Well," she says to Eric, like he should have started running toward the car the minute her skinny silhouette appeared in the distance, "why are you standing here? You've got US history in thirty."

"Bye, Eric," I say, but he's already started to retreat and doesn't hear me.

"What the fuck, Brynn?" she growls when he's out of earshot. "I was flipping out. I mean, after Lucy? You should have known I would have a panic attack."

I try not to listen too closely when my sister talks. Engaging with her never ends well. "Don't bring her into this. I'm sorry."

"And what were you guys even doing? Drunk driving? I was watching his position on the phone and it made no sense at all."

"You track him?"

"Of course I track him! Everyone does." The sand's still soft from the washed-out tide, and I watch my footprint fill in with water. "I just—I don't know what you need, Brynn. I don't know how to help you."

"You're making me sound crazy. I'm not crazy." A group of seagulls dips over our heads and we both look up, a habit from having our food stolen as kids. She used to get so mad that she would pick up spears of driftwood and chase them down the beach. "Remember when that one dangled your bag of carrot sticks right over your head?" I ask, hoping we can change the subject. "He was so mean."

She sticks a middle finger up at the sky. "They're all mean! They're evil birds!"

"What did you call them? Devil pigeons?"

"No, crapbags with wings, I think." She laughs. I can't remember the last time I heard this laugh, bright and free of bitterness. "C'mon," she says. "Let's make sure my delinquent son gets back to school." We pick our way over the piles of stiff seaweed, swatting away the flies with our hands. "It's not fair that he likes you so much," she says.

"He just likes me because I'm not you." The first steps of the boardwalk appear, and we start to climb the planks that lead over the sand dune. I can see Eric in the lot below now, leaning against my sister's locked car.

The wind blows my sister's hair into her face and I lean forward to lift the strands from her cheeks. When she looks back at me, her eyes are narrowed. "I feel like you're a different person now."

"In a bad way?"

"No. Just in a new way. It's not good and it's not bad."

You can always count on her to dodge a straight answer. "I think I would like to be a different person. I think that sounds good to me."

She nods in her terse, serious way. "Okay, well, what does this new person want to do?"

"What, you mean in my life, generally?"

"No, I mean right now."

"I thought I was in the doghouse."

She starts walking ahead and then waves her hand impatiently like I should know to follow her. "Oh, fuck it. I was just pissed because you and Eric got to have this fun heist together." She reaches for my arm and rocks it back and forth like a rope. "I want to be cool, too."

The ramp's incline steepens and we start walking faster. The wind off the water pushes us toward the pavement like a pair of hands at our backs. At the bottom of the boardwalk, I turn to look back at the hills of sand, the saw grass bursting up in brittle spikes. You can't see the ocean. But I know that on the other side of the pale slopes the seagulls are shouting, the waves returning, our starfish embracing her rock. The salt threads through the air like pollen. I wish Lucy were here to see it all.

"So where are we going?" she asks.

I squint my eyes so that everything fuzzes to streaks of color, blurred strips of blue and yellow and green. It's like turning the present into an impression, a memory. Which I guess is what happens with every new second of our lives.

After her first seizures, Lucy stopped asking, What happened? Instead she would go: Where was I? Like that lost time was a solid place. Like it still existed, somewhere. Like if she wanted to, she could return to it. And I'd feel jealous when she said that, because I knew I could never follow her.

"Home," I say. "I think I want to go home."

My sister snorts. "That's not very new."

"It is," I say. "I haven't been home in a very long time."

AT THE OLD HOUSE, I climb the stairs to Lucy's wing. I've been up only once, shortly after it happened, to clean. She hardly ever let me in her room, not even to drop off the baskets of laundry I so generously washed and folded. After all, she belonged to Charlie. He was the one who bought her that first set of paintbrushes, the thick watercolor pad from the art store, the waxy pencils whose tips felt like melted candle. Sure, I took her to the MFA, but mainly because it was an affordable and educational activity that turned her face away from a screen. Instead, I was the one who bought her the math workbooks, the SAT guide, the graphing calculator as big as a cell phone. Let her be who she is, Charlie said. But he didn't understand. There was only one reason why he got to be who he was. Me.

The top step of the ladder squeaks under my bare feet, and I close my eyes before entering her floor. What am I so afraid of? I don't believe in ghosts. Still, I have to force my eyes open. I expect to feel differently, taking in her twin bed and scratched desk and stained bureau (why did she never use coasters like I asked?), but I'm unmoved. Lucy doesn't live here anymore. And neither do I.

But then I turn to the white sheet stretched across her wall, hiding the bumpy ridges of her painting that she worked on for God knows how long. Charlie was the one who gave her the okay to use our house as her canvas, back when I was at a conference in New York. I was so angry when I returned that I almost carried an old tub of white paint up from the basement, but Charlie told me she'd never forgive me if I erased her work, and I realized he was right.

The sheet comes off with one easy tug. I've never been a creative person, and I have no idea how one interprets art instead of simply enjoying it, but I do know that these shimmery dunes, opaque but shining, make me feel something. Like I'm wandering through the stickiest part of her mind, which, no matter how hard I tried, I never understood. I walk to the wall and press my cheek to the acrylic, which is so sleek and cold it feels like glass against my skin. Below, the garage door opens. Charlie. The front door scrapes against the floor.

"Brynn?" he shouts. "Are you here? You parked like a maniac."

"I'm upstairs."

His steps vibrate up the bones of the house, rumbling the dried paint. A brief pause by the ladder. I can see him surveying it the day we intended to clean her room, the way he put one hand on a slat and turned to me. I can't do it, he said. But today, he climbs.

"What are you doing?" His head emerges from the square in the floor.

"Exploring."

He heaves himself up with a flurry of gasping breaths. I guess I shouldn't have believed him when he said he quit smoking. He comes to stand beside me and extends one finger to trace a spike of paint. "I have them."

I hold out my hand and he places a flash drive on my palm.

"Are you sure you want to see?" he asks.

I step back to take in the whole painting, and, like a kaleido-scope, it shifts into something new yet familiar, the same story in someone else's mouth. "Yes," I say. "I'm ready."

ACKNOWLEDGMENTS

This book was made possible by a constellation of people who supported me throughout its writing and publication. What follows is but a portion of the people who have transformed this novel and its writer for the better.

Duvall Osteen, my remarkable agent, walks the tightrope of art and business like a seasoned acrobat. You shepherded this novel through its many forms with heart, humor, and much-needed faith. And because you believed this book deserved to be in the world, I did, too. Thanks also to the brilliant Kelsey Day and Katie Barasch at Aragi, whose impeccable organization made this process seamless.

Emily Bell, my sharp-eyed editor, saw this book for what it was and what it could be. Your combination of editorial rigor and unwavering belief challenged and buoyed me throughout revision. What a gift to work with someone who makes creative risk-taking feel so comfortable.

Everyone at Zando has supported *Women and Children First* in ways above and beyond what I imagined. Caolinn Douglas was instrumental to the novel's editorial evolution and my smooth introduction to the publishing process. Maya Raiford Cohen kept this work and its writer on track with skill, patience, and kindness. Sarah Schneider ensured that this manuscript went from a Word document to the book you now hold in your hands. Chloe Texier-Rose and Sara Hayet worked tirelessly to share *Women and Children First* with readers of all types. Molly Stern and Sarah Jessica Parker showed enthusiasm from acquisition to publication that I'm deeply grateful for.

I think, not infrequently, that one of the greatest fortunes of my life has been the teachers I've encountered, particularly those who encouraged my writing at a young age. At Commonwealth: Eric Davis, Mara Dale, Judith Siporin, Catherine Brewster, and Mary Kate Bluestein. At Penn: Karen Rile, Max Apple, Deb Burnham, Jamie-Lee Josselyn, Al Filreis, and Buzz Bissinger. Thank you for telling me to keep going.

The Vanderbilt MFA program provided both creative and financial support as I began this project. Carla Diaz, Sam Rutter, Kelsey Norris, Mark Hamlin, Elena Britos, Madelin Parsley, and John Shakespear read early versions of these chapters and helped me understand what I was trying to accomplish. Lorrie Moore, Lorraine López, Nancy Reisman, and Tony Earley provided invaluable feedback and expanded my ideas of what fiction could do.

Many institutions and people gave me places to work and learn free from financial burden. When I was in the earliest stages of this novel, Buzz Bissinger and Lisa Smith opened their home and nourished me with conversation and incredible meals. Aspen Words, the Sewanee Writers' Conference, the Squaw Valley Community of Writers, and the Juniper Summer Writing Institute provided scholarships to their programs, gifting me not only space and time but workshops with mentors and peers.

Writing can be a volatile and lonely process, and I'm grateful to my friends, who have offered guidance, compassion, and laughter throughout the writing of this book. Special thanks are due to Allie and Sherry, who have been there since the beginning, who celebrate my wins as though they are their own, and who remind me how true friendship makes even your most hidden parts feel seen.

My parents, Monice and Neil, called me a writer since I first started sketching comics in Mom's studio. To have grown up in a household where art-making was seen as a necessary and legitimate pursuit is a gift I didn't fully recognize until I became much older. Thank you for the books you put in my hands, the museums you took me to, the dreaming you encouraged. I never had any doubts about becoming a writer because you always insisted it was possible.

Matthew, you have been, and continue to be, my partner in the truest sense of the word. This book largely exists because, in my darkest moments, you overrode my doubts with your unshakeable certainty of its worth. Your love makes the world bigger, and me braver.

Finally, a note. The story of Rebecca and Abigail in Marina's chapter is based upon the (supposedly) true story of Rebecca and Abigail Bates of Scituate, Massachusetts. I heard this story many times growing up, in many different iterations, from loosely remembered oral narrations to detailed picture book pages. The duration of the tale reminds me that the actions of two girls can have a lasting effect on many. Thank you for reading about the ten women that precede these acknowledgments; their stories belong to you now.

ABOUT THE AUTHOR

ALINA GRABOWSKI grew up in coastal Massachusetts and holds degrees from the University of Pennsylvania and Vanderbilt University. Her writing has appeared in *Story*, the *Masters Review*, *Joyland*, the *Adroit Journal*, and *Day One*. She has received scholarships from Aspen Summer Words, the Sewanee Writers' Conference, the Squaw Valley Community of Writers, and the Juniper Summer Writing Institute. She lives in Austin, Texas.